TIGER WITH
A HUMAN SOUL

BARBARA BISCO

Barbara Bisco

Black Lotus
blacklotuspublishing.com

ISBN: 978-0-9560276-2-7

Typeset in Goudy by Lawrence Mann
Printed and bound in Great Britain by
CPI Group (UK) Ltd.
Croydon, CR0 4YY
Registered under the Companies House Act
Number 2,196,742
www.cpibooks.co.uk

Published by
BLACK LOTUS PUBLISHING LTD.
25 Belsize Crescent
London, UK NW3 5QY
Registered under the Companies House Act
Number 5,928,807
www.blacklotuspublishing.com

Black Lotus has been registered as a Trade Mark
with the UK Patent Office

A CIP record for this book is available from the British Library

Papers used by Black Lotus Publishing Ltd. are natural,
recyclable products made from wood grown in sustainable forests.
The manufacturing processes conform to the environmental
regulations of the country of origin

FOR MY HUSBAND AND DAUGHTER

TABLE OF CONTENTS

IN THE TIME
OF THE RAJAS

Java 800 A.D.

Suhitra wound a protective cloth round her arm, picked up the baby tiger and murmured affectionately, 'Now, you naughty thing, you can chew on my arm all you like.' She was the daughter of the raja's animal keeper and understood the ways of the creatures in her care.

The cub, drowsy in the heat of the tropical noon, made only half-hearted efforts to take her up on her offer before snuggling down contentedly in her arms.

'That tiger's going to bite you one of these days,' predicted Surya, a boy who had been watching her from the vantage point of a nearby hill. He preferred to keep a safe distance between himself and any wild animals, even small ones.

'No he won't. He thinks I'm his mother.'

Surya looked doubtful. 'What're all those scratches and bruises on your other arm then?'

'Love marks. He just likes to play, that's all. He doesn't realise I don't have thick skin and lots of fur the way his jungle mother would.'

'I think you'd better get married and have a human

baby,' Surya advised.

'No thanks, I like this kind of baby better,' she said, giving the little beast a hug.

'I'm getting married soon,' Surya declared proudly, 'so I'll probably have a real baby.'

'You,' she exclaimed, laughing, 'you're still too young.'

'No I'm not, I'm almost sixteen and anyway, my father's already arranged it.'

'Who -' she began, but the cub, with a sudden surge of energy, leapt to the ground and began pulling at her sarong with his already-impressive teeth.

'She's a goldsmith's daughter from Srivijaya,' he replied, ignoring the antics of the little tiger. 'My father's already started making an amulet for me to give her at the wedding.'

'Is she pretty?' Suhitra asked absently, too busy detaching her sarong from her charge's mouth to pay much attention. When her first attempts didn't work, she picked up a stick and challenged him to his favourite sport, a lively game of tug-of-war.

'Oh, she's famous for her beauty all over the Island of Gold,' Surya boasted, although he hadn't met her and had no idea what she looked like.

He was annoyed with Suhitra for not being impressed by the fact that he was about to become a man while she was still a mere child, probably no more than thirteen.

But, of course, she didn't care about anything except her animals. Well, she'd soon grow out of all that and then – too bad for her. No one but a poor rice farmer or a palace slave would want to marry the daughter of an animal keeper, someone who spent her days cleaning filthy cages.

Surya wandered over to sit on a nearby rock, one that still offered a view of Suhitra's tussle with the little tiger but provided a better location for pondering the inequities of life.

It was only right that someone like himself, the son of a goldsmith, should travel to foreign kingdoms and do important things like carving gold rings for the fingers and toes of the raja and his wives. He had earned his place in the social order because of the things he had done in his previous lives; everyone knew that.

One day, if he were good enough, he might even be allowed to carve the designs on the offering bowls that would be laid at the feet of the gods. Still, it did seem a pity about Suhitra. He almost wished... he caught himself before he could finish the thought. The important thing was to accept your place in the overall scheme of things and that meant accepting other peoples' places too, even that of an animal keeper's daughter.

In all honesty, his place wasn't all that high. He wasn't a noble, he was just lucky because he liked his position so well. He couldn't think of anything more thrilling than taking a simple nugget of unworked gold and transforming it into an ornament fit for a queen or an offering bowl worthy of a god.

'Ouch,' he cried, jarred from his reverie by the feeling of teeth sinking into his ankle. He leapt up and shook his leg as hard as he could but the more he moved, the more tenaciously the playful predator held on.

'If you just stand still, he'll probably lose interest and let go,' Suhitra said, unsympathetically.

The suggestion was a good one and the cub, apparently deciding that it was wasting its hunting talents on an unworthy victim, soon relinquished its hold and set off in the direction of an inviting grove of bamboo.

'Look at your leg, it's bleeding,' Suhitra exclaimed and, moved to helpfulness by his obvious distress, made up for her initial heartlessness by unwrapping the cloth from her arm and winding it round his ankle.

While she was doing this, a strand of her long black hair accidently grazed his hand and sent a tingling sensation through his veins; one that drove the pain in his ankle from his mind.

Sensing the change in him, Suhitra immediately drew back in alarm, straightened up and ran after the tiger. She knew all too well that if her father suspected she was letting a higher ranking boy, or any male at all, fool around with her, he would marry her off to any man he could persuade to take her. And that would mean the thing she dreaded most in the world: separation from her beloved animals.

After that day she took care to avoid Surya.

This proved quite easy to do. A divine first son was born to the third wife of the raja, the god-king of Mataram, an incarnation of the great god Shiva. The entire palace, from the raja himself down to the lowest slave, went mad with joy.

Surya's father, Widjojo, was deluged with commissions for rings, necklaces, hair ornaments and bracelets to be given to the mother of the celestial infant. An elaborately carved gold box was ordered to hold the placenta. This would be buried under the left side of the palace door so it could continue to protect him after his glorious birth, as it had done while he was still in his mother's womb.

Surya nearly burst with pride when his father, under the pressure of so much work all at once, let him carve an amulet shaped like a tiger claw to tie around the baby prince's neck. If the amulet was perfect, it would endow the royal child with the strength, ferocity and courage of this most formidable of carnivores.

Fully aware of the importance of this undertaking,

Surya poured all his time and effort into it. He had little leisure time in which to watch the tiger cubs, no matter how attractive their keeper. On the few occasions when his father allowed him a brief respite, usually in between tasks, he was able to wander in the vicinity of the animal cages. But he was left disappointed as Suhitra, for reasons that baffled him, wasn't anywhere in sight.

The pressure on Widjojo, and hence on Surya himself, intensified as the day of the ceremony approached – the one that would celebrate the 35th day of the infant's life. The heirlooms handed down from previous generations of rulers were brought out to bedeck the raja, his queens, the princes, princesses, noble relatives, high priests and even the royal elephants and horses. The newly commissioned gold ornaments had to be ready as well.

When the all-important day arrived, towering piles of rice in the shape of mountains were brought out, pig, goat and chicken meat was roasted on sticks over charcoal fires, spicy stews simmered in pots, succulent fruits were displayed on lacquerware trays and the air was filled with the scent of flowers. No one in the palace - nobleman or commoner, freeman or slave - was denied a share in the festivities.

Surya spotted Suhitra in the crowd shortly before the ceremony was to begin and lost no time in going over to her.

'How's the tiger cub?' he asked.

'You mean Abimanyu?'

'Who?'

'The one you saw me playing with that day. He nipped you in the ankle, remember? His name is Abimanyu.'

'I never heard of a tiger having a name,' Surya said scornfully.

'All of ours have names; besides Abimanyu, there's Gatotkaca, Kumbokarno, Arimbi and Banowati.'

'How come you don't take the one I saw, Abimanyu, to play near the bamboo grove anymore?'

'Too busy.'

'I bet Abimanyu's not too busy,' Surya pointed out.

Suhitra suddenly liked this boy. Anyone who could see things from a tiger's point of view was her sort of person.

It was curious though. She had known Surya all her life although she hadn't actually seen him very much. He had come to look at the animals once in a while but he had been different ever since his last trip to Srivijaya. She had noticed him watching her, not only that day when he had told her he was getting married but several other times too. That morning when she had been feeding the gibbons, for instance, and the day the new orang-utan had arrived - the one that had been sent as a gift from a raja near the River of Diamonds. It had taken quite a while to soothe it and Surya had kept staring at her in a funny kind of way.

Still there was something really nice about his smile, she thought, it seemed to go all the way up to his eyes. And she really liked the way he seemed ready to understand things about animals. Surely there couldn't be any harm in talking to him in the midst of a crowded festival? She would just have to be sure that her father didn't see her and misunderstand, that was all.

'We have a new tiger,' she told him.

'Another cub?'

'No, a big one, probably five or six years old.'

'How did you get it?'

'He just walked into a rice field right outside the palace.'

Surya had trouble believing this. 'A tiger wouldn't come that close,' he protested.

'This one did. Lots of animals come down from Mt Merapi when it starts making those rumbling sounds and if they get hungry enough, they'll go anywhere.'

'It's not rumbling now,' Surya pointed out, 'and I've only seen a few showers of sparks since I've been back.'

'It's been enough to affect the animals,' Suhitra insisted.

Surya considered this. 'But how did your tiger, the new one I mean, get into the palace?' he asked.

'One of the guards spotted it, so my father and three slaves went out, threw a net over it and brought it in.

One of the slaves was chewed up a bit in the process, just his arm and a piece of his leg though, so he probably won't die.'

'He might have wanted that arm and leg.'

Suhitra looked at him quizzically. Whoever thought about what a slave wanted? What a strange boy this was. Still, he was very kind.

'How did the raja get his other tigers?' Surya asked.

'Gatotkaca, the oldest, was born in the palace. That was ages ago when my mother was still alive. She used to carry him around in a sling like a human baby and tell everyone he was my little brother. All the others, except Abimanyu, were brought here after their mothers had been killed. He was born here like Gatotkaca.'

Suddenly, Suhitra felt her father's sharp eyes on her, so she hastily cut the conversation short and went over to join a nearby group of giggling girls who were eating coconut-flavoured rice cakes.

It was evening before Surya caught sight of Suhitra again. He was at the back of the raja's open-sided audience hall with his father and two visiting goldsmiths, waiting for a performance of a *wayang* shadow play to begin, when he noticed her standing next to a large banana stalk that held the leather puppets that would be used that night.

Surya managed to catch her eye and smile at her once or twice but Suhitra, conscious that her father was nearby, didn't let herself return his greeting.

Gradually, more and more people filled the hall and the haunting tones of a traditional gamelan orchestra drifted through the palace. The puppet master took three puppets from their places on the banana stalk and held them up against a buffalo hide screen in the middle of the hall. An oil lamp suspended overhead cast the shadows of the leather figures onto one side of the screen; this allowed the people assembled on one side to see the actual puppets, while those on the other side saw the shadows.

Suhitra had had trouble deciding which side to choose. She always enjoyed watching the colourful puppets and she liked to see the dance-like movements of the puppeteer but tonight, she somehow felt like losing herself in the mystical world of the shadows. She found a place on a straw mat on that side of the screen and was soon caught up in a time-honoured tale of princes and princesses, gods and mortals, ogres and demons, played out against a background of the unresolved struggle between good and evil.

The goldsmiths had decided to watch the actual puppets and Surya was soon too absorbed in the plot to think about anything else. Then a princess called Suhitra, her skin the colour of gold, appeared on the screen and jolted him back to the real world and to thoughts of the real-life Suhitra.

What had inspired her lowly parents, animal keepers who were barely above slaves in the social order, to choose such a glorious name for their baby daughter? How had they dared to do it? The legendary princess had golden skin and delicate features; a girl who was destined to clean out the animal cages could never be anything like her.

The real-life Suhitra had skin that was dark brown from exposure to the sun and she didn't behave at all the way somebody of noble birth would. He had seen her large black eyes shine with happiness, sparkle with mischief or occasionally flash with anger; all emotions a real princess would have had the good manners to conceal. Then there was the matter of her clothes. Not only were they shabby but they were often dirty from the paws of the animals she handled every day.

Yet whenever Princess Suhitra appeared on the screen, he found his thoughts drifting back to the flesh and blood Suhitra and to that moment when she had knelt at his feet and wrapped the long cloth around his ankle.

The real-life Suhitra was prey to no such distracting thoughts as she watched the play progress, nor did she notice the passage of time until late that night when, during a long and violent battle scene, she decided to go over to the other side for a while and watch the puppets themselves rather than the shadows.

After going around the end of the banana stalk, she paused for a moment to watch the dance-like movements of the puppeteer and Surya gasped when he looked over and saw her; she was bathed in a golden glow from the lamp shining on the leather screen.

He was almost too astonished to breathe. Could it be that the Suhitra he knew was actually more than she appeared, that the little girl of the animals was an incarnation of the Princess Suhitra of long ago?

He shook his head in momentary awe and bewilderment. What terrible thing could the lovely princess have done in her previous life to have brought her so low in this one?

A scene of dastardly court intrigue was being played out on the screen. Unable to answer the question of Princess Suhitra's possible misdeeds, Surya gave up and allowed the intricacies of the plot to distract him.

Meanwhile Suhitra, who had always loved the *wayang*, found that her attention kept drifting towards Surya. Would he smile at her again, she wondered. It was better that he didn't. Did she even want him to? Rather than answer the question, she went back to the side of the shadows.

It didn't occur to Surya that he wasn't the only one whose eyes had been on Suhitra at the moment when the golden light had washed over her. He wasn't the only one who had seen a connection between the princess in the *wayang* and the little girl of the animals. The raja's brother, Prince Baliputra, had also been struck by it. In spite of the fact that the girl was merely the daughter of the dirty fellow who took care of the animals, he began making plans for her.

The entire kingdom, even the gods and goddesses themselves, celebrated the birth of the royal infant. On the night following the *wayang* performance and every night the following week, the goddess of the mountain and the sea - Nyai Loro Kidul - proclaimed the glory of the baby prince by sending a shower of fire into the sky from her dwelling-place deep within Mt. Merapi.

Then one afternoon the earth itself trembled and the jubilation at the court changed to consternation. Could it be that the powerful goddess was angry?

A tidal wave smashed across the shore at nearby Parangtritis, the goddess's ocean home just off the southern coast of the kingdom. Four villages were entirely washed away.

Rumours that some of the sacred rituals to appease Nyai Loro Kidul had been neglected began to gain credence; these ceremonies were of critical importance because she was the celestial wife of the raja. It was only the mystical relationship between these two divine beings - the god-king of Mataram and his consort, the goddess of the mountain and the sea - that kept the kingdom safe.

Their wedding had been solemnized by a grand procession around the base of Mt. Merapi, the goddess's earthly home, when the present raja had succeeded his father to the throne. Once a year, trailing back into the distant recesses of history and legend, it had been the sacred duty of the ruler to reaffirm his commitment to their union. He did this by offering himself to her in the form of all his carefully preserved nail and hair clippings from the preceding twelve months. These were taken to the edge of her watery home at Parangtritis and tossed into the waves for her pleasure, to the accompaniment of elaborate rituals and prayers.

But Nyai Loro Kidul, sometimes known as the Green Sea Goddess, was a demanding consort. The entire kingdom lived in fear of her power, anger and jealousy.

As it became clearer to everyone that the kingdom was in grave danger, extra ceremonies - many of which had long fallen into disuse - were performed to propitiate the various deities that held dominion over the lives of the people. Special offerings were brought to Nyai Loro Kidul off the coast at Parangtritis and other gifts were presented to her at the base of Mt. Merapi. At the Temple of Prambanan, the air was thick with the scent of incense carrying the prayers of the faithful to the great gods, Brahma, Vishnu and Shiva.

The intense activity didn't end there. Pilgrims scaled the heights of the Buddhist temple at Borobudur in their quest for salvation. Some members of the privileged elite even pursued the swifter path to enlightenment and subsequent nirvana offered by a Tantric sect. It was achieved through the heightened awareness and intensified sensory perceptions induced by human sacrifices and sexual orgies.

Several slaves disappeared from the palace but they weren't missed by anyone who mattered.

Widjojo received an order from the raja's brother to carve a golden handle. This was for the priests at a Tantric temple to use as the sacred implement to deflower virgins in special ceremonies.

The feverish religious activity appeared to bring good results. Fewer and fewer sparks poured out from the top of Mt. Merapi, the earth stopped trembling and the treacherous sea stayed within its proper bounds.

Yet as the weeks passed, people remained vaguely restless. More and more animals, seeming to sense danger, moved from the higher to the lower slopes of the mountain, while some of the more intrepid ones even found their way into the town. The temples remained scenes of incessant offerings and prayers.

Widjojo, deciding that his son was old enough

to begin working on important ceremonial objects as well as jewellery, allowed him to do some of the carving on the handle of the deflowering implement that the raja's brother had commissioned. This would make merit for the boy in the eyes of the gods and could improve his lot in his next incarnation. In any case, new orders were flooding in and he needed any help his son could give him.

Surya was thrilled with this elevation in his role. The only trouble was that, images of Suhitra bathed in the golden glow of the lamplight still wafted through his dreams at night. His father's increased demands meant that he no longer had time to spend hanging around the animal cages on the chance of running into her.

Yet he couldn't get her out of his mind. Sometimes his desire to see her would be so intense that he would get up before dawn, go down to the stream near the gibbon enclosure and hide behind the large clump of bougainvillaea in the hope of watching her take her morning bath. The sight of Suhitra drenching herself with pails of water, making her sarong and breast cloth cling to her in the most exciting way, left him floating with happiness and aching with longing for the rest of the day.

One morning while he was watching her, a gibbon swung onto one of the bamboo bars of its cage and, discovering that the bar had come off in its hand, it gave a cry of gleeful astonishment. The delighted little ape instantly gripped the adjacent bars with its other hand and one of its feet and successfully squeezed itself through to freedom. The young animal, brimming over with the mischievous nature of its species loped across the ground, leapt onto Suhitra's back and then swung on the long wet strands of her hair.

'Ouch,' she cried, 'let go! Get down!'

But the naughty creature, who loved to tease, only pulled harder.

Forgetting about keeping out of sight, Surya rushed over to pull the little beast away but the gibbon, thrilled that another playmate had come to join the fray, reached out his free hand and seized the newcomer's hair. In the ensuing whirlwind of flailing arms and legs, Surya missed his step and fell down at the water's edge, bringing Suhitra and the gibbon down with him. The startled ape immediately took off and Surya found himself half-lying on top of Suhitra.

'Are you alright?' he asked, breathlessly.

'I think so.'

'Are you sure?' he persisted, running a hand over the contours of her body.

'Yes, at least, I would be if you weren't crushing me.'

'Oh,' he exclaimed, turning red and rolling off her but not actually getting up. Instead he moved to one side and ran his fingertips along the line of her eyebrows, then over her eyelids and across her cheekbones.

She stayed quite still for a moment, knowing she should get up but not wanting to so, taking her cue from him, she reached up, touched his face and smiled.

A wave of almost unbearable pleasure raced through him. He lay motionless, scarcely daring to breathe for fear of breaking the spell as he felt the tips of her fingers drifting down to his neck and roaming over his back with a touch so light it almost seemed like a dream.

A roar from the cage of the oldest and largest tiger brought this heaven to an abrupt end by producing an instant change in Suhitra. She pushed him aside with a ferocity that astonished him and leapt to her feet.

'What's the matter?' he cried.

'That's Gatotkaca.'

For a moment Surya was baffled. Then he remembered that the tigers she took care of had names. 'You mean that really big tiger?'

'Of course, who else would roar like that?'

'Another tig –' he began.

'No, I recognise his voice. The others would never sound like that.'

'Why not?'

'Because Gatotkaca has a human soul and he's protecting me,' she exclaimed, in great agitation.

Surya had heard about the transfer of human souls

into the bodies of animals, especially pigs and tigers, but he had never actually had any contact with one of these extraordinary creatures. It made him nervous to feel that he had come so close to offending one. Still, he couldn't help being a little dubious. 'How do you know it has a human soul?' he demanded.

'The *dukun* told me.'

'How did he know?' he asked, a little nervously. It was common knowledge that *dukuns* had special insights into the spirit world and the word of one was never supposed to be questioned.

'I had told him about Gatotkaca, that my grandfather had been the one who had taken care of him until he had become too ill to carry on and that was when I started doing it. Since he's the oldest tiger, I always fed him first. I was doing that just at the moment when my grandfather died and you can't imagine what happened.'

Surya couldn't.

'A huge scorpion came up that close to my leg,' she continued, spreading her palms a little bit apart. 'It didn't hurt me though because Gatotkaca saw it, peed right on it and drove it away. Isn't that amazing?'

Surya nodded.

'My father said I should tell the *dukun* about it so I did and he explained that when my grandfather's soul left his body, it entered Gatotkaca's and was continuing to protect me, in much the same way he always had. Except, of course, my grandfather wouldn't have killed the scorpion by peeing on it. He would have hit it with a rock or something.'

'I'd like to have another look at that tiger,' declared Surya, now convinced that this was an extraordinary animal.

When they got to the cage, Gatotkaca, who had been pacing up and down, stopped and fixed Surya with a hostile stare.

'And there was another time he protected me,' Suhitra went on.

'When?' asked Surya, peering into the creature's large amber eyes, hoping for a glimpse of its human soul.

'Just before my father and I were supposed to go to my uncle's village for my cousin's hair-cutting ceremony, we didn't go. Gatotkaca stopped us.'

'How did he do that?'

'He appeared to me in a dream and although I couldn't quite get his exact words -'

'Words,' exclaimed Surya; this was more than he could believe.

'Maybe not words precisely,' Suhitra admitted. 'More like a roar but the kind of roar you can understand.'

'Maybe you can,' Surya declared truculently. 'I don't know who else would.'

'I don't know about that but I could tell Gatotkaca was warning us not to go and when I asked the *dukun* about it, he said it was a very clear sign and we would be foolish to carry on with our plans.'

'Why?'

'Well, you know what happened, don't you?'

'No.'

'My uncle's village is over near the temple at Borobudur, that's where they had that terrible cholera epidemic, you know.'

Surya didn't but pretended he did.

'It broke out on the very day we would have arrived there. Nearly half the people in the village died and we probably would have too.'

Surya was suitably impressed. This was definitely a tiger to be treated with respect.

The pressure on Surya was intense in the days that followed. He needed to focus all his attention on his work but he couldn't get Suhitra out of his mind. So many things about her puzzled him: the golden aura that had seemed to envelope her on the night of the *wayang* performance, the delicate outline of her features - more like those of a princess than like someone even a highly-placed slave might look down on - and the way she seemed to understand strange things, like tigers with human souls. What about her own soul, he wondered. What qualities from a previous life must linger there?

Certain that he would become demented if he let himself worry about these things, he forced himself to concentrate on the graceful figures he was carving on the deflowering handle.

One night he saw Suhitra in a dream. She was feeding great bloodstained lumps of meat to Gatotkaca and gradually, as he took them one by one from her hand, the brown of her skin changed to a radiant gold. Her shabby clothes turned into finely woven silk and the long protective cloth she wrapped around her arm when she played with the baby tiger was transformed into a band of pure gold with the head of Kala, the protector of the Temple of Prambanan, carved on it.

The dream haunted him throughout the following day, so much so that in the evening he went to see the *dukun* about it.

He found the old man sitting on a low wooden platform in front of his house, quietly chewing betel and apparently so deep in thought that Surya was a little hesitant about disturbing him.

But the *dukun*, sensing the presence of a visitor,

quickly became alert and listened intently to the account of the dream.

'The meaning of the dream is clear,' he said and, after a short pause, went on to confirm what Surya had suspected all along. 'In a former life, Suhitra was a royal princess, a very high and noble princess perhaps a queen. But she did something very bad. She has now been reborn into a very low level of the social order and must lead a life of penury and hardship to pay for her sins in that previous existence.'

The *dukun* fell silent for a moment while he carefully placed an areca nut and some lime on a betel leaf and rolled it into a shape vaguely resembling a cigar. Then he continued.

'It happens in certain cases that the soul clings to some characteristics of its body or its circumstances from an earlier life and this appears to have been what has happened in Suhitra's case.'

'Oh,' said Surya, not wanting to be rude but wishing the *dukun* would tell him something he didn't already know. So what should I do?'

'Do? Why should you do anything?'

Surya's mouth turned down at the corners but he didn't answer.

'I see,' said the *dukun*, in voice that was kind but had a warning.

23

Surya felt a sudden chill race down his spine. Could those ancient eyes have penetrated his secret thoughts?

'You must stay away from this girl,' the old man said. 'She brings to this life traces of a lineage that is far too high for you. And remember, she has a powerful protector, a tiger with a human soul. If you use her in the way you might use an ordinary servant girl, she will destroy you.'

Surya had feared an answer of this sort. He wanted to argue but managed, with some difficulty, to restrain himself. No one argued with a *dukun*; that would be unthinkable. All he could do was thank the holy man and leave with a firm resolve to put Suhitra out of his mind.

As the weeks passed, Abimanyu grew too big for Suhitra to pick up and hold so she began taking the tiger cub for walks through the palace grounds, controlling it with a collar and leash her father fashioned out of buffalo hide.

Much to her surprise, and not entirely to her father's pleasure, the raja's brother Prince Baliputra took a fancy to the animal and sent orders for her to bring it into his presence nearly every afternoon.

But then, Suhitra tripped over a rock, fell and sprained her ankle one day while she was chasing a gibbon that had escaped from its enclosure. It left her leg swollen and painful, so her father had to take over the task of giving the cub its exercise and taking it into the royal presence. This substitution did not appear to please the prince and as soon as Suhitra was able to limp along beside the young tiger, she was required to resume her duties.

Things went well until the day when Abimanyu took an unaccountable dislike to Prince Baliputra, snarled at him and bit him on the hand.

Word was sent down to the animal keeper that the visits were no longer required. He was terrified that his daughter would be blamed for the animal's offence.

He endured several days of tormented waiting before he allowed himself to relax a little. No order for retribution had been issued, not yet anyway. Still, he decided that he must take what precautions he could to protect Suhitra and that meant finding her a husband who lived far away from the palace, as quickly as possible

Luckily the festival of Durga Puja was approaching. With its elaborate procession of people, horses and elephants to the Temple of Prambanan, it would give him an opportunity to beseech the goddess for help in finding a husband for Suhitra. He considered Durga, the fiercest of the great god Shiva's wives, to be his special patron. She rode a tiger, possessed a fiery spirit and held a weapon in each of her eight hands so she could drive away the forces of evil.

With the help of such a powerful protector, he would surely be able to secure a good husband and a good life for his daughter.

With that thought in mind, he took three pieces of silver out of his meagre savings and used it to buy new clothes for himself and Suhitra, as well as offerings of fruit and flowers for the goddess.

Preparations for the festival began before dawn on the appointed day with the trainers grooming the royal horses and the mahouts taking the royal elephants to bathe in a nearby stream. Brightly coloured paint was brought out to serve as makeup for the faces of the animals and fine cloths were draped across their backs, while golden necklaces and anklets were hung around their necks and placed around their legs.

The raja rode to the temple on the back of the largest and most impressive elephant. Other nobles, some mounted on royal animals, others conveyed in elaborately decorated sedan chairs, followed throughout the day. The divine infant, the child of his youngest and current favourite wife, was cradled on a silken pillow in his nanny's arms and made the journey on an elephant that was only slightly smaller than his father's.

Lesser mortals, including the goldsmiths, went on foot but the journey passed in a dizzying flash for Surya. He had had a glimpse of the baby prince just as the nanny was adjusting one of the silken cloths around him and had seen that the heavenly child was wearing the tiger claw amulet Surya had carved for him. It had been the most thrilling sight of his life.

Suhitra's father, Nakula, mindful of how important the day could be in arranging his daughter's future, had been among the earliest of the pilgrims to arrive at the temple. He had managed to get a place close to the image of the Durga when she was taken from her niche in the chapel of Lord Shiva and he stayed close to her as she was carried seven times around the temple.

It was not until dusk had fallen and the crowd was beginning to disperse that Surya caught a glimpse of Suhitra. Had the goddess endowed her with a special radiance for the day's celebrations, he wondered, or was it just that she was wearing a new sarong that hugged her hips and legs and made her seem different? She had a new breast cloth too, he noticed, and it made him think of the way she had looked during the wayang performance when the lamplight had been shining on her.

He was no more able to stay away from her than he could keep her out of his dreams. He didn't give a thought to the *dukun's* warning as he walked over to her.

She was talking to two other girls in front of the chapel

27

of Ganesha, the elephant-headed god, but she hurried away when she saw him coming. She was mindful of what her father might say if he saw her with a boy, today of all days.

'What's the matter?' he asked, refusing to be rebuffed. Catching up with her, he blurted out, 'You look different today, not like someone who takes care of dirty animals.'

Her eyes flashed with anger, her animals weren't dirty and she told him so.

Surya's vision of her as a noble princess faded. No well-bred Javanese lady would ever show her emotions like that but then he should be glad Suhitra was acting like a coarse peasant girl. It gave him a chance to reassume the feeling of superiority he had always had when he was with her. After all, he was a skilled craftsman, some might even say an artist, and what was she? A nobody. Still, he could afford to be kind.

'You look sad today, in spite of being all dressed up.' he said. 'Is something the matter?'

She nodded.

'My father is asking the goddess to help find a husband for me.'

'You want one, don't you?'

'No,' she said emphatically.

'I thought all girls wanted husbands.'

'I don't.'

'You know what I think?'

'No, and I don't care. I don't care about anything anymore.'

This outburst was so unlike anything the semi-deified Suhitra of his dreams would have said that he reacted by declaring, 'You'll be lucky if your father can get an orang-utan to marry you.'

'I'll be luckier than the girl who's going to marry you anyway.'

Surya's furious reply was stifled by the arrival of Nakula looking as happy as a man who had just stumbled across buried treasure.

'Wonderful news, my daughter,' he exclaimed, almost breathless with excitement. 'The goddess is bestowing a blessing on us that is magnificent beyond all our dreams.'

Suhitra's face turned to stone. She knew what this blessing must be.

'A rich man, my daughter, a rich rice farmer. He owns five water buffalo and enough good rice land to feed more than twenty people and he is willing to marry you. I met him at the very feet of our special goddess. He had watched you praying and asked me about you. He is rich, just think of that, rich! You will have a wonderful life. You will –'

He broke off, nodded and bowed to a man whom Suhitra thought must be at least thirty-five and who held a small boy by the hand.

'It's not him, is it?' Suhitra asked with a shudder. 'He's so old.'

'No, no,' Nakula said, laughing uproariously. 'That's not him, that's his son and his grandson.'

'But you can't marry me to a grandfather,' she cried in horror. 'You wouldn't do that, would you? It would be too awful. I couldn't bear it.'

'Don't worry, child,' her father said soothingly, 'you'll only see him in the dark so what does it matter? In the daytime he'll be too busy counting his bags of rice and his gold to pay any attention to you. And in nine months you'll have a fat baby to take care of. That will be better than of a lot of animals, won't it? You'll have plenty of good food to eat and other wives to share the work. A year from now you'll be thanking me.'

'No I won't,' Suhitra insisted, stubbornly, 'and I won't marry him.'

'There, there,' Nakula said, determined not to let her rudeness dampen his spirits. She would soon think differently. After all, a rich husband, lots of babies, what more could any girl want?

'You've always been a good child,' he said confidently. 'You'll do as I tell you.'

'Not his time,' she cried, and before her father could stop her, she flew off in the direction of Durga's sanctuary.

After pushing heedlessly past the people queuing on the narrow steps, she threw herself down in front of the image of the special deity, now returned to her place in the incense-filled dimness of the interior, and pleaded.

'Oh great Goddess who rides a tiger, please help me. Show me how to escape this terrible marriage. Don't make me sleep in the same bed as some wrinkled old man, a grandfather with no teeth and horrible sagging skin and no hair. I'll die before I'll let someone like that feel me and touch me and make a baby inside me. But I don't want to die, I want to live.'

'Oh, great Goddess, I want to be like you, have a brave heart like yours, tame tigers and kill demons like you do and,' she looked up longingly, at the weapons in the goddess's eight hands, 'and I want to have a powerful sword like yours.'

But then what would be the use of that, she realised, for who could she kill? Not her father, that would be unthinkable. Not this dreadful husband, the retribution would be too terrible. Not only would she have to pay with her life for such a horrific crime but she would suffer the anger of the gods through countless future incarnations. Didn't the priests say that a woman should treat her husband like a god no matter how dreadful he was? Surely she would be better off just killing herself? But every time she tried to think about that she came up against the same obstacle, she wanted so much to live.

She put her forehead down against the cool stone of the sanctuary floor and let the tears of despair flood down her cheeks, until eventually she felt some of the goddess's fierce courage seeping into her heart.

She didn't notice that by then everyone else had left the little chapel and she was alone in the quiet darkness.

Her father hadn't tried to follow her. He had been pleased to see her go and seek the counsel of the goddess. She was only a child and it was natural that the thought of marriage, especially to such a rich and important man, should frighten her. Durga would make her realise her good fortune. Hadn't the goddess already blessed the marriage by arranging today's meeting?

With all the pride and elation of a man who knew he was favoured by the gods, he strolled among the remaining worshippers and spread the news of his daughter's good fortune.

Surya, temporarily paralysed by the conflicting emotions swirling around within him, hadn't followed her either. Her outspoken defiance had shocked him. Rudeness like that wasn't at all in keeping with the behaviour of an incarnation of a princess. On the contrary it showed her to be an ordinary mortal like himself, only much lower in the social order.

Yet somehow her passionate rebellion had inflamed

his desire for her, whipping it up to the point where lurid images of a lecherous old man enjoying her naked body were tearing him apart.

Shaking his head in an attempt to drive these awful pictures from his mind, he slowly made his way over to Durga's chapel and lingered near the stone elephant-fish at the entrance until he was sure that everyone, apart from Suhitra, had left. Then he climbed up the steep stone stairs and went into the shadowy interior.

At first he was barely able to make out Suhitra's prostrate form but when his eyes adjusted to the gloom, he knelt down beside her and caressed the silky strands of her now-disordered hair.

'Suhitra,' he said in a soft whisper, almost as if he wished to prevent the goddess from hearing, 'don't be sad. I won't let you marry that old man, I promise you I won't.'

'You,' she exclaimed, turning to him in surprise. 'What can you do about it?'

'I can marry you.'

She looked at him in astonishment. He was rather shocked at this suggestion himself.

'But you're already engaged,' she pointed out.

'I'll ask my father to break it off.'

'He'll never agree.'

'He might.'

'He wouldn't let you marry someone like me even if

you weren't already engaged.'

'Yes he –'

'There's no point in lying,' she said firmly. 'I'm not a fool. I have some idea of what's possible and what isn't.'

'I guess I know what's possible too,' he admitted sadly. Then, taking her hand and running it along the side of his face, he said, 'I just wish I could be the one to marry you instead of just standing back and letting some rich old man do it.'

Hearing the sympathy in his voice, seeing the distress in his eyes and feeling that at least she had a friend, Suhitra impulsively put her arms around his neck and pressed her tear-stained face into his shoulder.

The gesture set him on fire. He pressed her to him, stroked her hair and ran his hand down her back.

The pleasure she felt at his touch drove everything else from her mind until, suddenly remembering they were in the presence of the goddess, she gasped, 'No, stop, you mustn't.'

'But I'm not about to –'

She didn't wait to hear what he wasn't about to do. Instead she leapt up, flung herself down the steps and went in search of her father. Left alone, Surya carried on kneeling at Durga's feet and began to pray.

'Oh powerful Goddess,' he murmured, 'you who rides a tiger and holds a weapon in each of your eight hands.

Won't you regard Suhitra as your special daughter and protect her? She takes care of tigers and is almost a mother to one. And she is watched over by a tiger with a human soul named Gatotkaca. Please don't let her virginity be sacrificed to the pleasure of that lascivious old man.'

And in spite of the goddess's ferocious appearance, Surya was convinced he could see a slight smile of understanding cross her face. Reassured, he left the sanctuary with a feeling of hope. Things might work out somehow.

The news of Suhitra's good fortune quickly spread around the palace. It was quite extraordinary for someone in her position to become the wife, even the fifth or sixth wife, of such a rich and important man. As a result, both she and her father were treated with a new respect.

The wedding was to be formalized with minimal ceremony as befitted the low status of the bride and the number of senior wives of the groom. Nevertheless, astrologers were consulted to determine the day and time of the wedding and Suhitra was to receive a pair of gold earrings from her prospective husband.

A day scarcely three weeks away was declared the

auspicious one and Suhitra woke up each morning with a greater sense of desperation as it approached.

Her father proved implacable in his insistence that she go through with the marriage and this drove her thoughts to the possibility of running away but, however she looked at it, this means of escape never led to a happy outcome. Starvation, prostitution, or some kind of slavery would be the inevitable result so she could only hope that the old man would die or forget about her before the wedding.

Occasionally she even allowed herself to believe that Surya's father would prove unexpectedly understanding and allow him to marry her. Horrid as he could be at times, at least he was young but she never held on to that hope for more than a few seconds at a time.

In fact, the master goldsmith had been outraged at the mere suggestion of such a marriage. The boy must be mad to think it might be possible! He would ignore the impudence of such a request this time, shameful though it was, but he wanted to hear no more about it.

Suhitra didn't know that there was yet another person in the palace who wasn't pleased by her 'good fortune'. The raja's younger brother, Prince Baliputra, had not forgotten her and, after some serious reflection, came up with a very different plan for her.

Although essentially a Hindu, the prince had become a member of a Tantric sect, a legacy from the preceding Sailendra dynasty which offered a rapid route to individual salvation and one where it was not necessary to live through numerous incarnations to attain it.

It was believed that a mystical union with the Ultimate Spiritual Reality could be achieved through the delirious exhilaration, heightened perceptions and fevered ecstasy induced by the spilling of human blood or the union of men and women in sexual orgasm. The door to paradise would then stand open for the privileged few who had been wise enough to have participated in the orgiastic rituals.

To that end, the throats of three slaves had been slit in a special ceremony on the night of the last full moon.

Prince Baliputra, more than most people, was still disturbed by the sparks that were shooting into the sky from Mt Merapi. Although they were shooting at a reduced rate, he felt that more must be done to appease the gods. A generous gift from him, one of extraordinary beauty and value, would surely please them. What could be better than to offer a girl who had lingering traces of a previous life within her, ones that gave a golden glow to her skin and highlighted the delicate features and graceful movements that set her apart from others of her status? The moon would be full and round again in twenty days and he would offer Suhitra to the gods.

The prince smiled as he pictured her, freshly bathed and dressed and wearing jasmine flowers in her hair, like a bride being led to the altar. He pictured her legs spread apart, her arms pinioned down by the chanting priests and a freshly oiled deflowering instrument shaped like an erect phallus plunged into the soft feminine centre of her body. After she had been opened in the sacred ritual, he would be the first one, apart from the high-priest of course, to enjoy her. For an exquisite moment they would become one with the creative force of the universe and only then would the lower ranking participants in the rites be given a chance to have their turn with her.

A great many people were expected to attend the ceremony and Prince Baliputra congratulated himself on his forethought in arranging for the deflowering of two other girls in the same ceremony. It would, he thought, be inauspicious for his special gift to die before the night was out.

He sent word to Widjojo that it was very important for the deflowering implement to be ready by then, so the already-overworked goldsmith turned the task of carving its decoration over to his son.

Surya tried to push thoughts of Suhitra out of his mind and focus on the fine detail required by the work but he managed to anger his father nonetheless by repeatedly asking to be released from his engagement to the girl in the Kingdom of Gold.

Shortly before sunset on the night of the full moon, Prince Baliputra sent a servant woman named Jumwati to Suhitra with orders that she was to follow her. Wondering what it was all about and thinking it must be something about Abimanyu, Suhitra did as she was told.

Much to her surprise, Jumwati led her to the palace gate. A cart, drawn by a pair of large bullocks and occupied by two other girls about her age, as well as two older servant women and a driver, was waiting and Jumwait told her to get in.

'Where are we going?' Suhitra asked.

'To Chandi Mahadewa.'

'Where is that?'

'Not far, you'll see.'

'But why?'

'Because that's where Prince Baliputra says you're to go.'

Knowing that disobeying the prince would be no laughing matter, she hastily climbed in.

The cart was just pulling away from the gate when Surya rushed out calling, 'Wait, wait for me.'

The cart didn't wait but the bullocks refused to be

hurried and Surya soon caught up with it, threw in a small package and climbed in after it.

'What are you doing here?' Suhitra asked.

'Delivering this,' he said, indicating his package and smoothing out the coarse cotton it was wrapped in. 'My father said I have to give it to the priest at Chandi Mahadewa myself. He doesn't dare trust anyone else with it.'

'What is it?'

'A new implement for deflowering a virgin. I carved the handle myself and it's going to be used in a ceremony tonight. I'd show it to you but I don't want these other people to see it.'

'Why not?'

'They might try to steal it. The handle is pure gold so it's worth a fortune.'

Suhitra nodded with understanding. She didn't like the look of the two serving women, nor of Jumwati for that matter.

Thinking Suhitra looked genuinely disappointed, Surya decided that he absolutely had to show it to her. After all, the carving on it was the best work he had ever done and he was justly proud of it.

'Let's go over there,' he said, nodding towards a corner of the now-lurching vehicle.

She agreed and, when they were sitting with their

backs to the other passengers, he pulled back a little bit of the wrapping and revealed a small section of the precious handle.

Suhitra gasped when she saw it. The figures on it were so exquisitely carved that they seemed to spring to life.

'It's Lord Shiva and his consort, Parvati,' explained Surya, thrilled by her obvious admiration.

'It's the most beautiful thing I've ever seen,' she told him, without exaggeration.

'Shhh,' he said, quickly wrapping the cloth around it again.

'Can't I see the rest of it?'

'No,' he returned firmly and then, suddenly curious, asked, 'What are you doing here anyway?'

'I don't really know.'

'But you must.'

'I only know that Prince Baliputra ordered me come. He likes the tigers so it may have something to do with Abimanyu or it might be about my hateful wedding. I keep feeling there has to be a way out of it somehow but I don't know how. Every plan I think of turns out to be just as dreadful as the marriage itself or even worse. And now, on top of everything else, I think Gatotkaca, our oldest tiger, is sick. This morning he wouldn't –'

But Surya was no longer listening. The mention of Prince Baliputra had filled him with terror. If Suhitra were being summoned to Chandi Mahadewa to clean the courtyards or take care of the animals, she would know why she was going. And a brother of a raja wouldn't care about her wedding to some peasant farmer, no matter how rich the man was. A man like that would only care about Suhitra for one thing.

Surya suddenly felt he wanted to crush the deflowering implement, golden handle and all, between his hands. The thought that he had worked on it himself, longing for Suhitra all the time, when it would actually be used to –

Oh God, he couldn't let himself think about it. But he would have to think about it and think hard. What other hope would she have?

It occurred to him that Prince Baliputra might not be very interested in tigers; seeing Abimanyu might have just been an excuse to see Suhitra. But why would he have needed an excuse? Surely he could have just sent for her when he wanted her and dismissed her when he didn't. And if he was interested in her himself, why was he sending her to all those randy monks at Chandi Mahadewa when they were likely to fuck her to death during their horrible ceremony?

He had heard rumours of what went on in the temples where Tantric rituals were practised and, like everyone else, he had observed that slaves and servants who were taken there usually didn't come back. He had heard the stories that boys told each other about what happened to the virgins there but had never been so audacious, or so foolish, as to question the actions of the priests.

Now, a realisation of what would almost certainly happen to Suhitra swept over him with horrific clarity.

Surya leaned over the side of the cart and threw up.

Something about the raja's brother kept nagging at him as the water buffalo lumbered on. Could Prince Baliputra have noticed Suhitra the way he had on the night of the *wayang* performance, noticed the strangeness of someone in her low position being covered with a golden glow that brought out a delicate, almost aristocratic, quality in her appearance?

Suddenly he put it all together. Vestiges of nobility handed down from a previous life would make her a glorious gift for the gods, one so extraordinary that it would go a long way to assuring salvation for the prince.

'Jump out,' he whispered hoarsely in Suhitra's ear, 'run, get away as fast as you can. Go to the old man who wants to marry you.'

'But why –'

'Hurry, you've got to go now while you still have a chance. And it has to be before the old man realises how risky it'll be to let you in.'

'I'd rather die and anyway, why should I?'

'You probably will die if you don't go now. Listen,

Suhitra, I think the deflowering implement I made may have been meant for you.'

Her eyes widened in astonishment as she took in the implication of his words.

'So you see, you've got to get away now, quickly, before we get there.'

'I don't believe it. Prince Baliputra has always been nice to me. He didn't even complain when the tiger bit him. He would never send me to the monks for anything like that. It must be something to do with my wedding.'

'Don't be so easily taken in.'

'I don't believe I'm being taken in,' she insisted stubbornly.

'You don't understand,' he protested, exasperated that he didn't seem to be getting through to her. 'There're going to be lots of men, all kinds of men, at that ceremony tonight and it won't be just the priests who'll have sex with you, the others will too. None of them will care what happens to you after they've finished and even if you live through it, you'll just be another temple prostitute. You don't want that, do you?'

But before she had a chance to answer, Jumwati, curious to know what Suhitra and the goldsmith boy were talking about, came over and planted herself firmly between them.

At that point the cart rounded a bend in the road. The tall spire of a stupa came into view and Surya realised in despair that Suhitra's chance was lost.

The bullocks were drawn to a stop at the gate of the sacred precinct and Suhitra, along with the two other girls, was taken down off the cart and led away to a bathing place.

All Surya could do was hand over his package to a young priest who was waiting near the entrance to receive it. Even if he didn't give it to them, he knew they wouldn't cancel the ceremony for the lack of a new deflowering implement. He just wished he could get the thought of what it would be used for out of his mind. But he had known about that all along, he reminded himself, he just hadn't thought it would be used on Suhitra. That changed everything.

Absorbed in his dark thoughts Surya walked over to a banyan tree, sat down in its resplendent shade and absently took out the knife he had tucked in his sarong. It was his favourite possession, so sharp it could be used for incising gold, and he took it with him everywhere. Usually he enjoyed running his fingers along the flat side of the blade, feeling its shiny surface between his fingers and visualizing the master-carver he would one day become. But now, for the first time, it did nothing to lift his spirits so he returned it to its protective covering, put his head in his hands and succumbed to a wave of hopeless misery.

No one seemed to notice him.

He asked himself over and over again how he could have so blithely set about carving that golden handle, without thinking about what it was going to be used for. How could he not have questioned the necessity of the sacred rituals? The priests said they were needed, but were they? Would those rites and ceremonies really stop the fire from coming out of the mountain or keep the earth from trembling beneath their feet? Would they really open the way to paradise for those who participated in them?

The learned priests, the ones who understood and controlled the mysterious forces of the universe, said they would, and they had read the sacred texts so they must know. How could a simple goldsmith like himself know enough to question their teaching? He could read a little, even write a bit, but most of his time had been spent learning how to fashion a nugget of gold into an object of even greater beauty than the raw material itself. What was this knowledge compared to that of the priests?

And what if Suhitra had followed his advice and run away from her part in the ceremony? Would they both have suffered the retribution of the gods through countless future lives? He shuddered at the thought. Or was it possible that the priests were wrong, that the mountains would spit fire and the earth would tremble whether slaves were sacrificed and virgins were used as prostitutes or not?

Surya broke out in a cold sweat as the incredible

sacrilege of these thoughts dawned on him. Surely he would be struck by lightning or swallowed up by an angry demon? He braced himself and waited in terror for it to happen.

It didn't.

Eventually he allowed himself to breathe more easily and was able to take in the scene around him.

A number of ragged musicians were straggling into the compound and beginning to practise their instruments when a priest appeared from a small wooden building behind the main sanctuary and, spotting Surya, questioned him sharply about who he was and what he was doing there.

'I'm the goldsmith who carved the handle of –'

He broke off, finding it difficult to say the words, 'the deflowering implement.' Before the priest had a chance to tell him to leave, he added untruthfully, 'Prince Baliputra ordered me to wait for him here.'

Instructions from such an exalted source could not be countermanded so the priest returned to his other duties, leaving Surya alone with his desperate thoughts.

The musicians settled into a serious practice session and the rhythmic beat of their instruments, mostly percussion, reverberated through Surya's veins and inspired him with a new determination. If he could just find Suhitra, he might be able to figure out some way to help her escape.

Her confidence in Prince Baliputra must surely have been shattered by this time, so she would cooperate and it might be possible to work something out.

He was right about the trust. Within minutes of being taken to a bathing place at the back of the compound, she had realised how wrong she had been and the coarse jokes of Jumwati and two other servant women had done nothing to cushion her disillusionment. Quite the contrary, they had soon filled in the details that Surya had omitted.

Horrified but unable to see a way out, she allowed herself to be bathed in scented water, dressed in a silk sarong and draped with a breast cloth embroidered with gold thread. Jasmine flowers in her hair completed the effect.

In despair she beseeched her special goddess, Durga, for help but no help came. She sent out a silent call to her other protector, Gatotkaca, but he too seemed to have abandoned her.

Deciding that she would have to rely on herself, she looked around frantically for a way to escape but didn't see one. Then she was pushed, along with the other two freshly bathed and dressed girls, into a small windowless room and left there under the watchful eyes of Jumwati and her companions.

Time lost all meaning as they waited, though there were thin open spaces between the slats of the walls that told them it was now dark. After a while, the other two girls lapsed into a state of numbed acquiescence but Suhitra never stopped racking her brain for a way to escape.

Then, although it seemed that everything was hopeless, she felt an inexplicable lightness of spirit. She didn't know that it was the very same moment that Gatotkaca's human soul left its body.

But Suhitra's father knew. Nakula heard the majestic animal give its final roar, a sound of anguish mixed with triumph as if, in shedding the confines of its feline body, the extraordinary creature was attaining a higher plane of existence.

The sound so filled him with wonder that, as he rushed toward its source, he did the unthinkable and left the door of Kumbokarno's cage ever so slightly ajar.

News that one of the full-grown tigers was at large in the palace grounds quickly drove everyone, except Nakula and a few unfortunate slaves who had no choice, into firmly barricaded rooms within their own pavilions.

The crisis delayed the arrival of Prince Baliputra and several of the nobles at the Tantric temple. The evening's rituals and ceremonies couldn't begin until they got there and the late start to proceedings was viewed as an ill omen, one that sent waves of apprehension through the ranks of the priests.

But to Surya, pacing the compound at Chandi

Mahadewa, every moment's delay gave him a little longer to find a way out for Suhitra. He just kept telling himself that there had to be one.

His first bit of luck came in the form of an indiscreet temple boy who pointed to a thatch hovel behind the main sanctuary and said, 'She's in that hut over there.'

Surya's first thought was that the walls looked so flimsy he could cut a small hole in one of them and talk to her through it. Even though she was only a girl, she might be able to help him figure something out. But he quickly thought better of this plan. He would be heard and seen and taken away and then he would lose what little power he had to help her.

Still, he thought, just letting her know that he had found her might keep her going until he could devise some kind of plan. He'd have to be careful though, no one must suspect he was talking to her.

He dealt with the situation by strolling back and forth in front of the hut, chanting the names of the raja's tigers as if he were reciting the mantras of a secret cult. 'Gatotkaca,' he began, as loudly as he dared and then went on to reel off the names of the others, 'Arimbi, Abimanyu, Kumbokarno, Banowati.' Each time he finished the list, he started over again. It was just lucky that the tigers were named after well-known characters in the *wayang* plays so they were easy to remember.

Suhitra, instantly alert at the sound of Surya's voice, suddenly recalled the moment in the bullock cart when he had shown her a bit of the golden handle and said that if the people around them saw it, they might want to steal it.

It only took a moment for the rudiments of a plan to burst forth in her imagination and, without bothering to fill in the details, she went over to Jumwati and whispered, 'Do you want to be rich?'

'Rich,' the servant woman cackled loudly enough for everyone to hear, 'stupid girl, who wouldn't want to be rich? I'd buy me some good rice land and a strong young husband to work on it and throw away that useless sack of bones I'm married to.'

Her fellow servants shrieked with laughter.

'I'm serious. I can show you a way to get really, really rich,' persisted Suhitra, still trying to keep the conversation to a whisper.

'You,' Jumwati jeered, 'what can you show me? You can't show anybody anything.'

'Yes I can. I know where there's something that's made of pure gold, something that's worth a fortune and it's right here in this temple. We can steal it, run away to a foreign country and sell it for lots and lots of money.'

Jumwati narrowed her eyes and regarded Suhitra suspiciously for a moment, then she spat on the floor to indicate her opinion of the plan. But Suhitra was too desperate to let herself be put off.

'It's the golden handle for the deflowering implement, the one that will be used in the ceremony tonight. I've seen it and,' she paused for a second, not quite certain how much she could persuade Jumwati to believe, 'I know where it is and how we can get it.'

Catching a flicker of interest in Jumwati's eyes, she decided to give full rein to her imagination.

'There's a kingdom I've heard about,' she said. 'It's far away from here, way over near the River of Diamonds. No one will find us there. We'll go up to the north coast, travelling by night, and then take a boat. I'll be your daughter and when we get there we'll sell the handle and live like royalty for the rest of our lives.'

'Don't bother me with your nonsense,' Jumwati snapped, but Suhitra could see that she had aroused the woman's curiosity so she went on filling her ears with tales of how easy it was all going to be and how luxurious their life would be when they reached the River of Diamonds.

When her imagination flagged, the sound of Surya chanting the names of her tigers gave her the encouragement she needed to go on. And when she felt she could interrupt her narrative for a moment or two, she would reply by chanting the tigers' names back to him, pressing her palms together as she did in the hope that Jumwati and the others, too ignorant to recognise the names of the characters from the *wayang*, would think she was praying.

Gradually Jumwati's greed began to gnaw away at her prudence but still she maintained her stance. 'Your plan is stupid. We'd starve before we got far enough away to sell such a precious thing.'

'No we wouldn't,' Suhitra argued. 'I'm young and there will always be men along the road, even more at the port too, so I'll be able to get money for us.'

'How do I know you won't just keep it for yourself?'

'Because you'll have the golden handle tied under your sarong.'

Jumwati turned this possibility over in her dull mind and Suhitra sensed that victory was near.

'But first I'll need a ratty old sarong,' Suhitra told her. 'And a broom and a handful of dirt. Quickly, before it's too late.'

Jumwati hesitated.

'Jewels, fine clothes, delicious things to eat, you want them don't you?' Suhitra reminded her. 'But you must hurry. We don't have much time.'

Jumwati wanted them enough to overcome her suspicions about Suhitra's story so she slipped out the door and returned a few minutes later with the required objects.

The sarong, worn to the temple by one of the other girls in the hut, was suitably tattered and dirty so Suhitra put it on, ripped the jasmine flowers from her hair and smudged her face and arms with dirt. Taking the broom, she went out into the compound and, sweeping the ground in front of her, looked around for Surya.

He saw her first and gasped, she hadn't been bathed and dressed like a sacrificial virgin after all. But then, he wondered, why had she been brought here?

She swept a path over to him as quickly as she dared, Jumwati following closely behind her.

'What are –' he began.

'Shhh,' she returned and, leaning close to his ear, whispered an outline of her plan.

'Don't tell him anything,' Jumwati hissed.

'I have to,' Suhitra returned, 'we need his help.'

'They took it in there,' he told her, with a nod in the direction of the sanctuary. 'It's probably on the high altar by now.'

She immediately turned towards it but he caught her arm in warning.

'The place is full of priests, all in there praying. They'll never let you get anywhere near it but I might just be able to manage it. Wait for me at the temple gate, outside it if you can.'

'Don't you dare try it, you cheating whore,' rasped Jumwati, who had managed to catch the gist of what he was saying. 'I'll shout, I'll tell everyone you are a thief and you're trying to escape with the sacred treasure. You'll never get through that gate alive, not unless you give me the handle first.'

'You wouldn't fare any better,' Surya pointed out. 'You're the one who's supposed to be guarding her.'

'Yes I would, I'd be the one who caught her,' Jumwati returned, with more certainty than she really felt. 'I'll get a big reward.'

'Okay, forget the gate,' Surya said, just in case she was right. 'Wait here, I'll go in and get it. You wouldn't stand a chance.'

'The old hag,' he added, indicating Jumwati, 'better wait here too. Stand near the wall where no one's likely to notice you.'

Surya left them and hurried over to the massive sanctuary door, wanting to get there before his courage failed him. He pushed against it but an angry young priest sprang forward. 'You can't go in there!'

'I have to, it's a command from the raja himself,' Surya replied, grasping at the first excuse he could think of. 'He wants his name engraved on the new deflowering handle.'

The priest regarded him suspiciously and continued to block his entrance. Surya saw that he needed to improve his story.

'It's because he can't be here tonight and he wants it to be known that the deflowering implement is a gift from him.'

The priest didn't quite know what to make of this explanation.

'It's so that his spirit can be here,' Surya continued, 'and since I'm the goldsmith who did the carving on the handle, I'm the one he ordered to engrave his name on it.'

The priest thought this sounded reasonable and the very thought of not carrying out the raja's wishes wasn't something he could risk. 'I'll speak to the High Holy One about it,' he said.

He meant for Surya to wait outside but by the time he realised that he hadn't, the sanctuary door had swung closed and they were both inside.

His first thought was to get the boy out but, realising this would be likely to cause a scuffle and that he might be blamed for it, he decided to ignore Surya's presence and hope the other priests would be too intent on their prayers to pay much attention to him.

Surya, hoping the same thing, didn't like the look of the rows of maroon robed priests he saw sitting cross-legged on either side of a large flat altar; the altar on which –

He couldn't bear to think about it, especially not in this room – the flickering oil lamps, the sandalwood-scented smoke and the chanted mantras gave a terrible reality to the plans for the night.

When the young priest was within earshot of His High

Holiness, the abbot, he relayed the message from the raja and the unusual request it contained.

His High Holiness did not like the raja who had previously lent his support to other temples and priests but never to Tantric cults such as his own. It was only the raja's younger brother, Prince Baliputra, who had been active in the practice of Tantric rituals. A request from the raja could not be dismissed lightly but there were times when even a god-king had to give way to the high priests. After all, weren't they the ones who controlled every aspect of life through their knowledge and practice of the sacred rituals? Weren't these the very rituals that made the sun rise, the rain fall and the winds blow? Without these essential elements, would the rice grow, would there be food or water, would even the glorious raja himself survive?

Clearly the answer was no. The power of the high priests surpassed that of any earthly power.

After His High Holiness had assured himself on this point, his eyes fell on the brazen boy standing next to the young priest. How had he dared to penetrate these sacred precincts during the preparations for an important ceremony? He waved his hand and signalled for the intruder to be taken away and appropriately punished.

Almost instantaneously, Surya was surrounded by four maroon-clad priests who, with a strength unlikely to have been acquired in prayer, pinioned his arms behind his back and dragged him to the heavy door. Terrifying pictures of slaves who had been sent to the temple and never been seen again flashed through his mind and gave a vital impetus to his imagination.

'But the raja's gift,' he gasped, ostensibly addressing his words to his immediate captors but speaking loudly enough for His High Holiness to hear. 'If the raja's commands aren't followed, the temple surely won't receive his magnificent gift.'

In his panic, Surya had lighted on His High Holiness's favourite subject; gifts. And very large gifts such as those a raja might bestow, were the most enthralling of all. It was good to have a brother of the raja, like Prince Baliputra, take a personal interest in the temple but gifts from him, welcome as they always were, would surely pale in comparison with the munificence of gifts from the raja himself. With careful manipulation, a substantial part of such a gift could be diverted into his own personal coffers.

A hint of a smile flickered across the holy countenance as he reflected that the raja was welcome to have his name carved on the high altar itself if it led to an agreeable flow of gold coins in the right direction.

After a few murmured words to an acolyte, Surya's arms were freed and the young priest who had brought him into the sanctuary was ordered to take the deflowering implement from the altar and give it to him.

Suhitra and Jumwati gasped in astonishment and relief when they saw Surya, escorted by the priest, come out of the sanctuary with the precious object in his hand.

'I need some light if I'm to do this work,' Surya told the priest, in the arrogant tone he felt befitted a master craftsman, 'and a place to sit.'

The priest eyed Jumwati and ordered, 'Get a mat for the goldsmith to sit on.'

Realising she had no choice but to obey, she was motioning to Suhitra to follow her when the priest thwarted her plan.

'And you,' he said, turning to Suhitra, 'bring a lamp.'

'Actually that one will do,' Surya interjected, pointing to one not far away, 'just have it brought closer. And I want the ground swept before I put down a mat.'

Suhitra was pressed into service for these tasks and Jumwati reluctantly went off alone to fetch a mat.

Surya, mentally sizing up the distance between Suhitra and the temple gate, wondered just how to get her through it without arousing suspicion. It wasn't very far but it wouldn't be easy and he'd have to think of something before Jumwati got back.

A continued obsession with cleanliness was the best strategy he could come up with so, after berating Suhitra for the abysmal state of the compound, he declared that the stone walkway between the sanctuary door and the temple gate was too dusty for Prince Baliputra's feet.

'Sweep it,' he ordered, with an imperious wave of his arm.

The true purpose of this command was not lost on Suhitra. Conscious that she must look like she was just trying to make the place spotless for the occasion, she made her way towards the gate as quickly as she could.

She was almost there when she heard Surya say, 'I think I hear the Prince and his retinue coming.'

The priest, keeping a close watch on him, cocked his head to listen. He didn't hear anything but still wanted to be the first to greet the illustrious group from the palace, so he hurried towards the gate.

'There, that's the top of the Prince's umbrella,' Surya cried, dashing around in front of the priest, 'just beyond the bend in the road, see?'

The priest didn't see.

'You're not tall enough,' Surya suggested. Pointing to a slight rise in the ground on the other side of the dirt track in front of the temple, he added, 'We'd be able to see better from over there.'

'And sweep away this dog shit in front of the gate too,' he shouted over his shoulder to Suhitra as they started across the road, 'Prince Baliputra is nearly here.'

No sooner had the credulous priest reached the spot in question than Surya darted around behind him, pulled out the knife he used for incising gold and drove it through the back of the unfortunate fellow's neck. Blood spurted out in an arc of scarlet as the priest fell unconscious to the ground.

'Quick,' Surya told Suhitra, 'before anyone can get us.' Seizing her by the hand, he ran for his life, for her life, for the two of them together, faster than he would have ever thought possible.

They ran for what seemed like forever along the narrow dikes that criss-crossed the flooded rice fields, past the thatched storage huts high on stilts and around the occasional shrine. Then with pounding hearts and bursting lungs, they forced themselves to run some more. Eventually there came a point when Suhitra couldn't go any further.

'Stop,' she panted, 'I just can't –'

She didn't need to say any more because Surya was exhausted too. Nevertheless he looked around nervously as he slowed his pace. 'No one's following us yet,' he observed with relief.

'What are we going to do?' she asked. 'We can't just keep running and running and –'

'I know,' replied Surya, who had been too intent on just getting away to think about anything else but as he was catching his breath, he considered their situation.

'That plan you made with Jumwati,' he said after

a few minutes, 'wasn't so bad.' Of course, he didn't like the part about her getting money from men along the way but that wouldn't be necessary. He could steal enough food to get them there. 'Maybe the thing to do is to get to the North Coast.'

'But how? It's so far and I can't run anymore, at least not for a while.'

'Remember what you told Jumwati,' he said, glancing around uneasily. He was well aware that they still weren't far enough from the temple to relax. 'You said you'd travel at night and find places to hide and sleep during the day. But we can't just stand here, we've got to get further away.'

'I can't –'

'Yes you can. You've got to. But we won't run for a while, just walk.'

Taking her firmly by the hand, they trudged on through the seemingly endless night. The approaching dawn was beginning to cast a purple light on the horizon when they saw the outline of a village in the distance.

'Fruit trees,' exclaimed Suhitra, suddenly conscious of how hungry and thirsty she was. 'There'll be fruit trees.'

'And maybe a river,' added Surya, whose major problem was thirst. 'But we've got to be awfully careful.'

Luck was with them. When they got close to the village, they saw that the houses were strung out along a narrow waterway. In a burst of energy, they rushed over to it, cupped their hands, lifted the water to their lips and drank it in greedy gulps, letting some of it escape through their fingers and splash across their dirty faces and torn clothes. Then, finding a papaya tree, they picked one of the fruits, took it behind a rice-barn at the edge of the village and devoured it ravenously. Nothing in their lives had ever tasted so good.

With the worst of their hunger appeased, sleep was what they wanted more than anything else but Surya was afraid they were too close to the village for that. 'Someone would be sure to find us,' he predicted.

'But I just can't go any further,' protested Suhitra.

Surya didn't think he could either, not much further anyway, although he didn't like to admit it. The problem was that they just weren't safe here. 'We've got to find a better place than this,' he insisted.

'But where?'

'I don't know,' he said, looking around gloomily. Brightening at the sight of a thatch-roofed platform in a distant paddy field, he added, 'Over there.'

Suhitra followed his glance and regarded what she saw with horror. The platform was built on slender bamboo poles that, as far as she was concerned, were so tall they reached halfway up to the sky.

'But we can't possibly climb up there,' she exclaimed.

'Of course we can. It's meant to be climbed, it's

a watchtower,' replied Surya, who had seen others like it on his travels. 'People go up there to look out for flocks of birds that would destroy the crop.'

Suhitra was relieved. 'It won't be a good place for us then,' she said, 'not if people are going to find us there.'

'But nobody's going to go up there now.'

'How do you know?'

'Because the rice still hasn't flowered, the birds won't be able to steal it yet. Come on, let's give it a try.'

'But how –'

'We just use those slanted cross bars, the ones that hold the thing together, and climb from one to the other.'

'We're not gibbons, you know,' Suhitra muttered, but then realising that if they did get up there they wouldn't have to run any further, she dropped her objections.

Managing to call up the strength for a final desperate sprint, she actually reached the foot of the tower ahead of Surya.

The sight of it from this new vantage point sent her into a panic. It looked so fragile, so flimsy and so very, very high, even higher than the spires of Prambanan, that she knew if she stopped to think about it, she would never get up there.

But she couldn't let that happen, so with a childish recklessness that thirteen years of life hadn't yet extinguished, she pulled her sarong up to her thighs, drew it between her legs and tucked it in at her waist, just as she did when she was mucking out the animal cages.

'You'll never catch me,' she called down to Surya as she scrambled up the cross bars. 'I'm the fastest gibbon in the tree.'

Up and up and up she went until an ill-advised glance down at the ground made her stomach lurch and her head spin so much that she nearly lost her grip.

Recovering in the nick of time and telling herself that she wouldn't look down again, she resumed her upward progress. The trouble was that the higher she went, the more she could feel the tower swaying with every move she made.

Where was Surya anyway, couldn't he climb any faster? Being alone up here was horrible.

A picture of Gatotkaca came into her mind and she wondered if his extraordinary soul could reach out to her in this terrifying place. She was beginning to doubt it when, in reaching for the next cross bar, her hand touched the floor of the lookout platform instead.

It took her a moment to appreciate the difficulty of being under the platform rather than on it, but her arm muscles were strong and her desperation acute so she managed to swing a leg over it and pull herself up, only to discover that a waist-high wall of rattan bordered the platform on all sides. This kept her from establishing more than a precarious foothold until, to her relief, she spotted a place where successive seasons of rain and wind had done some damage. By skirting around to it, she was able to reach the relative safety of the enclosed area.

Now, she thought, if Surya would just hurry –

A moment later he was there beside her. She threw her arms around him with an enthusiasm that nearly knocked him over and, blissful with relief at not having to run anymore that night, they sank down exhausted onto the platform floor.

'Look at that,' Suhitra gasped after they had lain quietly for a few minutes, 'the most beautiful thing is happening.'

Surya looked and saw a curious shower of red sparks shooting out of the mountain but he was really too tired to care.

'You don't suppose Mt Merapi is spitting fire because of us, do you?' she asked.

'Of course not, what would we have had to do with it?'

'We ran away from the temple, didn't we? That might have made the gods angry.'

'Perhaps,' he said doubtfully, 'but I don't think so. I wonder if those priests, the ones who were planning that terrible ceremony tonight, were really holy men at all.'

'They weren't much like the priests at Prambanan,' she agreed.

'They might even have been devils dressed up like

priests,' he suggested. 'You never know.'

'Do you really think so?' Suhitra asked, eager to seize on this theory. 'We'll be alright then, won't we?'

'Absolutely,' he said, though he was really not as sure as he sounded. Putting the thought of divine retribution out of his mind, he drew her into the circle of his arms and gave himself over to the need for sleep.

Soothed by his nearness, she snuggled up against him the way she had seen two of her gibbons do as they were falling asleep, and neither of them stirred until the sun had driven away the terrors of the night.

It was near the middle of the day when Surya opened his eyes. At first he couldn't imagine where he was, nor could he account for the astonishing fact that Suhitra was sleeping next to him.

Then his memories came flooding back and with them came the problem of how they were going to get to the North Coast without being caught and killed for what they had done.

He lay there worrying until Suhitra, dreaming that her tigress, Arimbi, was rubbing up and down against Kumbokarno, began to mirror the cat's seductive movements, stretching and sliding along the full length of his body until his heart was pounding and his cock was straining up towards the sky.

Barely able to believe what was happening, he let his

hands run over her breasts, along her hips and thighs and into the dark softness between her legs, drawing her ever further from the misty world of sleep.

She responded by pressing her lips first to his mouth and then to his cock, not with the shy hesitation of a young girl but with the wild abandon of the animals she cared for.

They loved and slept, loved again and slept again throughout the glorious afternoon, unaware of the gigantic burst of fire that was coming out of the mountain and turning the sky to flaming red. Conscious only of each other, they didn't see that a scarlet tongue of lava was rushing down the slopes of the volcano towards the fragile pillars of their watchtower. Nor did they hear the panicked cries of the villagers and the animals as they tried in vain to escape the boiling avalanche.

It was only when a wave of molten rock tore at the bamboo poles of their hiding place that Surya and Suhitra realised they had indeed displeased the gods and - in a mystical mind-blowing moment - love and terror, death and life, were fused together as they were consumed by the fiery lava.

IN THE TIME OF THESULTANS
Java 1970 A.D.

August 12, 1970

Darling Mike,

I am so excited I can barely stand it.
The pilot has just announced we will be
landing in Yogyakarta in fifteen minutes. Can
you believe it? After dreaming about Java for
so long, I'm actually going to have ten whole
months to explore it and get to know it.

The funny thing is that I suddenly feel
a little scared. What if it isn't at all like
I imagined? What if nothing goes right? What
if it's all too different and I just can't fit in?
What then?

The one thing I'm really sure about is
that I love you madly. If only you were here
with me now, I wouldn't be worried about
anything. Still, every time I look down at my
finger and see the ring I feel gloriously happy.

Let's not wait until you finish law school to get married. Let's do it as soon as I get back to Philadelphia.

Masses and masses of hugs and kisses,
Tess

August 16, 1970

Darling Mike,

I can't begin to tell you how absolutely lovely everything is here. The head of the Southeast Asia Foundation and his wife, Mr and Mrs Wilson, met me at the airport and insisted I stay with them until I found a place of my own. I have one now and moved in yesterday. A professor at Gajah Mada University (that means Wild Elephant University isn't that a great name?) found it for me. It is a simple little room in a local family's home and it's absolutely surrounded by flowering trees. Delicious-looking papayas are hanging from the branches just outside my window. How cool is that? The electricity is an if-maybe sort of thing. Sometimes it works and sometimes it doesn't so I have an old-fashioned oil lamp on my desk.

People are always drifting in and out of the house and, as a result, I'm still not sure exactly how many people actually live here but these are the ones I'm sure about: a really sweet old couple who look absolutely ancient, their two grown-up sons and their wives, their daughter (who isn't married) and their three adorable grandchildren. I think that's all but I could be wrong. With so many people around, it's hard to tell. Right now a bunch of neighbourhood children are staring at me through the window.

I just wish you were here enjoying all of this with me.

Tons of love,
Tess

August 20, 1970

Darling Mike,

Today is the first day since I've been here that I've felt a bit down. I think part of the trouble is that everybody speaks Javanese when they're talking to each other so I'm always left out of family conversations. They only use Indonesian when they're talking to outsiders. Of course, that's exactly what I am, an outsider, but it's not very nice to be reminded of it all the time. And on top of that, I've discovered that my Indonesian isn't nearly as good as I thought it was which is a bit of a shock.

One thing that's disappointing is that nobody at Gajah Mada seems to know what to do with me. When I tell them I'm here to do research on the kingdom that built Prambanan, they just smile and tell me that nobody knows much about it. What kind of Master's thesis am I going to come up with if the only help I get is a sort of pitying smile? There's no way I'd dare tell them that what I really want to do is find the palace and the treasures of the ancient kings of Mataram.

They would laugh their heads off. Of course I couldn't tell anyone in my department at home about that part either, they wouldn't have supported my application for a grant. No serious archaeologist would. I haven't told anyone but you.

Another thing that doesn't help is that I'm so hungry all the time. The family gives me plenty to eat but it's all cooked in this dreadful coconut oil that has a vile smell and tastes absolutely disgusting.

Anyway, the awful truth and I hate to admit it, is that with the mood I'm in at the moment, I'd like nothing better than to be back in Philadelphia with you, preferably in bed.

Thousands and millions of hugs and kisses,
Tess

September 3, 1970

Darling Mike,

I'm sitting in the university library as I write

73

this. It is a large airy room with huge windows on either side so that the breeze, when there is one, can flow through it. Unfortunately the only thing flowing through it at the moment is the broiling sun and it feels like the inside of an oven in here.

I should be scouting around for stuff that will be useful for my thesis. After all, I've been here over three weeks now, but somehow I can't seem to get down to it today.

I wish I blended in more with the other students but, to begin with, just the way I look sets me apart from everyone else. I'm about a foot taller than the Javanese girls and I even tower over a lot of the men. And my colouring makes matters worse. Everyone here has beautiful dark eyes, silky black hair and lovely honey-coloured skin so my blue eyes and nondescript brown hair stand out a mile. And my skin seems so pale compared to everybody else's that I must look like a ghost to them but I know that if I tried to get a suntan I'd just turn into one enormous freckle and end up looking even worse.

I read your last letter about a hundred times and I'm hoping –

Tess looked up from her letter at the sound of excited voices coming from the quadrangle in front of the library. She turned to the boy sitting next to her and asked him in Indonesian what was going on.

At first he said that he didn't know but after listening a moment longer, he added that it was something about a tiger. At least, that's what it sounded like to Tess.

Convinced that she must have misunderstood, she asked, '*Harimau?*'

It was the Indonesian word for tiger.

The boy nodded but before she had a chance to ask him anything more, he jumped up and rushed out the door.

Tess hesitated, uncertain whether to follow him. Even in Java, where improbable things seemed to happen every five minutes, she really couldn't believe there was a tiger just outside the library. Still, something must be happening and she was curious, so she hurried over to see what it was.

The only unusual thing she noticed at first was that lots of people were milling around talking excitedly to each other. A police cordon was being set up in front of the Food Science Building on the other side of the quadrangle and a throng of people were pressing up against it in order, she supposed, to peer inside.

Suddenly being tall was a good thing as she could see over most people's heads. The trouble was that what met her eyes was not a pretty sight.

A man covered in blood was being carried out of the building, heaved into a bicycle rickshaw and pedalled away.

There didn't seem to be anything more to see after that but, to her surprise, the crowd didn't dissolve. She kept hearing the word that sounded so much like tiger but must be something else.

She looked around for someone who might be able to explain what was going on and saw an American she had met in the Southeast Asia Foundation office. He was an anthropologist, she recalled, so he should understand what all this was about.

'Gary,' she called, making her way through the crowd towards him.

'Barry,' he corrected with a genial smile, 'Barry Gellert. And you're Teresa Dickenson, right?'

'I hate the name Teresa,' she said. 'I always try to get people to call me Tess.'

'Okay, Tess,' he agreed.

'Can you explain what all this is about?'

'You won't believe this but I swear it's true. There's a tiger in the Food Science Building.'

'You don't mean roaming around free,' she protested.

'That's exactly what I mean. It seems to be checking the place out, wandering around like it's some kind of invited guest.'

'You can't be serious.'

'I've seen it myself, stripes and all, every inch a tiger.'

Tess regarded him balefully. She didn't like being played for a fool. On the other hand, he looked like he was really nice. His eyes sort of lit up when he smiled and she liked that. It made her wonder if, preposterous as it seemed, he was actually telling her the truth.

'Look,' he said, seeing the sceptical expression on her face, 'I promise I'm not making this up. I swear I got the shock of my life this morning when I saw it.'

'You mean you were in there with it?'

'No, I was just going by the building when a bunch of guys came leaping out the windows, running like all the fiends of hell were after them. Something was obviously scaring the shit out of them and I wanted to find out what it was. It was pretty obvious they weren't going to stop and tell me about it so I figured I'd have to see for myself.'

'You can't have actually gone in there after all that?' she exclaimed. He surely couldn't have been that much of an idiot.

'God no, I just popped my head through the window and damned if I didn't see it, pacing up and down in front of the blackboard looking positively professorial, like it was about to give the class a lecture on zoology or something.'

Tess laughed. 'I'd have thought the lecture would have

been on William Blake,' she said.

'You lost me there,' he returned, baffled, 'why him?'

'Tiger, tiger burning bright; in the forests of the night', she said, quoting the first line of the poem, 'remember that?'

'Vaguely. It sounds familiar but I have to admit it didn't exactly spring to mind.'

'Who was the man who didn't get away in time?' she asked, changing the subject. 'The one who was taken away in the rickshaw all covered in blood?'

'He was the cleaner. Just doing his job, poor guy, but he sure as hell was in the wrong place at the wrong time. He looked like he had been pretty badly mauled.' Spotting his friend, Kanwa, in the crowd, he called, 'Is this an ordinary event around here, wild animals turning up without an invitation?'

'Happens all the time,' Kanwa returned, with a laugh. 'Three or four signed up for my class just yesterday.'

Then, seeing Tess and afraid she might think he was serious, he added, 'No, this is a real first. I can't remember anything like this ever happening before.'

'What I don't understand,' Tess said, 'is how a tiger could just wander through a city like Yogyakarta and turn up in a university building.'

'Animals are smart,' Kanwa said, 'sometimes smarter than people. They know when a volcano is about to erupt and they come down off the mountain looking for a safer place.'

'But Mt Merapi doesn't still erupt, does it?' Tess gasped.

'I'm afraid it does, every few years.'

'But it's so close,' she said, with an instinctive shudder, 'I can see it from the terrace in front of the house where I live, at least I can in the mornings before the cloud cover settles in. Don't people worry about living so close to an active volcano?'

'It's okay,' Kanwa assured her, 'the lava never comes down this way.'

'Why not?'

'I guess we're just lucky here in Yogya,' he said, and then turning to Barry, asked him how his project was going.

'It's going exactly nowhere at the moment. Trying to get accurate information in this country has to be the world's most thankless task. People just tell me what they think I want to hear, or what the village headman wants them to say, or what they've decided would make them look good. It drives me crazy.'

Tess, surprised to hear an anthropologist talk like this, was trying to think of ways to present the Javanese in a better light when a small van with the words *Kebun Binatang* displayed on the side drew up in front of the Food Science Building.

Half a dozen men jumped out of it, climbed over the

police cordon and took up positions at the classroom windows.

'Who are they? What are they going to do?' Tess asked.

'It looks like they're from the zoo,' Barry said. 'I expect they're going to shoot the bastard with some darts.'

Tess gave a cry of outrage. 'You can't mean –'

'Just sleeping darts,' Kanwa put in hastily, 'so they can take it to the zoo.'

To Barry's surprise, this prospect didn't seem to make Tess feel much better. 'Hey, what's the matter,' he said. 'Isn't that a damn sight better than killing it?'

'I'm not so sure,' she replied truculently.

'Well, they have to do something with it,' Barry pointed out. 'They can't just hand it a notebook and a pen and send it into class. I mean, suppose it gets hungry in the middle of a lecture and feels like a quick snack? The professor might look up and find that he was missing a student.'

Barry's hopes of drawing a laugh from Tess came to nothing because, just at that moment, the heavily sedated tiger was brought out on a makeshift stretcher and shoved unceremoniously into the waiting van.

The sight of the majestic creature being subjected to such ignominious treatment tore at Tess's heart. Tears welled up in her eyes at the thought of the fate that lay ahead of it, a life of degradation in the zoo behind the bars of a cage.

'Hey, aren't you taking this a little hard?' Barry asked, beginning to wonder if this girl was some kind of mental case.

'He looked dead,' Tess said flatly.

'You'd look pretty dead too if someone had just jabbed you with a snoot-full of knock-out drugs,' Barry declared. 'Stop worrying. He'll come round soon enough and be as right as rain.'

'I hope he doesn't,' she cried. 'He'd be better off dead than locked up in some horrible cage for the rest of his life.'

'Bullshit! After all this kerfuffle, he'll be famous and get the royal treatment. In tiger language that means plenty to eat, the best accommodation on offer and a guaranteed introduction to the tigress with the sexiest stripes in the zoo.'

'I just wish that were true.'

'Why is it,' Barry asked, turning to Kanwa, 'that beautiful women never believe anything I say?'

The jokey question annoyed Tess. She knew she wasn't beautiful and hated it when men, boys, whoever, tried to score points with her by suggesting she was.

What she didn't take into account was her lively spirit - at once animated and thoughtful, mischievous and sensitive - that sparkled in her eyes and gave a quixotic loveliness to her face. Barry was not the first person to mistake this for beauty and she did him an injustice when she thought him insincere.

'Barry's right, you know,' Kanwa said, interceding on his friend's behalf. 'The tiger's going to be fine. But if you'd like to see for yourself we could all go to the zoo one day next week. My little girl, Sonja, loves animals and when I tell her what happened here today she'll want to see the tiger. And it will be a good chance for you and my wife Mini to get together.'

'I've got to work,' Barry objected.

'Have you forgotten where you are?' Kanwa demanded. 'This is Java not America, nobody here works after one or two in the afternoon.'

'Yeah, that's one of the best things about it,' Barry said, acknowledging that his friend was right. 'Okay, you can count me in.'

'Thursday afternoon then,' Kanwa suggested, 'how does that suit you? Mini, Sonja and I can pick up Tess and we'll meet you at the gates of the zoo at... shall we say 3 o'clock?'

'Sounds good,' Barry said.

Tess agreed.

'Well, I'd better hit the library,' Barry groaned, looking down at his watch. 'Are either of you going that way?'

'No, I'm going back to my office,' Kanwa said, 'so I'll see you on Thursday.'

Remembering that she had left her notebook in the

library, Tess fell into step beside Barry. 'Kanwa's English is awfully good,' she remarked, when he was out of hearing.

'Yeah, that shows what a little pillow talk will do. That was my wife's theory anyway. Mini is a Filipina so her English is virtually that of a native speaker and I think that's mostly what she and Kanwa speak at home. He met her when he was at Ateneo University in Manila. He's a very bright guy and he bagged a fellowship to do his degree there. She's no dummy either, you'll like her.'

The library seemed even hotter to Tess than it had earlier so she responded with enthusiasm when Barry strolled over to her table and asked, 'Do you have any interest in getting a cold drink?'

'I'd kill for one,' she said.

'Come on then. I've got Big Red, that's my motorbike, just outside so we can whiz down to Jalan Malioboro and get one. I know a place that's actually got a refrigerator. The drinks aren't exactly arctic but they're the coldest thing around.'

'That sounds great but –'

'But what?'

'I've never been on a motorcycle and I don't know –'

'It's high time you got on one then.'

'No, really –'

'Come on, just take a look at Big Red before you decide you don't like the idea. You don't have to get on if you don't want to.'

Since the parking place for motorbikes was practically on her way home and there couldn't be anything too scary about just looking, Tess agreed. But by the time they got to the far side of the sun-drenched quadrangle she was so hot and thirsty that that she was thoroughly prepared to risk her life for a cold drink.

'There it is, that's Big Red,' Barry announced, at the sight of his prize possession. 'It doesn't look scary, does it?'

'No,' she lied, thinking that it looked very scary indeed.

'Here, give me your books then,' he said and, after strapping them onto a rack behind the seat, told her, 'Now hop on.'

She hesitated, deterred this time not by the prospect of being thrown beneath the wheels of an oncoming bus but by the length of the miniskirt she was wearing. It was one of her shortest and clearly not made for hopping on and off motorbikes.

'Do you want to ride sidesaddle like the Javanese girls or would you rather try it American style?'

'American style, I guess.'

'Good, it's safer. You're less apt to go shooting off if we hit a bump.'

She didn't find this very reassuring but, deciding to ignore it, she climbed onto the seat behind him and put her hands gingerly on each of his sides.

'Hey, you've got to hold me tighter than that,' he said.

She clutched him harder, so hard in fact that, after a very bumpy start, he exclaimed, 'Jesus, you don't have to cut me in two.'

She relaxed her grip a little while they were going through the quiet streets around the university but tightened it again when they turned out into the terrifying traffic on Jalan Solo.

Trucks and buses driven at death-defying speeds ruthlessly asserted their claim to space on the road, leaving the smaller vehicles like vans, motorbikes, bicycle rickshaws, regular bicycles, oxcarts, and the occasional horse drawn carriage to cope as best they could. Passenger cars were rare. Pedestrians had last priority of all and were forced to the very edge of the road.

Tess was thoroughly petrified and could only hang onto Barry as tightly as possible. By keeping her eyes firmly on the back of his neck, she could try to pretend the chaotic scene around her wasn't happening.

When they got to Jalan Malioboro, the traffic was just as heavy but it didn't move at the same breakneck pace. Nevertheless, when they finally pulled to a stop at an open-fronted café, Tess breathed a sigh of relief that she was still alive.

'How was that for a ride!' Barry demanded. 'Pretty damn great or what?'

'Great, if you don't mind being absolutely terrified,' she said with a laugh. 'I can see why it's mostly teenagers who ride them.'

'That may be true back home but not here. It's transport for the whole family in Java, everyone from grannies to babies piles on together.'

They found a table under a whirling ceiling fan in the café. 'What do you want to drink?' he asked.

'Anything cold will be heaven.'

Sadly her hopes for anything of the sort were dashed when the waiter informed them that the fridge was broken and nothing was cold. He offered to bring them ice instead.

'No thanks,' replied Tess, mindful of the parasites that were likely to be lurking in it. 'I'll just have a warm Coke then.'

Barry, who wasn't worried about the little nasties, ordered a beer on ice for himself.

'You can't put ice in your beer,' Tess cried, horrified.

'I admit my drinking companions back at Cornell would have –'

'Cornell, is that where you went to college?'

'No but I was there for graduate school, you've got to hit the booze pretty hard if you want to keep from freezing your butt off up there.'

'It's not that bad,' she protested.

'How do you know?'

'I spent three weeks there once.'

'Not in the winter, I take it.'

'Late January, early February.'

'God, whatever possessed you to do that?'

'I wanted to use the Wason Collection for a paper I was writing. It was on the Majapahit Kingdom here in Java and there aren't many places where you can get information about it.'

'I expect there aren't many people who want to know about it either,' he observed. Then, banging his fist down on the table, he exclaimed, 'The Wason Collection, that's got to be it. I knew I had seen you somewhere before but I couldn't think where. It's been bothering me all morning.'

'You have a short memory. We met last week in the Southeast Asia Foundation Office, remember?'

'That's not what I'm talking about, I mean quite a while ago. When were you at Cornell anyway?'

'1968.'

Barry looked perplexed. 'That's no good then. I had finished my thesis and hightailed it out of there by that time.'

'Could you have gone back for some reason?'

'No, I was doing slave labour laying bricks for a union-busting construction company in New Jersey.'

'Why would anyone with a Ph.D. in anthropology do that?' Tess asked, shocked. She was not entirely sure she believed him.

He laughed. 'The Ph.D. was to keep the draft board off my back until I was twenty-six. The bricklaying was to get money for an extended honeymoon on the way out here.'

'Well at least you had a lovely reason.'

'It had its moments but we needn't go into that. What I want to do is figure out where I could've seen you. If not Cornell, then where? You don't remember by any chance, do you?'

'I'm afraid not. Does it really matter?'

'No, it's just kind of weird, knowing something happened yet not being able to remember it.'

'It's probably just that I look a bit like someone you used to know,' she suggested.

'I guess that could be it,' he agreed, without conviction, 'but whatever possessed you to do a paper, or whatever it was, on a farfetched topic like the Majapahit Kingdom?'

'It's not really all that farfetched, not for me anyway. I've always had a thing about Java.'

'How did that happen?'

'My Aunt Saskia got me started on it. She was born in Java when it was still a Dutch colony and lived here until she was about 11. That's when the Japanese came and put her whole family into prisoner of war camps. Aunt Saskia and her mother were sent to one, her father and brothers were put in a different one and died there.

'Then after the war,' Tess continued, 'Aunt Saskia went back to Holland with her mother but it turned out that it wasn't anything like the wonderful place she had dreamed about when she was in the camp. It was miserably cold and at first there was barely enough to eat.'

'Sounds rough.'

'I guess it was. Anyway, that was more or less when she developed this life-long case of homesickness for Java, for the Java she remembered before the Japanese came. But she married my uncle and came to live in the States and never did get back here.'

'Homesickness isn't usually contagious. How did she manage to pass hers on to you?'

'With her 'Java stories' - she told them to me from the time I was little. They were about heroes and ogres and kidnapped princesses and all sorts of things like that. I just thought of them as fairy tales but now I realise they were the stories from the Javanese shadow plays, the *wayang*. Sometimes she would just ramble on about her childhood with her gibbon and her parrot and her leopard cat in a place where it was always summer. That was the best of all. I always felt like I was stepping into some kind of magical world when I went to her house and got to listen to her. None of her kids were at all interested so the two of us became very close.'

'Okay, I'm beginning to see where you're coming from.'

'Then one Christmas when I was in high school, my uncle gave her a book called *Ancient Indonesian Art*. It was full of pictures of Prambanan and Borobudur and some of the temples in East Java. I used to pore over it whenever I got a chance. The faces and the clothes and the decorations on the relief carvings absolutely fascinated me. Aunt Saskia didn't really know much about ancient times there so I asked my teachers at school but they knew even less, I mean zero.'

'It wasn't a hot topic around my neighbourhood either.'

'Wasn't it?' she said, laughing. 'Anyway, the fact that nobody, or at least nobody I'd ever met, knew anything about the civilization that had built these incredible temples made them seem terribly mysterious and exciting. I used to imagine what it would be like to be swept back in time, to be a Javanese princess with jewels in my ears and around my neck and even on my toes, just like the ones in Aunt Saskia's book.

'Anyway, it was really that book that made me want to be an archaeologist. I had visions of finding the lost palaces of the ancient Javanese kings, especially the palace of the raja who had built Prambanan. That was my favourite temple, you see, and I was convinced that it would have the most glorious treasures.'

Her eyes lit up at the memory of this fantasy but she quickly broke off, embarrassed, and said, 'Of course, all this must sound awfully childish and silly.'

'No,' he said, not entirely truthfully. 'In any case, it's a damn sight better than the things I spent my high school years thinking about.'

'Why, what did you think about?'

'Sex mostly, but sometimes about hitting home runs or twisting my brother's head off.'

'That's dreadful!'

'Oh we tolerate each other now, sort of. It was just that he's barely a year older than me and always did just a little better than me in absolutely everything.'

'Surely not everything?'

'Well, all the important stuff like math and science and sports and getting girls and all that sort of thing, the things guys really care about. So you can see it wasn't too great having Mister Fucking Perfect for a brother and having him sweep up all the kudos while I came panting in at second best.'

'What's he doing now?'

'He's a stockbroker raking it in on Wall Street so, of course, that means he's not doing a little better than me, he's doing a hell of a lot better.'

'But being an anthropologist is so much more interesting,' she protested.

'Do you think so? I'm glad somebody does.'

'Don't you? Why else would you be here?'

'Simple. You had your Aunt Saskia, I had my Uncle Sam. He pointed his famous finger at me and gave me a choice between marching into a jungle with a gun and a pack of C-rations and letting the Viet Cong shoot holes in me, or heading out here to this jungle with a notebook and pencil and not dodging anything but malaria, typhoid and a swarm of internal parasites.'

'Aren't you exaggerating a bit? I mean, you certainly can't call this a jungle can you?'

'No but some of the flora and fauna around my village reminds me of the jungle.'

'Couldn't you have gone to graduate school in something you liked a little better than anthropology and still gotten your deferment?'

'Yeah, I was an idiot,' he admitted. 'I guess it was just that anthro seemed like the farthest thing away from business school which is what John, my genius brother, had been headed for since the age of five.'

'But business school only takes two years,' Tess said, after doing some quick arithmetic, 'how come he wasn't drafted after that?'

'Like I said, he was always smarter than me. He managed to get his knee mangled in a football tackle in high school so the army didn't want him.'

The bitterness in Barry's voice was beginning to make Tess uncomfortable. 'What made you decide to come out here?' she asked, in an effort to get onto less emotionally-charged ground. 'I know anthropologists tend to work in uncomfortable places but couldn't you have found one that you might like a little better?'

'Probably but a very persuasive post-doc from the Southeast Asia Foundation came my way, you know, one of those little treats for crazed masochists who've finished their Ph.D. thesis and want to inflict a little more agony on themselves.'

'You don't seem like the sort of person who'd be much of a masochist. What's your project about, anyway?'

'You don't want to know.'

'Yes I do, tell me.'

'Just some rubbish about social constraints on technological change.'

'Could you elaborate on that?'

'You must be the only person in the world who would want me to. Most people would be halfway out the door before I'd finished the first sentence.'

'I'm just curious as to what the world's most reluctant anthropologist would choose to write about.'

'Okay, you asked for it,' he said, and embarked on a sardonic description of his project, peppering it with comical impersonations of the people in his village and painting an hilarious picture of himself as the awkward stranger who doesn't understand what's happening and gets everything wrong.

Tess was weak with laughter by the time he wound up his topic and suggested they should probably be going.

'Where do you live?' he asked. 'I'll drop you off.'

'You don't need to, I can take a rickshaw.'

'It's no trouble. You live out near Gajah Mada, don't you? That's practically on my way.'

She nodded and a few minutes later found herself once again facing the prospect of getting on Big Red.

Jalan Malioboro, which had been crammed with traffic when they arrived, was now almost deserted, the offices and shops lining it closed for the daily one-to-five siesta. The only signs of life were provided by a group of boys lounging on the other side of the street.

Aware that they were staring at her, Tess remembered she was wearing a very short skirt and wondered how she was going to climb on Big Red without giving them ringside view of her panties, blue ones that day, she remembered.

One glance at the leering boys was enough for Barry to take in the situation so he kicked down a footrest on the side of the bike and said, 'Here, you'd better ride sidesaddle like the Javanese girls.'

She did and it made all the difference. With her view no longer blocked by the back of Barry's neck, she could enjoy the passing scenes of Yogyakarta as it lay, sun-drenched and lethargic, in the hazy heat of the early afternoon.

She was almost sorry when Big Red pulled up in front of her house.

'Don't forget the zoo next week,' Barry called after her as she started down the gravel path to her door.

'Don't worry, I won't.'

Not certain just what she thought of him, she turned and watched him shoot off down the pot-holed street. He seemed like such a mass of contradictions, it was hard to know what to think.

She sidestepped the problem by thinking about the tiger instead. What a brave and adventurous creature it was and how amazingly smart, heading straight for the Food Science Building like that. She couldn't wait to write and tell Mike about it. He'd never believe it though, not in a million years.

When the day for the visit to the zoo arrived, Kanwa and his family came by for her in two rickshaws; she was to go with Mini in one of them, Kanwa would take four-year old Sonya in the other.

Tess could see immediately that Mini would be very easy to like. Her manner was warm and friendly and, by the time they arrived at the zoo, Tess knew her life story. She knew that she had grown up with her five brothers and three sisters in the mountain town of Baguio in the

Philippines, and that her parents hadn't liked the idea of her marrying Kanwa and going to live in a foreign country but she had been very naughty and done it anyway.

But Mini didn't only ramble on about herself, she wanted to know about Tess's childhood in Connecticut and her life as a university student. But when Tess began to tell her about Mike, she exclaimed, 'Oh, I'm so sorry to hear that, I was hoping you and Barry would like each other. I thought you sounded like you'd be perfect for him.'

Tess wasted no time in correcting this impression. 'Barry's not at all my type,' she declared firmly, 'and anyway, he's married isn't he?'

'Not anymore.'

'What happened?'

'His wife couldn't take living in a Javanese village; no electricity, no running water and absolutely no one who spoke English, apart from Barry, of course. You can't really expect an American girl to put up with all that and Cynthia was the last sort of person to do it.'

'Did Barry take it hard when she left?'

'I don't know. He never talks about it, not even to Kanwa, but I don't think he could be very happy about it. After all, it must be lonely out there and he doesn't –'

But Tess didn't get to hear any more because their rickshaw drew up in front of the gate to the zoo and Barry called out, 'You're late.'

'Rubber time,' laughed Mini. 'You're in Indonesia now, not America. Anyway, we're not very late are we?'

'I think we're doing pretty well,' Kanwa said, looking at his watch. 'It's only twenty past three.'

'Where's the tiger?' asked Sonya.

'I'm eager to see it too,' Tess told her as they all set off down one of the shady paths that laced its way to the zoo.

Tess's first thought was what a beautiful place it was but before long she began to see a darker side. Green and cool, it was indeed lovely for the visitors - she didn't change her mind about that - but it was a sad place for the zoo's four-legged residents.

'Those cages,' she cried, 'they're so small and cramped. It's dreadful.'

'Everyone in Java lives in small places,' Kanwa explained, 'almost everyone, and you can't expect the animals to live better than the people do, can you?'

'No, I suppose not,' Tess agreed reluctantly.

When they reached the area where the big cats were kept, Kanwa found out from an attendant which tiger had been the intruder, or in Tess's view the hero, at Gajah Mada.

She could have wept when she saw it. The animal was pacing up and down in an enclosure so small that it couldn't take more than four or five steps in any direction without having to turn around.

'That cage,' she said, wishing she could batter the ghastly thing down, 'is barely big enough for a mouse.'

Kanwa gave a nervous laugh, Mini smiled sympathetically, Sonya looked distressed and Barry said, 'Hey, don't let it get to you.'

'I can't help it,' she said, struggling to fight back tears. Letting her emotions get the better of her wouldn't do anything to help the tiger. She would just look like more of a baby than Sonya and how embarrassing would that be? 'It must be so awful, being a prisoner like that.'

At the sound of Tess's voice, or so it seemed, the tiger came to an abrupt halt right in front of her, sat down on its haunches, fixed her with its amber stare and let out a roar so loud and imperious that it reverberated throughout the zoo.

Startled but quickly regaining her composure, Tess held the magnificent creature's gaze long enough, she hoped, to let it know how much she admired its beauty, strength and spirit.

She felt certain that it understood.

Then the extraordinary moment passed. Once again she saw the tiger as others might see it, a caged and defeated animal for whom all hope, pride and freedom were confined to the distant past.

This time, Tess didn't succeed in keeping back her tears. Not wanting the others to see she was crying, she turned and hurried on ahead of them down the path.

Sonya, who had been badly frightened by the tiger's deafening roar, also burst into tears. Mini's effort to console her combined with Kanwa's attempts to distract her prevented them from noticing Tess's flight. Only Barry realised that something must be wrong and followed her.

'Hey, what's up?'

'Nothing.'

'Bullshit, something is.'

'It's just that everything's so terrible.'

'Can you narrow that down a bit?'

'You have eyes, don't you,' she said, suddenly angry that she had to give an explanation. 'Can't you see what they're doing to that wonderful tiger, locking it up in a horrid little cage like that?'

'Well, you know what would happen if they unlocked it, don't you? Your wonderful kitty cat would thank you by gobbling you up for a mid-afternoon snack.'

'That doesn't mean they should put it behind bars with barely enough room to move for the rest of its life.'

'I wish the animals in this place had better conditions too,' he said, 'but you're talking like that tiger was a person and it's not. It's got four legs and a tail and some very impressive stripes.'

'I can see that, I'm not blind. But I think it has some human qualities too.'

'What gives you that idea?'

'I can see it in his eyes.'

'You can imagine it, you mean,' Barry corrected.

'No,' she said firmly, 'it's something more than that.'

The sight of a bougainvillaea-covered stall with bottles set out in front of it made him realise how thirsty he was and, seeing no chance of having a rational argument with this girl, he said, 'Come on, let's get something to drink. With any luck, they might have something beside that sickeningly sweet orange stuff the Javanese think is so great.'

They didn't.

'Oh well,' Barry said, 'I'm thirsty enough to settle for just about anything wet, how about you?'

Tess said that she was too.

'You know what your problem is?' he said, when they were seated at a low wooden table with their drinks.

'No, what?'

'You've got too much imagination. You see an animal and you endow it with all sorts of human qualities that it doesn't actually have.'

'But I don't usually —'

'Now take me for instance,' he said, 'I've got no imagination at all and that means I don't get bogged down in a shitload of useless sentimentality.'

'Maybe it also means you have no feelings,'

she suggested.

'I hope you're right about that, it's feelings that make life hell.'

'Does that mean yours have been badly hurt?'

'No, I take care not to let that happen,' he said.

'Not ever?' she asked incredulously.

'Never.'

'Not even when your wife went back to the States?' she blurted out, realising too late that the question was completely out of order. 'Oh God, I can't believe I said that, I'm really, really sorry.'

'Don't worry, it was one of the best days of my life. We were driving each other crazy. But that's enough about me. Let's go find the gibbons, they're far more interesting.'

There were times during the next few weeks when Tess could scarcely believe that her dream had come true and she was actually in Java. Then there were the other times, the ones when she was hard-pressed to fight off a sense of isolation and disappointment. Yes, she was in Java but it wasn't quite the Java of her dreams.

For one thing, there was the family she lived with. She wanted to think of them as her Java family but she was having trouble doing it, they treated her with a formal politeness that didn't allow her to forget she was a guest. When they spoke to each other they used Javanese rather than Indonesian so, unless she was being spoken to directly, she was effectively excluded from the normal round of domestic chatter.

The grandfather and grandmother of the family, known as Bapak and Ibu, were kind but they were old and, as far as Tess could see, never went anywhere or did anything. The two grown-up sons who lived at home were immersed in their own concerns and had little time for her. The older one was married and taught economics at Gajah Mada and his wife was invariably occupied with her three small children and sometimes with the offspring of friends and relatives as well, all of whom liked to stare at Tess from a distance but rarely seemed inclined to talk to her. The younger son was a medical student who always seemed to be out somewhere or studying in his room.

The family offered her food and shelter for a sum that was princely by Javanese standards but it did not offer her companionship or a sense that she belonged.

Attributing a good part of her loneliness to the language barrier, Tess resolved to learn Javanese but she had problems with its hierarchical nature. Speaking High Javanese to some people and Low Javanese to others, based on a complicated formula of relative age and status, was difficult for her. To begin with it was hard to know exactly what anybody's status was and, more importantly, it was hard for her to come to terms with the idea of talking down to people who might, for whatever reason, be perceived as inferiors. It was too great a violation of her basic sense of justice, so she soon abandoned her efforts and simply concentrated on improving her Indonesian.

One thing that was not disappointing was the early morning parade of people passing the house; women in long batik skirts and tight, fitted tops on their way to the market, some carrying babies in batik slings on their hips; men, a number of them in western clothes but others in sarongs, on their way to work and children in their blue and white school uniform on their way to a day in the classroom. Tess usually started the day with a cup of tea on the terrace in front of the house so she could watch it all. This was the Java of her dreams, although in her imagination she had been a part of it and absorbed into the colourful fabric of Indonesian life, not sitting separately like a spectator in a theatre. With the realisation that this would almost certainly continue to be the case, a sense of disenchantment with the whole idea of coming to Java began to weigh on her spirits.

One day, after lingering longer than usual over her morning tea, Tess decided to pull herself together and fight against the feelings of exclusion and isolation that were depressing her. She would go out to her very favourite place in Yogya, well, just outside of Yogya actually.

It was the one that had captured her imagination ever since she had seen the pictures of it in Aunt Saskia's book – the ruins of the ancient temple at Prambanan.

She had been to see it once already but another prowl around the beautiful neglected temple should be just the thing to lift her spirits.

Her memory of the trip out there was rather daunting though, involving as it did a bone-shaking ride in a rattletrap old bus that didn't have brakes or shock absorbers and, in all probability, would have a ruthless, speed-crazed maniac for a driver.

It would be worth it though, she decided, because once she got there she would be in the Java she had dreamt about for so long, wandering through the deserted courtyards of the temple, running her hands over the beautiful low-relief carvings, picking her way amongst the stones that had fallen from the crumbling walls and mentally putting them back where they belonged.

And she would have the fun of seeing it all in her mind's eye, the temple filled with people dressed in their best clothes bringing offerings of fruit, flowers and incense to their gods. These powerful beings watched over them and protected them but if they were angered or neglected, they could make the earth tremble beneath their feet or send streams of red hot lava down the mountain to punish them.

It wasn't far to Prambanan and in a little over an hour she was actually there, standing in the central courtyard looking up with a mixture of awe and sadness at the sanctuary of the great god, Shiva.

How could the kingdom that built this beautiful place have vanished, just like that, into the shadows of a long-forgotten time? What terrible catastrophe had driven the people away from a place that must have been sacred to them? And what had gone through their minds when their gods had failed to protect them? Had they even had time to think about those things or had the disaster struck so swiftly that it had precluded all thought?

She thought the latter seemed more likely. After all, if the Kingdom had been destroyed by something that had happened slowly, surely there would have been time for someone to write about it. An inscription would have been found somewhere and the archaeologists at Gajah Mada would have been able to tell her about it.

With this settled, as far as she was concerned anyway, she went back to visualising the temple complex as it must have been in the days of its glory. She was so absorbed in the mental pictures she was conjuring up that she leapt with fright when she heard a voice behind her say, 'I think you're Tess.

Turning, she recognised Professor Subandi from Gajah Mada and went into a momentary panic. She would die if he could read her mind. She wanted to give the impression that she was viewing Prambanan with the analytical eyes of a serious archaeologist, not the romantic eyes of a girl who had been captivated by the pictures in her auntie's books.

To her great relief, Professor Subandi's next words revealed no special talent for mind reading. Instead, in a voice filled with incredulity, he asked, 'Are you here by yourself?'

For an instant Tess wondered why this was so surprising but then she remembered how rarely the Javanese ever seemed to do anything alone. 'Yes,' she said, 'I like to wander around on my own.'

'I understand but I like it best to come to this place with someone who also sees its beauty. Come, I will explain the panels to you.'

Tess was about to protest that she was already familiar with them but fortunately stopped herself in time. What a fool she would be to miss hearing what one of the most respected archaeologists in Indonesia had to say about them.

It was a decision she didn't regret.

As they strolled through the temple compound, they paused in front of each of the relief carvings so the professor could recount the event that was being illustrated. His knowledge of the ancient Hindu epics, the Mahabharata and the Ramayana, was so vast and his insights so brilliant that through the power of his narrative he almost brought to life the gods and heroes, ogres and animals, princes and servants portrayed in the famous stories .

'This has been the most interesting morning of my life,' Tess declared later, when they were having something to drink in a little stall outside the temple compound.

'You like? Good. Many people, tourists, Indonesians, they come here, look around, go home. They do not appreciate. I am glad you come to Java and are interested in archaeology.'

'So am I,' Tess agreed.

'You come my house. I have many books. You can read Dutch, yes?'

'A little. I took two semesters of it before I came here.'

'Good. Most books in Dutch but not all. You read Indonesian?'

'Yes but it's still a bit difficult for me.'

'I have books in Indonesian, books in English. I will show you when you come. You write your thesis on what?'

'I'd like to write it on the civilization that built this temple,' she said hesitantly, 'a social and cultural history of the Mataram Kingdom.'

'Not good,' he declared, shaking his head in disapproval.

Tess's heart sank. 'Why not?'

'Nobody knows exactly where that kingdom was. Where was the capital, where was the palace? There is nothing left of it now so you will not find anything for your thesis. Better you write about the Majapahit Kingdom in East Java - bigger, later, more information available. That way you have enough material for your thesis.'

Tess fought back the temptation to confide in this kind man and tell him about how determined she was to find the capital, though of course she wouldn't mention her hope of discovering the riches of the raja's court as well. That would just be setting herself up for ridicule.

'The trouble is that it's the Mataram Kingdom that really interests me.'

Professor Subandi considered this for a moment and then suggested a compromise.

'Why not broaden your topic to include the Hindu-Buddhist Kingdoms in Java? That way, maybe you will find enough information for your thesis.'

'But '

'I know,' he said with a smile, 'you are someone who like beauty and Borobudur is not so beautiful like Prambanan but it is bigger and has more relief carvings for showing life in the classical period. It gives you the opportunity to show they are special Javanese style, not just copy of Indian art like some books say. That's very important, it will make a good thesis.'

'I'll think about it,' she replied tactfully.

They took the bus back to Yogya together and as they were parting, Professor Subandi repeated the invitation to come to his house.

'When?' she asked.

'Anytime,' he replied, with the Javanese vagueness she was having trouble getting used to. Before she could reply, he hailed a bicycle-rickshaw and was gone.

In spite of the casual manner with which the invitation had been issued, Tess took it seriously. She knew that the calling hours in Yogya were from five to seven in the evening and that everybody who was not already out visiting someone else would be prepared to offer sweet tea and conversation to any visitor who dropped in.

She waited a few days and then tried to call on him but he wasn't home.

On a second try she had better luck. His wife brought out the expected glasses of tea, his children peered at her from behind the safety of their mother's skirt and Professor Subandi himself showed her the promised books. She borrowed two of them.

Borrowing and returning books gave her an excuse for repeated visits and her host was clearly delighted to have long conversations with someone who shared his enthusiasm for antiquities. Sometimes, when other students or professors from the archaeology department were there, she brought the subject around to the Mataram Kingdom and to the question of where the centre of it might have been.

'It was probably in Magelang,' one professor said.

'Semarang,' declared another.

There were also suggestions that it might have been in the area around Borobudur or perhaps somewhere near Prambanan or maybe within the boundaries of present-day Yogya or even as far north as Tegal. One archaeologist was convinced that the kingdom had had several different capitals at different times.

Tess took a great interest in this last possibility. It would explain the assortment of ideas about the capital's location without assaulting her own conviction that, at least at the time of its mysterious disappearance, the royal palace had been near Prambanan. She had to watch what she said though. It would be too embarrassing if anyone suspected that her ideas were based on a feeling no matter how strong it was, rather than on any real evidence.

It was so different when she was with Mini; she could say whatever was on her mind. Mini's Filipina-style warmth and fluent English made her wonderfully easy to talk to. As well as offering Tess the kind of friendship she wasn't finding among the more reserved Javanese, Mini often acted as a sort of cultural bridge. America had left such a strong stamp on her country that she almost felt as if its culture were her own, while her marriage gave her a valuable window on Indonesian life.

Darwati, a student at Gajah Mada and the youngest of Mini's numerous sisters-in-law, was frequently in the house when Tess stopped by for a chat and, intrigued by the idea of a conversation between two foreigners, made an effort to understand as much of it as her limited English allowed.

Mini was never timid about trying to arrange the world to her liking. She decided that a friendship between Tess and Darwati would be a great way of improving her sister in law's English as well as teaching her new friend more about Indonesia, and it was therefore something she should encourage.

The best way to do this, she decided, would be to get Tess to give Darwati English lessons. Kanwa's father could probably be prevailed upon to pay for them, although of course it would have to be at Javanese rates. That would be low by international standards but Darwati could make up for it by showing Tess around Yogya.

Tess fell in love with the idea right away but staunchly refused to take any money for the lessons. Darwati was more hesitant about it all. She had never actually spoken English with anyone except Mini and she didn't consider her to be a real foreigner. Not only was she part of the family but she wasn't one of those big scary-looking people with ghostly white skin, creepy blue eyes, strangely coloured hair and horrible fierce tempers. Mini didn't look very different from an Indonesian. She had had to learn their language and their ways of doing things but it hadn't taken her long to fit in. A true foreigner like Tess, no matter how nice she seemed, would never really fit in, at least not in the same way.

Mini was vaguely aware of Darwati's feelings but wasn't easily deterred by obstacles she considered minor. She merely directed her persuasive talents to overcoming them. She coaxed, she cajoled and she engaged in a little verbal arm-twisting until eventually Darwati agreed to go to Tess's house for three lessons a week.

The first few sessions didn't go well. Darwati was consumed by shyness and seemed to lose all power of speech while Tess, convinced that it would be easier to extract a few English sentences from a statue, would have given the whole thing up as a bad job if it hadn't been for Mini's insistence that, given a little time, it would all work out.

Fortunately, things became more relaxed by the fourth or fifth lesson. Darwati discovered that Tess wasn't inclined to fly into murderous rages over small things and probably not even over large ones. Tess found out that her pupil did have a voice after all, one that, in spite of the limitations of her English, she could use to express a surprisingly individualistic outlook on life for someone who had been brought up on the customs and traditions of Java.

Tess even began to suspect that underneath her outward adherence to the rigid Javanese codes of politeness and acceptable behaviour, Darwati harboured a spark - possibly quite a strong spark - of wayward mischievousness.

Gradually, the pretence of lessons was dropped in favour of showing Tess around Yogya and just having a good time. They browsed in the shops along Jalan Malioboro, perused the goods on sale in the market, ate in little restaurant stalls, climbed through the dilapidated water castle behind the sultan's palace and admired the batik paintings produced by the colony of artists there, visited dimly lit houses where tireless women drew on the skill of centuries and the patience of saints to produce intricately designed batik cloths. One day they even hired a driver and horse drawn carriage and went to the silver working village of Kota Baru. On Saturdays they took Darwati's little cousin out to the School for Classical Dance and watched her have her lesson.

During their afternoons together, Darwati could scarcely hear enough about Tess's life in America, the freedom she had had to do whatever she liked and, most enthralling of all, the relationship she had with Mike.

'I like the way it is alright to have a boyfriend,' Darwati declared enthusiastically.

'But some girls here have boyfriends too, don't they?'

Darwati considered this for a moment, then replied hesitantly, 'Yes, but not the same, not so free.'

'How about Gajah Mada students?' Tess persisted. 'I'm sure I've seen them with boyfriends or girlfriends.'

'Sometimes,' Darwati agreed, 'but I think their parents do not know.'

'Do you have a boyfriend?'

'No!'

'You're blushing.'

'What is that?'

'Your face is turning red,' Tess said, with a laugh.

Hastily putting up her hands to hide her cheeks, Darwati shook her head vigorously and insisted, 'No, I do not have.'

Tess was certain she was lying but didn't want to pry so she let the subject drop and enquired about the possibility of seeing a *wayang kulit* puppet show instead.

'We must wait,' Darwati told her.

'Wait for what?'

'Until special thing comes.'

Tess, feeling she must have missed something in all this, looked blank so Darwati explained, 'Rich men pay for the performance when there is marriage or circumcision or some special thing, so we must wait.'

Tess sighed. Javanese vagueness about when things would happen was a constant source of frustration for her but she told herself she would just have to get used to it.

Over the next few days Tess found herself wondering about Darwati's supposedly nonexistent boyfriend. She actually felt a bit hurt that her friend hadn't trusted her enough to tell her the truth.

Oh well, she thought, Darwati will tell me when she's ready and in the meantime, I don't have to know.

It wasn't long before she found out.

They had arranged to go to the dressmaker together at five o'clock the next afternoon but when half past five turned into six and Darwati had still not come by for her, Tess worried that something might have happened. Was she sick or had she had some kind of accident? Mini would surely know, so the thing to do was stop by her place and find out.

'She went to visit her auntie,' Mini explained.

Tess frowned. That was funny, she thought, Darwati hadn't said anything about it yesterday.

'When is she coming back?' Tess asked.

Mini shrugged.

'In a few days, I guess.'

'But she's missing her classes,' Tess pointed out.

'I know. Kanwa doesn't like it when she does that.'

'Does she go off like this very often?'

'Sometimes.'

Tess had already learned that classes at Gajah Mada were conducted on a rather casual basis, with frequent absences on the part of professors as well as students. Still, it would be fun to tease Darwati about her mysterious disappearance when she came back.

'You didn't really go to visit your auntie, did you?' Tess asked when she saw her again.

'Yes, I did.'

'That's funny, why did I think a boyfriend had something to do with it?'

Darwati suddenly looked quite agitated.

'Not funny,' she protested.

'Then there is a boyfriend,' Tess said, with a laugh.

'No, there is not.'

'I bet there is.'

Darwati, not used to dealing with direct confrontations, gave up.

'How did you know?' she asked.

'I just guessed.'

'You will not tell Kanwa, will you,' Darwati asked, in alarm, 'or Mini?'

'Of course not if you don't want me to. But why is it such a secret?'

'Indonesia is not same as America. Kanwa feels responsibility to me.'

Tess accepted this but went on to ask, 'What's this boyfriend's name anyway, is he a student too?'

The question opened a floodgate that had been locked for far too long. Secret revelations poured out, things Darwati had been dying to talk about for months but hadn't dared. Now, in this American friend who, like herself, had a boyfriend, she found the perfect confidante.

'Oh no, he is not student,' Darwati said. 'He's too old, more than thirty but very handsome. His name is Sigit. He lives in my auntie's village, out near Prambanan. He works at the airport, assistant manager, and one day soon he will be manager. Then after a few years he will go to Jakarta and be manager there. That is a very important job, he will be rich.'

'You could tell Mini about him, couldn't you?' Tess suggested. 'After all, Kanwa was her boyfriend before they got married. Mini even told me that her parents weren't happy about it because he wasn't a Catholic. And they didn't like the thought that he would be taking her to live far away where they would hardly ever see her.'

117

'Philippines is not like Indonesia,' Darwati said emphatically. 'Philippines is like America. Young people do what they want.'

Tess had never been there and didn't know so she didn't pursue the point.

Confidences about boyfriends, however, soon began to flow both ways. The amazing qualities of both Mike and Sigit were extolled and the closeness between Tess and Darwati grew in importance to each of them.

Although there were a few other foreigners living in Yogya, Tess's contact with them was intermittent at best. For the most part, they were older, married and deeply involved in their own projects so she was able to establish only a limited rapport.

As a result she was particularly glad when, one very hot afternoon, the sound of Big Red coming to a stop outside the house made her look up from an article she was reading that Professor Subandi had lent her.

A moment later she saw Barry's head poking through the window.

'Can I interest you in going down to Malioboro for a Coke?' he asked.

'Yes,' she said, with enthusiasm, 'that would be great.'

The suggestion couldn't have come at a more welcome time. It had been one of those days when it hadn't been easy to convince herself that Java was the greatest place in the world. Hovering rain clouds had darkened the skies for most of the afternoon and then left without bringing anything like a cooling shower. The temperature in her room had risen to levels generally associated with the outer corridors of hell and, as so often happened, the electricity was off so she couldn't even use her tiny fan.

Just to make a bad day even worse, everything on the table at lunch had been cooked in the hated coconut oil. When, still hungry, she had come back to her room only to find that the Silver Queen chocolate bars she kept for such emergencies had turned into chocolate soup and soaked through six pages of thesis notes.

She would have welcomed a visit from Satan himself if he had rolled up on a big red motorbike and suggested something long, wet and possibly cold.

'Hop on then and we can zip down there.'

'Give me a couple of minutes. I need a quick bath, I'm too hot and sticky to live.'

'Okay, take your time.'

Astonished as she had been by the Javanese custom of taking several baths a day, she now couldn't imagine going anywhere without washing first.

Even so, the Indonesian way of doing this still seemed a bit like an adventure to her, standing next to a large vat of water and pounding the surface with a tin dipper to send the goldfish living in it, some of them as much as six inches long, scurrying over to the far side. Only then could she be fairly confident that no slithery, scaly creature would be in the water she poured down her back.

The very idea that fish lived in the bathwater had horrified her at first but when she learned that they were there to eat the mosquito eggs, she had accepted their presence as a clever, if somewhat quirky, method of insect control.

Now she was used to it so she happily splashed water over herself, changed into a fresh yellow mini dress and left her hair to flow down her back instead of putting it into its usual plait. She was feeling cool and refreshed when she met Barry in the garden a few minutes later.

He thought she looked great and told her so.

'You sound surprised,' she said, feigning outrage for a moment and then laughing.

'I wasn't, really,' he protested, getting on Big Red. He waited for her to settle in behind him and then took off.

A shock greeted them when they arrived at the café; the drinks were actually cold.

'Can you believe it,' Barry exclaimed, 'they must have fixed the fridge. I swear there's nothing like being buried in the wilds of Central Java to make you appreciate the amenities of civilization.'

'Yogya's hardly the wilds,' Tess returned. 'It's the

centre of Javanese culture, at least, that's what the people here say.'

'Over in Solo they wouldn't agree. They think they're the ones who are in the centre of things. Unfortunately, no one could think my village was the centre of anything except possibly rice paddies. If you don't believe me, come out and see for yourself.'

'I'd like to,' she replied, with more enthusiasm than he had expected. 'I haven't actually been out in the countryside yet, no further than Prambanan anyway.'

'Lucky you.'

Ignoring this, she asked, 'Is it far?'

'To my village? It takes about half an hour on Big Red.'

'How about on the bus?'

The question elicited a loud guffaw from Barry.

Seeing that she looked a little hurt, he explained, 'Sorry, it's just that it's kind of funny to think of taking a bus to a place that hasn't got a road.'

'How do you get there then, can Big Red fly?'

'Sadly no but he's a real whiz at zipping along the dikes between the paddy fields.'

'Not everyone in the world has a motorcycle,' Tess pointed out. 'What do those people do?'

'Not everyone in the world comes to my village but anyone crazy enough to want to takes the Yogya-Solo bus out past Prambanan, then changes to a creaky little market bus filled with more chickens than people and eventually slogs his way through the paddy fields on foot.'

Tess had to admit this sounded rather daunting. 'Well, I'm not sure –'

'Don't worry, I've got to come into Yogya on Saturday morning anyway. I'll pick you up around lunchtime, we'll grab a bite to eat somewhere along the way and then let Big Red do his stuff along the dikes between the rice paddies. It'll take you about five minutes to see the whole village from top to toe so I can easily get you back in time for whatever thrills you've got planned for Saturday night.'

'Don't worry about that,' she said ruefully. 'I haven't had any thrilling Saturday nights since I've been here.'

'Mine have been pretty tame too.'

'Did it ever strike you that Javanese style social life isn't much fun?' she asked.

'Strike me! It's hit me like a ton of bricks, all that sitting around with gruesome little glasses of sweet tea. Deadly!'

'And not being able to drink it until it gets cold and someone finally says –'

'*Monggo, monggo,*' he said, finishing the sentence for her. 'And the damnedest thing is that you can't demolish more than half of it or they think you're some clod without any manners who doesn't get enough of the sickly sweet stuff at home.'

'Ridiculous, isn't it,' she said, laughing.

'Totally but I'm surprised to hear you say that.'

'Not as surprised as I am to hear you say it,' she returned, with emphasis on the pronouns.

'Why?' he asked, genuinely baffled.

'You're the anthropologist, you're supposed to like submerging yourself in different cultures.'

'Well, I like it marginally better than I like the idea of submerging myself in the US army and putting bullets through a bunch of toothless Vietnamese grannies but that's about as far as it goes.'

'Fair enough but now it's your turn to explain. Why did I surprise you?'

'You won't be offended, will you?' he asked, wondering if he was going to regret this conversation.

'I don't know,' she shrugged, 'try me.'

'Well the thing is, I had you pegged as one of those people who thinks everything about Java is wonderful just because it's different from whatever it is they're trying to escape back home.'

'But I'm not trying to escape anything, quite the opposite actually. I feel like I've been drawn to something here. And that's especially true at this point in my life because it means being away from Mike for nearly a year and,' she added, tragically, 'we only just got engaged.'

'Maybe you're one of those people who get engaged and then run like hell to escape the consequences,' he suggested. 'God knows that's what I should have done.'

'Why didn't you break it off then? Isn't that what engagements are for, to give you time to change your mind if you want to?'

'Wrong, the purpose of engagements is to let the noose slip around some poor guy's neck so softly and gradually that he doesn't notice what's happening until, zap! He's standing in front of an altar somewhere mumbling, 'I do'. And he's not allowed to leave the building until he's signed away his freedom, his finances and his balls.'

'That's a dreadful way to think about it,' she exclaimed, appalled.

'No, just an accurate way, if you'd ever been married. You haven't, have you?'

'No.'

'If you had, you'd know what I'm talking about.' Then as if seeing her with fresh eyes, he added, 'You're a girl, I sort of forgot.'

'Thanks.'

'Well it's an important point because it puts you strictly in the enemy camp when it comes to talking about marriage.'

'I don't see why.'

'Look in the mirror then, you might find out.'

'There isn't one here. And anyway, I'm already engaged so you're safe, if that's what's worrying you. I promise

I'll never try to marry you. That means I can be neutral, sort of a human Switzerland, while you do all the ranting and raving you like.'

'Why do I get the feeling you're not taking me seriously?'

'I've no idea but there's something I can't help being curious about. Was your ex some kind of witch or are you this bitter because you're still in love with her?'

'Still? That suggests I was in love with her in the first place.'

'Weren't you?'

'Not really.'

'Then I think you were a rat to marry her and deserve whatever you get.'

'You're no human Switzerland,' he growled, 'you're on her side.'

'In the absence of more facts, I probably am. Why did you marry her anyway?'

'Some stupid reason, thinking with my dick, I guess. She didn't exactly hurt the eyes.'

'That's not a very romantic attitude.'

'I'm not a very romantic kind of guy, although compared to my brother, John –'

'You mean he has an even less romantic nature?'

'That's putting it mildly. The only thing he cares about in a woman is her outer packaging.'

'Yuck,' she said, with a shudder, 'I hope no girl's been

stupid enough to marry him.'

'Not yet but –'

'You mean that's about to change?'

He nodded. 'In a couple of months, the day after my divorce comes through.'

'That's a coincidence, sort of.'

'Not exactly. He's marrying my wife.'

When Barry rolled up in front of her door on Saturday, Tess greeted his arrival with mixed feelings. Although she hadn't fallen off Big Red yet, she wasn't altogether confident about her ability to stay on it all the way out to his village. Terrifying as the speed-crazed traffic on Jalan Solo was likely to be, the thought of what might await her when they going along the dikes was worse. She would rather fall into the path of an oncoming bus than into a flooded paddy field filled with poisonous snakes and other horrible creepy crawlies. Still, she managed to put these dire fantasies out of her mind and look like she wasn't scared a bit when she clambered onto the bike.

One of her fears came all too close to being realised, not in a flooded paddy field but in the open-sided restaurant where they stopped for lunch.

She was, to her surprise, actually enjoying the curried jackfruit Barry had persuaded her to order when a snake charmer with a python draped over his shoulders sauntered down the narrow aisle between the tables. Just the sight completely put her off her food but then, only inches away from her, the man slipped on some sauce that had been spilt, lost his balance and very nearly sent the python slithering into her lap.

She leapt away in horror as Barry grabbed the man by the elbow, steadied him and – Tess couldn't believe her ears when she heard this – offered him a few rupiahs to let her stroke the revolting creature's clammy skin.

'There's no way I'm going to do that,' she cried, feeling sick at the very thought.

'Come on, just give it a try,' he urged. 'It won't be half as bad as you think and it might keep you from getting so freaked out about snakes.'

But his attempt at persuasion fell on deaf ears and in the end, he simply had to send the man and his python on their way.

Back on Big Red she decided that she didn't like Barry as much as she had thought. Anyone who would want her to touch that ghastly python just couldn't be that much of a friend. How insensitive could he be?

Nevertheless, she managed to put the incident out of her mind and enjoy the coolness and the feeling of the wind in her face as they rode along. She wasn't even bothered about the possibility of falling off; after the python, nothing seemed very scary.

She was almost sorry when Barry brought Big Red to a stop underneath a papaya tree at the edge of his village.

'It's beautiful,' she exclaimed, surveying the cluster of small wooden houses topped with thatched roofs, all shaded by luxuriant vines and flowering trees.

'Do you think so?' he replied, genuinely astonished.

'Yes, it's like stepping into a picture book.'

'We must go in for different kinds of books then.'

'Which house is yours?'

'That one,' he said, pointing to one of the closer ones. 'Not quite the presidential palace but at least it's away from the centre of the village so I can occasionally get a modicum of privacy.'

'And over there, is that a river or something?'

'In the rainy season I guess you could call it that. Right now it's more like an oversized drainage ditch but don't tell Derek Kent I said that. He and his bunch are working on a project involving the entire river system in the area and this pathetic little stream is actually part of it. You must have met the Kents in Yogya by now, haven't you?'

'Not yet.'

'You will. Anyway, Derek and a couple of other Brits are working on plans for a dam. But forget about that for now. I want you to meet my girlfriend.'

'I didn't know you had a girlfriend living with you.'

'Didn't I mention her?'

'No.'

'Well, come and meet her. The two of you should get on famously, at least if you can overlook her shortcomings as a hostess. She's not likely to pour you a beer or do anything helpful like that, she doesn't for me, although she'll drink one fast enough herself if she gets her hands on it.'

They had just reached Barry's house when a charcoal-coloured gibbon on a long chain swung out of a mango tree and leapt onto his shoulder.

'Here she is. Let me make the introductions. Tess, this is Marilyn; Marilyn, this is Tess.' Ruffling the little ape's hair, he put an affectionate arm around her and explained, 'In a moment of wishful thinking I named her after Marilyn Monroe.'

'Wasn't that a bit of a stretch?' Tess asked, laughing.

'You can say that again.'

Marilyn, using Barry's right arm as a tree branch, launched into an assortment of gymnastic feats to impress their guest. Sadly this didn't elicit quite the admiration she felt she deserved so she climbed back onto Barry's shoulder and began going through his hair looking for lice or other biteable insects.

'Sorry old girl,' Barry said, removing her from the vicinity of his head, 'but if you're nice, I'll bring you an orange.'

Marilyn was not in a cooperative mood. Instead of letting go, she pressed herself up against his back, wrapped one of her long hairy arms around his neck, folded a similarly hirsute leg around his chest and held on for dear life.

'A banana?' he cajoled hopefully but it seemed that Marilyn didn't take bribes. 'Okay,' he warned, 'you're in for it.' And reaching around behind him, he began tickling the naughty little creature's stomach.

She wriggled and squirmed in delighted anguish then, when she had had enough, leapt to the safety of the mango tree.

Barry flung open the door to his house and said, 'It's not much but here it is. I hope you won't think it's too awful. Marilyn's a terrible housekeeper.'

Tess followed him into what she assumed was the sitting room, although the few pieces of furniture were piled so high with books and papers that there was scarcely anywhere to sit. A typewriter was balanced precariously on the edge of a table and the window, she noticed with surprise, didn't have any glass in the panes.

'It's –' She floundered, at a loss for adjectives.

'I warn you, it gets worse,' he said cheerfully. 'That black hole ahead of you is the bedroom. You've got to go through it to get to the kitchen.'

Leading the way through the darkness, he navigated

a path between a double bed and a roughly hewn wooden chest then, going down two steps into a tiny courtyard, he indicated an open-sided lean-to with a kerosene burner and a tin sink that had some dishes drying next to it and said, 'Our glorious kitchen.'

'No wonder Marilyn doesn't like to cook,' Tess said, looking around.

'If you want to take a bath or go to the john, you go back there,' Barry said, indicating a corrugated metal structure on the other side of the courtyard. 'If you feel like a bath, you go in here,' he said, pushing open a green door and revealing a vat of water and a tin dipper. 'For your other personal requirements, the blue door is the one you want.' And with this, he opened the door to a closet-sized space that had a platform shaped like a human foot on each side of a hole in the floor.

Tess thought that, apart from the whimsical shape of the platforms, it was an arrangement she was used to by now.

'That's all there is, folks. This concludes the grand tour of the split level ex-urban home of Barry and Marilyn.'

Turning back to the kitchen, he asked, 'What can I offer you? I'm afraid the menu's pretty limited; warm beer, hot tea, tepid water - boiled, of course - or some fruit. Marilyn's cooking isn't something I'd want to inflict on you and mine isn't much better. Unfortunately the prospects for anything else look pretty dim unless - hang on a minute, there are some rice cakes in this cupboard. They shouldn't be too bad, sort of like Rice Krispies glued together with a little cement. Want to try one or would you rather have a tour of the village first?'

'A tour,' she said promptly.

As she retraced her steps towards the front door, Tess kept an eye out for any lingering evidence of the absent wife but the only signs of feminine habitation she came across were an overturned bottle of Shalimar under the bed and a pair of batik curtains at the window.

I can understand how this place might have depressed her, Tess thought. But when she glanced out the window she was struck by the timeless beauty of the surroundings and wondered how she would feel about living here, not with Barry of course but with Mike. Would this village, its spartan little cottages half hidden by the profusion of greenery and flowering trees around them, cast a spell over someone who might be susceptible to that sort of thing, someone like herself?

'You know,' she said, turning away from the window, 'this view must not have changed for a thousand years.'

'Yeah, that's the trouble with it,' he agreed.

Ignoring him, she added, 'I almost envy you, being an anthropologist and living in a place like this. It must be lovely.'

'You gotta be kidding.'

'No I think it could be heavenly. For a little while anyway.'

'More like the other place, the one down below, if you ask me. You'd get fed up pretty damn quickly if you were sentenced to staying here for more than five minutes.'

'Possibly,' she conceded.

'Definitely. Believe me I know. But never mind about that, I better take you to meet the headman. It would be bad form if I didn't and I don't want the *dukun* to turn me into a pig or a cockroach or something for not following local customs.'

Tess, with mock solemnity, agreed that that would be a very bad thing.

They had only gone a short way down the shaded path that served as a main street for the village when a little girl with a younger sibling a batik sling on her hip came over to Barry and said something to him in Javanese.

To Tess's astonishment, Barry not only answered her in Javanese but went on to have an extended chat.

'I didn't know you could speak Javanese,' she told him admiringly when they were on their way again.

'Got to.'

'Why, don't the people here speak Indonesian?'

'The younger ones do but if you're trying to write the definitive work on technical change, or the lack of it, in a Javanese village you've got to talk to the old people.

And if they're women, that pretty much means using the local lingo. Also if you want to tease the kids or, more cynically, use them as a way of getting closer to their families, you've got to do it in a language they understand. And they generally don't start learning Indonesian until they get to school.'

When they reached the headman's house, Barry resorted to Javanese again and called out the traditional greeting, '*Monggo, monggo*.'

The headman's wife, Ibu Wati, came to the door, welcomed them with a nearly toothless smile and told her daughter-in-law to make tea and fry some cassava chips for their foreign visitors. She also tried unsuccessfully to push several small children towards Tess but they were too suffused with shyness to do anything but hide behind her sarong. The youngest one was more than shy, he thought this strange foreign woman was a witch and fled in terror.

This elicited a burst of laughter, not only from Barry but from Ibu Wati and several other betel-chewing women in the room.

Barry, deciding he might as well put his time to good use while they were waiting for the headman, embarked on a charm offensive, flirting outrageously with the old ladies and joking around with the children.

He only shifted into Indonesian when the headman got back and Barry introduced Tess. However the conversation soon drifted to local matters in which she had little interest so she tried her best to talk to her kind hostess.

It wasn't easy though, as they barely had even a language in common, so she responded with enthusiasm when Ibu Wati drew her over to see some photographs pinned up on a wall.

Barry was in one of them, standing next to a willowy blonde woman who looked like she had just stepped off the front page of *Vogue*.

Could that possibly be his wife, she wondered, finding it almost inconceivable that anyone so well dressed and so perfectly groomed had lived, even for a short time, in Barry's bare little bungalow? How had she managed to get so clean in that miserable hole of a bathroom or put on her makeup without a proper mirror?

If she's really Barry's ex, Tess reasoned, she must have been a magician.

She was glad when they finally started on their tour of the village. If it had been conducted without interruption, it would surely have been completed in the five minutes Barry had predicted but he stopped to chat with practically everyone they passed. She couldn't help noticing that they all seemed to like him.

'This is our *jamu* lady,' Barry explained, after exchanging a few words with a girl carrying a basket full of bottles on her back. 'She's got medicines and potions for everything from cholera to unrequited love.'

Tess had seen a number of *jamu* ladies in her neighbourhood in Yogya. There was even one who came around regularly bringing a murky-looking concoction for Ibu, one said to keep skin looking taut and young. Tess thought it looked positively poisonous but she had to admit that something was keeping Ibu looking a good deal younger than her sixty-three years.

Urged on by Ibu and persuaded by the fact that it smelled of cinnamon, she had agreed to take a sip of it one day but had vowed she would never take another. It was so bitter she had barely managed to choke it down.

Today, however, spurred on by a suspicion that Barry wouldn't have anything good to say about traditional medicines, she felt a perverse impulse to defend them.

'Some of those potions might not be too bad,' she said, 'at least, not if they're mixed with boiled water.'

Before Barry could fulfil her expectations and take issue with this, he noticed a little boy creeping up behind them apparently intent on touching Tess's honey-coloured hair. He was pretty sure the little fellow just wanted to see what it felt like but he intervened anyway, catching hold of him by the scruff of the neck, growling something at him in Javanese and sending him on his way.

'Okay, that's pretty much the whole show,' he said a few minutes later when they had effectively circled the village.

'What do you say, we go back to the house and break out a room temperature beer? I'm afraid there's no hope of a cold one.'

'Anything wet will be good.'

When they got back to the house, Barry hastily swept a mess of books and papers off of two chairs, said 'back in a minute,' and disappeared in the direction of the kitchen.

He was back before long with the promised drinks and what he had called the cement rice cakes. 'Sorry about these,' he said, looking at them dejectedly, 'but I'm afraid they're about all I could find in the cupboard.'

'Don't you ever eat?' she asked.

'Actually I do, thanks to my neighbour, Ibu Tini. She comes in the mornings, does the laundry and cleans up a bit. And she's not a bad cook. It's vaguely edible anyway.'

'Did your wife cook when she was here?'

'She boiled some water once but the flame on the kerosene burner is a real bitch to control. It shot up and caught the ceiling on fire so that pretty much put a stop to her culinary efforts. But then she was sort of like Marilyn, fun to play with but not much use around the house.'

'That's not a very flattering comparison.'

'I know but fortunately I don't think Marilyn heard.'

'You must've been a real horror to be married to.'

'Cynthia would agree with you about that.'

'Was she an anthropologist too?'

'God, no. She was, and still is, I expect, an aspiring actress.'

'Good heavens. What in the world would someone like that do out here?'

'Who knows,' he said, with a shrug. 'What do women ever do?'

'Marilyn really is the perfect girlfriend for you, I can't think of anyone else who would put up with your medieval attitudes.'

'Yeah, I get along with her a lot better than I did with Cynthia, that's for sure.'

'What I can't understand is why a beautiful actress would come out here in the first place. It doesn't make sense.'

'She was under all sorts of romantic illusions about love under the coconut palms, thought it would be a real turn on. But when she realised it was just sex with a boring clod of a husband in a godforsaken hovel a thousand miles from nowhere, she very sensibly decided not to stick around.'

'I think I have a few romantic illusions about what it would be like to live here for a while too, especially if I could do a few things to fix up this house, but I know Mike would go crazy in five minutes. I don't think he could even survive in Yogya for more than a week or two.'

'And you accept that?'

'Of course. I can't ask him to live a life that he's clearly not suited for, can I?'

'Maybe not but isn't that what he's going to ask of you?'

She looked surprised at the thought. 'No,' she said, 'he isn't going to ask anything weird or unexpected, just the normal sorts of things. He's going to be a lawyer, hopefully in New York or somewhere that's got lots of colleges where I can teach, so everything will be fine.'

'Suppose he gets a job with some Wall Street firm and you get a great offer from the University of California, then what?'

'Then we'd spend a lot of time in airports,' she said, laughing at the mental picture of them taking turns dashing through terminals with armfuls of books and papers.

'You've got things all planned out then.'

'What's wrong with that?'

'Just about everything. If it all goes according to that plan, there will be no surprises on the way and it will be deadly dull. If it doesn't, which it probably won't as most long-term plans don't, then where will you be? It's likely to be somewhere that doesn't suit you at all. And in your case, there's another problem and it's a biggie.'

'Oh, what's that?'

'The plan doesn't suit you.'

'Why not?'

'It's too conventional. People who follow their dreams

to distant tropical islands, like Java for instance, aren't going to be happy living with someone who can't hack that way of life.'

'Are you really talking about yourself rather than me?'

'Who knows? Maybe I am.'

They fell silent for a moment and then Barry, looking out the window, said, 'We'd better get a move on. Those clouds over there look like the kind that build up into a serious rain and it's no fun getting caught on Big Red in a downpour.'

They were just getting up to leave when a little girl appeared at the door, a three-tiered Tiffin carrier in her hand. After mumbling a few words in Javanese to Barry, she handed it to him and left.

'Shit,' he exclaimed, 'why does this always happen? I can't wiggle my big toe without somebody trying to make me do something else.'

'Can't you just put the food in the kitchen and eat it later?'

'Not if I value my life. That little girl was the headman's granddaughter and she said the food was a present for you from her granny. If we just charge out of here without bothering to eat it, or without pretending to eat it, it would be a major insult and my name will be mud.'

'But wasn't it lovely of her to do that,' Tess exclaimed, touched. 'Of course we must take the time to eat it. Never mind the rain, it won't kill us to get a little wet. Let's see what she sent.'

'Okay. Hold on a minute though, I'll get us some plates.'

When he was back, she saw that he was carrying a bottle and two glasses as well as two shallow bowls made of tin.

'Ever tried this stuff?' Barry asked, reaching for the bottle.

'What is it?'

'A weird kind of rice wine, Chinese I think. It's a little on the sweet side but it's slightly sparkling and not too bad when you get used to it. Since we're stuck with eating this little snack, I figure we might as well do what we can to liven it up.'

While he opened the bottle and filled their glasses, Tess explored the contents of the Tiffin carrier and, finding crisp fried soy bean cakes with red chilli peppers, cabbage leaves and garlic in a sweet soy sauce and fluffy white rice, she suddenly remembered that, thanks to the snake charmer, she had left most of her lunch on the plate.

This little snack looked rather inviting, or that's what she thought until a whiff of the ever-present coconut oil sent her stomach into somersaults before eventually settling back into its usual mealtime state of reluctant resignation.

She managed to swallow a few bites, then turned her

attention to the wine and the hilarious imitations Barry was doing of people in the village. He knew just how to use his posture, his voice and his facial expressions to capture the essence of whoever he was mimicking and soon had her in gales of laughter.

Not even the dreaded coconut oil kept her from enjoying the impromptu picnic and because the wine was sweet and slipped down easily, she didn't notice how strong it was.

By the time the effects began to kick in, the clouds overhead had darkened and rain was beating down on the roof.

'Well that's it,' Barry declared with a glance out the window, 'unless you've got a life and death reason to get back to Yogya in the next hour or two, we'd better wait this out.'

'It may be Saturday night,' she returned with a sheepish laugh, 'but that doesn't mean I'm doing anything. This is Java, remember.'

Although she would rather die than let him know it, she secretly didn't mind being holed up into this remote cottage with Barry, held prisoner by the sheets of water pouring off the eaves of the thatch roof. It was actually rather exciting, even more so when it began to get dark and Barry lit the three kerosene lamps in the room.

'If you want things a little brighter, I'll pump up the

Petromax,' he offered, 'but I warn you, it makes it hotter than hell in here.'

'Oh no don't. I hate those dreadful things, they give off such a harsh light. I don't understand why anyone wants to use them when they could have kerosene lamps instead.'

'To see better?' suggested Barry.

'Well I wouldn't,' Tess declared firmly. 'I'd much rather have the lovely soft glow you get from a kerosene lamp.'

'Suppose you wanted to read something?'

'I'd wait 'til morning.'

'Christ, I should have married you,' he said with a laugh. 'You're the only girl I know, American girl that is, who might actually be able to hack it out here.'

'Why is it you always fall in love with the wrong people,' Tess mused, 'not just you, I mean everybody.'

'Why, have you fallen in love with the wrong person?'

'I don't know, I never thought about it until this afternoon.'

'Come to any conclusion yet?'

'Well yes, sort of. About half a second ago. I decided Mike's exactly the right person for me.'

'And what convinced you, may I ask?'

'Sitting here in the lamplight with this beautiful village just outside, cut off from the rest of the world by the rain, it's like being in a dream or stepping into a fairy tale or something. And you can't live on dreams, can you? Even if

I were here with Mike instead of you, no offence, I expect the beauty and the magic of it all would vanish when the reality of village life set in. And speaking of reality, I think I'm being absolutely devoured by mosquitoes.'

'Hold on, I'll get you some insect repellent and light one of those Chinese coils.'

He was back a moment later with a bottle of greenish-brown liquid in his hand.

'Here, put this on,' he said, taking off the cap and handing it to her.

'Yuck,' she exclaimed, drawing away, 'that smells revolting. It looks disgusting too.'

'It is, but you want to revolt the mosquitoes, don't you? This stuff does the trick. Just regard it as sort of a two-for-the-price-of-one sort of thing, you get to repel two species at once, mosquitoes and people.'

'The problem is, I don't want to repel myself as well,' she returned, gingerly dabbing a little on her bare legs.

'Come on, don't be such a baby. Put a little on your shoulders at least.'

'That's too close to my nose.'

'Give me the bottle,' he said, taking it from her and rubbing a generous amount on her arms, shoulders and the back of her neck. 'There, that's not so bad is it?'

'It's horrible,' she insisted, and was about to say a few more things along this line when a particularly aggressive mosquito came diving towards her open mouth and would have flown in if she hadn't closed it quickly.

This was enough to make her give up her resistance.

'Well now that my nose has gone numb,' she said, 'that stuff doesn't seem so bad. I must say, you're actually rather good at rubbing it on. You don't give massages by any chance, do you?'

'I might, on special request.'

'It's tempting.'

'That gives me an idea, a game we could play until the rain stops.'

'What kind of game?'

'It's called Mike and Cynthia.'

'What in the world are you talking about?'

'A game, it's an easy one to play. You pretend I'm Mike and I'll pretend you're Cynthia and, until the rain stops, we'll pass the time in the way we would if it were true.'

'Just 'til the rain stops?'

'Just 'til then.'

He was surprised that she hadn't turned the suggestion down flat, even more astonished when he saw her smile and lean, ever so slightly, towards him.

But the moment passed and the next thing he knew, she was drawing away.

'Sorry, I'm not very good at pretending,' she said, 'my imagination doesn't stretch that far.'

'Never mind, it was just an idea,' and looking around, he added, 'I think Cynthia left a pack of cards around here somewhere. We can play gin rummy instead.'

Tess, who wasn't an enthusiastic gin rummy player, hadn't much chance to wonder about her choice before the rain, like so many tropical downpours, stopped almost as suddenly as it had started. In less than an hour, they were able to climb on Big Red and make their way back across the paddy fields then on to the busy road to Yogya.

They were mud-splattered and dirty when Big Red pulled up in front of Tess's door but neither of them minded. The ride into the wind with the air, fresh and cool from the rain, blowing in their faces, had left them in high spirits and their afternoon together in the village had driven away the sense of isolation that been haunting both of them.

The next day proved far too eventful for her to think about feelings of isolation or anything else.

When she stopped by the Foundation office to see if there was a letter from Mike, she discovered the two secretaries and the accountant talking excitedly to each other.

'Have you heard?' Ninik, the head secretary, asked the moment she walked in.

'Heard what?'

'About Mr Wilson.'

'No, what happened?'

'He has malaria, a very bad case apparently, and he's in the hospital.'

'I thought he looked like he might be coming down with something when I saw him a few days ago,' Tess replied. 'Remember, he was sort of flushed and said he had a headache but I thought it was probably just the flu.'

'The doctor said malaria,' Ninik continued. 'They are sending him to Singapore this afternoon, maybe he will not come back.'

'He's not going to die, is he?' Tess cried, alarmed.

'I don't think so,' Ninik said reassuringly, 'but Mrs Wilson thinks they are too old to live so very far from good medicine. She does not want to come back.'

'It's the first time I've heard of anyone getting malaria here in Yogya,' Tess said.

'A few people get malaria here but not very many. But Mr and Mrs Wilson went to Pelabuhan Ratu, remember, and there is a lot of malaria on the south coast.'

'What's going to happen to the office?' Tess asked.

'I don't know, maybe they send a new man.'

Jettisoning her plan to spend the morning in the library, Tess went over to the Wilson's house and found a thoroughly distraught Mrs Wilson flinging things into half a dozen open cases.

'Is there anything I can do?' Tess asked, after hearing the latest account of Mr Wilson's condition.

'Oh my dear, that would be wonderful. I've been up since three o'clock this morning and I hardly know what I'm doing anymore. But do have a cup of coffee with me first. I think I'll collapse if I don't have one and maybe a little toast along with it.'

'I can't imagine how the office will get along without Mr Wilson,' Tess said honestly, when they were seated on the veranda with the mid-morning snack between them. 'It'll come to a standstill.'

'Oh not for long,' Mrs Wilson assured her. 'We were planning to retire at the end of this year, you know. I think we must have told you that.'

Tess nodded.

'A very nice young man, Philip Dunhill, has been planning to come out here soon anyway so he could learn the ropes before we left. It will be harder for him now without Bill to show him things but he'll manage somehow, perhaps you can help him settle in.'

'I'll try,' Tess said doubtfully, 'but I don't really know anything about running the office.'

'You don't need to. Ninik knows how things are done and Philip is an extremely bright young man. Still there are bound to be a few things about life in Yogya that it will be nice to ask another American about.'

Tess promised to do what she could, spent the rest of the morning trying to inject some order into Mrs Wilson's packing and then, in the afternoon, went with her and a very jaundiced-looking Mr Wilson to the airport.

At the sight of their plane taking off Tess had a sudden childish feeling of being abandoned. Until that moment she hadn't realised quite how nice it had been to know they were there for her if she needed them. There had been times, not many but more than she would like to admit, when she had welcomed the chance to escape the strangeness of Java by dropping in on them. They were always ready to offer her a cup of tea or a meal or, best of all, a cold drink. They actually had a refrigerator, something she had never appreciated before. She fervently hoped that the 'nice young man' would prove to be as much like Mr Wilson as possible.

That hope was soon dashed. Tess knew from the moment she saw him walking across the tarmac at the airport that he wasn't going to be like Mr Wilson at all.

It had been easy to pick him out from the other disembarking passengers because he had been the only American or European man dressed for business rather than for sightseeing. By the time she and Ninik, the official welcoming committee, had finished introducing themselves she had taken a virulent dislike to Mrs Wilson's 'nice young man'.

One of the most startling things about him, Tess decided as they bounced around in the rattletrap taxi taking them into town, was his eyes. They were blue but such a pale blue that they almost seemed to be devoid of colour, especially when set against his swarthy skin and dark hair. The most disturbing thing she found about his eyes though, was that they didn't change expression when he smiled.

In spite of this negative first impression, it wasn't until she stopped by the office the next day hoping for a letter from Mike, that she felt she had a reason to hate him.

His initial greeting when he saw her was almost cordial.

'Come, have a coffee,' he said, motioning towards the open door of his office, 'and tell me about your thesis. What are you working on and how far along are you?'

Before she had much of a chance to answer, he settled himself comfortably behind his desk and said, 'I used to dabble in archaeology myself, back in my graduate school days. I even worked on an excavation in Turkey for a few months. Of course I've shifted gears now, as you can see, but archaeology is still high on my list of hobbies.'

Is he being patronising, Tess wondered, or am I just

being too touchy?

'Now tell me,' he said, 'just what are you interested in?'

'The Mataram Kingdom, the first one that is.'

'Oh, and when and where was that?'

'Here in Central Java in the eighth and ninth centuries, around the time Prambanan was flourishing.'

'That sounds like it might have potential. What aspect of it are you focusing on, political, economic, what?'

'Mostly social and cultural actually.'

The look he gave her was so sharp it made her feel she was facing a sort of intellectual panther, ready to pounce on her ideas and rip them to shreds.

'Sounds a bit fuzzy, I think you might want to sharpen up your focus. And in any case, I didn't realise there was an excavation going on at the moment.'

'There isn't.'

'Then where are you getting your data? What kind of sources are you using?'

'I'm still looking at possible –'

'You don't sound very well prepared,' he snapped. 'You can't just pull your data out of thin air, you know.'

'Thank you for that,' she retorted, 'but there's a wealth of material already out there on the temple walls. Anybody can see it if they look but nobody has analysed it yet, it's in the low relief carvings. And a lot can be deduced or inferred from other monuments and stone sculptures, and from bronzes that have been excavated too. And then there are the accounts of Chinese travellers who visited the kingdom during that time, nobody has really done anything with them yet and –'

'Do you read Chinese?'

'No,' she said defensively, 'but I read Indonesian and Dutch, plus some of the writings have been translated into English.'

'Where was the centre, the capital of this civilization you seem to be so taken with?'

'That's what I hope to find out,' Tess answered too quickly. The moment the words were out of her mouth she regretted them.

'You mean you don't know?' he gasped, making no attempt to hide his astonishment.

'I think you'll find that no one seems quite sure,' she replied, trying to keep her voice as well as her temper under control, which was no easy task as she was becoming increasingly angry.

'But you think you're going to solve the mystery, do you?' he said, sarcastically.

'I'm going to try.'

'May I ask how?'

Damn him, she thought, it wasn't easy to fight off a terrifying feeling that the ground was being pulled out from under her but, with a supreme effort, she managed to look him in the eye and say, 'I don't know yet.'

'What in the world could those people in the New York office have been thinking,' he demanded, 'giving you a grant when you didn't have a coherent research plan?'

His tone was so scornful that it made her want to pick up the heavy brass ashtray on his desk and throw it at him, either that or dig a very deep hole for herself and never come out.

But she did neither. Instead she snapped, 'If you really want to know, I suggest you write and ask them.'

'That's not likely to do us any good,' he replied coolly. 'Our problem now is to figure out how, on the basis of so little groundwork, you can cobble together a minimally adequate thesis. I believe you've got only ten months to do it so we'd better get on the stick.'

'We? Funny choice of pronouns,' she said. 'I'd have thought my thesis was strictly my problem.'

'Then you wouldn't have been entirely correct. Since I'm in charge of this office, the work that comes out of it will be seen, to some extent at least, as a reflection on me. And I think it's only fair to warn you now that if you need more time for your project, and it certainly looks to me like you might, I won't be able to authorise it, at least not unless it holds out some chance, however small, of success.'

'That's quite alright with me,' she declared, and flinging

her plait over her shoulder she got up and started for the door.

'Tell me one last thing before you go,' he said. 'What do the archaeologists at Gajah Mada think of your topic?'

It was agonising not to be able to say they thought it was wonderful but it would be too embarrassing to be caught in a lie. And she would be caught, Yogya was too small a place for the truth not to come out.

'Professor Subandi has been very helpful,' she equivocated, trying to put the best possible face on things, 'even though he thinks I'll have trouble finding enough hard data.'

'Who else is taking an active interest in your work?'

'Unfortunately you seem to be.'

Momentarily taken aback by this response, he said, 'I'm sorry if I've hurt your feelings but surely you can see that it was in your best interest. A few frank words early on could save you from going back to the States with an ill-thought-out thesis, one that would never be accepted by your committee.'

'I have no intention of going back with an ill-thought-out thesis,' she told him, her voice shaking with rage.

'That's alright then,' he said, and was about to turn back to the papers on his desk when he added, 'Oh, one more thing before you go. I'm looking for someone to teach me Indonesian, someone who can come by the house or the office for an hour every day. Do you know anyone who might be interested?'

'No.'

'I have a book of Indonesian lessons,' he continued, as if he hadn't heard her, 'so all I'd need is a native speaker, preferably someone who knows a bit of English. A Gajah Mada student would do.'

Tess was just about to repeat that she didn't know anyone who would be interested, when the thought of Darwati made her change her mind – the girl's love of shopping seriously exceeded the limits of her finances.

'Actually, I do know a student who might want to do it,' she said. 'I'll ask her and let you know.'

'Good, let me know when I can meet her. In the meantime, feel free to drop in if there's any way I can help you.'

Tess went over to Mini's house that afternoon and presented the plan to Darwati but the thought of having a one-on-one conversation with a foreign man so terrified her that she refused to consider it.

If Mini hadn't caught a few words of their conversation, the whole thing probably would have ended there. But she did hear and immediately brought her opinion to bear on the subject.

'But of course you must do it,' she exclaimed. 'It'll be every bit as good for your English as it will for his Indonesian but the difference is, he'll be paying you.'

Frightened rather than encouraged by this aspect of the situation, Darwati repeated, this time with renewed urgency, 'No, I cannot.'

'Don't be silly,' Mini insisted, 'of course you can. I'll help you prepare the lessons if you want. I'm learning Indonesian myself so I have a good idea of what he'll want to know. And I'm sure Tess will help you too.'

'I will if I can,' Tess agreed, trying to overlook the fact that this would be helping Philip, albeit indirectly, at the same time.

'There, you see,' Mini said confidently, 'everything will work out perfectly.'

'But I speak English with you and Tess,' Darwati protested, 'that is enough.'

'No it's not,' Mini argued, 'not if you want to be a secretary in a foreign company and make lots of money like we planned. You have to be able to talk to all kinds of people, some of them nice and some of them not so nice, and this is your chance to start. Then once you improve your English and make your typing a little better, all you will need is a few good contacts. This man, Philip, can be your first one. It will all happen, you'll see. You'll make lots of money and be able to go to the dressmakers and the gold merchants as often as you like and not worry about what things cost. But you have to be able to speak English and talk to foreigners to make this happen.'

Both Darwati and Tess looked sceptical, Darwati because she doubted her abilities and Tess because she doubted the likelihood of achieving the glorious outcome Mini described.

'You'll make at least ten times what you would working for a Javanese or a Chinese,' Mini went on, reading Tess's thoughts.

Tess nodded, knowing this was true.

'But I cannot go there by myself,' Darwati cried, horrified at the thought.

'You won't have to. Tess will introduce you and stay with you the first few times,' Mini offered generously.

This was more than Tess was prepared to do. She was beginning to regret that she had ever mentioned the lessons at all.

'I'll take you there tomorrow and help you arrange the times and agree on what he'll pay you, that sort of thing,' she agreed reluctantly, 'but after that you've got to go by yourself, that is if you decide to give it a try. You can always change your mind after you've met him. I promise I won't try to get you to go back if you don't want to.'

Tess was feeling extremely uncomfortable by this time,

sending her friend into the lion's den seemed like an awful thing to do. On the other hand, if she were completely honest about what a bastard Philip was, Darwati wouldn't even give the lessons a try. So in the end she just let matters stand and hoped for the best.

Mini knew Darwati well enough to be reasonably sure how she would handle the prospect of the lessons. She wouldn't come right out and say no to Tess, that would be rude in Javanese society. She would go along with the plan for the moment even though she had no intention of actually following through with it. In Java this was not deceit, it was just good manners.

The thing to do, Mini decided, was to make sure that Darwati had no way of getting out of her side of the agreement so she arranged for Tess to pick Darwati up at the end of her Modern English Novel class and take her over to Philip's office for their meeting.

Darwati's heart sank when she saw Tess waiting at the classroom door. She knew her fate was sealed, at least for the initial visit.

But it all went surprisingly well. Philip greeted them pleasantly, went out of his way to be friendly to Tess and made a real effort to put Darwati at her ease. But the important thing, the thing that made all the difference, was the dazzling sum he offered for the lessons; 500 rupiahs an hour.

Darwati was speechless when she heard it and Philip, mistaking her silence for reluctance, hastily raised his offer to 600 rupiahs.

For riches like that, Darwati would have given language lessons to an army of demons and ogres or, scarier still, to an entire legion of colonial soldiers sent out from Holland to keep order in Java.

When everything had been settled and they were on their way through the outer office, Darwati had a reassuring chat with Ninik who said that none of the men she had worked for had exploded in murderous rages, sprouted fangs or done unspeakable things to the women who worked for them.

She was beginning to take heart at this news when Barry, who admittedly didn't seem very frightening either, breezed in to pick up his monthly cheque.

'Have you met the new guy yet?' he asked Tess.

She nodded.

'What do you think?'

Glancing around to make sure that Darwati and Ninik were absorbed in their own conversation, Tess made a quick thumbs-down gesture.

Barry responded with a grimace, then shrugging his shoulders said, 'Oh well, who cares? He's just a paper-pusher really. He won't make any difference to me.'

'He might to me,' Tess said gloomily.

'How?'

'I don't want to talk about it, not here anyway.'

'Okay, how about if I stop by your place this afternoon? Will you be home around three?'

'Yes, that'll be –'

'Mail for you,' interrupted Tukiem, the other secretary, handing several letters to Tess. Turning to Barry, she added, 'Mr Philip wants to meet you. Please come to his office.'

Tess's face brightened at the sight of the last envelope. 'A letter from Mike,' she announced happily to whoever might be within earshot.

'See you later then,' Barry said, and followed Tukiem into Philip's office.

It was after four o'clock and the afternoon sun was generating its usual heatwave in her room by the time Tess actually heard Big Red sputter to a halt in front of the house.

'Guess I'm a little late,' Barry told her through the open window.

'Are you? I didn't notice,' she replied indifferently.

'That's not very flattering,' he growled, and vanished into the house.

He reappeared in her room a moment later. 'Good God,

don't tell me you actually live in this oven,' he exclaimed. 'What's the temperature in here anyway?'

'I don't know, somewhere between roast and bake I expect,' she replied apathetically.

'Jesus, maybe my little country retreat isn't so bad after all. I'm going to tell Marilyn that she'd better start appreciating the cool breeze we've got blowing through the place out there.'

In a futile search for a comparable wave of fresh air, he draped himself across the windowsill, hung there in a sort of U-shape gasping for air until he felt he had made his point, then pulled himself back into the room.

'I had a long talk with Philip after you left,' he said, launching into the subject of his visit, 'and I must say he's a damn sight smarter than Wilson.'

'How can you possibly know that after one quick conversation?'

'It wasn't all that quick and it was definitely long enough to see that the guy's no fool. He's done his homework, that's for sure. He knows a lot about the area already and he's only been here two days.'

'You're easily impressed.'

'And you're not?'

'Not in this case anyway.'

'Okay, I agree he's a little short on sweetness and light but does that really matter? What gave you the idea he was such a bastard anyway?'

Tess repeated the gist of her conversation with him and concluded, saying angrily, 'He implied that I was a total waste of space, that my thesis was going to be worthless and that I'd better forget about everything that interests me and change my topic entirely. What's more, he actually came out and said that I could forget about any possibility of an extension no matter how badly I might need it. Not that I really care about that, I don't want one anyway.'

'Aren't you building a few tactless comments up into a lot more than he really meant?'

'Just the opposite, I'm ignoring them completely. I'm even doing him a favour and finding him a language teacher, although he doesn't deserve it. And it's a pretty awful thing to do to Darwati. He'll probably eat her alive.'

'Hey, what's the matter with you today? I've never seen you like this. Give the guy a chance.'

'Why should I? He didn't give me a chance.'

'Maybe he's just a woman-hater,' Barry suggested.

'Is that supposed to make me like him better?'

'No, but it might keep you from taking what he said so personally.'

'A fine friend you are,' she retorted, 'I thought you'd be on my side.'

'Look I'm not on any anybody's side. It's just that I got along with him, you didn't. Let's leave it at that.'

There was a moment's silence while they glared at each other and then Tess said, 'I hate to be rude but I've got work to do.'

'Okay, fine. Big Red's getting a little restless out there.'

'You'd better not keep him waiting.'

'Don't worry, I won't.' After knocking a stack of papers off her desk in his haste to leave, then reaching down to pick them up, he continued.

'You know, if you've really got work to do, I don't mind being given the heave-ho. But if you're just in a snit because I said Philip wasn't such a bad guy, then I think you're being a hell of a poor sport.'

'Think what you like, I don't give a flying fuck.'

'Don't worry, I will,' he said, taken aback at her vehemence and wondering what in the world had got into her today. He had certainly never heard her use language like that before.

Then, deciding Tess's silly moods weren't his problem, he pushed the door open and was halfway through it before turning to growl, 'Goodbye,' and caught sight of the expression she was no longer bothering to conceal.

Dumbfounded by the utter dejection he read in her bearing, he said, 'Hey, why are you letting that guy get under your skin like this? It's not like he can actually cut off your grant or anything. All he can possibly do is keep you from getting an extension and you don't want one anyway. You and Mike are getting married, remember?'

He could scarcely have said anything worse.

'Ever heard of second thoughts?' she asked.

'Why, are you having them?'

'No but Mike seems to be.'

'What makes you think that?'

'His letter, the one I got this morning.'

'He's probably just in the throes of one of those panic attacks typical for the human male at the thought of a wedding. It's a pretty scary prospect, so what can you expect? A guy feels the noose tightening around his neck and gets attacks of all kinds of things, life-threatening cases of cold feet or oxygen deprivation, you see the poor fellow gasping for air and all that sort of thing but it generally comes right in the end. The blushing bridegroom manages to pull himself together and toddle down the aisle. Just ignore the stupid letter, that's my advice.'

'It's the bride who walks down the aisle, silly,' Tess pointed out, 'not the groom. He just stands there.'

'An ominous sign of his role in years to come.'

Tess decided to ignore this.

'Anyway, Mike hasn't actually changed his mind.'

'Then what the hell are we talking about?' Barry asked, in exasperation.

'He just wants to postpone the wedding,' she returned, as though it were a truly odious crime.

'Any particular reason?'

'So he can finish law school first.'

'Well, there's something to be said for that.'

'No there isn't, I'd get a job so it would be fine.'

'Some guys don't like living off their wives.'

'Idiots! If you love each other, things like money don't matter. It's being together that's the important thing and if you have that going for you, then everything else falls into place.'

'That's just romantic bullshit.'

'No, it isn't. In any case, the fact is that Mike has changed his mind about our getting married next summer.'

'Maybe it's occurred to him that love is more fun if you've got a roof over your head and a bite or two to eat on the table.'

'Oh you know all about it, do you?'

'No, but there are some things any moron can figure out.'

'Like what?'

'Like the fact that the fairy tale romance you seem to have in mind would barely last through the honeymoon. Real life love, and by that I mean the varnish people use to gloss over their sex drive, doesn't work like that.'

'You must not ever have loved anyone, not really,' Tess said.

'Not in the silly romantic way you're talking about.'

'Oh, just in a varnish-for-your-sex-drive sort of way?'

'It does sound a little crass when you put it that way,' he admitted. 'But I'll make a bet with you.'

'What kind of bet?' she asked suspiciously.

'The kind where it will be a while before we know who wins. I bet that twenty years from now, that'll make it 1990, you'll look back on your ideas about love and be amazed that you ever could have been so idealistic and impractical.'

'Okay, I'll take that bet. My ideas about love aren't going to change, at least not very much, so what do I stand to win?'

'A magnum of champagne with a red ribbon tied around it, delivered to you in person wherever you are. We'll crack it open together and drink to the meaning of life and the glory of love. And if the guy in your life, the one who's made this glorious outcome possible, looks thirsty enough, we can even give him a drop or two. But you have to understand, all this is only in the very unlikely event of you winning.'

'It's not unlikely at all,' she argued, 'but just in case that doesn't happen, what do I have to do?'

'Send me a cheque for whatever a can of beer costs twenty years from now.'

'But that's absurd!'

'Not when you consider the odds. You're playing

a long shot, a very long shot, so if you win, you win big. I'm going with the favourite, so of course I don't stand to collect very much.'

'Okay, but how are we going to know who the winner is?'

'Clearly we've got to keep in touch and what's more, and this is the dicey part, we've each got to rely on each other to tell the truth.'

'I'm okay with that,' she said, 'so you'd better start saving up for the champagne. I can taste it already.'

'Deal then?'

'Deal.'

'Good. I'll start saving tomorrow but in the meantime I'd better be off. I told Derek Kent I'd bring his maps back this afternoon. You know the Kents, don't you, Mary and Derek?'

'Sort of, I met them for about five minutes once at the Wilson's.'

'They're really nice, you'll like them. In fact, why don't you come along with me now? They generally have a good supply of cold beer on offer. Then I'll buy you a Chinese dinner before I bring you back to this furnace you live in.'

'Actually I could use a break,' she said, brightening at the thought. 'And you're right about it being dreadfully hot in here.'

'Come on then, Big Red must be chomping at the bit

by this time.'

'Impatient beast,' she said, with a laugh.

The cooling breeze that a ride on Big Red inevitably generated had thoroughly refreshed her by the time they pulled up in front of the Dutch colonial house where the Kents lived.

Mary, a pixie-like woman with sparkling blue eyes, greeted them at the door and invited them in, saying, 'We're just having tea.'

'I was kind of hoping for a beer,' Barry replied.

'I think we can find you one,' she replied cheerfully, as she led them into a large comfortable room where Derek and their daughter, a pale little girl with eyes that seemed too big for her face, were defying the afternoon heat with steaming cups of tea and slices of delicious-looking coconut cake.

Barry took one look at it and said, 'Maybe I'll have tea after all. Cake and beer don't go so well together and there's no way I'm going to pass up anything that looks that gorgeous.'

'Have tea and cake first, then a beer,' Mary suggested.

'Good idea,' Barry agreed enthusiastically.

'We're expecting your new Foundation Representative, Philip Dunhill, to drop by this afternoon,' Mary said.

'He's an old friend of ours, you know. We were all in Turkey at the same time.'

'He was working on an excavation not far from our irrigation project,' Derek explained. 'That was a number of years ago but I don't suppose he's changed much since then. Quite a decent chap, you'll like him.'

'But you must have met him already,' Mary said. 'You can imagine how surprised we were when we heard that he was going to be the replacement for David Wilson. And now he's here even sooner than we expected. It's amazing, isn't it, the way the same people keep turning up?'

'Lucky we haven't led a life of crime,' Derek quipped. 'We'd never be able to escape our guilty past.'

Tess tried to conjure up a picture of Derek as some kind of thief or murderer but failed completely. His eyes were too kind, his middle too large and his air of conservative respectability too profound to make it possible. It was even harder to imagine Mary, with her ready smile and generous hospitality, as anyone with evil intent so Tess didn't spend much time trying.

'It's such a pity Philip never married,' Mary continued, 'but often the nicest men don't, you know.'

'I don't know where you got that idea,' Derek protested.

'It's rather odd when you think about it,' Mary continued, undaunted by the interruption from her husband, 'slavery is illegal but marriage is still condoned, I mean, look at me.'

Everybody did.

'I don't think you illustrate your point very well, my dear,' Derek said reproachfully.

'You mean just because you don't keep me tied up in the kitchen with nothing but a few old rags to wear,' she demanded, laughing, 'that doesn't mean anything. I have to deal with a daughter who has no school to go to, a husband who wants to eat English food in a place where the meat is so tough you can scarcely get a knife through it, servants who are constantly disappearing for the weddings or funerals of a thousand imaginary relatives. I mean the gardener's father died twice last year, can you believe that?'

Nobody could.

'I only have two air conditioners for a house with five bedrooms,' she went on, the lilt in her voice belying her complaints, 'a hot water heater that's perpetually broken and – oh,' she squealed, interrupting herself gaily, 'someone's at the door. It must be Philip!' Leaping up, she rushed out to greet him.

Tess watched in amazement, wondering how anyone could be so happy to see that fiend in human form. Derek, too, in his low-keyed, less exuberant way, seemed just as pleased to see his old friend.

It was turning into a really strange day as far as

relationships with people were concerned, Tess decided. First there had been Mike's letter, one that any fool except Barry could see meant that his feelings for her had gone from torrid to tepid. Then the one friend in all of Java she felt she could relax and really be herself with, Barry, had gone over to the dark side or, at least, had declared his neutrality when all she wanted was an ally in the looming war between herself and Philip. And now to her annoyance, Mary and Derek, whom she had quickly come to like, were treating that viper like some kind of visiting raja.

She had really been enjoying herself until he came along but now, with the conversation centring on him and all the great things he had been doing in the last few years, the afternoon had been spoilt.

That's what she was thinking about when the little girl, who was equally uninterested in Philip's glorious accomplishments, came over to her and asked, 'How do you spell hippopotamus?'

Startled, Tess suppressed a smile and told her.

'Do things like that bother you sometimes?' the child asked.

'Like what?'

'Like how many 'p' s there are in 'hippopotamus'.'

'Not really,' Tess replied, trying to look like she took the question seriously, 'at least not recently. Do they bother you?'

'Sometimes. Words with double letters, or words that might have double letters, bother me because I can never remember whether they have them or not, except of course the ones in my name.'

'What is your name?'

'Didn't Mummy tell you?'

'I don't think so.'

'Do you want me to tell you then?'

Tess suppressed a stab of exasperation.

'Yes please.'

'It's Holly, with a double l.'

'Mine's Tess,' she returned, and then added, 'with a double s.'

Holly broke into a delighted smile, seeming to regard this as a sign they were members of the same club. 'Do you want to see the spelling words I had today?' she asked, adding ruefully, 'I got two wrong though.'

'That doesn't matter, I'd like to see them anyway.'

Thinking that anything would be better than sitting there listening to Philip being idolised, she let Holly lead her down a corridor to a small room with two desks.

'This is where I do lessons,' Holly said, indicating a small desk with books, papers, pencils and crayons laid out on it in neat rows, 'and that's Mummy's desk,' she added, pointing to a larger one covered with a jumbled heap of similar school necessities.

Odd that it isn't the other way around, Tess thought, but then everything to do with Holly seemed a little unusual.

'Next year I'm going to back to England to boarding school,' Holly said, taking a paper filled with neatly written words, two of which had been misspelled and were underlined in red ink, from the heap on her mother's desk.

'These are the spelling words I did this morning. Do you want me to show you some of my school books too?'

Tess said that she did and as she thumbed through them and Holly chattered away beside her, she became so intrigued by this strange and voluble child that she was startled when Barry poked his head around the door.

'Hey, what are you two jabbering about? We'd better be going if we want to stop for some chow on the way.'

'After that enormous piece of cake you ate?' Holly exclaimed.

'Watch it, kid,' warned Barry. 'That cake was only the beginning. I eat little girls too.'

Holly stuck her tongue out at him but still kept well out of his reach.

'Are you going to come again?' she asked Tess as she followed her back down the corridor.

'If you want me to.'

'When?'

'I don't know. Sometime.'

'Yes, you must make it soon,' urged Mary, joining them at the front door. Then, seized with an inspiration that encompassed Barry as well, she added, 'Why don't you both come for dinner on Thursday night?'

'Great, I'd love to,' Barry, always ready for a good meal, replied with enthusiasm.

'Lovely. Philip's coming then too,' Mary added.

'I'm not sure I'll be able to,' Tess put in hastily.

'Of course you can,' Barry said, thinking she was being an idiot to turn down a good dinner just because of Philip. After all, it might be just what she needed to make her see the guy in a different light. 'What are you planning to do on Thursday night that you can't do some other time?'

Embarrassed and furious, Tess felt her imagination completely freeze up but not wanting to be rude, she opted for the Javanese way of dealing with awkward situations. She thanked Mary and said she would come, even though she had no intention of actually doing so.

What the hell, she told herself, she could always develop a sore throat or bubonic plague at the last minute.

It was Philip himself who threw a spanner in her plans. Tess ran into him in the office the day before the proposed dinner and, to her surprise, he offered to pick her up and drive her to the Kents'.

'Thanks but you don't need to,' she replied, 'I like taking rickshaws.'

'I don't think it's a good idea for you to take them alone at night.'

'I've done it before.'

'Not when I was around.'

'I did manage to run my own life before you were here, you know, and I've no intention of stopping now.'

Scooping up her mail, she would have swanned off if he hadn't delayed her by saying, 'Hold on a minute. You don't happen to know why Darwati always acts like she's so damn scared of me, do you? I swear I've never been anything but nice to her yet she seems to think I'm some kind of ogre. For the life of me I can't think where she could have gotten that idea, can you?'

'No,' said Tess, hoping she looked innocent. 'It's funny because Darwati is usually very perceptive about people.'

Philip was on the point of growling that she wasn't so fucking perceptive about him but Tess was already halfway out the door by then so he turned his attention back to the papers on his desk.

As the morning grew hotter and the air conditioner struggled against the rising temperature in the room, Philip found his thoughts returning to Tess. He had never encountered anyone with a less focused project and he was going to have a devil of a time pounding the thing into any kind of shape. Yet instead of being grateful for his help, the little twit had got it into her head that it wasn't any of his business. That certainly wasn't going to make things any easier.

A major dose of tact was going to be called for and that had never been his strong point, especially where women were concerned. He might as well face it, the few relationships he had managed to make time for in his busy life had been short-lived and fairly disastrous.

Working his way through college, his sights set on getting the highest possible grade average, hadn't left him with much time or money for socialising, and graduate school, with its nose-to-the-grindstone pressure, hadn't been any better in that respect. In any case the remarkable thing about Ph.D. programs was their dearth of attractive women. He would be prepared to swear that none of the female graduate students in his department, gorgons all of them, had any idea what a comb was. As far as he could make out, they vied with each other to see who could look like the greatest fright.

When he had finally finished his degree and left the academic world behind him, his girlfriend situation hadn't improved very much. Nor, thanks to the clawing competition within the Foundation, had his workload decreased to any noticeable extent. It always amazed him when businessmen suggested that working for a non-profit organisation must be quite relaxing. It was dog-eat-dog if you wanted to get to the top and the top was, most emphatically, where he wanted to be.

The reason Tess's vague and romantic approach to her thesis annoyed him so much was that if he were going to keep his career progressing from strength to strength, first-class work had to come out of the Yogyakarta office under his stewardship. There had been too many dud projects on Wilson's watch, the old fellow had probably been doddery by that time. In any case, he had been so close to retirement that he probably hadn't tried very hard or cared very much.

It was different for him. Yogyakarta was exactly the right launching pad for the Foundation's expanded operations in Indonesia and he, Philip Dunhill, was exactly the right man to preside over it.

The political turmoil of the '60s was now a thing of the past and a stable government that was interested in upgrading the quality of its human resources was firmly in control. This meant that the scope for an increased Foundation presence throughout the country was limitless and there was no way he was going to let a golden opportunity like that slip through his fingers. He could already visualize himself as the Number One man in a whole network of Foundation offices spread across the entire archipelago.

Of course it wasn't going to be handed to him on a silver platter. The Yogyakarta venture had to be a stunning success to make it happen. The turkeys left over from Wilson's regime would have to be shaped up or killed off as soon as possible. Fortunately there was one exception, the project that guy Barry Gellert was working on, looked very promising. He just wished he could say the same about Tess's half-arsed little venture. If anything were to come of that, he'd have to take hold of it and massage it into shape himself.

It was bad luck that Tess wasn't a man. Girls were so touchy. They couldn't take the truth the way men could and that made them harder to handle. He'd have to map out a careful strategy, coax her along and win her confidence. And it would really help if he could get her to like him. He could see that she didn't and that her feelings were going to stand in the way of his plans if he didn't manage to turn them around. It was a real pain that women were ruled by their emotions rather than by their intellect, even when they had one. He supposed Tess did have one but she was too feminine to be easy to deal with. Getting her to see things his way was going to be tricky. Still, it might be rather entertaining too.

Tess, after leaving the office, only thought about Philip long enough to pronounce him a paternalistic, self-important pig before glancing down at the envelopes in her hand and seeing Mike's handwriting on one of them. Almost daring to hope it would say he had been drunk, off his face, out-of-his-mind when he had suggested postponing the wedding, she ripped it open and scanned the letter inside.

It didn't say that at all.

It went into detail about a case in his Torts class, emphasised the superhuman pressure he was under and described the monumental hangover he had had after a beer-blast on Saturday night. When she got to the closing line and read that he hoped she was still having a whale of a time in Java, she crumpled the letter into a ball and shoved it into the bottom of her bookbag.

She wondered what had happened to Mike. How could he have changed so much in just a few months? They used to understand each other so well, share each other's interests, want the same things in life. Now it seemed like all he cared about was getting good grades in what must be the world's most boring subject and partying with his beer-guzzling friends. As for telling her the things she wanted to hear, that he loved her, that he missed her, that life would be totally meaningless until they were together again, well, there certainly wasn't any of that. It was true he had signed it 'love Mike' but that was probably the way he would sign a letter to one of his aunts or his grandmother.

To hell with him, she thought. He's turned into a robot and who can love a robot? Not me. Barry's wrong about my having a lot of imagination. If I did I might be able to persuade myself that Mike still loved me the way I want to be loved. But to a logical, rational mind like mine, it's all too obvious that if he still loves me at all it's in a tepid, half-hearted sort of way. And who needs that kind of love, for God's sake?

Pursuing this line of thought but now focusing it on Barry, she asked herself, who needs a friend like that? He had let her down too. A real friend would be firmly on her side, supporting her against Philip and not just taking the easy way out by mouthing rubbish, like agreeing to disagree. What a rat he was.

Were there any men in the world who weren't pigs or rats, she wondered, frowning as her mind darted back over the different phases of her life. Her father had been kind enough when he wasn't off somewhere doing important things and Uncle John had always been nice to her when she had gone over to look at Aunt Saskia's Java books. But her high school class, the male half of it anyway, had been made up entirely of unpleasant zoological species: reptiles, worms and warthogs.

Of course there had been David, she remembered with a smile. He had been spending the summer with his dad and stepmother and little half-sister. It had been like some kind of miracle when he had just fallen off his bicycle into her front yard one afternoon. Her mother had been out shopping so she had brought him into the house, put Mercurochrome on his scraped leg, made a cold compress for the rapidly rising bump on his forehead and wound a bandage round his ankle in case it had been sprained.

The treatment had ended with a pitcher of lemonade and she had found out that he was a major in archaeology at the University of New Mexico. He had even been on a dig the previous summer. She could still remember the fascinating things he had told her about the ceremonial room, he called it a kiva, that they had been excavating. Apparently it had all sorts of paintings on the walls and had been the place where Pueblo Indians held their sacred rituals way back in the fourteenth century. There had been skeletons too and weird objects used in traditional rites, plus lots and lots of pieces of broken pottery called shards.

She had listened enthralled to everything he had been able to tell her about it all and it proved to be the first of many afternoons when he cycled past her house. She had decided to spend more time riding her bicycle too and they agreed that the street between their houses was the best place for getting up a good speed. For some reason they always seemed to find themselves there around the same time and, as his stepmother worked in the afternoons and his little sister spent that time at day care, David's house was the natural one for them to go to for something to drink after cycling. He had wanted to take her to the movies but her parents had had the ridiculous and infuriating idea that she was too young to go out with a college boy. She had pointed out the fact that she would be fifteen in just a month but they had held firm and that had been the end of that – sort of.

They still saw each other in the afternoons and one day, when she knew Aunt Saskia would be at the hairdresser, they had even climbed in the window and pored over the books on Java together. He had agreed that it was the most fascinating place in the entire world and they had made plans to go there together when he finished college.

Then one day, as the month of August was drawing to a close, he had impulsively leaned down and kissed her and it hadn't been long before he was doing much more than that. Within a few days of that first touch, one that had electrified them both, they had lain naked on his bed together and during the last week of that glorious summer they made love every afternoon.

They wrote to each other for nearly a year after he had gone back to New Mexico but his father and stepmother had moved away before Christmas and she had never seen him again.

Still, he was probably the only male in the world, the

only young one anyway, who wasn't horrible.

Tess let her mind drift back over the ones she had gone out with at university. There had been that reptile, Mark, the first year, then there had been a sort of sophomore slump until she met George. He hadn't been too bad actually, not if you liked grizzly bears anyway. In all fairness, he really hadn't been more than five or ten pounds overweight and he wasn't all that hairy, just a little bit up and down his back. But he had a round face and an unquenchable thirst for beer so it didn't take a fortune teller to predict what his shape would be like in 10 or 20 years. Then there had been the swimmer, Sam. When it came to looks he was the best of the lot but he had been a little short on stimulating conversation. Plus he had had that ghastly habit of getting up at five in the morning for swimming practice.

In truth, by the time she met Mike in her last year, she had been getting so fed up with the male menagerie parading through her life that she had tried very hard, perhaps too hard, to convince herself that she had finally found the right one.

The discovery that Mike was very far from being the right one was therefore a nasty shock.

The first thing she needed to do, she decided, was figure out whether she really needed a man in her life at all. Maybe she didn't. For years she had just assumed she did but that may have been silly. After all, what would she really need one for except sex? And what was the point of having sex if it just made you unhappy? It did have its moments, she had to admit that and she would probably miss it, to tell the truth she missed it already. How many months had it been since she had been with Mike? More than three. It seemed longer but that might be because so much had happened during that time.

Not letting herself think about sex had to be the first step in this new 'don't need a man in my life' regime, so she quickened her step in the direction of the archaeology lab and immersed herself in some stone inscriptions from the Mataram Kingdom that had been found near Tegal. She went on to skip lunch, spend the entire afternoon painstakingly recording and analysing any clues they offered about the life in the ancient kingdom, and didn't let herself think about sex, Mike, men or anything like that even for a second.

When she got home that evening she was surprised to find Darwati waiting for her, looking nervous and miserable.

'What's wrong?' Tess exclaimed, forgetting that in Java it was rude to come directly to the point.

'Nothing.'

'That can't be true, something obviously isn't right.'

Darwati looked more distressed than ever. She didn't know how to handle a direct contradiction. The people she knew always pretended to believe you, even when they knew you were lying, it was the polite thing to do. Now caught in this uncomfortable situation, all she could do was repeat, 'Nothing.'

'Come on,' Tess cajoled, 'we're friends, aren't we? You can tell me.'

Darwati was longing to tell her, that was why she had come, but now that the moment was at hand, talking about it was more difficult than she had imagined.

'Is it something to do with Sigit?' asked Tess, fairly certain that it must be.

Darwati nodded.

'Does he think you shouldn't see each other anymore?'

'Oh no,' she cried, 'he loves me very much.'

'What is it, then? You're not –'

'Oh no, not that,' Darwati protested, vehemently.

'What then?'

'There is a girl in my auntie's village, a very bad girl. Everyone knows she is bad and now –' Darwati's eyes grew large and tragic as she related her news. 'Now this bad girl wants Sigit.'

'But it's you he loves,' Tess pointed out reassuringly, 'so there's no problem, is there?'

'Yes there is,' Darwati cried, with uncharacteristic

assertiveness, 'a very big problem.' Lowering her voice to a murmur, she explained, 'This bad girl has a powerful *dukun*. He is up on Mt Merapi, near Kaliurang.'

'But surely you can't seriously –' Tess managed to catch herself before she made the mistake of smiling.

She had heard about people going to a *dukun* for help in matters of love. Their power as diviners, healers and practitioners of black magic was regarded with awe and fear. They could, if properly requested, make someone fall in love with you or ensure that the object of your affections didn't stray. That was the relatively benign side of their art but there was also a darker one. They were reported to know the potions and the incantations that would enable you to get back at a rival, or even remove one from the scene altogether. This 'black magic' was illegal but as the law was near-impossible to enforce, it was generally ignored.

Reminding herself that it wouldn't do to make light of any of this, Tess said, 'Don't worry. If Sigit really loves you then the *dukun's* spells won't have any effect, you'll see.'

Darwati didn't argue but polite disbelief was written all over her face so, in an effort to raise her spirits, Tess suggested they go to the cinema. A film about bloodthirsty, sex-starved ghosts was playing that Darwati had said she wanted to see.

Tess had been less than enthusiastic about going,

not only because of the subject matter but because she dreaded the thought of spending two hours in the stifling atmosphere of a non-air-conditioned theatre. But today she wanted to humour her friend so she agreed to go.

Sadly her magnanimous gesture was poorly rewarded; the seats were infested with bedbugs.

Several days later when she was halfway through her usual breakfast of fried rice with chilli peppers, she remembered that the Kents' dinner party was that evening.

Damn it, she thought, she would have to find a phone. As she had to tell Mary Kent she was sick, she couldn't exactly make the call from the office.

She hastily ran through a list of things that could be wrong with her, things that didn't have visible symptoms, require hospitalisation or last very long. Bubonic plague failed on all counts and, in any case, might be slightly over the top.

Eventually she settled on a stomach problem. People in Yogya had them all the time so it was easily believable and, with any luck, it would be over in a day or so. It didn't quite pass the 'no visible symptoms' criteria but it was unlikely that anyone would press for details.

Confident that she had the situation under control, she paid a visit to the one neighbour who had a telephone and chatted with her long enough, she hoped, to conform to Javanese ideas of politeness. But when she was finally able to dial the Kents' number, her ears were assaulted with a harsh zinging sound that her kind hostess, hovering near the phone in order not to miss anything, explained meant the line she was trying to reach was out of order.

She would just have to write a note which might be better anyway. But before she sat down to do it, Tess realised that she wouldn't have any way of getting it to them. She couldn't exactly deliver it herself when she was supposed to be throwing up every five minutes and she couldn't get a rickshaw driver to take it because she didn't actually know the name of their street or the number of the house.

She wondered how she could have been such an idiot. Everyone knew that telephoning in Yogya was an if-maybe proposition at best. How could she have forgotten that? All she could do at this point was stay home and leave the Kents to deal with the empty place at the table.

But that was a really shabby way to treat people, especially ones who had been so nice to her. She would just have to hope they would think there had been some kind of emergency and she hadn't been able to get through on the phone. She'd apologise all over the place, grovel when she saw them and spare no revolting detail about just how ill she had been. In the meantime, she'd better stay home.

She couldn't risk letting Philip, Barry or worst of all one of the Kents, see her roaming around in perfect health.

Somehow the day seemed to crawl by. The idea that she couldn't go out made her want to do exactly that and as the afternoon progressed she could have sworn that the temperature in her room had soared to unprecedented heights. Could her conscience be joining forces with the elements to increase her misery?

She tried to tell herself that accepting an invitation and then not turning up was such a Javanese thing to do that the Kents must surely be used to it by now. But there was a catch to that line of reasoning, of course, she wasn't Javanese so they wouldn't be expecting that sort of thing from her.

The more she thought about what she was doing, the worse she felt about it.

Damn Philip, she fumed, it was all because of him that she was sitting here hating herself this way. It was his fault! Or was it? Wasn't she the one who was responsible for what she did or didn't do?

To hell with him, she told herself, she wasn't going to let him provoke her into being horrible to someone who hadn't been anything but nice to her. Mary Kent had invited her to dinner and she was going to go.

Suddenly her room didn't seem as hot and claustrophobic as it had before. She bathed, put on a pale green mini dress and brushed her hair, letting it hang loosely over her shoulders and down her back. She was just finishing her makeup with a touch of pale blue eyeshadow when, to her surprise, she heard Big Red pulling up in front of the house.

'I thought you might like a lift,' Barry said as he came into the room.

'Thanks but isn't it still a bit early?'

'Yeah,' he agreed. 'The thing is, my day's all shot to hell. Everyone I wanted to see was out so I figured I might as well come on over here and chew the fat with you for a while before we go to the Kents'. You haven't got a cold beer, have you? I could kill for one right now.'

'I'm afraid that's not on offer. You can have a coke or a Green Spot though.'

'If it's cold, lead me to it.'

'Sorry, we don't have a fridge.'

'Finish putting on your war paint then and let's go round up a beer on Jalan Malioboro. I swear, the temperature in this room beats the seasonal average in hell.'

'Sorry you're uncomfortable but then I don't recall inviting you.'

'You're quite the little snapping turtle today,' Barry observed cheerfully. 'You know, I think living in this place is warping your character. You used to be quite likeable but now, well, it wouldn't surprise me if you started growing cloven hooves and a long forked tail.'

'You're full of compliments today.'

'I know. Marilyn never appreciates them but I was hoping you'd be different. Unfortunately you seem to be even worse. At least Marilyn doesn't answer back.'

'That's too bad, it might do you good if she did.'

'What's got into you today? I thought we were friends.'

'So did I.'

'What's the problem then?'

'Philip,' she replied.

'What's he got to do with anything?'

'I don't see how you can be Philip's friend and mine too.'

'Why the hell not?'

'Because he hates me.'

'Don't be ridiculous. He doesn't hate you. Why should he? What have you ever done to him?'

'I don't know, well I do know actually. He thinks I'm an idiot and he's had it in for me from day one. You should hear the way he talks to me, it's unbelievable. And I'm sure he's going to do everything he can to sabotage my thesis.'

'Bullshit, there isn't any way he could do that even if he wanted to.'

'He can keep me from getting an extension and I'm sure that's what he has in mind.'

'But you told me you didn't want one,' he reminded her,

191

'so what's the problem?'

'I didn't want one when I said that but I do now. Everything's going so much more slowly than I planned and after that letter from Mike, I'm not in any mood to rush home.' Picking up her brush and sweeping it through her hair with long angry strokes, she continued. 'Just thinking about him makes me furious.'

'Don't think about him then,' Barry suggested, then watched her in silence for a few minutes before exclaiming, 'Will you stop that!'

'Why?'

'Because I'm asking you to.'

'That's no reason.'

'Yes it is,' he argued, 'it's the best reason.' And coming up behind her, he grabbed hold of the brush and wrestled it away from her.

'Give me that,' she cried, struggling to get it back.

'Shhh, don't scream. Your landlady will think I'm attacking you.'

'You are attacking me, sort of.'

'No I'm not, I'm just going to brush your hair.'

And with long rhythmic strokes that began at her temples, followed the contours of her head and went down to the middle of her back, he ran the brush through her hair.

Tess felt her resistance evaporate and simply gave

herself up to the exquisite pleasure of the moment telling herself, or trying to tell herself anyway, that this was no different from being in the hands of the world's most fabulous hairdresser.

But it was different, she knew.

And when, a few minutes later, he set down the brush, pushed his hands up under the full weight of her hair and began kneading the back of her head, a bolt of electricity shot through her, rippling down her spine to the most sensitive part of her body and lingering there like the fervent touch of a lover.

Then Barry, reminding himself that getting involved with this crazy girl was a really bad idea, brought the moment to a close.

'You're not so different from Marilyn after all,' he teased. 'She likes being brushed too.' Before Tess could think of a sufficiently scathing retort, he added, 'We'd better get going if we want that cold beer.'

The ride on Big Red through the fading light of early evening went a long way towards restoring a mood of friendly camaraderie, and by the time two refreshing glasses of beer had been set down in front of them, they were drifting into the ever-compelling topic of life in Java.

It was only after they had called for the bill and were getting ready to leave that Barry, with uncharacteristic awkwardness, muttered, 'You know, I've been doing some more thinking about that prick, Philip, and as far as I'm concerned he can go to hell.'

'Good,' Tess said, and hurried out to Big Red ahead of him, not wanting him to see her revelling in her victory.

When they pulled up in front of the Kents', her upbeat mood fell victim to a wave of second thoughts. Should she really have come tonight? But when Holly, who had been watching for her from the living room window, came rushing out to meet her, Tess was glad she hadn't let any fits of cowardice get the better of her.

A warm welcome from Mary, followed by a brief altercation between mother and daughter about just whose guest Tess really was, made her feel even better.

'But I want to show her the story I wrote today,' Holly protested. 'It's about digging up treasures and that's what she likes to do, it's her very, very, very favourite thing.'

Sadly for Holly, Mary's response was firm.

'Later,' she said. 'You must at least give her a chance to sit down with a drink first.'

But Tess, touched by the look of disappointment on Holly's face, suggested, 'I might just take a quick look at it and then –'

Before she could finish the sentence, Holly was pulling her down the passage to the schoolroom.

The story was about a little girl who found the jewels from a lost castle buried in her garden.

'I only wish I could be so lucky,' Tess said with a smile.

'You can't always find lost treasures just like that,' Holly explained helpfully. 'Sometimes you have to go looking for them.'

Tess couldn't disagree with this.

'Have you ever found any?' Holly asked.

'No, I haven't been as lucky as the little girl in your story.'

'But have you ever looked for them?' she asked.

'Not in my garden but I look for them almost every day,' Tess told her, 'that's why I'm here in Java, although I don't always go out and about looking for them. Sometimes I just look for clues about them in books.'

'When you do go out looking for them, can I go with you?'

'Maybe sometime.'

'Does Mummy know that's what you're doing here?'

'I suppose she does.'

'Was she surprised when you told her?'

'I don't think so.'

'I bet Uncle Philip will be surprised when I tell him.'

Tess shuddered. The prospect of Philip hearing her project described as a childish treasure hunt was ghastly beyond belief.

In an attempt to rein in the damage, she put her forefinger to her lips and said, almost in a whisper, 'Shhh, let's not tell anyone. Let's keep it our secret. That way it will be more fun when you come with me.'

Holly was thrilled. What could be more exciting than having a secret with Tess and a secret about a treasure, too?

'I'll never, ever tell anyone,' she promised. Perhaps because she was a lonely child, growing up in an alien culture, she was actually very good at keeping secrets.

They got back to the living room in time to hear Mary introducing two more guests, Elizabeth and Felicia, who had come out from the UK the previous week and would be teaching English at Gajah Mada .

Derek gave them a warm welcome, Philip said something coolly appropriate and Barry announced that he hoped they'd brought plenty of Lomotil and insect repellent out with them.

'What's Lomotil?' Felicia asked.

'Haven't you heard of it? It takes care of what we Americans call Montezuma's Revenge, also known as Delhi Belly. We're still looking for some genius to come up with a name for the Indonesian version.'

Holly piped up, 'How about the Java Jig?'

'Stop that, both of you,' scolded Mary, laughing. 'It's very naughty of you to frighten new arrivals like that.'

Both Elizabeth and Felicia chorused that they weren't frightened at all.

'That's the spirit,' Derek said approvingly.

Noticing Tess in the doorway, it occurred to him that she had missed the round of introductions so he set about making that right, finishing by saying, 'She's at Gajah Mada too.'

'Are you in the English Department?' Elizabeth asked.

'No, archaeology, doing research for my Master's thesis.'

'What are you doing it on?'

'That's still something of a mystery,' Philip replied, before Tess could think of the best way to describe it.

'Oh do tell,' exclaimed Felicia eagerly. 'I love mysteries.'

'It's on the Mataram Kingdom in the –' said Tess, quickly jumping in before Philip had a chance to answer for her.

'Never heard of it,' interrupted Felicia.

'I have,' said Derek. 'It was an Islamic kingdom in Sumatra sometime around the fifteenth century.'

'Oh, I thought you meant a real mystery,' cried Felicia, disappointed, 'a murder or something.'

'The Islamic one was actually the second Mataram Kingdom,' Tess explained. 'I'm working on the first one, the Hindu one. It was –'

'Unfortunately,' Philip interrupted, 'Tess didn't get the direction she needed back at the University of

Pennsylvania so hasn't quite pinned down her topic yet. But she has come to the right place. The two of us are going to put our heads together and come up with a splendid topic.'

'We're not going to do any such thing,' Tess cried, digging her fingernails into her palms to keep from clawing the self-satisfied expression off Philip's face.

'What the fuck do you think you are doing,' Barry growled, in an undertone that only Philip could hear, 'talking about Tess's project like that? You'd better take it back and apologise, actually do more than apologise, grovel.'

'What's the problem?' exclaimed Philip, looking both surprised and amused. 'I'm doing Tess a favour, offering her a lifeline. If we team up we can probably salvage her thesis, if not ' He grimaced but then added, 'Fortunately, I used to be something of an archaeologist myself so I'll enjoy getting into it again, doing what I can to oversee her work.'

'There's no way we're a team,' cried Tess. 'We never have been and never will be. My thesis is my project, not anybody else's and,' she added, looking Philip directly in the eye, 'what you think of it is a matter of complete indifference to me.'

'Of course it's your project,' Philip said soothingly, still perplexed by her hostile reaction to his generous offer. 'I'll just be available as a resource person whenever you need me.'

'Are you going to help Barry with his project too?' Mary asked, in an attempt to defuse the obvious tension.

'No need,' Philip replied. 'He's getting along fine without me.'

'It's kind of the other way around actually,' Barry said. 'I'm going to be helping him sort out the mess his office is in, step in and run things whenever it looks like the place is falling apart, be his resource person.'

'We'll see about that,' Philip replied sharply.

'It looks like resource people aren't in very high demand around here,' Derek observed.

'I wish I had one,' sighed Felicia. 'My boyfriend, Paul, was my resource person at home but he won't be coming out here until March or April.'

'I don't think that's quite the kind of resource person Philip or Barry have in mind,' Elizabeth said.

Felicia, wondering why Elizabeth always thought she knew everything, flashed her a look of repressed irritation. Of course the poor thing must be thirty-five if she was a day, needed to lose at least a stone and didn't have a great boyfriend like Paul, or any boyfriend at all, as far as she knew. That explained a lot.

'Paul is a professional photographer,' she added, mistakenly assuming everyone would want to know.

'How lovely,' Mary exclaimed. 'Perhaps we can ask him

to take some pictures of Holly before she goes back to England. Children change so fast, you know.'

'Oh, he's not that kind of photographer,' Felicia said, hastily. 'He takes pictures of wildlife and nature and that sort of thing.'

Mary's disappointment showed on her face.

'His pictures have been published in lots of magazines,' Felicia went on to inform her audience, 'but what he really wants to do is a piece for *National Geographic*.'

Sensing that Paul's career goals weren't arousing much interest, Felicia singled Tess out as the one person who deserved to hear more about him. After all, she had a more sensitive face than the others.

Tess, who would cheerfully have listened to the accomplishments of the devil himself if they saved her from Philip's observations about her thesis, welcomed Felicia's description of the camera safari that she and the divine Paul had been on in Africa.

When they all moved into the dining room, Tess hung back to see where Philip would be sitting before finding a place at the opposite end of the table but her careful manoeuvring came to nothing. He asked Felicia to change seats with him and the next thing she knew, he was firmly ensconced beside her.

'You look really nice tonight,' he told her truthfully.

After a minimally polite reply, Tess turned away

from him and focused her attention on what Mary was saying about their recent weekend at the beach at Pelabuhan Ratu.

Philip didn't have a chance to further his 'Tess strategy' until the soup dishes were cleared away and a beautiful-looking roast was set on the table. While Derek was carving, Philip leaned over to Tess and said, in a low voice he hoped no one else would hear, 'I like that dress you're wearing tonight, it really suits you. Do you always choose clothes that match your eyes?'

To his utter mortification, Mary heard him, laughed and exclaimed, 'But her dress doesn't match her eyes! It's green, a sort of apple green, and her eyes are blue.'

Everyone looked at Tess's eyes and then at her dress.

'I can't tell blue from green,' Barry announced cheerfully.

'I've heard of people like that,' Derek said, 'but you're the first one I've actually met.'

'My grandmother says you can't trust people with green eyes,' put in Felicia, 'but it can't be true because Paul's eyes are green.'

'I don't care if the guy's peepers are purple,' Barry whispered to Elizabeth and they both laughed.

Felicia heard him, felt hurt and decided that he wasn't as attractive as she had thought, not really a candidate for a quick fling before Paul arrived.

Barry, for his part, would have preferred to have a quick

fling with Elizabeth who not only had a sexy figure with lots of curves but a good sense of humour as well.

In Philip's eyes, Elizabeth wasn't particularly sexy, nor slim enough or young enough to suit him, but when it came to someone to talk to he had to give her a high rating as she was intelligent and interesting.

Derek would have agreed with the high rating. He thought women were at their best in their thirties, young enough to be attractive but old enough to have something to say that might possibly be worth hearing.

Tess's instinctive reaction to Elizabeth was that she was the sort of person you could trust while Mary, with her usual warmth and generosity, had already decided that Elizabeth was lovely.

Felicia, who saw her as overweight, dowdy and clearly past it, couldn't understand why anyone and particularly anyone male, would want to bother with her.

As the dinner progressed, Philip grew increasingly proud of the way he was seizing opportunities to pursue his 'Tess strategy' while still giving due attention to the general conversation. He made a point of telling everyone how well Tess spoke Indonesian, how knowledgeable she was about the Javanese people and how helpful she had been in finding him a language teacher.

Tess heard all this praise with astonishment. She wondered if the cocktails, followed by the wine that was not often seen in Java, had been too much for him. He didn't look like it had gone to his head but she couldn't think of any other explanation. In any case, it wasn't really worth thinking about because he was sure to revert to his usual, horrible self the next day.

Mary breathed a sigh of relief when the sarong-clad servants padded in to take away what remained of the main course. Happily, no one had seemed to notice that the roast lamb was really roast goat. It had turned out that Felicia was a vegetarian and Elizabeth had been too embroiled in conversation, first with Barry and then with Derek, to pay much attention to what she was eating. The others, with the possible exception of Tess, had been in Java long enough to have forgotten what real lamb tasted like and they must know that it simply wasn't available in Yogyakarta.

The meal was rounded out with bread and butter pudding, which Elizabeth and Derek attacked with enthusiasm. Felicia barely touched hers because it was fattening and the three Americans, none of whom liked it very much, ate just enough to be polite.

When everyone had finished, they all streamed back to the lounge for coffee and a splash of cognac, Tess's very favourite tipple. It was delicious and she was thoroughly enjoying her second glass – Derek, ever the perfect host, had been quick to notice that she was in need of a refill – when Philip seized on another chance to further his Tess strategy.

Turning to her as casually, as if they were a couple who had been together for years, he said, 'I'm afraid it's time for us to go. Tomorrow's a work day, you know.'

Tess looked pointedly at her half-finished drink and said, 'Actually, I'm not ready yet.'

'Of course you're not,' Derek agreed, eyeing her glass. 'Mustn't waste good cognac.'

'I'm afraid I've got a lot to do tomorrow,' Philip said testily, 'and I really must get an early start.'

'Me too,' Elizabeth said regretfully, 'but it's been a lovely evening.'

'Perhaps you can give Elizabeth and Felicia a ride then?' Mary suggested, turning to Philip. 'They live near Gajah Mada so that can't be very far from you, can it?'

To his annoyance, he had to agree that it couldn't.

'I wouldn't mind staying for another round myself,' Barry said, casting a hopeful eye in the direction of the decanter, 'so I'll take Tess home.'

'She won't be very comfortable on that bike of yours,' Philip snapped. 'I can take all three girls in the car.'

'I'll be fine on the bike,' Tess declared.

'Okay then, if you're sure,' Philip said, trying to show some enthusiasm for this plan. It wouldn't do for anyone to think he had wanted to take Tess home and been rejected.

After dropping off Elizabeth and Felicia, Philip went over the events of the evening in his mind and decided he really needn't be bothered by Tess's initial resistance to the idea of their working as a team. It was always hard for anyone to admit they needed help. He'd just be patient, carry on saying all the right things and she'd come around. He had gotten off to a good start tonight, she'd just been a little surprised by it all and hadn't quite known how to react but a little time would take care of that.

Helping Tess with her thesis and basically doing the thinking part of it for her would be a good way to relax in the evenings. Archaeology had been his first love, though he had focused on the area around the Mediterranean. He didn't really know anything about what had gone on in Asia but directing Tess's little project would give him an incentive to find out.

Tess's thoughts when she got home focused not on the evening but the afternoon. Barry had scarcely touched her, she reminded herself, he had just brushed her hair in pretty much the same way he brushes Marilyn's. He said so himself. It didn't mean anything. He just wanted to be friends, that's what's important, and he showed it in the way he put Philip in his place tonight. She could handle that slimy bastard by herself and she didn't need anyone's help but it was still nice to know Barry was on her side.

That night as she drifted off to sleep, she dreamt of speeding through the night on Big Red holding firmly onto Barry.

I've got to stop dropping by Tess's place so often, Barry told himself when he failed to fall asleep that night with his usual alacrity. The last thing he needed at the moment was to get involved with this zany girl. What he wanted was a human equivalent of Marilyn, someone good for a little fun but who wouldn't complicate his life.

The trouble was there weren't many girls like that. He guessed that was why some men went to whores, especially in places like Bangkok or Manila where the professionals managed to look like they hadn't already been screwed by six other guys already that night. But the whole scene put him off. He was just stupid enough to want a woman who was going to go wild for his gorgeous self, the idea that she would be doing it for money just ruined things as far as he was concerned. And this was Yogyakarta, not Bangkok or Manila. Most of the girls here, at least the ones he had seen standing along Jalan Solo waiting for some truck driver to stop, were so small and half-starved looking he couldn't for the life of him see how a guy could get a kick out of having it off with them. The desperation of some fourteen-year-old kid or an old hag - who probably wasn't much more than thirty but looked eighty because of the god-awful life she had led - just didn't do it for him.

What the hell was he doing lying here thinking about whores anyway? I'm sex-starved, he thought, that's my problem but I don't see any way out. When women are around they make my life hell and when they're not – fuck, why should life be so damn difficult?

'You up there,' he said to a God he wasn't at all sure he believed in, 'why didn't you make humans more like starfish? Why is it that one of those lucky creatures can get his rocks off just by dividing himself in two whenever the mood takes him whereas human males have to put up with all kinds of crap from their females? How come you let those stupid starfish get off so easily and you leave me here to suffer?'

Jesus Christ, Barry said to himself, now I know for sure that Java is driving me bananas. What kind of no-hope loser lies in bed having fantasies about the sex lives of starfish? If ever anyone was ready for the loony bin, it's me.

There was only one thing to do about it. He'd get out of Java for a while, have a change, go some place that had a little life to it. Jakarta? No, that was really just a bigger version of Yogya. Singapore? No, too strait-laced for the kind of vacation he wanted. Bali? Yeah, that might be just the ticket. He could go there over Christmas, find some Australian chick who was looking for a good time and give her one she wouldn't forget in a hurry.

Just the thought of this made him feel better and in a few minutes he was asleep, dreaming about nearly-naked Australian girls sunning themselves on Kuta Beach, just waiting for him to arrive.

Two days later he parked Big Red outside the Garuda Airlines office, went inside and, to his surprise, saw Tess in the queue at the ticket window.

'Going somewhere?' he asked, strolling over to her.

'To Bali for New Year's, I hope,' she said. 'Although it seems like everyone else in Java has the same idea so I'm not sure I'll be able to get a ticket.'

'I'm off to Bali too but I'm going for Christmas so I guess I won't see you there. New Year's is a big deal in my village so I've got to be back for it, swing into my best 'participant observer' routine, you know.'

'I'm staying here for Christmas, spending it with Mini, Kanwa, Sonia and Darwati,' Tess said. 'According to Mini, Christmas is really big in the Philippines and the celebrations start a couple of months ahead of time. She says she misses it all so we're going to try to make it as much fun for her as possible.'

Changing the subject, she added, 'Do you know anything about places to stay in Bali, outside of Kuta I mean? After two or three days on the beach, I want to go up to Ubud and maybe even on to Besakih.'

'Not me, I'm going to stake out a spot on Kuta Beach and stay there.'

Tess gave him a pitying look. 'Then you're going to miss out on some of the best things about Bali.'

'Like what, for instance?'

'The temples, the dances, the festivals - all that sort of thing. I thought they'd be at the top of any anthropologist's to-do list of Bali.'

'Then you'd think wrong. This particular anthropologist is knee-deep in village culture, he's surrounded by it morning, noon and night. What I need is a vacation that's a real change, not just a postman's holiday.'

'I never thought of it that way,' she acknowledged.

'It's the only way,' he said firmly. 'As a matter of fact, you archaeologists don't know how lucky you are. Your stuff stays in the ground until you get a shovel and dig it out, it doesn't suddenly turn up on your doorstep just when you least want to see it. But anthropology walks around on two feet, calls out *monggo, monggo* in front of your house at six in the morning, peers in your window when you're sprawled out on the bed in the buff and brings you revolting things to eat that it has cooked up. It's a dog's life and I'm going to get as far away from it as I can while I'm in Bali. You'll have to do enough of the culture-vulture stuff for both of us.'

'No problem,' she agreed, 'I'm looking forward to it.'

Within a couple of hours of arriving in Bali, Barry found a cheap hotel, had a refreshing swim and took a stroll along the beach to check out the feminine fauna.

He hadn't gone very far before he spotted a girl with long blonde hair and a figure that was right out of his midnight fantasies. She had undone the top of her bikini and was lying face down on a towel.

He had definitely come to the right place, he could see that, so he sauntered over to her and casually sat down on the sand.

'Great beach,' he remarked after a few minutes.

There was no reply.

'Where are you from?' he asked.

Once again he was greeted with stony silence.

'How about a swim?' he asked.

She turned her head to face the other way.

'I just got here a couple of hours ago,' he persisted. 'Do you know any good places to eat?'

She sat up, smiled sweetly at him and threw a handful of sand in his face. Then she turned and lay back down again.

There was only one sensible course of action after that, Barry decided, and that was to retreat. Hoping for a more encouraging response from some other chick, he wandered on down the beach.

The next girl he spoke to was a determined shell collector who was splashing along the water's edge looking for something exciting to add to her collection. She was decidedly friendlier than the sand thrower but she made him think of the Great White Whale in *Moby Dick* so he left her to search for the perfect conch by herself and looked around for someone else to approach.

It wasn't his lucky day. There were plenty of attractive girls around but they all seemed to be with someone already or to have gone to a charm school for snapdragons or to claim they had other plans, whether real or imaginary he didn't know.

After several hours of discouraging results, he had dinner by himself in a stall near the beach and began to wonder if Bali really was all it was cracked up to be. Two pretty Indonesian girls made a play for his attention as he left the restaurant but he was pretty sure they were professionals so after a brief chat, he moved on.

He was wondering where the Kuta Beach nightlife

he had heard about could be when he came across an open-fronted shack that boasted a small bar, a lively band, three Batak singers and a narrow space that served as a dancefloor.

As far as Barry was concerned its main attraction, its only attraction, was its lively clientele. That was enough to lure him inside and order a drink in the hope that Kuta Beach wasn't going to be a total write-off.

A group of girls who sounded Australian were laughing and drinking at the next table. He watched them for a while and noticed that a couple of them kept looking over at him. Feeling encouraged, he went over and asked the prettier of the two if she would like to dance.

He was in luck. She was a good dancer and told him over the pulsing rhythms of *Hey Jude* that, as it was the last evening of their holiday, they were planning to stay up all night and make the most of it.

The only problem was that after a while she began to show the effects of the astronomical number of drinks she had had. When she was too far gone to keep time to the music, they went back to his room, threw off their clothes and fell onto the bed together. Just as he was poised for the final glorious moment, she pushed him off her, ran naked down the hall to the loo, and was sick.

She didn't seem quite as attractive to him after that and when morning came, he wasn't sorry to tell her he hoped she had a good trip home.

By the second day after Christmas, Barry was beginning to feel a little fed up with Kuta Beach. He had scored a couple more times, once with an Australian girl who was island hopping from Darwin to Singapore in order to get a cheap flight on to London, then with a Pan Am flight attendant who, in a change from her usual stop-over in Bangkok, had come to Bali for what she called her 'Christmas in paradise.'

He had said goodbye to each of them with essentially pleasant memories clouded by only the mildest of regrets, and was now wondering whether or not he really wanted to make another foray along the beach, repeat what was becoming a rather overworked routine and risk having more sand thrown in his face.

But what the hell, he was here wasn't he? He foresaw a long dry spell for himself when he got back to Java so he might as well check out the bikini-clad fauna while he could.

It was still only half past ten when he arrived at his favourite viewing spot but several appealing girls were already browning themselves in the sun. It was a little early in the day to make a move on any of them so he decided to have a swim, then relax and soak up a few rays.

He had barely started into the waves when he noticed that they were considerably bigger and stronger than they had been the last few days. They came crashing onto the shore with a ferocity he hadn't expected and he could feel, at least he thought he could feel, the tug of a menacing undertow.

Looking around, he could see that only a few strong swimmers, mostly guys, were in the water. Any pretty girls, probably aware that this was a beach where the surf was known to be treacherous and lifeguards were non-existent, were staying close to the water's edge.

Barry wasn't a bad swimmer but he didn't kid himself that he was any kind of aquatic Superman, so he went back to the undemanding pastime of watching girls.

The only trouble was that, as the middle of the day approached, the heat of the sun combined with the pounding of the waves began to have a slightly hypnotic effect on him. He allowed himself to be lulled into a pleasant trance until a sudden quickening of people's steps and a change in the tone of their voices alerted him to the fact that something was very wrong.

He sprang up and glanced around just in time to see three men, Aussies by the look of them, setting an unconscious girl face down on the sand. Someone was barking instructions about expelling the water from her lungs while a heavily tattooed bystander was yelling,

'Watch out, you idiot, that's her hair you're treading on!'

'Good God,' gasped Barry, his eyes fixed in horror on the girl's long rope of a plait, 'it's Tess.'

Desperately trying to remember everything he had ever learned about life saving, he rushed over and would have flung himself into the task if another Aussie, this one with the muscles of a world class wrestler, hadn't grabbed hold of him and ordered, 'Stay back, can't you see these guys know what they're doing?'

Barry did see. He also saw, as the men turned her over and began mouth to mouth resuscitation, that the girl was not Tess.

Weak with relief, he allowed himself to be pushed back into the crowd and ended up next to a man who was saying, 'You've got to hand it to the Aussies.'

'Yeah,' agreed Barry, in spite of the fact that none of their attempts to breathe life into the unresponsive form seemed to be working.

From time to time a gush of water would spill from the girl's mouth and a surge of hope would sweep through the onlookers, generating frantic calls for towels to stave off the chill of death. But eventually, when no sustained movement occurred, quiet murmurs of 'too late' began to circulate amongst the crowd.

Barry was having trouble coming to terms with the violently contrasting images surrounding him - the brilliant sun shining on the blue water, a girl in a yellow bikini whizzing by on water skis, a group of none-too-sober guys having a beer blast on a boat anchored just off shore, children building a sand castle well out of reach of any oncoming waves and the happy shouts of tourists too far down the beach to know that death had struck their seaside playground that morning.

These scenes of carefree pleasure somehow had the effect of intensifying the tragedy for Barry.

'See, you can't get away from me,' he could almost hear an angel of death saying, 'no matter where you go, no matter what you do, I'm waiting.'

Only three or four members of the little group gathered around the motionless form had actually known the dead girl, yet everyone shared a sense of desolation mixed with a sudden awareness of their own mortality, as they waited in near silence for the ambulance to arrive from Denpasar.

It came and within minutes it was gone.

The crowd dispersed and soon there was no sign that anything but light hearted holiday antics had ever happened on that beautiful beach.

Barry decided that he badly needed a beer. He felt shaken. The girl's resemblance to Tess was still disturbing him. Everyone knew Kuta was a dangerous beach, there were stories of drowning there all the time, but did she know that? The very thought of Tess, who imbued everything in Indonesia with a kind of fairy tale loveliness, spending several days here by herself horrified him. He could easily imagine her not taking the dangers of Kuta Beach as seriously as she should. She was always taking all the wrong things seriously; Java, archaeology, her relationship with that arse, Mike, to name a few. But when it came to the right things, you never knew how she would react. Would she take the power of the ocean seriously? Maybe but he wouldn't bet a lot of money on it.

Glancing down at his watch, he saw that it was only a little after eleven. Good, he thought, that should give him enough time to go back to the hotel, change out of his wet things, rent a motorcycle, stop by the airline office to get his return ticket pushed back to a later date and still get to the airport in time to meet the daily flight from Yogya.

'What are you doing here?' Tess asked in astonishment when she saw him. 'I thought you were supposed to be back in your village by this time.'

'I should be leaving this afternoon but I just couldn't face it,' he said, trying to sound casual, 'so I changed my ticket. Bali kind of gets to you, you'll find that out. And since I knew you'd be coming today, I thought it would be easier to catch up with you here than down on the beach somewhere. Where are you staying anyway?'

'No idea, I thought I'd just find a place once I got here. Any suggestions?'

'My hotel isn't too bad, not if you think about how little I'm paying for it. Do you want to take a look?'

'Why not?'

'Is that all you've got?' he asked, glancing at the small case she had with her.

She nodded. 'I didn't think I'd need much.'

'Good because I've got a bike outside,' he said. 'Not Big Red, of course, more like his baby brother but it should do.'

Picking up her case, he led the way out through the throng of hopeful porters, vendors, taxi drivers and pickpockets waiting just outside.

'You'd better ride American style this time,' Barry said when they got to the section of the car park reserved for motorbikes. 'That way you can balance the case across your lap.'

'But if I do that, how can I hold on to you?'

'Easy, any able bodied orang-utan could do it.'

'In case you haven't noticed, I'm not –' she protested, laughing.

'Okay, just try to think like an orang-utan and you should be alright.'

'I'm not sure I can do that.'

218

'You can if you try, just put your arms around the case and then grab onto me.'

'But if we bounce or something I might –'

'Then you'll go flying off.'

'I think I'll take a taxi,' she declared, surveying the array of rattletrap vehicles waiting nearby.

'Are you crazy? These taxi drivers are bandits of the first order.'

'Why, what do they do?'

'They name a price that doesn't sound too bad, you agree and then when you're out in the middle of some Godforsaken rice field, they stop and jack up the amount to something like quadruple what you originally agreed to.'

'Suppose you refuse to pay it?'

'They chuck you out and let you walk the rest of the way, at least, that's what they say they'll do and they probably would. In any case, it's a dead certainty that you'd never meet up with any of your bags again.'

'Then how did I get the idea that Bali was some kind of paradise?'

'A rumour spread by people who don't know much about the place. But don't worry, you just have to overlook a few things that's all. Even the Garden of Eden had a snake that was something of a killjoy. So be a brave girl, you can do the orang-utan reach if you try.'

Fighting back a sense of trepidation, Tess climbed

on the motorbike and tried her best to think like an orang-utan. Despite the fact she nearly bounced off each time they sped over a bump or swerved to avoid a pothole, they arrived at their destination with life and limb intact.

'Yes,' the manager of the hotel said in response to Barry's enquiry, 'we have very nice room for your friend.'

Tess was a bit shocked when she saw it. Barely large enough to contain a wooden bed, it was ugly enough to put off all but the most aesthetically challenged occupant. Its minimal comforts comprised only a coarse white sheet, a coverlet made of striped towel-like material and a greying mosquito net that dangled drunkenly from a strand of neon pink plastic twine.

She thought it was a room tailor-made for the holiday from hell.

The manager, oblivious of the signs of dismay on her face, proceeded to make things worse by flinging open a pair of shutters and showing off the 'view'. But all she could see was the next house, a mere two or three feet away, so this only served to depress her further. When he announced, not without a semblance of pride, that the bathroom was just down the hall on the right, Tess shuddered. She wasn't looking for luxury but this place was more than she had bargained for.

Making a fair guess at what she was thinking, Barry said, 'I'll trade rooms with you if you want. Mine's not a whole lot better but it's a little bigger and it looks out on the street. You can even see the ocean if you stick your head far enough out the window. It doesn't exactly get a five star rating but it's probably about the best you can find without going to a higher price range.'

'Well,' she began uncertainly, 'I did come to Bali for the temples and the beach, not to sit around a hotel room but –'

'Yeah, that's what I figured too,' Barry broke in before she had quite come to a decision, 'at least as far as the beach goes. Come on and see if my room strikes you as any less gruesome.'

She did and it was just enough of an improvement to make it tolerable.

'How's the food around here?' she asked, when she had deposited her case on the bed. 'I'm starving.'

'The Balinese food is great. Just stay away from anything that sounds American like hamburgers or spaghetti.'

'Not too good?'

'Poisonous but put yourself in Uncle Barry's hands and you'll be fine.'

Tess wasn't entirely sure about that but she was hungry enough to give almost anything a try.

A few minutes later they were seated at Barry's favourite eatery, a food stall not far from the hotel, digging into a boiled vegetable salad smothered in peanut sauce, pork-fried rice and slices of fresh pineapple and papaya.

Tess had to admit that he had known what he was talking about when he said the food was good.

'Ready for the beach?' Barry asked when they had scooped up everything on their plates.

'Actually, I'd rather do a bit of exploring first. Beaches are pretty much the same everywhere but Bali is something special.'

For once Barry thought this culture-vulture tourism was a good idea. The morning's tragedy had put him off the idea of sun, sand and surf, especially surf, for a while.

He didn't kid himself that he would be able to keep up that attitude forever but he could at least try to prolong it. After all, the beach was a bad idea for reasons that had nothing to do with the hazards of the ocean. He was sure the sight of Tess in a bikini wouldn't exactly hurt the eyes and he didn't want her falling prey to some guy like himself who was canvassing the place for an easy lay.

After all, Tess was his friend and what were friends for if not to look out for each other? If this meant something of a postman's holiday for himself, then what the hell. Soaking up a little Balinese culture wouldn't kill him.

He'd already had it off with three and a half girls while he'd been here, one had got a nosebleed just before the critical moment so he counted her as half. That should keep him going for a while. And he was an anthropologist, for God's sake, traditional cultures were supposed to be his thing. It would be embarrassing if he ever had to admit that he had been to Bali and hadn't thought about anything but sex the whole time

Taking in a few temples wouldn't kill him, he told himself, as they left the food stall, turned away from the beach and started down the road in the direction of the rice fields.

They hadn't gone very far when their way was blocked by an oncoming procession of Balinese girls dressed in colourful sarongs and balancing offerings of fruit and flowers on their heads. A group of men followed close behind them, bare-chested with checked cloths covering the lower part of their bodies and flowers tucked behind their ears. Everyone was dancing and chanting as they went along.

Tess could scarcely believe her luck in coming across some kind of festival so soon after arriving.

'What do you suppose the occasion is?' she asked.

'Who knows but it looks like it might be fun, if a village bash is your kind of thing.'

'Maybe it has something to do with the New Year.' Tess suggested.

'A bit early for that, isn't it?'

'Perhaps a wedding then,' she said. 'Everybody looks so happy.'

'That's something I never understood about weddings.'

'Grouch,' she scolded, giving him a sharp pinch. 'Look, those men over there are carrying some kind of statue. I think it's supposed to be a bull or something.'

'It's got four legs anyway,' he agreed, 'but with those flowers all over it, it could be anything.'

'There's something underneath it too,' she pointed out. 'What do you suppose it is?'

'Beats me,' Barry replied, without much interest.

'A bull,' she said, when the procession got closer to them, 'that must be what it is. What else would have horns like that?'

They watched in silence for a few minutes and then Tess said, 'That thing below it couldn't be a coffin, could it? It's that size and shape.'

'I wouldn't think so,' he said, not altogether truthfully. He knew the Balinese had some pretty weird ideas about funerals but he'd had enough of death for one day and wanted to get her off the subject. 'With all this singing and dancing, it's more likely to be something else.'

'I expect you're right,' she agreed as the procession,

which had been moving quickly, caught up with them, enveloped them and then passed on ahead.

'Let's follow it,' Tess cried. 'Then maybe we'll find out what it's all about.'

Barry was fairly certain that he knew and, as he was even less enthusiastic about funerals than he was about weddings, he tried to discourage her. This was supposed to be a vacation!

'If it really is a funeral, or even if it's not, these people might not appreciate an intrusion from gaping tourists,' he warned, hoping this aspect of the situation would put her off.

But Tess was fascinated by this glimpse of traditional Balinese life she was being treated to so effortlessly and was hungry for more.

'They didn't seem bothered by us a minute ago,' she pointed out. 'They barely seemed to notice us at all.'

'That's different, we were just walking along an open road, not crashing their festival or ceremony or whatever it is.'

'Yes but suppose we just stay at the back and leave the second anybody seems annoyed?' Seeing that Barry did not look enthusiastic, she added, 'But you don't have to come if you don't want to. I remember the way back to the hotel.'

'That's okay, I'll come with you,' he said, not wanting to

go back to the beach and not sure what else he would do.

The procession skirted some rice fields then turned into a small temple compound, where a signpost near the gate gave Barry some faint hope of derailing this little excursion into the world of Balinese culture.

'You don't have your period or anything, do you?' he asked.

'What in the world –'

'That's what,' he replied, pointing to the sign in clearly printed English stating that menstruating women were forbidden from entering the temple.

'Fortunately I'm okay,' she said and, to his dismay, breezed through the gate.

'Shit,' he muttered under his breath as he followed her inside.

It didn't take Tess long to see that, notwithstanding the singing and dancing, the coffin-like object was exactly what she had originally thought it was and the ceremony was a funeral. But nobody seemed to object to their presence so they found a place at the back of the crowd and watched what was going on.

Barry even forgot to be impatient with the distinctly anthropological turn his holiday was taking and watched the proceedings with a fascination equal to Tess's.

Prayers were said and the body of the dead man was lifted out of the coffin and placed on a funeral pyre.

Holy water was poured over it, a lit torch was set to it and the motionless form, along with the flower-bedecked figure of the bull, was engulfed in flames.

Tess was still revelling in the good luck that had brought them to this ceremony when the acrid smell of burning flesh began to permeate the air and made her think they might not have been so fortunate after all. Waves of nausea washed over her and she had fight to keep her rebellious stomach under control but she was so determined not to miss anything that she managed it. She glanced over at Barry and saw that he also looked a little green but wasn't saying anything about rushing off.

Fortunately a gentle breeze came along and helped diffuse the stench.

Then the most amazing moment of the incredible afternoon occurred. The bull collapsed on top of the body, long tongues of fire encircled the dead man's head, a resounding pop emanated from the skull and a cry, not of sorrow but of jubilation, rose from the assembled crowd.

'They sound happy,' Tess gasped, barely able to believe her ears.

A girl standing next to them overheard and explained, 'We very happy now because grandfather's soul is free.' Seeing that Tess still looked shocked, she went on to tell her, 'When person die, soul stay near body until cremation. Then fire make body pure and soul can go free, go to heaven, so we feel much happiness.'

'But aren't they sad that the person died?' Tess asked. 'Won't his family miss him, his friends too?'

'Yes they miss him but just a small while. They meet him again in new life. Old body no good anymore, sick. Soul born again in new body, more better. Everyone very happy.'

Even though the girl, Lakshmi, had been working at the Bali Beach Hotel for two years, she was still taken aback at the trouble foreigners had understanding some of the most basic things in life.

'When that happens, when someone is born again in a new body, do you recognise them?' Tess asked.

Lakshmi looked doubtful. 'Maybe sometimes,' she said, 'but not so very often.'

'Do people ever remember who they were in another life?' Tess wanted to know.

'I not know anyone who remember but sometimes maybe remember little bit, I think so.'

Before Tess could come up with any more questions, Lakshmi was called away by a group of friends.

Interested though he was, Barry wasn't altogether sorry to see her go. This conversation about ghostly beings leaping about from one body to another was freaking him out. What he was ready for right now was a return to the world of the living, hopefully accompanied by a cold beer.

Tess did not have the same reaction. Intrigued by everything going on around her, she was remembering something one of her science teachers had said at school. It was about matter being neither created nor destroyed but only transformed.

If that were true about matter, why not about souls? Why shouldn't there be some non-material part of you that didn't shrivel up and die, or drift up to some celestial paradise somewhere, when your body did? And why shouldn't that part of you, call it your soul, be reborn right here on earth.

The question was still at the back of her mind when, several hours later, she was having a beer with Barry in the nightclub where he had met the vomiting Australian girl.

'Do you suppose,' she conjectured, 'that these people could be attuned to some special truths about things?'

'These people,' laughed Barry, indicating the none-too-sober dancers and drinkers around them.

'No, you idiot, the Balinese people.'

'What kinds of things?'

'Oh I don't know, life and death and living again in a new body, that sort of thing.'

'You've got to be kidding.'

'No, I'm serious. You can't just assume that because we come from a more technologically advanced country, we know more about those things than they do.'

'I'm not assuming anything,' Barry said impatiently. 'I'm just not getting carried away with the first off-the-wall idea I meet up with on my vacation, that's all.'

'You certainly take the cake as the world's most ethnocentric anthropologist.'

'What I am is the world's most reluctant anthropologist and I'm trying to be on vacation,' he said, 'but you're not making it any easier. Come on, let's dance.'

Taking her by the hand, he led her out onto the tiny dancefloor.

'You're a good dancer,' he said after a few minutes.

'You sound surprised,' she teased.

'Actually, I am.'

'Why, do I strike you as some kind of heffalump?'

'No, it's just that I had you pegged as someone who'd spent more time in libraries than on dance floors.'

'Most people who dance in the evenings do something else in the daytime, don't they?'

'I guess you're right,' he agreed but somehow he was surprised all the same.

He was even more surprised when, after a few days of exploring temples and watching dances - extraordinary ones, he had to admit - that were staged in the temple compounds, Tess said, 'I wonder if –'

'If what?'

'If we could somehow fit our bags, and ourselves, on a motorcycle.'

'Why would we want to do that?'

'So we could go to Ubud for a couple of days.'

'You mean that artists' colony up in the hills?'

She nodded.

'With both our bags?' he asked doubtfully. 'I don't see how.'

'Well, with just one bag then?'

'Mine? Sure, no problem. It'll be bit hard on you though, going without any clothes.'

'Selfish! We could share a bag and leave the other one at the hotel.'

'Nice for the thieves.'

'I don't have anything worth stealing, do you?'

'Not really.'

'What's the problem then? If the manager says he'll take care of it, it will probably be safe enough and if it isn't –'

'What I don't understand is, what's the point of going there? What's the great attraction?'

'Isn't it obvious?'

'Visible as a black cat on a moonless night.'

'The point is that there must be more to Bali than this area around Kuta. So much that we've seen so far has been laid on for the tourists. I'd like to get away from it for a bit and find the real Bali, wouldn't you?'

He was on the point of saying that he wanted to get away from village life not go looking for it, when the thought of the drowned girl on the beach stopped him. Hadn't his fear that Tess wouldn't take the dangers of the Kuta Beach surf seriously enough been his reason for staying on here? Well, what better way to sort out that problem than getting her away from the ocean? In any case he was getting tired of tramping around temples, it would take several hours to get to Ubud and a day on a bike might be a pleasant change.

'Okay,' he agreed, 'let's go. When do you want to start?'

'How about right after this?' she said, looking down at her half-finished breakfast of fried rice with an egg on top.

'Suits me,' he said.

Tess had a bad moment when she realised that taking even one bag would mean a repetition of the uncomfortable and possibly dangerous 'orang-utan reach' all the way up to Ubud.

Fortunately the kind hotel manager had a better idea. After disappearing into a back room, he returned with a long strip of plastic rope and tied the bag onto the back of the motorcycle.

'You sit here,' he told Tess, indicating the

barely-adequate space he had left for her between Barry and the impromptu luggage rack.

It was a little cramped but Tess managed to wedge herself into it, telling herself that it was better to be a bit squished than to have to balance the bag across her lap and reach around it to hold onto Barry.

The ride was all that Barry hoped it would be and they had been whizzing down the narrow road between the paddy fields for some time when he felt a sharp thump between his shoulder blades.

'What are we going to do about lunch?' Tess shouted in his ear,

'You just finished breakfast.'

'That was ages ago and besides, I wasn't as much of a pig as you were. You probably won't be thinking about food again for days.'

'Okay, okay, let's keep an eye out for somewhere that looks promising,' he returned.

It was quite a while before they saw anywhere, promising or not promising, that offered food but eventually they came across one and screeched to a halt in front of it, sending a group of goats, including two baby ones Tess thought were adorable, scurrying to safer climes.

'This place doesn't look too bad,' Barry said, hoping that it wouldn't be.

'It would have to be really awful to put me off,'

Tess said. 'I'm starving.'

'You'd better curb that appetite of yours when we get to Ubud,' he warned, 'or there won't be enough space on the bike to bring you back.'

'Beast,' she said, finding a table and sitting down ahead of him.

A waiter came over to them and announced proudly, 'Two dishes today, fried rice and –'

'But we had that for breakfast!' Tess cried in dismay.

'Fried rice,' he repeated firmly, 'and goat meat saté.'

'I guess we can't be too picky then,' Barry observed. 'We'd better go for the goat meat saté.'

'No way,' Tess said, outraged. 'Just think of those cute little goats we just saw. I'm having the fried rice.'

Shortly after they left the restaurant, the gradient of the road turned sharply upwards and didn't level off until they neared the tree-lined streets of the little artists' colony.

As a result of the shade and the altitude, the air in Ubud was wonderfully refreshing and Tess peered excitedly into the open-fronted Chinese shops as they rode down the main street. They passed a temple made of the distinctively Balinese combination of red brick and grey stone and then rode by a similarly hued building that looked more like a small palace.

Scarcely two minutes later, they had left the centre of the town behind them and were whizzing along a winding road to – well, they didn't quite know where.

A sign saying 'Art Gallery and Hotel' prompted Tess to cry out.

'Let's stop and see the art gallery and we can check out the hotel at the same time.'

'If it actually exists,' Barry said, pulling the bike to a halt in front of the gallery and looking around, 'but I don't see anything that looks like a hotel anywhere.'

'It must be somewhere,' Tess reasoned. 'I'll ask in the art gallery, shall I? They must know.'

'Okay, I'll wait here.'

He hoped the hotel hadn't been torn down or anything, he could probably get a cold beer there but he couldn't for the life of him figure out where it might be. All he could see, apart from the art gallery, was a deep ravine covered entirely with trees and shrubs that looked more like a hostelry for apes and lizards than for people.

Apparently he was wrong.

Tess was back out of the gallery in a flash, gave him a thumbs-up, darted down a path into the ravine and quickly disappeared into foliage.

Barry was never very good at waiting and soon became restive. He would have looked around for a place to lock up the bike so he could go after her, if a boy with a snake and monkey show hadn't come down the road. The antics of the little primate kept him amused for a while although the snake, lethargic in the midday heat, remained coiled up in its box and did nothing to add to the entertainment. After a few minutes Barry grew bored, tipped the boy and sent him and his menagerie on their way.

This left him with nothing of interest. What the fuck was Tess up to anyway, he was wondering, when a group of women came by with astonishing amounts of fruit and flowers balanced on their heads. Either the weight of their loads or the deficiencies of his charms, he figured probably the latter, meant they largely ignored him.

He hoped for better things when some pretty Balinese girls came up the road. His initial efforts to chat them up were met with smiles and giggles but, possibly due to that same lamentable shortfall in his animal magnetism, further attempts at conversation met with an even less encouraging response and a few minutes later, they too were gone.

He growled to himself; what could possibly be taking Tess so long? He was considering locking up the bike, untying the bag and going in search of her when he saw her hurrying back up the path.

'Where the hell have you been?' he demanded.

'In heaven,' she replied, her eyes shining. 'I've just been looking at the most beautiful, magical hotel I've ever seen.'

Her enthusiasm had to be wildly excessive and for some reason this annoyed him. 'I don't see any hotel at all,' he snapped, 'magical or otherwise.'

'Well I promise you there is one and one of the most fantastical things about it is the way that it's hidden from the world.'

'How can you hide a whole hotel?'

'Each room is its own separate cottage, built entirely out of local materials, on the side of a deep ravine, one that's covered with masses of trees like this one. The hotel blends in with everything and practically looks like it grew there.'

'Seems unlikely,' Barry grumbled.

'Come and see for yourself if you don't believe me. Everything is really simple, no electricity or running water, nothing that would take away from the lost-in-the-woods atmosphere. Best of all, each cottage has a stupendous balcony that overlooks the thickest, deepest, greenest bit of forest you've ever seen. When you stand on it and look around, you can't help but believe that Bali really is 'the morning of the world' just as people say.'

'I'm not a morning person,' Barry muttered.

'Oh don't be such grouch,' she scolded, but she was too happy to be silenced by his testy response.

'Not only is the whole hotel tucked away where you can't see it from the road,' she went on, 'but none of the cottages can be seen from any of the others. When you're there you feel like you're the only person in the world, or the only one apart from your very own houseboy. Each cottage has one and there's a special doorknocker that you bang on when you want him to bring you something.'

'Like a cold beer, you mean, or don't they have fridges in this earthly paradise?'

'It didn't occur to me to ask,' she said with an indifferent shrug, 'but they're sure to have beer. That's the important part, isn't it?'

'I guess so,' he admitted grudgingly.

'A red-headed Australian girl called Phoebe is the owner's girlfriend and she's really nice. She's been telling me all about Walter Spies.'

'Who?'

'The German painter. Apparently this used to be his house. Come on, you've got to see it. If we don't stay here I'll die of disappointment.'

'How much does it cost?'

'I forgot to ask,' she confessed, 'but whatever it is –'

'We'd better find out before you get too carried away.'

Tess disappeared down the path again and came back looking utterly crushed.

'Why so tragic?' he asked.

'It's expensive,' she said, 'very expensive.'

'Like how much?'

Even after this preparation, he was shocked when she told him.

'For a place that hasn't got electricity or running water,' he exclaimed incredulously, 'you gotta be kidding.'

'I wish I was. But think about it, why would you need things like that when you have your own room boy to bring you kerosene lamps, fill your bathtub and basically provide you with anything you want?'

Barry was unimpressed. 'It still sounds like a great big rip-off to me,' he replied.

'If you'll just come and see how beautiful it is, you'll understand how I feel,' she insisted.

'I don't have to understand, just knowing how much a night here would cost is enough. We'd have to be crazy to shell out that much for a hotel when Ubud must be teeming with other places to stay.'

'They won't be like this,' she said, disconsolately.

'You never know,' he replied, waiting for her to climb back on the bike. 'Anyway, let's go and see what we can find.'

His optimism proved to be short-lived. They investigated lots of hotels, most of them considerably better than the one where they had stayed in Kuta, but they all struck Tess as dreary and depressing.

'You know,' she said, when they had stopped for a beer

at an open-sided stall along the main street, 'I've been thinking.'

'First time for everything,' he said, trying to tease her into a more upbeat mood, 'but better make sure you don't overdo it.'

'Don't be rude. I've been thinking about how much better it would be to share a room in a place that was fantastically, unforgettably beautiful than for each of us to crawl into some dingy little hole of our own.'

'If you're still thinking of that art gallery place,' Barry said, doing some quick mental arithmetic, 'forget it. It would still come out miles over budget, at least for me.'

'But if it were just for a night or two,' she protested, 'that wouldn't be so disastrous, would it? It wouldn't be that much more than we were each spending in Kuta –'

'Didn't they teach arithmetic where you went to school? It would be a hell of a lot more than we were paying in Kuta.'

'Well maybe,' she conceded, 'but the problem is that you haven't seen it yet. If you had, you'd understand how totally worth it would be.'

'I doubt it.'

'If you take a look at it – it won't take us more than five minutes to get back there – and you're still convinced it isn't worth the money, I promise I won't say another word about it.'

'If that's what it takes to keep you from going on about it anymore, I'll have a look. Just finish your beer and we'll be off.'

'Never mind about the beer,' she said, pushing it towards him, 'you can have it if you want. I'm ready to go.'

Tess was right, it didn't take them long to get back to the 'magical' hotel. This time Barry locked the bike, left it under the supervision of the gallery manager and followed Tess down the narrow path into the ravine.

The vegetation on each side was so thick that Barry was actually surprised when he suddenly found himself standing in front of a small wooden cottage. A staircase led up to a wide balcony that spanned the entire front of the cottage and Tess scrambled up without bothering to look around and see if anyone was there.

'Come on,' she called. 'The place is empty at the moment and the view from here is fabulous. You can see over the tops of the trees and all the way down into the ravine. There's even a lovely little babbling brook, I mean, I suppose it babbles at the bottom. Come and see.'

He did and although his aesthetic sense had always been a bit on the rudimentary side - at least that's what one of his ex-girlfriends had claimed - he was transfixed by the compelling beauty of the vista that lay before him.

'Okay, I admit it, this place is pretty damn gorgeous,' he exclaimed, gazing out at the scene in front of him. 'I can almost understand why you're making such a fuss about staying here.'

'You mean you agree?' asked Tess, pretending not to have noticed the word 'almost'.

'I agreed that it's beautiful, the scenery I mean. I didn't agree that forking over a preposterous sum to stay here is such a great idea. And anyway, we haven't seen the inside yet. It might be ghastly, you never know.'

Tess did know, Phoebe had shown it to her, but she didn't want to antagonize Barry at this point so she decided not to argue. Instead she said, 'The owner's girlfriend has the key. I'll go find her.'

Left alone with nothing particular to do, Barry strolled over to the balcony rail and surveyed the scene in front of him. A soft mist was settling over the far side of the ravine, entwining itself amongst the trees and giving an almost dreamlike quality to the atmosphere.

Intrigued by its progress, Barry found that the longer he watched it the less capable he was of looking away. It reminded him of something but annoyingly he couldn't quite remember what. It certainly couldn't have been anything to do with this place because he had never been here before. There were mists and forests in other places in the world so he must be thinking of one of them, maybe one he had been to when he was a kid or it might even be like somewhere he had seen in a film. That was probably it, there was a kind of vague, otherworldly quality about it that made it seem a little unreal, more like some filmmaker's fantasy than an actual place.

No, that wasn't it, he remembered now. The Kents had a guidebook to Bali and he had thumbed through it one day while Mary was quelling some crisis in the kitchen and Derek was reading the riot act to Holly for letting the cat into his study. He hadn't seen it and had sat on it and the resulting yowls, scratches and, worst of all, the nasty bite he had received, meant that he couldn't sit down anywhere for a while.

Remembering this made Barry feel much better, there was nothing strange about a good picture in a guidebook. He wasn't left to think about these things much longer anyway as Tess soon came back, bringing Phoebe with her who opened the cottage door for them.

A quick glance around was enough for him to see that, although the room was simple to the point of stark, it had an austere loveliness about it. Such furniture as there was had been fashioned entirely from wood or rattan and the glassless windows were curtained only by the green of the outside foliage.

Even so, at the ridiculous price being asked the place was definitely rip-off heaven and he wasn't entirely sure that Tess's interesting suggestion of cutting down the cost by sharing a room was such a good idea. It certainly had its appealing aspect, such as the prospect of a midnight romp under the mosquito netting, but it was likely to lead to a greater involvement with Tess than he really wanted at this point. He liked her, liked her a lot and she was certainly very attractive but with some of her off-the-wall ideas about things, he had a feeling that a relationship with her could be hard work. That wasn't what he needed at this point; after Cynthia, he felt ready for a girl who was easy to be with and wouldn't complicate his life.

The good thing about his quick flings in Kuta had been that they were with girls he wasn't likely to see again so they were pretty much problem-free.

Actually, he thought suddenly, gazing out into the mist and noticing that it was now creeping up their side of the ravine, if staying here meant so much to Tess and it seemed that it did, what did it matter if it was a little hard on the wallet? They wouldn't stay long and what the hell, they were on vacation, weren't they?

'If you still want to spend a night or two here,' he said, turning to Tess, 'I guess it's okay with me but we don't need to crowd into one room. We probably each need our own space.'

'Fantastic,' she cried, throwing her arms around him in her enthusiasm, 'you won't regret it, I promise.'

Barry had barely disentangled himself from this unexpected bear hug when he was startled by a banging sound just outside the door.

'That must be the doorknocker,' Tess cried, dashing out to see who was there.

Barry, wondering what was going on, followed her out on the balcony and saw that Phoebe was holding up a wooden figure, one that had a curiously hollowed out section down its middle. It was highly stylized, painted in vivid colours and very definitely male; a long red stick, appropriately placed, left no doubt about its gender.

When she saw Tess and Barry she pulled the stick out, inserted it in the figure's hollowed out section, repeated the banging sounds and then reattached it in the place where a ready-for-action dick could be expected.

'Now it's your turn,' Phoebe said, laughing and handing the figure to Tess.

Tess giggled but didn't hesitate. She gave the red stick a quick tug, pulled it from its designated place, inserted it in the vertical slit in the figure's mid-section and began beating loudly.

Both girls thought this was hilarious but Barry had a hard time keeping himself from cupping his hands protectively over the corresponding part of his own anatomy.

'Do you two little fiends really find the idea of pulling

the poor guy's dick off so damn funny?' he demanded.

'If it's a long red one like that we do,' Tess returned, making no effort to stifle her laughter. 'But I'm just practising using the doorknocker. Here,' she added, when she had returned the red stick to its place, 'you can have a go if you want.'

Barry most emphatically did not want to have a go.

'No, thanks,' he said, 'that's strictly a toy for man-eating females.'

Tess was about to take issue with this when a boy materialised out of nowhere, smiled, greeted them in Indonesian and asked if they would like anything.

'This is Krishna,' Phoebe explained. 'He will be looking after you while you're here. He heard the doorknocker and thought you were calling him.'

'I must say, a cold beer would be nice,' Barry replied, and proceeded to translate this information for Krishna's benefit.

'With ice?' the boy asked.

'Why not?' Barry said. He'd just drink it quickly before the ice melted.

Tess told Krishna that she would like a fresh lime and soda and then, turning to Barry, exclaimed, 'Isn't it going to be absolute heaven staying here?'

'It might not be too bad,' he admitted not wanting to confess that, astonishing as it was, he too was falling victim to the compelling charm of this place.

When they had finished their drinks, they spent the rest of the afternoon exploring the ravine, following winding paths through the tangled vines and greenery and playing with the monkeys they found tethered near one of the discreetly hidden bungalows.

Sunset comes at the eastern edge of the time zone and the Balinese heat had begun to fade when they reached the little stream at the bottom of the ravine. Still, the cool clear water felt good on their feet as, shoes in hand, they followed it to the point where it was joined by a rivulet of water that bubbled down the slope, emptied into the brook and formed a shallow pool.

'What fun,' Tess cried when she saw it, 'our own secret swimming place. I wish I could just plunge in right now.'

'Do it then,' Barry urged.

'My bathing suit's up in the room,' she replied glumly.

'Anyway, this water's pretty damn cold,' he said, 'and it would feel a lot colder if you had more than just your feet in it.'

'I wouldn't mind,' she said staunchly, although she knew she really would.

'I bet it's not chlorinated,' Barry warned.

'How can you think about horrid things like chemicals

when you're in a paradise like this?'

Barry didn't dignify this with an answer.

'It looks like this must have been a natural pool originally, with the water flowing into it from up the upper slopes and then out again through that opening down there,' he said, pointing to a V-shaped rock formation on the lower rim. 'It looks like it has been lined with concrete and those rocks around the edge didn't get there by themselves. Somebody must be taking care of it so maybe it does have chlorine in it, after all.'

'There you go again; chemicals. When did you become so obsessed with them?'

'When I found out the hard way that vomiting and diarrhoea weren't a lot of fun. In any case, I'll just play it safe for now, wait and sluice myself with water when I get back to the luxury of my Neolithic bathroom.'

The water won't be any more pristine up there, Tess thought, but decided not to mention it. Instead she merely said, 'Good idea, I'll do the same thing.'

Feeling cool and refreshed after a bath, Tess was reading on the balcony when the sound of someone on the stairs alerted her to the arrival of a visitor.

'How does anybody get anything to eat in this place?' Barry called.

'Don't you remember, you just bang on the doorknocker and Krishna will come and see what you want. If it's dinner, you tell him and he'll bring it.'

'He didn't look like much of a cook to me.'

'He doesn't have to be, he just passes the word along to Phoebe and she takes care of it. Then he brings it here when it's ready.'

'Okay but you'll have to do the doorknocker bit. Grabbing hold of a long red dick just isn't my sort of thing.'

'What makes you think it's mine?'

'You're a girl, aren't you, so be a good kid and give that impressive cock a quick tug.'

Tess shot him her fiercest death stare then went over to the doorknocker, removed the required section and rapped Barry sharply over the head with it before banging it in the designated slit.

Krishna's appearance was almost instantaneous.

The dinner was tonight chicken paprikash, he told them.

There didn't seem to be any other choice so they agreed that it sounded good and Barry announced that he wanted a beer.

'One for you, too?' he asked, turning to Tess.

'Heavens no,' she cried, 'this is a gin and tonic veranda if ever there was one so that's what I'll have, anything else would be sacrilege.'

Turning to Krishna, she gave him her order.

His usual smile evaporated and he was forced to explain that some American guests had finished the gin four, or maybe it was five, days ago. He looked sadder still when Tess questioned him about other possibilities. It seemed the bar had subsequently been depleted by visits from three Brits, five Australians and a troop of Boy Scouts who had come to Bali for an international jamboree.

'What do you have then?' she asked.

'Bintang beer and Balinese cocktail.'

'What's in it?'

'Very good,' he told her, smiling happily.

Her efforts to coax more specific information out of him just yielded repetitions of this assurance so, for lack of a better option, she chose the Balinese cocktail.

'Oh, I know that stuff,' Barry said, recognising the short bulbous bottle when Krishna brought it. 'I've had it in my village. It's like a rice wine, sweet but drinkable if you're really desperate.'

'I don't think it's that bad,' Tess said, after taking a cautious sip, 'in fact, I almost like it.'

She found it tasted better and better as the short tropical twilight faded into the early Balinese dark.

'See, there are advantages to being on the eastern edge of a time zone,' Barry claimed, 'and one of them is that it gives you more drinking time.'

When Krishna came back again, bringing them

kerosene lamps and spicy smelling coils of insect repellent, they ordered a second round.

'Do you suppose we're the only guests here?' Tess wondered, when he had gone in search of the requested refills. 'We didn't see anyone else this afternoon and I didn't think any of the other cottages looked occupied.'

'If we're the only ones, it might mean they'll bring dinner faster,' Barry said hopefully, 'and I'm starving.'

'I can't imagine that it will be very fast,' Tess replied, thinking it best to prepare him for the worst. 'If they have to start from scratch heating up the charcoals and all that, it might take ages.'

It did.

By the time their dinner arrived, Tess had polished off her second drink and Barry had worked his way through two more beers so they ordered another round. After all, they had to drink something with dinner, didn't they?

When Krishna had gone, Barry peered down suspiciously at his plate. 'Any guess about what this is supposed to be?' he asked.

'Chicken paprikash, remember,' Tess said, regarding it uncertainly, 'and it does look a little bit like it.'

'It looks more like some kind of Balinese style chicken and chillies to me,' Barry said, 'with some garlic and onions and other stuff thrown in.'

'And they've put it on rice instead of noodles,' Tess

observed, 'but I suppose that will be just as good. Are you brave enough to try it?'

'Why not? I'm hungry enough to bite into anything that's not going to bite me back.'

Tess regarded hers a little more warily but, after tasting it, she decided it really wasn't bad. 'In fact,' she declared, 'it's really very good.'

Barry attacked his plate with enthusiasm, found that he liked it and was just scraping up the last few bites when he looked up and said, 'I think it's beginning to rain. Lucky we've just about finished this dinner.'

Tess didn't see anything lucky about it. She gloried in the cool breeze that was suddenly wafting across the balcony, lowering the temperature and bringing with it a fine mist mixed with a light shower.

'Just think how lovely it feels,' Tess cried, holding both arms out to the refreshing drops.

'But my food, what's left of it anyway, is getting wet and so am I,' Barry moaned. 'Let's go inside.'

'Do you dissolve in water?'

'I might and what's left of my chicken paprikash will turn to chicken soup pretty soon if I stay out here.'

'Don't be ridiculous, all you have to do is move back a little so you'll be under the overhang and you'll be fine. You can pretend you're an Indian raja.'

'Why would I want to do that?'

'To enjoy the things a raja enjoyed, one of them anyway.'

'Like a harem of beautiful women, you mean?'

'No, silly, like the one who had a special pavilion built just for watching the rain.'

'And how would that keep the rest of my dinner from getting wet?'

'It wouldn't but it might keep you from worrying so much about it.'

'I'd worry about it a lot less if I had another beer,' Barry said, regarding his empty glass with gloom. 'How about exercising your charms, or maybe your muscles, on that big red dick you seem so crazy about and getting Krishna to bring me one?'

'How about doing it yourself?'

'Since you're being so unhelpful, I guess I'll have to.'

'It won't be very nice for him being dragged out in the rain,' she said.

'A minute ago you were claiming the rain was lovely,' Barry pointed out, as he took the doorknocker off its hook and began banging on it.

Krishna, holding something made of straw over his head to keep off the rain, appeared almost straightaway and took Barry's order. Nothing was mentioned about more wine for Tess but Krishna thoughtfully brought some anyway.

253

'That boy's like some kind of genie,' Tess marvelled when he was out of hearing, 'always there to give you whatever you want, almost before you know you want it.'

'You don't mean you actually like that stuff you were drinking, do you?'

'It's not too bad, I just think of it as a Balinese version of a cocktail.'

'All I can think about right now is that I'm getting soaked,' Barry complained.

The shower that had been so gentle a few minutes earlier had, almost without warning, turned into a ferocious downpour.

'Come inside,' Barry shouted, over the sound of the huge raindrops pelting down on the wooden floor of the balcony, 'before we're half-drowned.'

'No, I love it out here.'

'Suit yourself, I'm going in.'

'Wimp!'

'You're pissed and –'

'Probably but who cares?'

'And you're nuts.'

'All the better! Being smashed and crazy is a lot more fun than being sober and sane.' And before he could stop her, she flew down the balcony steps and disappeared into the thick green foliage.

'Hey,' he called, 'come back.'

She didn't respond.

'Tess, for Christ's sake, show some sense,' he shouted. 'Get back here.'

The only reply came from a chorus of black and orange lizards, accompanied by a troop of frogs.

Fuck, he growled to himself, when I catch her I'm going to strangle her. And with this delightful thought, he grabbed the tray that Krishna had used to bring his dinner, held it over his head in lieu of an umbrella and took off down the path after her.

The sudden burst of rain had, with tropical capriciousness, tapered off to a drizzle by the time he finally found her and he hoped her manic phase was equally on the wane.

She looked calm enough, he thought with relief. Perched on the edge of the little pool at the bottom of the ravine and apparently not minding a bit about the rain, she was happily splashing her feet in the water.

His first impulse was to sit down next to her but he was reluctant to get his shoes or jeans any wetter than they already were. Then, deciding it was a little late to worry about that, he went ahead and sat down.

'What the hell got into you up there on the balcony?' he demanded. 'Why did you run off like that?

'I really don't know,' she replied, with a careless laugh, 'maybe it was the Balinese wine or maybe there's something magical in the Balinese air, who knows? The wonderful thing about it was that for a few minutes I was on the most exciting spectacular mind-blowing high you can possibly imagine. All the colours around me, what I could see of them in the dark, seemed incredibly vivid. And the sounds of the forest took on a whole new tone, one that was strange and beautiful and terrifying all at once. They seemed to surge through me like bolts of electricity. My reaction to everything was intense beyond belief, it was like I was on the verge of some extraordinary experience but then somehow it never quite happened, the amazing mind-blowing experience, I mean.'

Barry stared at her in dismay. Had she completely flipped out?

'All the intensity just sort of faded away and left me feeling shivery and damp.'

'I'd say you're a lot more than damp,' he observed, 'half drowned would be more like it. You'd better get out of those wet clothes. A cold in the head wouldn't be such an amazingly wonderful experience.'

'No, it wouldn't,' she acknowledged, 'but there's no way I'm going to let my life be ruled by stupid, boring things like colds in the head.'

A moment later she astonished him by giving a practical demonstration of this attitude by tugging at her jeans, throwing off her top and plunging into the pool in only her bra and a pair of lacy panties.

He started to shout something along the lines of 'are you crazy' but stopped himself abruptly. What kind of bloodless no-hoper would complain when a pretty girl started taking off her clothes?

'Come in,' she called from the pool. 'The water's arctic but if you can just think like a polar bear, you'll love it.'

'I haven't the foggiest idea how polar bears think.'

'Jump in, this water might give you a clue.'

'Thanks but no thanks.'

'Wimp!'

He pretended not to hear her.

'Slug,' she taunted, splashing water over him with her foot, 'scaredy-cat.'

She splashed him again, this time with better aim and he got thoroughly drenched.

'You'll be sorry for that,' he cried, and forgetting his earlier fears about the chlorine, or lack of it, he stripped down to his boxer shorts, leapt into the pool and took his revenge by giving her a thorough ducking.

Determined to leave no doubt about who was calling the shots, he declared that he could swim faster than her, proved it, was challenged and proved it a second time. He announced that he was a shark, chased her across the pool, caught her and let her escape for the fun of catching her again.

After a few rounds of this, he forgot about being a shark in his excitement at feeling her nearly-naked body sliding up and down against him, so he set about repeating this part of the game without bothering about the rest.

Somewhat to his surprise, she didn't try to stop him as his hands travelled up and down her back, along her thighs and underneath the lacy panties to the soft hidden place they concealed. And letting his fingers linger there, he played with the soft petals and the hard little nub he found.

The panties were a nuisance so he slid them down over her thighs and legs then pulled them off entirely and tossed them, along with her bra and his boxer shorts, into the grassy undergrowth around the pool. With that done, he picked her up and swirled her around until she was balanced horizontally across his arms with only her face and toes above the surface. He started to kiss her lips but, in a flight of whimsy, reached down, took hold of one of her feet, and kissed her toes instead. Then he put her big toe in his mouth and sucked on it but his breath, coming fast and hard as it was doing, tickled the sole of her foot. She wriggled and squirmed in her attempt to get away but his hold on her stayed firm and in the struggle she let her face slide beneath the surface of the water, swallowed more of the pool than was good for her and came up coughing, spluttering and, for a moment, feeling a bit disoriented.

Blurred images wafted through her mind as she brushed the water from her eyes. A temple much like Prambanan, a cone-shaped mountain spitting fire, lush rice fields with a dark-eyed boy running through them, all flashed through her consciousness in an instant. At first she thought the boy was alone but then a girl seemed to be running with him, a girl so young she was barely more than a child. And as the scene became clearer, Tess had a curious feeling that the girl she was looking at was herself.

Barry, in the meantime, lost interest in her toes and let his hand travel back to more exciting, more hidden, less tickle-resistant parts of her body, unaware that his touch was blending in with Tess's illusions about the dark-eyed boy and not realising that, with her eyes closed, she was merely giving herself up to the pleasure of the moment, unconcerned about whose fingers were finding their way inside her.

And then the hand wasn't there anymore. Opening her eyes, she saw that the dark-eyed boy seemed to have disappeared and it was Barry who was there in the pool with her. He was floating on his back, allowing his towering cock to soar halfway up to the sky and silently inviting her to give him the pleasure that he had been giving her.

She did more than that. After gazing at him quizzically for a moment, she firmly drove the dark-eyed boy from her mind then slipped her hands deftly around his enormous erection, let her fingers play on it like a piano and at last, brought her mouth down over it.

She was convinced that, in a curious sort of way, it didn't really matter whether it was Barry or the dark-eyed boy who was floating there in the pool with her, it didn't matter because they were actually the same person.

For a moment she found this reassuring but then it began to strike her as terribly unsettling, so much so that she suddenly pulled away from him, swam to the edge of the pool and climbed out.

Barry, in a fervour of excitement by this time, could scarcely believe what was happening.

'Hey, what's the matter? What's going on?' he cried, watching in astonishment as she did her best to wrap her wet top and jeans around herself and ran up the path towards their cabin.

'Wait!' he called, but she didn't.

'Shit,' he muttered and, with a feeling of outrage, he scrambled out of the pool, grabbed his clothes, held them in front of him and raced after her.

'What the hell is this about?' he demanded, catching up with her on the balcony outside her room. 'What happened out there?'

She didn't answer.

'You're shivering,' he said, drawing her inside, finding a towel and rubbing her like a wet dog. 'Let's warm you up and then you've got to tell me what made you cut and run like that.'

'Nothing happened.'

'What do you mean nothing happened? One minute you were making me feel like I had landed in the middle of the world's most glorious Shangri-La and the next, you were taking off like you had all the fiends of hell at your heels. Don't try and tell me nothing happened. Something did and I want to know what it was.'

'It's hard to explain.'

'Try.'

'You'll think I'm crazy or something.'

'Nothing new about that.'

'The thing is,' she began, ignoring his last remark, 'what happened was so strange that I don't really understand it myself. But it didn't just happen when I ran off, it happened before that. It happened when I, when we were, you know.'

'I don't know, that's the problem.'

'It was when we were in the pool and you said you weren't a shark anymore, it felt like you weren't really Barry anymore either. I mean you were and you weren't, if you see what I mean.'

'No, I don't see.'

'Suddenly there was something about you that made you very different, not your usual self at all; and yet at the same time you were someone I knew.'

'At least that part figures, you do know me.'

'No, no, I mean a different person, someone I loved.'

'But that guy wasn't me.'

'No, it was –'

'Mike,' he said, finishing her sentence for her so he wouldn't have to hear her doing it, 'out there in the pool, I kind of forgot.'

'Oh, it's not Mike,' she said, looking at him in surprise.

'Who then?' he asked, taken aback at this revelation, 'not that it's any of my business.'

'I don't know actually,' she said, trying to sort out her thoughts but not succeeding.

'What do you mean you don't know? If you're so damn crazy about someone, you must have some idea who he is.'

'I know it sounds ridiculous but I swear to you, I don't.'

'You're not making any sense.'

'Listen, I know this sounds crazy but I didn't explain it very well because I don't understand it very well myself. I can promise you though, I wasn't pretending you were somebody else. It was like you really were somebody else but at the same time you were still you. Do you follow me?'

'No.'

'Let me put it like this. I suddenly had a really, really strong feeling that you were more than just you, it was like you were you and another person, a totally different person as well. Does that make it any clearer?'

262

'No.'

'It was as if I saw some aspect of you, a really important aspect that I'd never seen before.'

'You did, my dick.'

'There's no point in talking to you if you're going to be like that,' she cried in annoyance.

'Never mind about how I'm going to be,' he flung back angrily. 'Let's talk a little more about you and how great it was before you opened your eyes to the fact that it was just friendly old Barry lying there with his dick in the air.'

'Don't be horrible.'

'What the hell am I supposed to be, all sweetness and light when I hear that some screwy chick was pretending I was someone else?'

'I'm not just 'some screwy chick' and I wasn't pretending you were somebody else, you really were somebody else. I don't know why you're being such a beast about it.'

'I should have thought it would be pretty obvious and if it isn't, tough. I'll be damned if I'm going to stay around explaining it to you,' he retorted, heading for the door.

Pausing as he passed the doorknocker, he pulled out the red stick and tossed it into her lap. 'Here, next time you feel like playing with some guy's cock,' he said, 'try this one.'

A moment later she heard his footsteps going down the stairs.

They both woke up cross and tired the next day and failed to drink in the magical beauty of the Balinese morning. With an exchange of little more than hostile looks, they managed to cram their belongings into the shared bag.

There's nothing like sex to spoil a good friendship, Tess thought, and it was a shame because she really liked Barry, in spite of how awful he could be sometimes. It had been a big mistake to let things go as far as they had last night but even so, she didn't see why he had to act like a bear with a sore head just because she wasn't claiming to be wildly in love with him.

She supposed she shouldn't have taken off her clothes but how could she have known it would matter so much? It wasn't as though she were some sort of femme fatale who could drive men wild by offering them a glimpse of her naked body. Admittedly more than a glimpse had been on view last night but she couldn't exactly be expected to go swimming with her clothes on.

In the future maybe she would go skiing when she wanted a vacation; she wouldn't be likely to start shedding her clothes in the snow.

Remembering a school trip to Vermont and the fun that she and the dishy ski instructor had had one very cold night, she decided that a little winter weather wasn't that much of a deterrent to a good time after all.

Seeing the mischievous sparkle that lit up her eyes at the recollection, Barry was furious. She's feeling damn pleased with herself this morning, he thought bitterly. Well, she had a right to. She had certainly made a fool out of him. His big mistake, he reasoned, had been staying on here in Bali just because of Tess and he was damned if he was going to hang around any longer. If he could get on today's flight back to Yogya, that's exactly what he would do.

Or was it really such a good idea? Maybe Marilyn's company wasn't what he needed right now. Another stroll down Kuta Beach, one without Tess, might be a better option. He would just screw the first willing chick he came across and if she had a face like a gorilla and a vagina like a bear-trap, never mind. He'd close his eyes and '

'You look like you're thinking deep thoughts,' Tess teased.

He ignored her.

'Care to tell me what they're about?'

'No, they're none of your business.'

She digested this rebuff in silence for a few minutes but then, since he didn't seem likely to hold out the first olive branch, she decided it was probably up to her.

'Is there any chance of us being friends ever again?' she asked.

'About as much as finding a snowball in hell.'

'Don't you even want to try?'

'No.'

'Neither do I,' she lied and, without looking to see whether or not he was coming with her, went to pay her bill and say goodbye to Phoebe.

She found her in the kitchen learning how to make a fiery looking pork dish called *babi bumbu Bali* and told her that they would be leaving in a few minutes.

'But that's terrible,' Phoebe exclaimed, 'you haven't had a chance to see anything here yet.'

'I know,' Tess agreed, casting a baleful look at Barry who had followed her up the path.

But Phoebe, determined to make them give Ubud at least a little of the attention it deserved, launched into an extensive account of all the interesting things they would be missing, beginning with a *legong* dance at the Pura Taman Sarasawati temple that night.

'It's the one you passed on the main street on your way here,' she told them. 'The dancers are all little girls and virgins, at least they're supposed to be. They're so young that they probably are. It's really beautiful and if you can possibly stay on an extra day, I swear it will be worth it.'

'Sounds exotic,' Barry said. 'I don't think I've seen a virgin since I left John Foster Elementary School.'

'Don't pay any attention to him,' Tess told Phoebe, 'he

has a warped sense of humour and he's in a very grouchy mood but I might stay on for a couple of days by myself. I'll probably have a better time without him anyway.'

'Thanks a lot,' Barry retorted. 'I hope you enjoy your walk back to Kuta.'

'I probably will, who knows what adventures I'll have along the way?'

'There's no reason you would have to walk,' Phoebe assured her. 'There are lots of buses down to Denpasar and you can easily get another one onto Kuta from there.'

'Great,' Tess said, and then added regretfully, 'I might have to find somewhere else to stay though. I don't think I can afford another night in this place.'

'The hotel isn't full,' Phoebe reflected, 'and my friend – you see, this is his place, not mine – sometimes offers people a discount so I suppose I could offer you one. Perhaps something like forty per cent? That's the most I've heard him give anyone but I don't think he'll mind. He's in Surabaya for a few days and he left me in charge so –'

Phoebe broke off as the sound of laughter mixed with feminine voices drifted down from the entrance.

'That must be our new guests,' she said, hurrying off to greet them, 'back in a mo'.'

'Gee, this place is romantic,' a voice drawled, heavy with the inflections of the American South.

'It sure beats that dump we stayed in last night,' a sultry

alto replied.

'There was supposed to be a swimming pool here but I don't see it,' someone complained in petulant tones.

'It might be down there somewhere,' suggested a girl with an optimistic outlook, 'hidden in that mess of trees.'

'We'd better find out before we check in,' warned the alto. 'I want to make sure I don't lose my tan.'

'I didn't fork over all that money for a bikini wax just to stay hidden behind a lot of trees,' declared the petulant one.

'Why don't we just go back to Kuta?' said the alto. 'That's where the action is. This place looks totally dead.'

'Don't you ever think about anything but sex?' demanded the thick southern drawl.

'Not very often,' the alto admitted.

'What's a vacation for if not to have a little fun?' asked the petulant one.

'We've come to Ubud to see the temple dances and prowl around the art galleries, that sort of thing,' declared the optimist.

'Better you than me,' the alto said. 'I want to do my prowling when there are some good-looking guys around.'

'We're about a foot taller than most of the Balinese men,' the petulant one was reminding her as their voices faded into the distance.

Barry, who had heard all of this, promptly added one

more option to his list of possibilities.

Why go down to Kuta, he thought, when there are plenty of sure things right here in Ubud with the added satisfaction of getting off with one of them right under Tess's nose?

He chortled gleefully at the thought and, turning to her, said, 'You don't need to buy that bus ticket down to Denpasar just yet, I might be staying on another day or two myself.'

She burst out laughing. 'Those girls who've just arrived wouldn't have anything to do with this decision, would they?'

'Maybe they would and maybe they wouldn't,' he replied. 'In any case, I'm going to have a swim, soak up some sun and possibly even do a little socialising.'

'Well if you get raped by a hoard of sex-mad females, don't expect any sympathy from me.'

'No problem, I'll be too happy to need it,' he returned with a grin and watched as she flounced out of the room, set off in the direction of the art gallery and then abruptly turned back.

'How come you can suddenly afford to stay on another night here,' she asked, 'when up until now you've been making such a fuss about how much it costs?'

'I've decided I kind of like the place and at forty percent off, it might be worth it. After all what's more important, money or a little fun?'

She's jealous as hell, he told himself delightedly, and I haven't even done anything yet. After the little games she played last night, it's exactly what she deserves.

Thoroughly pleased with himself, he went back to his room, changed into his bathing things and sauntered down to the pool but when he got there he was disappointed, there wasn't anyone in sight. He decided he might as well have a refreshing dip anyway and, if he were lucky, something interesting might show up.

He splashed around for a while and was just beginning to get fed up with swimming by himself when three of the four girls appeared.

They were in high spirits and he had no trouble starting a conversation with them. They dissolved into gales of laughter at his jokes, feigned terror when he declared he was a shark and were unabashedly flirtatious when he caught them.

But they weren't hard on the eyes, so when they finished their romp in the pool, he quite naturally did the gentlemanly thing and rubbed suntan oil on their backs. This task actually kept him rather busy, as they seemed to need supplementary applications every few minutes.

When lunchtime came around they all declared they were hungry and decided to go out for a bowl of noodles together. In a stroke of brilliant timing, they ran into Tess just at a moment when all three girls seemed to be hanging onto him at once and generally treating him like some kind of film star.

Tess merely acknowledged his presence with a cool nod, cast a disdainful glance at the girls and swept on by.

By the time Tess had wandered through several temples, gone in and out of an assortment of galleries and shops, watched a group of craftsmen making leather puppets and paused for an ice cream, the afternoon was drawing to a close.

She wondered if Barry would be at the hotel when she got back. She sort of hoped he wouldn't but then, why should she care? What the slimy reptile did and who he did it with was of absolutely no interest to her.

Even so, she wasn't altogether sorry when she passed his room and saw that he was alone on his balcony with only a book and a beer for company.

'Where's your harem?' she called up to him.

'They've deserted me for a bunch of monkeys.'

'They've got better taste than I thought.'

'Thanks a lot.'

'Any particular monkeys?'

'Yeah, the ones in the *Kecak* dance down in Batubulan.'

'How come you didn't go with them?'

'I had gotten them all pregnant by then so what was the point? Anyway, if I want to hear a lot of simian noises,

I can just go home and talk to Marilyn.'

'The sirens from the swimming pool might have been more interesting conversationalists,' she suggested.

'It wasn't conversation I was after.'

She wished she could have said the same but after wandering through beautiful temples and interesting galleries all day and having no one to share them with, she felt desperately in need of someone to talk to. She was possibly even desperate enough for that someone to be Barry.

Well, she'd be brave, she decided. She'd show him that it didn't bother her what he did and that she wasn't remotely interested.

'You wouldn't like to invite me up for a fresh lime and soda, would you?' she asked, sounding as casual as she could. 'I'm dying of thirst.'

'Sure, as long as you do the doorknocker bit.'

A few minutes later she was sitting on the balcony, the longed-for drink at her side, and Barry was raising his glass to her, saying, 'Cheers,'

'Cheers,' she echoed.

'Friends again?' he asked warily, not entirely sure this would be a good thing.

'I suppose so,' she said, trying to agree without sounding too enthusiastic.

'Good, because I'm thinking about checking out those

dancing virgins Phoebe was telling us about. Do you want to come?'

She hesitated, very much wanting to see the dance but loathe to give Barry the idea that he could just pick up with her again when his preferred companions weren't available.

The lure of the temple dance won out.

'Yes, I'd like to,' she said.

Dusk was settling over the sandalwood-scented courtyards of the temple as, with a semblance of their former camaraderie returning, they passed through a massive grey stone and red brick gate into a seemingly magical world; one where the strangely haunting music of a traditional *gamelan* orchestra filled the air and the visitor was guided to the performance area by the flickering yellow light coming from hundreds of tiny oil lamps. Tess could almost feel herself being swept through the temple's shadowy passages as they walked along, carried back into the nearly-forgotten world of Hindu Indonesia. It made her wonder whether Prambanan had been like this a thousand years ago.

Why wouldn't it have been? The music that had been played there must have been much the same as the music she was hearing now, although she supposed it was played it at the slower Javanese tempo. And the suppliants at the feet of those ancient gods probably watched dances that were similar to the ones she and Barry were going to see tonight.

After all, it was the Javanese rajahs who had, with their courts and culture, fled the advances of Islam, bringing with them their gods, art, music and literature to blend in an easy syncretism with the traditional animism of their new home. Why shouldn't she feel their lingering presence in this temple, high in the hills of Bali?

Nevertheless, she couldn't help feeling that there was something eerie about the possibility and glancing downwards, she realised she was holding tightly onto Barry's hand.

'Are you trying to cut off the circulation in my fingers or what?' he teased.

'Sorry,' she said, with an embarrassed laugh but she couldn't be sorry for long because just at that moment, the first little dancers floated onto the scene. Others soon followed displaying all the loveliness and grace of the heavenly nymphs they were portraying and Tess was completely lost in the beauty of what she saw.

Barry was slower in succumbing to the allure of the diminutive dancers but as the evening progressed he became more and more captivated by their beguiling charm and their mastery of the art. As they bewitched him with flirtatious glances from their enormous eyes, enticed him with caressing motions from supple fingers and subjugated his heart with the beating of their angel wings, he became convinced that he had never seen such exquisite loveliness before.

'Jesus, I hope I'm not turning into some kind of filthy old man,' Barry muttered to Tess on the way back to the hotel.

'You don't seem like one,' she said, 'not like a filthy one anyway. Who could help falling in love those incredible little girls?'

Thinking that Barry could do with a bit of teasing, she added, 'Or it may just be that you were a Balinese in a previous incarnation, that would explain why you were so taken with them.'

'Not too likely,' he growled, but hastened to emphasise that watching little girls in temples, or anywhere for that matter, wasn't his sort of thing.

'Silly,' she said, 'I never thought it was.'

They said a rather stiff and self-conscious goodnight to each other when they reached the hotel, each remembering that the previous evening hadn't ended so well. Still Barry didn't feel quite ready to be by himself yet. He couldn't get the performance at the temple out of his mind and felt compelled to talk about it.

'Are you up for one more swig of that Balinese wine before you turn in?' he asked.

'I suppose so.'

'There was something about those little girls tonight, the dancers I mean, that has been bothering the hell out of me,' he began, when they were settled on his balcony with drinks and cassava chips in front of them.

She started to laugh but seeing that he looked serious, quickly adjusted her expression and asked, 'Whatever is it?'

'Just something I read for one of my anthro courses a few years ago about a temple ceremony on some Pacific island –'

'Bali?'

'No, not Bali actually, more like Tonga or Samoa or someplace like that.'

'What has it got to do with Bali then?'

'Hopefully not much, there are massive differences between the cultures of these islands but there are some similarities too and –'

'It would help if you told me what you were talking about,' Tess said, impatiently.

'Okay, sorry, it's just that temple priests in a couple of those places have come up with some pretty bizarre ways of relieving girls of their virginity and I can't help wondering whether something like that is going to happen to those little girls we saw tonight.'

'Like what?'

'Like finding a bunch of lecherous priests waiting to initiate them into the ways of the world.'

This time Tess actually did laugh.

'Of course not, this is Bali, things like that don't happen here. They will just grow up and get married like any other village girl. They probably won't be allowed to dance anymore, not that particular dance anyway. That's all.'

'They don't belong to the temple then?'

'Belong,' Tess repeated, confused, 'belong to whom?'

'The priests.'

'Of course not. Maybe you'd better forget about those anthropology courses, they're putting preposterous ideas in your head.'

'In this case maybe,' he acknowledged, 'but still, I can't help wondering about what kind of future those girls are going to have.'

'Just an ordinary one, I suppose, but if you really want to know ask Phoebe. She seems to know about everything that goes on here.'

'Okay, I'll just go see if I can find her. I won't be long,' he promised and in a flash he was gone, leaving her to wonder why he couldn't have waited 'til tomorrow.

He was totally obsessed, she thought, they were

adorable, their performance had been brilliant and anyone would have loved them but Barry seemed to be going overboard.

Even so, she had to admit that he wasn't the only one who was finding it hard to get the temple out of his mind; she was having trouble too. And as she went back over the scenes of the evening, her memory began to play tricks on her.

No longer was she merely watching the dancers, she felt as if she was one of them. At first it was wonderful to see herself there, performing for the gods, but then things began to take on a darker hue. The smoke spiralling up from the incense sticks seemed to take on human-like forms, the chords from the percussion orchestra vibrated with menace and the movements of the dancers became jerky and awkward. The smoky forms surrounded her, closed in on her, bore down on her, cut her off from everyone else, and one of them had some kind of gleaming instrument in his hand.

Panic overwhelmed her and she wanted to run, run as fast as she possibly could, so she did. She tore down the balcony steps, bumped into Barry and nearly sent him flying, along with the freshly poured glass of beer in his hand. The next thing she knew, they were both on the ground in a state of shock.

'What the fuck –'

'Sorry,' she gasped, catching her breath and rolling away from him. 'I didn't know what I was doing. It was like I was having some kind of terrifying nightmare or something.'

'People generally wait until they're in bed to have those, unless they're borderline lunatics to start with.'

'Are you just trying to be a beast? Anyone can have daydreams or fantasies, call them whatever you want, and they can be just as bad as nightmares, especially when they're as vivid as the one I just had.'

'Of course they can,' he said soothingly, 'but you're back in the real world now so try and put the whole thing out of your mind. Old Uncle Barry's here and he'll drive those imaginary bastards away.'

'Can you really do that?' she asked, clinging to him in a distinctly childish way for a moment and then pressing herself up against him in a way that wasn't childish at all. 'How are you going to go about it?'

'I'll show you,' he murmured, 'but not here.'

Forgetting about his better judgement, he drew her up the balcony steps and into his room, lowered the mosquito netting down over the bed and pulled her into the secret world it enclosed.

Still, he didn't entirely trust her. He didn't want to be left in the lurch a second time, so he held himself back until his cock was longer and harder than it had ever been and she was opening her legs to his exploring fingers.

When he finally plunged into her, a curious thing began to happen. It was as though in entering her body, he also entered her mind and, instead of driving her dream world away, he found himself inside it.

He was there with her in the terrifying temple, protecting her from a flash of shiny metal and a pair of ice-cold eyes. Then they were running, running so fast they could scarcely breathe, to escape the menacing forms that were pursuing them. As they raced along the dikes that crossed the flooded rice fields, the rhythm of his thrusts took on the rhythm of their running feet, faster and faster until their breath came in short desperate rushes and they collapsed together in exhaustion.

All too soon the magic of Bali was over and they were back in Java, picking up the threads of their lives again, although Barry did anticipate a few changes in his.

With the most important of these in mind, he climbed onto Big Red and rode into Yogya on the first Saturday afternoon after they got back, picked up Tess and took her out to his village.

A thoroughly disconcerting sight awaited them when they drew up in front of his house. Clearly visible through the living room window was the golden hair of someone neither of them expected to see.

It was Cynthia.

'Hello,' she called, coming to the door at the sound of the motorbike and greeting them as if she was the mistress of the house and they were guests.

'What the hell are you doing here?' Barry demanded.

'I just thought I'd drop in and see how you're getting along without me,' she returned airily.

'Dropped in,' he exclaimed, 'from New York! Who are you kidding?'

'You should be flattered.'

'I'm not.'

'That's good because I really just popped over from Singapore. Aren't you going to introduce me to your little friend here?'

'What I'm going to do, if you'll get out of my doorway, is get myself a beer,' turning to Tess, he added, 'I'll get one for you.'

Before either woman could reply, he stalked off to the back of the house.

'Come in,' Cynthia said graciously to Tess, 'I guess we'll just have to introduce ourselves. I'm Cynthia Gellert, Barry's sister-in-law, well, soon to be sister-in-law, that is. His brother John and I are getting married in April. We're just on a little pre-honeymoon honeymoon, a quick swing around the world to put us in the mood for marriage.

Now I want to know all about you.'

'I'm Tess ' she began coldly but before she could indicate that she had a last name, Barry stormed in, interrupted her by slamming a large beer bottle and two glasses down on the table and filled them so inexpertly that foam bubbled over the top and dripped in amber puddles onto the floor.

Cynthia, greatly amused by this performance, leaned towards Tess and said, 'It's really amazing that he's never learned how to pour a beer when you think of how much of it he drinks. Let's hope it doesn't give him a frightful case of middle-age spread in a few years. You know, I think I can already detect an increase around his middle since the last time I –'

'What the hell did you come here for anyway?' barked Barry, handing a glass to Tess, keeping the other one for himself and pointedly excluding Cynthia.

'Oh just a whim, perhaps a little nostalgia for old times,' she returned carelessly. 'After all, you can't be married to someone for nearly a year-and-a-half and then forget them right away, can you?'

'I can,' Barry declared, 'easily.'

'I don't believe you for a minute,' she purred, 'not after the great times we used to have together.' Turning to Tess, she added, 'What do you think? It wouldn't be possible, would it?'

'I wouldn't know,' Tess snapped, before saying to Barry,

'If you'll give me a ride out to Jalan Solo, I'll get a bus back to Yogya from there.'

'No you won't, you're the one I invited and you're the one who's staying. Cynthia can go back the way she came, to wherever it was she came from.'

'No problem,' Cynthia assured him cheerfully. 'I'll certainly do that but not just yet. I mean, after coming all the way from Singapore and changing planes in that frightful Kemayoran Airport, I couldn't think of staying less than two nights. I already have a reservation back on the Monday flight.'

Barry grimaced. 'Luckily, Yogya's got plenty of hotels. If John's bankrolling you for this misguided little adventure you can probably afford the Ambarrukmo. The room service there is sure to be a damn sight better than it is here.'

A mischievous sparkle came into Cynthia's eyes. 'You can't tell,' she said with a laugh, 'I might prefer what's on offer here.'

'Barry, can I talk to you for a minute?' Tess broke in.

'Sure,' he said, and led the way out to a shady spot next to Marilyn's tree house.

Tess let the little gibbon climb onto her shoulder and play with her enticing plait for a moment before saying, 'Look, I know this situation isn't your fault but it's certainly not my fault either and you've got to get me out of it.'

'Don't worry, I will.'

'I mean now.'

'But I don't want you to go now. I want her to be the one to go.'

'So do I but let's face it, it's going to take a fork-lift to get her out of here and in the meantime, I refuse to be subjected to the sordid little games you two are playing.'

'Look, I didn't mean –'

'I don't care what you meant. I just know that I'm not going back into that house while she is there and if you won't take me out to the bus stop on Jalan Solo, I'll walk across the rice fields and get there by myself.'

'Okay,' he said reluctantly, going over to Big Red, 'if that's what you really want, let's go. Climb on.'

She started to follow him and then let out a shriek. 'Ouch,' she cried.

Looking back, Barry saw that Marilyn also did not want Tess to leave and was thwarting her efforts by clinging firmly onto her plait.

'Let go, Marilyn,' he ordered sternly.

But the little ape, always delighting in a challenge, responded by putting one arm firmly around Tess's neck and using the fingers on her other hand to secure her grip on the beguiling rope of hair.

The ensuing fracas brought Cynthia to the door. 'Was that little monkey my successor?' she asked, mockingly.

'That is, until Tess came along.'

'Yeah, there've been a few improvements around here,' Barry retorted as, with some difficulty, he managed to detach the plait from the little primate's grasp.

Marilyn, on the verge of one of her legendary temper tantrums, sprang up onto the top of Barry's head, drawing hoots of laughter not only from Cynthia but from several passing children as well. Sadly, Barry's hair wasn't as much fun to play with as Tess's, so she settled for tugging on one of his ears instead, then scrambled across his head and twisted his other ear, eager to see if that drew the same reaction from the admiring crowd.

It did. Within minutes a dozen or more village children, the youngest ones unencumbered by clothes, gathered to watch the show. Marilyn warmed to her expanding audience by leaping onto the shoulder of a pretty girl selling herbal remedies. The girl was startled; she jumped to one side, sending one of her medicine bottles flying out of her basket and smashing it into a rock.

This delighted Marilyn who then proceeded to leap onto a little naked boy and begin playing with his penis, twirling it around first with one hand and then with the other until the little fellow, shrieking with terror, managed to get away, only to slip, fall and hit his head on the jagged edge of a broken bottle.

A crimson stream spurted out from a long gash above

the boy's ear as he fainted, whether from loss of blood, dizziness or hysteria, Barry didn't know. He only knew that Marilyn's misdeeds were his responsibility so, after a hasty conference with the boy's mother, he put them both on the fastest vehicle in the village; Big Red.

'God, whoever would have thought this would turn into such a hellish afternoon,' he muttered to Tess, as he kicked the starter, 'but with any luck, I won't be gone too long.' And before she could answer, he set off for the hospital in Yogya.

'Well,' Cynthia said, turning to Tess, 'there's not much point in standing out here is there? We might as well go inside and have some tea.'

Realising that she had no choice but to make the best of things, Tess decided that at least she could indulge her curiosity about this ghastly woman.

'How can you even boil water in this primitive kitchen?' Tess asked, after she had followed Cynthia back inside.

'It isn't easy. I nearly blew up the place the one time I tried it but fortunately Siti's back there doing some laundry for me, or she was before all the commotion broke out about that stupid monkey. She can make it for us.'

When Siti had been found and set to the task, Cynthia made herself as comfortable as the straight up and down furniture in the house allowed and said, 'Now tell me about you and Barry. Is he in love with you, or you with him?'

'No, we're just –'

'Fooling around?' suggested Cynthia.

Tess was annoyed.

'No,' she replied sharply, 'I wouldn't say that.'

'What would you say then?'

'I'd say it was none of your business,' snapped Tess.

'I'd say you were wrong about that. Who a man fools around with, and how involved he is with her, is very much a wife's business.'

'But you're not any kind of a wife anymore,' Tess reminded her.

'Is that what he told you?'

'It's not true?' Tess asked, trying to suppress the quick stab of pain at the possibility Barry had lied to her.

'If you take a long-term view of things, I suppose it's true. We want such different things in life that we could never really settle down and live together again. And Barry's sort of an oddball, you've probably noticed that by now.'

'Not really.'

'I guess all anthropologists are,' Cynthia went on. 'I thought I could get used to it and just live for the nights while we were in this hellhole. As you must have found out by now, Barry's no slacker in bed and if the days had just been shorter, a hell of a lot shorter, I might have been able to pull it off but,' she shuddered, 'this place was just too gruesome. I couldn't stick it out.'

'How come you came back then?'

'For the same reason I came here in the first place, jungle nights with the leading stud of the American Anthropological Association.'

'But aren't you about to marry Barry's brother?'

'Not for a few months yet.'

'I don't mean to sound puritanical or anything –'

Cynthia burst out laughing.

'You may not mean to but you do. Haven't you ever been engaged or anything?'

'Sort of,' Tess replied, uncertain just how to describe her current relationship with Mike.

Cynthia shrugged. 'Then you must know that being engaged doesn't mean you have to lock yourself into some kind of chastity belt,' she said.

'True,' Tess agreed, 'but it tends to rule out going to bed with your fiancé's brother.'

Cynthia laughed. 'I take your point,' she said, 'and ordinarily I suppose it would be true but our divorce papers haven't come through yet so legally Barry and I are still married.'

'And that means?'

'That means what difference could one more little get-together make?'

'It might make a difference to your fiancé.'

'Oh, him,' Cynthia returned airily, 'I doubt it.'

'Honestly, how can you possibly claim that Barry's an oddball when the one who's got seriously weird ideas is you? Of course it would make a difference to your fiancé.'

'Not if I don't tell him.'

'Somebody else might.'

'Who, you?'

'No but maybe Barry will tell him.'

'That wouldn't matter, he wouldn't believe it if it came from Barry.'

'Why not?'

'He'd think Barry was just trying to look like he had one-up on him, you know, pretend he's better at something than John is. And actually, at this one particular thing, Barry wins by a mile. Sex just doesn't interest John very much.'

'Then why is he marrying you?'

'For my brilliant intellect, incisive wit and not altogether repulsive appearance,' she ventured, with a laugh. 'He wants to impress his clients and friends with what a great guy he is and thinks that having me will do that. And then, of course, there's the real reason.'

'And that is?'

'It should be pretty obvious by now, or haven't you figured it out?'

'I guess I'm a little dense.'

'Shall we just say bit slow on the uptake? He's marrying me to get one-up on Barry. They've always been like that, ever since they were kids and this time,' she added, with a giggle, 'it's turned into a little game of volleyball with me as the ball.'

'Don't you mind?' Tess gasped.

'Why should I? It's great. I just bounce into John's court and collect a few credit cards and then bounce into Barry's and have a good romp in bed. It promises to be a very happy arrangement.'

'For all three of you?' cried Tess in amazement.

'Of course. John will have a trophy wife to parade on the cocktail circle and won't have to waste time doing boring things like chatting up attractive blondes or going through the motions of having sex.'

'Not ever?'

'Oh now and then, just to prove he can, but it's obvious he doesn't find it half as interesting as a company balance sheet. And Barry's just the opposite, sex is the only part of a relationship he cares about. So you see, we're going to be a very happy little triangle.'

'Are you sure about that? Barry didn't seem exactly thrilled to see you,' Tess reminded her.

'Oh, that was because I took him by surprise and anyway, he was never very glad to see me during the day.

Basically, he doesn't like me very much. We always fought whenever we were in the same room for more than five minutes, unless we were in bed. I think that's what made the nights so spectacular. There's nothing like a lot of pent-up hostility to make really great sex, don't you think?'

'No, actually, I don't.'

'Maybe you just haven't been lucky,' Cynthia said with note of sympathy in her voice. 'I think there are lots of people who –' She glanced out the window and broke off at the sight of someone going into a nearby house.

Following her line of vision, Tess recognised the girl with the basket of bottles on her back.

'Look, it's the *jamu* lady,' Cynthia exclaimed. 'She's got the most wonderful potions and cures. Do you ever take any of them?'

Tess shook her head.

'You should,' Cynthia advised, 'they're great. Some of them anyway.'

'Most people seem to think they don't work.'

'Some of them do. Hold on a minute,' and with this, Cynthia dashed into the bedroom and reappeared with a large handbag over her shoulder, saying, 'I want to catch her before she goes out again.'

Tess was surprised to see the *jamu* lady come to the door at the sound of Cynthia's voice, greet her with a warm smile and draw her inside.

It was quite a while before she came out again.

'Didn't you buy anything?' Tess asked, when Cynthia looked like she had come back empty-handed.

'Mixed up with that filthy village water? Heavens no. I just bought lots of the powders.'

'What kind of powders?'

Cynthia hesitated. 'The slimming one's quite good,' she said evasively.

'You don't need it,' Tess observed, with a touch of envy.

'Well, I want to stay this way. And while we're discussing figures, you'd better get Barry to lay off the beer. He won't have anything to do with *jamu* but I like his body the way it is. Let's keep it that way.'

'Wait a minute,' Tess protested, 'if you're suggesting a new kind of volleyball, with Barry bouncing from you to me, and back again, you can just forget it. I'm not playing.'

'Why not? Two interlocking triangles should be twice as fun as one.'

'No it won't because I'm not going to have any part of it.'

'Don't tell me you're in love with Barry?' said Cynthia, sounding shocked.

'No, fortunately.'

'That's good; being in love is hell. Leave it to the teenyboppers, a little suffering will do them good. But if you're not in love with Barry then what's your problem?'

'I don't have a problem. I just have an aversion to being manipulated by people like you, or by anyone for that matter.'

'You don't understand,' returned Cynthia soothingly. 'I wouldn't try to –'

'I do understand, except for one small thing.'

'What's that?'

'When you're still so involved with Barry that you'll come to this place which you apparently hate, why don't you mind more about my being here? I can't believe you really think your little volleyball games or triangles or whatever you want to call them, will turn everything into some kind of picnic.'

Cynthia smiled. 'Believe whatever you like,' she said generously. Then, seeing that was Tess getting up from her chair and starting for the door, she asked, 'Where're you going?'

'Home. I've had enough of this conversation. I'm not waiting around for Barry any longer.'

'How are you going to get there without Big Red?'

'How does anyone go anywhere from here? I'll walk across the paddy fields and catch one of those market buses going out to Jalan Solo. Then I can get a regular bus into Yogya.'

'That sounds pretty horrendous to me. I wouldn't want to do it.'

'You don't have to. You can wait here like some hungry predator, pounce on Barry the moment he walks in the door and have sex all night. I couldn't care less. Your sordid little triangles don't interest me at all. And if you have five minutes between orgasms, you can tell him that I never want to see him again.'

'I might if I think about it,' Cynthia laughed, 'but talking isn't really our thing.'

Tess endured the bus trip back to Yogya in a state of numbed semi-consciousness and spent much of the night trying to convince herself that Barry didn't matter to her. No man mattered and no man ever would, she was going to see to that. It was the only way to cope with life.

She woke up the next morning tired, in an extremely bad mood and not in any frame of mind to deal with Philip, so it was bad luck that he chose that particular day to invite her into his office for a coffee.

'Thanks but I just popped in to pick up my mail, then I've got to get to the library. I've masses to do.'

'Surely you can spare me five minutes?' he said, his tone showing that he didn't think anything she was likely to do was very important. 'Just give me a quick rundown on how your project is going, that's all.' Seeing that she was about to flee, he added, 'Ninik's just made some fresh coffee.'

'Okay, one cup,' she agreed, giving in to temptation, 'but only a very quick one.'

He led her into his office and asked her briefly about her holiday in Bali. Noticing that she displayed no equivalent interest in how he had celebrated the New Year, he got straight down to business. 'Do you have an outline of your thesis or anything like that you can show me?' he asked.

'No.'

He raised an eyebrow. 'Don't you think you should have one by this time?'

'Probably.'

'But you don't?'

'I do actually.'

'But you just said –'

'I said that I don't have one to show you. I didn't say that I don't have one.'

'May I ask why you don't want to show it to me?

'Yes.'

'I'm listening,' he said, testily.

'Because it's my project, not yours and it's still in the early stages. I'm not ready to show it to anybody yet.'

'Don't you think we're sort of in this together?' he suggested, trying to repress his irritation. She could be very annoying at times.

'No, I don't.'

'You can't mean that you're just going to hand in a final

version of your thesis without getting anyone's advice or comments along the way?' he exclaimed, his astonishment now outweighing his annoyance. 'Don't you think that's a little risky?'

'Very risky but that's not what I'm going to do.'

'Am I the only interested person who's being blocked out?'

'Yes, now that you mention it.'

'Why do you persist in regarding me as an enemy?' he demanded, genuinely bewildered.

'Because you've never treated me as a friend.'

'Come now, isn't that a bit harsh?'

'I don't think so.'

'Is there anything I can do to make you change your mind?'

'Not that I can think of at the moment,' she replied, standing up to go. 'Thanks for the coffee.'

Fuck, he muttered under his breath as she left, why was it so hard to get a good working relationship going with her? What was he doing wrong? Nothing, as far as he could tell she was just being difficult but she'd come around. There was no way he was going to let her make a hash of a project that could, if it were handled right, rebound to his credit.

Of course, there was some question about how much time and effort he wanted to put into the thing, maybe he should just write it off. He was intending to do that with a number of other projects Wilson had generated, not that this one was really his predecessor's fault. Some clown in the New York office had been responsible for selecting Tess for the grant.

An unsettling question suddenly came into Philip's mind. Why was he making such a big deal about this particular project? It couldn't be that it was Tess herself who interested him, could it?

An image of Tess as she had looked that night at the Kents came into his mind. Her hair, freed from that 'no sex please' braid, had been flowing down around her face and shoulders in a way that had made her look surprisingly attractive. Just imagining running his hands through it was giving him a hard-on. And there was something particularly exciting about the thought of a girl who only let her hair down for him to touch and not for anyone else.

Although there was that guy, Gellert; he might have touched not only her hair but a lot more of her as well. Hadn't the bastard stayed on in Bali several days longer than he had originally planned? He didn't like the idea of making a play for Tess and getting turned down for Barry, how humiliating would that be? No, he'd better play it cool, take his time and see how things went.

In any case, he'd better start thinking about something else or the morning would be shot before he was able to get any work done.

Having made the decision to put Tess out of his mind, he stuck to it, more or less, until noon the next day. But when Darwati missed his Indonesian lesson for the third day in a row, he decided to stop by Tess's place on the way home for lunch and see if she knew what had happened to her.

'She has an auntie who lives out near Prambanan,' Tess said, standing in the doorway and pointedly not inviting him in. 'Sometimes she goes to visit her and stays for a few days.'

'But she was there a couple of weeks ago,' Philip objected. 'Why would she go back again so soon?'

'I've no idea,' Tess replied, with an indifference she was far from feeling.

She was well aware that Darwati had been depressed recently, convinced that the spell the *dukun* had been casting on her adored Sigit was working. He had stopped encouraging her to spend more time at her auntie's place in his village and was 'so busy' at work that he hardly ever had time to come to Yogya anymore. They hadn't had any of their secret meetings at the zoo or been to the Colombo Night Club together for ages. And in the midst of a flood of tears, Darwati had told her that Sigit had been seen dancing with 'that bad girl' at the Colombo.

She didn't really think Darwati was about to die for

love or to do anything terrible to Sigit or even to 'the bad girl' although she did have a few nagging doubts about the latter of these possibilities. Darwati might just see her shattered romance in an overly dramatic light and waste what little money she had on getting the services of a *dukun* of her own, one who, for an outrageous sum, would be willing to engage in a little black magic on her behalf.

Black magic, Tess had learned, was illegal although the practice of white magic was okay.

'I just thought that because you two were good friends, you might have some idea what she's up to,' Philip said.

'That doesn't mean I know every detail of her life,' Tess snapped.

'No of course not,' he replied brusquely, the heat of the sun and the coldness of her manner making him uncomfortable. 'I just thought - well, maybe it's a good thing she didn't come today. The electricity in the office has been off all morning and it can be pretty miserable there without any air conditioning.'

Tess offered only perfunctory sympathy.

'In fact, I've been thinking of taking the afternoon off,' he continued, although the idea had really just occurred to him, 'going out to Prambanan and taking a look around.'

'You mean you haven't been there yet?' she asked scornfully.

'I had a quick look around when I first got here but I'd like to go again, specially if I could go with the local expert.'

'That should be easy enough, you know where the archaeology department is,' she replied, not caring how rude she sounded.

'Yes, but I thought maybe you could give me some special insights into the temple.'

Patronising bastard, she thought, and was fishing in her mind for a biting response when the sound of Big Red approaching made her change her mind abruptly.

Barry! How dare he think he could just climb out of bed with Cynthia one minute and come barrelling over here the next? But she managed to hide her anger somehow and put on a show of enthusiasm for Philip.

'I'd love to,' she said and before he could take in her sudden change in attitude, she was darting towards his car, apparently ready to start out that very instant.

The only problem with that was that he hadn't eaten anything since breakfast and he was hungry.

'Let's stop by my place and have some lunch first,' he suggested, swinging into the front seat beside her.

'Good idea,' she agreed, relieved that Philip had already slid the car into first gear by the time Big Red sputtered to a halt in front of the house.

'I'm off to have lunch with Philip,' she called to Barry

as they drove away.

'Wait, when can I see you?' Barry shouted after them, but Tess had turned away and with the car windows rolled up to keep the air conditioning in, she didn't hear him.

Fuck, he said to himself, as he kicked Big Red to a fresh start. Fuck Cynthia, and most of all, fuck me for being the world's greatest moron. How could I have let everything go so wrong so fast?

It had all started when he had taken that kid and his mother to the hospital, he thought, reviewing the events of Cynthia's unwelcome visit in his mind. They had had to wait forever for the kid's head to be stitched up and when they had finally got back to the village, he had barely been able to walk into his house before hordes of the boy's relatives had come calling on him to thank him for his wonderful rescue mission. This had made him extremely uncomfortable because he was well aware of the fact that it had been Marilyn's temper tantrum that had caused it all in the first place.

The good thing was that the relatives, with legendary Javanese politeness, had refrained from pointing this out. The bad thing was that he had had to be equally polite in return and this had meant plying the teeming hordes with endless cups of sweet tea while they talked over a hundred other subjects before getting to the real reason for their visit. This was the aspect of Javanese politeness that nearly drove him crazy.

By the time they had left, he had felt like it was the middle of the night and it probably was. Going to Tess's place, pounding on the door and waking up the family she lived with just hadn't been an option.

Cynthia, who viewed midnight as the beginning rather than the end of an evening, had been bored into something of a coma by the conversations in Javanese which she hadn't understood and which wouldn't have interested her even if she had. After the last guest had left, he had found her sound asleep, lying diagonally across his double bed, so he had just pushed her roughly to one side and slept until the usual sounds of screeching birds, barking dogs, squawking chickens and calling children announced the arrival of morning.

When he had opened his eyes Barry had looked at Cynthia's still sleeping form with surprise, then with distaste, then with a faint resurgence of that disastrous old attraction and finally, with a firm determination to put any ideas of that sort out of his mind.

The Cynthia phase of his life was over, thank God. He had woken up in more ways than one and had realised that he wanted more from a woman, much more, than he, or probably any man, would ever get from Cynthia.

The next dreadful thing that happened over the nightmare weekend had been that Cynthia had sprained her ankle, or that's what she claimed. He was convinced she had been lying, certainly he had never seen any sign of swelling. Still, she had insisted with mule-like stubbornness that taking even a single step plunged her into the most excruciating pain and that staying in a hotel all by herself would be unthinkable. How would she even be able to get to the dining room or anywhere else for that matter? She would go mad if she had to sit hour after hour in a cold impersonal hotel room. It would be like being shut away in some kind of solitary confinement but if he could spend just one more day with her, for old times' sake if for no other reason, it wouldn't have to be that way. She would be leaving after that and by the time they saw each other again she and John would be married and everything would be different. The whole idea of ending their relationship on an angry note was making her feel so sad. Wouldn't it be much nicer if they could spend one last beautiful day in their thatched cottage under the coconut palms and then say goodbye as friends? Wasn't that what he wanted too?

He had grumbled that he didn't care how it ended but he wasn't being entirely truthful. He would have given a good deal to be able to put aside the bitterness he felt whenever he thought of her and wondered whether this might be one way of doing it. What harm could there be in giving it a try?

The day had actually proved to be much like the idyllic one she had described. The only problem had been finding things to talk about but they never had had much to say to each other so when, at about six o'clock, she had suggested sending one of the village boys out to the Chinese Apothecary on Jalan Solo for some whisky, he had thought this was a good idea. They usually had a few bottles squirreled away somewhere and a little fiery liquid might oil the wheels of conversation a bit. Cynthia rarely drank more than a few sips of anything stronger than water enlivened by a slice of lemon. Alcohol was fattening and she maintained a nearly ceaseless vigil over her figure but this time she seemed to have put her perpetual diet on hold and had actually had several drinks. He had surpassed her by at least two to one, probably more like three to one, but hadn't realised he was getting a bit sozzled until she began taking off her clothes.

His dick had shot up like a rocket at the sight of a naked Cynthia naked lying seductively on the bed. Without thinking about Tess or his brother or anything at all, he had fallen on top of her and gone at her like some kind of wild animal and her response hadn't been exactly tame. They had gone on and on and on, with him turning Cynthia from one position to another while she teased and tantalised him with some playful strategies of her own. They must have spent eons of time building up to an erotic explosion yet somehow the eventual release had been disappointing, for him anyway, and he suspected it had been pretty much the same for her. They had fallen into a deep and exhausted sleep that had lasted until Marilyn's outraged demands for breakfast had woken them towards the middle of the morning. The little gibbon was an early riser and she had grown accustomed to a certain standard of service. The delay was not to her liking, nor was the return of Cynthia. They had never been friends and Marilyn saw no reason for that to change.

In the all-too-sober light of morning, Barry woke up to a few qualms of conscience about Tess. But considering he found himself in the throes of a life-threatening hangover whenever he thought about anything at all, he simply subscribed to Marilyn's view that the sooner Cynthia was out of the way, the better.

It had been with no reluctance at all that he had taken her to the airport later that afternoon, watched her board the plane for Jakarta and fervently hoped she wouldn't miss her flight onto Singapore for her reunion with John.

As he had climbed back on Big Red, he had toyed with the idea of dropping by to see Tess but decided against it. He had felt that if he waited a day or two it would make it easier to gloss over any mention of what had gone on with

Cynthia, put it down as ancient history and sweep it under the rug. Then hey presto! End of story, no harm done.

Having convinced himself that this would be the best way to handle a decidedly sticky situation, he had holed up in his village and let a couple of days pass before pulling Big Red to a stop in front of Tess's door – just in time to see her drive away with Philip.

Shit, he muttered to himself, what is she doing, going off with that guy when she hates him? She's going to be in for a hell of an afternoon. But he was wrong; it didn't turn out that way at all.

It occurred to Philip over lunch that it might be a good idea to talk about something else besides Tess's thesis for a while. After groping around for possibilities and starting a few subjects that promptly wilted, he happened to mention the excavation he had been working on in Turkey when he had met the Kents.

Tess had shown a remarkable interest in it and had immediately begun asking questions. As this played to both Philip's long-dormant interest in archaeology and his active interest in himself, the topic had carried them all the way through lunch and out to Prambanan.

By the time they arrived, Philip had discovered that Tess was actually a good deal more intelligent than he had thought and she was beginning to wonder whether he really was the big, bad ogre she had been imagining.

This suspicion was further reinforced by the interest he took in everything around him as they strolled amongst the temple's scattered stones and toppled stupas. He seemed particularly intrigued by the low relief carvings around the base of the Shiva sanctuary so she related the parts of the Ramayana story they illustrated, pointing out the carefully incised representations of Rama and Siti, of the ogre Rawana and the much-loved Hanuman with his monkey army.

The age-old struggle between good and evil lost nothing in her lively telling and Philip became increasingly captivated by the sparkle in her eyes as she spoke.

When they had gone full circle around the sanctuary, she led the way up a steep stairway into a windowless stone chamber. At first glance Philip thought the place was empty but as his eyes adjusted to the dimness, he realised that the image of an intensely war-like, yet somehow exciting, female deity - a weapon of death in each of her eight arms - stood in the centre of the room, gazing at them with the eerie calm of a thousand years of waiting.

'This is the goddess, Durga,' Tess explained, as if she were introducing a living, sentient human being. 'She's a consort of Shiva, she rides a tiger and drinks human blood.'

For some silly reason, Philip found himself shuddering at the thought. What kind of a wimp was he turning into, he wondered, hoping that his pathetic reaction was due to the unabashedly erotic quality of the goddess's voluptuous body in juxtaposition with the horrific weaponry she held.

Whatever it was, he became so caught up in the mystique of it all that he could almost see the presence of evil, crouching like a tangible substance in the shadowy recesses of the shrine.

'I'm surprised at how much you seem affected by all this,' Tess told him, when they paused to rest on one of the fallen stones in the inner courtyard.

'Why shouldn't I be? Archaeology used to be my thing, you know.'

'Yes, but I know lots of people in the field who spend all their time measuring and dating things and don't show any signs of feeling anything for what they're uncovering.'

'And you thought I was like that?'

'Yes, actually, at least I did until this afternoon. I would never have imagined you wandering around an archaeological site and being so caught up in what it must have been like a thousand years ago.'

'That's because you don't know much about me.'

'And what is it about you that would make me

understand?'

'I spent several years of my childhood wandering around a two thousand year old site, imagining what it had all been like when it was full of life.'

'You did,' Tess gasped, astonished, 'how come?'

'My dad was in charge of the American Cemetery at Carthage, the one for the men who were killed in the North Africa campaign.'

'Back in World War II, you mean?'

'Right, that's where they're buried. I went to the French school in modern day Carthage, but I had a tough time in the beginning. I didn't speak French and even when I had got over that hurdle I didn't fit in very well, so I was on my own a lot. Our house was just twenty minutes' walk from the ruins so I used to go there after school and prowl around a lot.'

'And tried to imagine what it had all been like,' Tess suggested, trying to fit this picture of a curious, rather lonely, child with the cold, matter-of-fact man beside her.

'Not the way you do with this place. I guess when it comes down to it I'm basically the measuring and classifying type. But I'd look for Roman coins, do scale drawings of the layout of the baths, trace out the streets, draw maps, all that sort of thing. There was hardly ever anybody around, usually there weren't even any guards, just the occasional tourist pottering about, so I really felt like I was discovering the place.'

He broke off with an embarrassed smile, not altogether comfortable with revealing this sort of thing about himself. Yet having started, he didn't find it so easy to stop.

'If you want to know the truth,' he confessed, 'I used to pretend I was Hannibal, the old amphitheatre was a great place to do that. The stage was Carthage, my castle was in the centre of it and the stone seats were perfect for the Alps because they were built into the hillside. They were really steep so I'd go charging up them with my sword and my elephants and leave regiments of dead Romans behind me at every turn. Then when I got to the top I'd make any Romans left alive, mostly women and children, swear perpetual allegiance to Carthage.

'So now you know what an idiot kid I was,' he said, peering down at her with an embarrassed laugh.

'I don't think you were idiotic at all,' she protested. 'It sounds like a wonderful way to spend your childhood.'

'I'm not sure many people would agree with you. In any case, it all came to an end when my dad died. My mother, sister and I had to go back to the States. It was a struggle to make a go of things there so I still remember that time in Tunisia as a sort of Golden Era.'

'Is that why you majored in archaeology when you got to college?'

'I guess so but it was a damn silly thing to do.'

'Silly,' Tess exclaimed, shocked, 'why do you say that?'

'Because it's not the thing to do if you want to make money.'

'But you wouldn't just sell yourself for money, would you?' she asked scornfully.

'Of course I would, so would anyone with any sense unless of course he had a nice little nest egg tucked away somewhere, either in a bank or in the form of an affectionate granny.'

'That's not true!'

He shrugged his shoulders.

'Well I wouldn't,' she continued, 'and I know lots of other people who wouldn't.'

'I dare say you do. Archaeology departments are full of them, eager young academics who think that the only thing they care about is pure research. But just wait ten years, or maybe fifteen, and count up how many have become instant Egyptologists because UNESCO's paying good money to salvage anything it can before the Aswan Dam floods the place; or how many of the chemists you knew in graduate school, really idealistic guys who were totally genuine about only caring for pure research, are working for pharmaceutical companies; or how many of your grad school friends from whatever department have chucked the academic scene and gone into business.'

'Your friends, perhaps, but not mine and definitely

not me.'

'Okay, not you perhaps,' he conceded. 'You'll be married well before fifteen years is up, though hopefully not to another archaeologist or one of the other saintly types you seem to know, guys who stick to their lofty ideals without a comfortable nest egg to fall back on. Just have a talk with them fifteen years from now and see how happy they are eking out a living on their meagre university salaries.'

Tess considered this for a moment.

'Don't you suppose most people have some regrets by the time they're middle aged, or probably a lot sooner than that? I mean, it's pretty clear you have some regrets about archaeology.'

'No I don't, not one.'

'I don't believe you. I can tell by your reactions, and by what you've said this afternoon that you still really love it.'

'I do love it although that's not the way I usually put it. I find it endlessly fascinating but that doesn't mean I'm not glad I had the good sense to keep it as a hobby and do something a little more lucrative for a living. I'm not the kind of man to sit around regretting things, if I want something I figure out a way to get it. It's as simple as that.'

'But if there isn't –'

'There always is, if you're prepared to do it.'

'Aren't you making yourself sound a bit ruthless?'

she said, half-teasing, half-serious.

'You've got to be if you're going to get what you want in life.'

The afternoon with Philip had a buoyant effect on Tess's spirits. When she went to bed that night she was able to fall asleep without giving Barry more than a passing thought.

Instead, her mind was occupied with the image of a little boy pretending to be Hannibal charging around the ruins of Carthage. Actually the Roman soldiers often looked a bit like Barry but that was okay because she had the fun of watching Hannibal cut their heads off. The odd thing though was that in spite of the threat of imminent decapitation, more Romans kept coming. Then she was in the dream with Hannibal, they were in a sort of castle and the Romans were pounding, pounding, pounding at a great wooden door and –

She woke up in alarm. Someone was rapping on the shutter of her window, a burglar, crazed killer, a Javanese ghost. Her blood ran cold at the thought and as the sound grew louder, she realised that someone was tampering with the shutter, trying to force it open. The next thing she knew she was hearing muttered oaths, they were in English so it had to be Barry.

Leaping up, she flung the shutter open so suddenly that he fell back into the garden.

'What are you doing here?' she hissed, in as loud a whisper as she dared. 'Don't you know it's the middle of the night? Go away.'

'But I just got here,' he protested, starting to climb in.

'And get your horrible foot off my windowsill.'

'I will, if you come out.'

'No way.'

'Then I'm coming in.'

'Don't even think of it,' she cried, panicking at the thought of how the family would react if they found a man in her room in the middle of the night. 'I'll come out.'

'Okay, but no treachery,' he warned, retreating from the windowsill but keeping his hand firmly on the shutter, he didn't trust her not to close it in his face.

'Don't worry, just because duplicity and deceit would spring to your diseased mind doesn't mean that everyone else would think that way.'

'Good God, what have I done to deserve all that?'

'You know very well what you've done,' she retorted, leaping to the ground on the outside of her window and hurrying to the far end of the garden out of earshot, she hoped, from the house. 'You've been having an orgy of nonstop sex with Cynthia.'

'What gives you that idea?' he gasped, as he followed her.

'I know you.'

'Maybe not as well as you think,' he said impatiently.

'Don't forget I know Cynthia too and she told me there's only one way the two of you spend your time together. It's pretty easy to figure out what that is.'

It was too dark for her to see the colour drain from his face as he choked out, 'Oh God, Tess, I –'

'After what we had together in Bali,' she interrupted, 'or at least what I thought we had –'

'Listen to me, Tess –'

'No! Why would I want to hear any more of your revolting lies?'

'I promise I won't lie to you but you've got to give me a chance to explain.'

'No, I don't. You don't deserve any more chances because you've already shown what a slimy reptile you are, nothing is going to change that.'

'Tess, I swear I don't understand how it happened but it was only once, not any kind of an orgy and I felt like hell about it afterwards.'

'Good, I hope you suffered agonies.'

'Go easy on me, Tess. You can't imagine how much I hate myself.'

'Yes I can, it's easy.'

A kerosene lamp flickered inside the house and Tess realised that their voices must have risen. A light sleeper could well have heard the unfamiliar sounds.

'Go away and don't ever come back,' Tess hissed, before darting back to the house, climbing in the window and locking the shutter behind her, 'not ever.'

Barry waited in the shadows while the grandfather of the family opened the front door, held up a lamp to survey the garden, satisfied himself that it was free of thieves and returned to bed.

After a number of futile raps on Tess's shutter, Barry dejectedly climbed onto Big Red and drove away.

When Tess woke up the next morning she was still seething with anger. The problem, she realised, was that she had been hoping against hope that Barry would have somehow convinced her that nothing had happened with Cynthia. It had been a faint hope but she had clung to it all the same. Now all she could do was face the brutal truth; Barry was just another member of the rat parade that had marched so ceaselessly through her life.

In an effort to think of something besides Barry's treachery, Tess decided to stop by and see Darwati. It would be a relief to focus on someone else's problems for a while.

Much to her surprise, she found that her friend's mood had apparently taken a turn for the better since she had last seen her. She was dying to find out what was responsible for this amazing change but Mini's presence in the room made it impossible for her to ask.

Instead she settled for saying casually, 'How are Philip's Indonesian lessons going?'

This provoked a burst of giggles from Darwati. 'He is a very funny man,' she replied.

'Funny,' exclaimed Tess, who had thought a lot of things about Philip but funny had never one of them, 'in what way?'

'He has very funny ideas about things,' she explained, and seeing that Tess would need some convincing she searched her mind for an example. 'Like volcanoes,' she said.

Tess still looked baffled so Darwati continued, 'He likes to talk about them and he has lots and lots of books about them.'

A little surprised to find herself defending Philip, Tess said, 'I don't think that's so funny, not when we're living in full view of one of the world's most active ones.'

'But it hasn't erupted for a long time, has it?' Mini asked, wanting to be reassured on this point.

'No, not for ages,' Darwati said airily.

'And how long is that?' demanded Tess, suddenly wanting to know.

'I don't know exactly, I was just a little girl the last time,'

Darwati returned, 'so I do not remember but my auntie told me.' Then, as if she were imparting something very significant, she added, 'and my auntie is from Muntilan.'

'Where's that?' Mini asked.

'On the other side of Mt Merapi. The fire from inside the mountain always goes down toward Muntilan.'

'I thought your auntie lived out near Prambanan,' Tess protested.

'I have many aunties.'

'Never mind about that,' Tess said, eager to return to what was really on her mind. 'The last eruption couldn't have been all that long ago if you can remember it.'

'I suppose not,' Darwati agreed indifferently.

'Doesn't it scare you to think the mountain is still alive,' Tess persisted, 'and that it might happen again?'

The question seemed to amuse Darwati. 'Oh, Yogya is safe,' she declared.

'It won't be if the lava flows down this way in the next eruption,' Tess pointed out.

'Never happen,' Darwati said confidently.

'You can't be sure of that,' Tess argued.

'Our Sultan is very good,' Darwati replied.

'But what does he have to do with volcanic eruptions?'

'He is married to Nyai Loro Kidul,' Darwati explained, as if that made everything clear.

It didn't. It only made Tess wonder if she had fallen

down a rabbit hole and was talking to the Mad Hatter or the March Hare.

'You see, Nyai Loro Kidul is the goddess of the mountain,' Darwati continued, 'and the Sultan is very good to her, so when the mountain spits fiery rocks in air they always go down the other side. You can see their path if you go there.'

'I thought Loro Kidul was the Green Sea Goddess,' Mini put in, emphasising the word 'sea'.

'She has two homes,' Darwati explained, 'one in the mountain, one in the sea.'

'I don't understand how the Sultan can be married to a goddess,' said Tess, trying to keep any hint of amusement out of her voice.

'In a very big wedding ceremony,' Darwati replied solemnly. 'The procession went all around the mountain.'

Tess attempted to digest this information, failed, set it aside and tried a new approach. 'You said the Sultan treated her well. How does he do that?'

'Every time he cuts his hair or his fingernails or his toenails, he saves all the cut off pieces for Nyai Loro Kidul. Then once a year he takes them down to Parangtritis and there is a big ceremony where he throws them into the sea for her.'

'What does she do with them?' Tess asked, feeling this conversation was taking her deeper and deeper into

Wonderland.

She takes them to her home in sea,' Darwati replied, with just a touch of impatience in her voice. She thought this should be obvious. 'So you see, he is a very good husband. He remembers her all the time. And she is a good wife too. She sends the fire from the mountain down along the Muntilan side so the people in Yogya never need to worry.'

'Well that's good to know,' Tess said, this time not troubling to conceal her smile or hide the amusement in her eyes.

Darwati, offended, turned to her sister in law. Although Mini wasn't Indonesian, she didn't seem like a real foreigner the way Tess did.

'Americans have such funny ideas about volcanoes,' Darwati said. 'Do you want to hear what Philip told me? I laughed and laughed when I heard it.'

Mini said she did.

'He thinks volcanoes come from plates.'

Both Mini and Tess looked startled.

'Special plates,' Darwati continued, 'not eating plates. They are called...' and hesitating over the newly-learned word, she pronounced it with extra care, 'tectonic plates.'

'What are they?' Mini asked.

'Very big plates that move around underground and sometimes have a big crash.'

She laughed delightedly at the thought, Mini looked sceptical and Tess wished she had been good enough in science to explain it all properly. She tried but wasn't very successful and as her audience quickly lost interest, she soon abandoned the attempt.

'What's up?' Tess asked, when a breathless Darwati rushed into her house a few days later.

'Diamonds.'

Tess couldn't believe she had heard right. She knew Philip was paying well for the Indonesian lessons but it wasn't enough to drape his teacher in gemstones.

'What about them?' Tess asked. 'Have any come your way?'

'Yes, from my old auntie. Did I tell you about her?'

'You have so many aunties, I can't keep track.'

Darwati laughed. 'My mother's mother had sixteen children, my father's mother only had seven but my grandfather's second wife had three and his –'

Tess cut short this flood of genealogical information by asking, 'Did your old auntie give you some diamonds?'

'I think so.'

'Don't you know?'

'Well she, my old auntie, was sleeping and they just popped out. She opened her eyes, said my name and died, so my other aunties say the diamonds are for me.'

'Hold on a minute,' Tess said, thoroughly confused. 'Where did the diamonds pop out from?'

'Her stomach.'

'But diamonds don't just pop out of people's stomachs,' she objected.

'Sometimes they do. It is a Sundanese secret. Do you know where Sunda is?'

'West Java,' Tess said promptly, 'around Bandung and Bogor.'

Darwati nodded. 'My old auntie was Sundanese,' she said, 'and she fixed diamonds into her stomach button to make my old uncle love her. That was a very long time ago but it was very powerful magic and it made my old uncle love her until he died. Now I will put the diamonds in my stomach button and make Sigit love me.'

'You can't be serious,' exclaimed Tess.

'Of course I am serious. Do you want to see? It's a secret really but you are just a foreigner so I'll show you.' And with that, she inched the waistband of her skirt down far enough to reveal a small diamond embedded in her navel. 'And there are three more, very small, under my skin just here,' she continued, tracing an arc along her lower abdomen with her finger.

Tess, scarcely able to believe her ears, cried, 'Oh, Darwati, you've got to go to a doctor right away and have

322

them taken out.'

It was Darwati's turn to have trouble believing what she was hearing. 'Oh no,' she cried, 'that would be very dangerous.'

'Of course, but having diamonds put under your skin was dangerous. You're likely to get a terrible infection.'

'Not that kind of dangerous,' Darwati explained impatiently, wondering why it was so hard for foreigners to understand anything. 'If they come out, I die.'

'You can die of an infection if they don't come out,' Tess argued. 'And as for them making Sigit love you, that's the most absurd thing I've ever heard.'

A steel-like quality, one Tess had never suspected Darwati possessed, manifested itself. 'It is not absurd and I won't have them out,' she declared. 'The diamonds are powerful magic and they have made Sigit love me already.'

'How do you know?'

'He told me.'

'Men can say anything.'

'What Sigit tells me is true. He does not see that bad girl anymore. He only sees me.'

'And how long do you think that will last?' Tess asked, feeling like a bit of a rat for putting it so cruelly.

'Forever and always.'

Tess sighed and then tried another approach. 'Even if I believed there was some mystical force associated with these diamonds, I don't think a relationship that results from tricks can ever be worth having.'

'You are a foreigner,' Darwati pointed out, unhelpfully. 'You just don't understand.'

And leaving Tess with an awful feeling that she had disappointed her friend, Darwati left.

Was anything going right, Tess wondered later that day, and decided that it wasn't. Perhaps the worst thing of all, she thought, was losing that affinity for Java and for everything Javanese that had been so important to her for so long. Or could it be that she was just viewing it sensibly for the first time? Probably that was it, she concluded, but instead of making her feel better, the possibility just made her feel worse and even more like an outsider.

Then there was Barry. It was still a bit of a struggle to put him out of her mind and to avoid any place where she might run into him.

As though things weren't ghastly enough, her work was going really badly. No matter how much time she spent in the archaeology section of the library poring over the material she found there, no matter how much she wore her dictionaries to shreds in her efforts to deal with the books and articles that were in Dutch or Indonesian, she could find absolutely nothing about the Mataram

Kingdom after the early part of the tenth century. It just seemed to have disappeared off the face of the earth. And what was worse, the more she read about the Kingdom up to that period, and there wasn't very much available, the more evidence she found to suggest that the capital hadn't been in the area around Prambanan at all. It had been somewhere along the north coast near Cirebon where it had had access to important nautical trade routes. A considerable amount of gold jewellery, as well as beautifully crafted gold and silver images of the gods that must have surely belonged to royalty, had been found in the area, giving added credence to the theory that Cirebon had been the capital.

But even though she didn't hate Philip all that much anymore, the prospect of admitting that he had been right all along was too awful to think about.

Glancing at her watch and seeing that it was a little after four, she decided to forget about the Mataram Kingdom for a while and go and see the Kents.

One of the good things about Yogya was that you didn't need an invitation or any kind of an excuse to go and visit someone, especially during the established 'calling hours' of five to seven. You could just drop in and if they were at home they would invite you in, if they were the Kents it would be highly likely that a piece of one of Mary's delicious cakes would be on offer too.

The teapot at the Kents generally made its appearance at four o'clock so, by stretching the Javanese calling hours just a bit, she could be stepping into their welcoming living room in just a few minutes.

She was.

'Look what I made,' Holly cried, holding up a homemade booklet that said 'United Kingdom' in uneven letters on the front.

'It looks like a passport,' Tess said.

Holly was delighted. 'That's what it is, it's for my bear.'

'I didn't know bears needed passports.'

'They do if they're going to boarding school,' Holly said. 'Do you have a camera?'

'Just an Instamatic.'

'Daddy has a real camera but it's broken, so could you take a picture of Fuzzy for his passport?'

'Sure, if you want me to.'

'When?'

'Tomorrow, if you like.'

It was agreed.

Tess came back with her camera the next afternoon and an appropriate background for the picture was set up in the schoolroom. Tess was just about to take her first shot when the sound of a male voice speaking English in the front hallway made her pause.

'Oh that's just Uncle Philip,' cried Holly, not wanting

the photo session to be put off, 'we don't need to bother about him.'

Tess wasn't eager to bother about him either. In spite of the fact that the afternoon at Prambanan had considerably modified her opinion of him, she felt that generating any enthusiasm for a passport picture for a bear would be beyond him and she didn't like the idea of his sneering at what they were doing. So she followed Holly's advice and carried on.

When Fuzzy had been duly photographed, Holly wanted Tess to see the large picture book her grandmother had sent, A *Child's History of England*. As they were thumbing through it, they came across a double page spread on Stonehenge.

'It's like a church for Druids,' Holly explained, 'but it doesn't have any roof. Do you suppose they can see God better that way?'

Tess wasn't sure about this.

'I think it would be scary to see God,' Holly said.

Again Tess was at a loss for a reply.

'I'm going to go to Stonehenge when I'm in England,' Holly declared, 'and see if I can find any secret messages from the people who built it. They might have written something in code on the stones.'

'I always knew I liked you,' Tess exclaimed.

'Why?'

'I think we're kindred spirits.'

'I think so too,' returned Holly, a delighted smile lighting up her small face at this unexpected idea. She was so suffused with pride and pleasure that she scarcely minded when her mother appeared at the schoolroom door a few minutes later and said that it was time for Tess to come and join the adults for a cup of tea.

'I hear you're going to organise a climb up Mt Merapi,' Philip was saying to Derek as Tess and Holly came within earshot.

'Yes, I think we should be able to get a fair sized group together, hire a guide and do it, although of course we'll have to wait 'til the end of the rainy season.'

'Do you really have to climb it again?' Mary protested. 'You came home half dead last time. I've never seen you so exhausted. You were a shattered wreck. You had lost your torch, dropped it or something and '

'I didn't drop it,' Derek interrupted, not appreciating his wife's description of him, 'the batteries went dead.'

'You don't mean to say you climb at night?' Philip demanded, aghast.

'We have to if we want to be at the summit at dawn.'

'Is that really so important?' Tess asked, sharing Philip's feelings about it.

'It is if you want to see anything before the cloud cover sets in. And in any case, it would be hard to carry enough water for a daytime climb.'

Holly, feeling that her father was leaving out all the exciting things about the climb, added, 'A man nearly fell into the crater last time, right into the boiling lava. Can you imagine? Daddy had to pull him out by his toes.'

'Rubbish,' Derek insisted. 'One fool leaned a bit too far over the edge so another chap and I grabbed his ankles for safety, that was all.'

Tess shuddered and Philip's face went a shade or two paler.

'Would you like to come with us?' Derek asked, turning to Tess.

'No thanks,' she replied hastily.

'You mustn't let this little horror put you off,' he said, with an affectionate nod at his daughter. 'It's perfectly safe. We had a couple of women along last time and they held up as well as the rest of us, better than some, in fact.'

'Well you certainly wouldn't have to grab me by the ankles,' Tess said, the very thought giving her a churning sensation in her stomach. 'There's no way I'd lean over the edge and look into the crater.'

'You wouldn't have to,' Derek assured her, 'although you might be tempted once you were there.'

Tess didn't say how very unlikely this prospect was.

'I'm with Tess,' Philip said. 'You wouldn't catch me leaning over the rim and looking into the thing either.'

'I'm glad to hear it. It's worth going just for the view from the top, it's magnificent,' Derek said. 'And of course, the whole thing is great exercise.'

He went on to tell them about the previous climb he had organised and, to Tess's surprise, seemed to be including her in the plans for the next one. Hadn't he heard what she had said?

'I'm definitely not going on that climb,' she told Philip when he was driving her home. 'The thought of going anywhere near the rim of an active volcano gives me the shivers, worse than that, it absolutely terrifies me.'

'It sort of scares me too,' he acknowledged, 'but that's the reason I'd like to do it, if I can.'

'Why, are you some kind of masochist?'

'No, I just don't like being afraid of things, that's all, and I figure that confronting deep-seated fears is the best way to overcome them.'

'That might be true for completely irrational fears,' Tess agreed, 'but when the danger is real, I'm not sure it's a good idea.'

'Yes, but unless I dangle myself over the edge like that idiot Derek told us about, and you can be sure I'm not going to do that, I don't see that there's any problem.'

'But it could erupt at any time, couldn't it, so why

would you want to be right where you'd get the worst of it?'

'I don't think it would make much difference whether you were just at the edge or back a few feet. And in any case, the volcanology station monitors seismic activity, which means it's pretty unlikely that it would go off without any warning. If there was any hint that something was going to blow, you don't think anyone would want to go ahead with the climb do you?'

'No, but are the volcanologists really that good, are their predictions really spot on?'

'I think they must come pretty close. Their instruments are so sensitive they respond to any pressure building up inside the mountain. But believe me, I'm as nervous about the whole thing as you are and you can be damn sure I'll check the latest reports before we set off on any climb.' He paused for a moment and then added, 'Do you want to know an embarrassing secret?'

Her first thought was that she didn't. Sharing a secret with someone created an intimacy between them that she didn't really want to have with Philip. Still, out of a combination of politeness and curiosity, mostly the latter, she said, 'If you don't mind telling me.'

'The fact is that just living in Yogya and seeing Mt Merapi looming up in the distance –'

'Not a very distant distance,' she put in.

'Right, in fact a damn sight too close for comfort, it

gives me the jitters.'

After another quick struggle between curiosity and intimacy, Tess replied, 'I'll let you in on my secret then, I sort of feel the same way.'

He shot her a quick glance, took one hand off the steering wheel, reached over and found hers. 'I'm glad I'm not the only one who has nightmares at the thought of being swept up in a torrent of boiling lava.'

'I promise you you're not,' she said, for some reason not minding sharing this secret with him. It actually made her feel better.

A few days later as she was splashing deliciously cool water from a large concrete vat over herself in a Javanese style bath, the unexpected sound of a car stopping in front of the house caught her attention. It was followed by an American voice speaking to Ibu in polite but rudimentary Indonesian. It was Philip.

Eager to find out what was going on, she hastily dried herself off, slipped on a fresh dress, gave her hair a quick brush and went out to find him waiting for her in the living room.

Ibu, whose language skills weren't up to dealing with English speaking visitors, mercifully glided off without even casting a look of disapproval Tess's way. She was a staunch upholder of the widely held belief that baths taken after dark made people sick.

'I hope you don't mind my dropping in on you like this,' Philip began, remembering how she had kept him standing out in the sun the last time he had stopped by unexpectedly.

'I'm glad you did,' she answered, realising with some surprise that it was actually true.

'I've been thinking about our volcano-phobia,' he began.

'Have you changed your mind about going on the climb?' Tess asked.

'No, just about –'

'About living so near Mt Merapi then?'

'Shh,' he whispered, with a horrified glance around him, 'we don't need to broadcast it to the world. People would laugh their heads off.'

'Don't worry,' Tess assured him, 'nobody in the house speaks English.'

'Are you sure?'

'Positive.'

'Well then, I had an idea that if you're free on Sunday we might just drive around to the other side of Mt Merapi. Darwati says there's a small road just before you get to a place called Muntilan that takes you right up to the base and from there you can see where a whole river of molten rocks and hot lava have come down.'

Tess shuddered. 'What a horrible idea,' she said.

'Not really, it's not as if the lava is still hot.'

'I still think I'd rather not see it, thanks. And I must say I can't figure out why you want to either.'

'Hasn't Darwati ever told you that business about the Sultan being married to the Green Sea Goddess?'

'And the lava always flowing down the other side,' Tess said, with a laugh.

'Right but I don't suppose you found it any more reassuring than I did so I thought a trip to the other side might –'

'Make us believe it?' teased Tess.

'Of course not,' he replied testily, 'but I thought that taking a look at the actual path of the lava might reassure us that Darwati had her facts right even if her reasons were a little off the wall. I mean, we'd see that for whatever reason the lava really does go down the other way and away from Yogya.'

'I'd rather just take her word for it,' Tess said, 'and try not to think about it. After all, there hasn't been a major eruption in seventeen years, not since 1954.'

'You thought about it enough to find that out,' Philip returned. 'but never mind about that. How about just going for a drive through the countryside, taking the turn-off toward Muntilan and having a look at the lava if we feel like it, giving it a miss if we don't? I promise not to press you either way. We could stop for lunch somewhere along the way and then come back to Yogya before the afternoon gets too hot. How does that sound?'

It sounds like fun, as long as you keep your promise. I don't know why I'm being so idiotic about it all but –'

'But what?'

'But since we'll be sort of skirting Mt Merapi, perhaps we'd better check with the volcanology station before we go.'

'If you want to know the truth,' Philip confessed, with a rueful smile, 'doing that has been in the back of my mind all along.'

Tess gave him an approving nod.

'The thing is,' he continued, 'I really don't have any suicidal tendencies, and even if I did, I don't think making my exit in by a wave of boiling lava would be a great way to go.'

Tess couldn't argue with this so, after they had arranged for him to pick her up on Sunday morning, he left.

Tess found the prospect of a few hours away from thoughts of Barry's treachery, the dreary progress of her thesis, and her general disenchantment with life in Yogya, so exhilarating that her companion for this deliverance could have been the devil himself and it wouldn't have mattered.

But as she had learned that afternoon at Prambanan, Philip wasn't all that much of a Satan after all and it would have taken someone far more annoying to destroy her pleasure in the drive through the beautiful Javanese countryside. Everything they passed, the flooded rice fields, lush and fertile from the recent rains, the simple wooden houses, their red tile roofs reflecting the light of the tropical sun, the sarong-clad children, younger brothers and sisters balanced on their hips, kept her from thinking very much about where she was going or who she was going with.

It was only when they actually turned down the narrow road that would take them to Muntilan that she could no longer put their unnerving destination out of her mind.

The scenery soon changed and so did Tess's mood. As the waterlogged paddy fields gave way to a thick forest of bamboo, one that seemed to enclose her in a stifling tunnel of green, she gave way to a moment of sheer panic.

Hoping for a sign that this growing sense of unease was affecting Philip too, she glanced over his way but was disappointed. He didn't seem to be thinking about anything but his car, navigating it along the deeply rutted road and minimizing the scrapes that were being inflicted on its paint job by the overhanging branches.

'Stop,' she cried, unable to keep her feelings to herself

any longer, 'I don't want to go any further.'

'But we're practically there,' he argued.

'You promised we could turn back if I changed my mind about going, remember?'

'I had no idea you'd wait to change it until there wasn't any place to turn around but I'll try.'

He did his best to make the turn but her protest had come too late. A living wall of trees and plants, undulating but unforgiving, gave him no choice but to press on closer and closer to the foot of the volcano.

Tess felt her whole body grow rigid as she gazed up at the scene of grey ash, giant boulders and cold hardened lava that twisted down the mountain. She tried to keep herself from picturing it as it had been when the rock strewn ash hadn't been cold but had been pouring down the mountain in the form of molten lava, rushing down to annihilate everyone and everything in its path.

Feeling a need for reassurance, even if Philip was the only person around to offer it, she moved closer to him and he responded by putting his arm around her.

'Maybe there's something to be said for Darwati's theory about the Sultan and the Green Sea Goddess after all,' he suggested, with a smile. 'Maybe his 'good husband' routine really is persuading Loro Kidul to send the lava down this side of the mountain away from Yogya.'

Tess considered the possibility for a moment, tried to

laugh but couldn't quite manage it and shuddered instead.

'Let's go,' she said, 'I actually don't like thinking about raging torrents of hot lava, no matter where it has gone or where it's going to go sometime in the future. It must be so awful for all the people and I can't bear to think of the animals caught in its way, it's too horrible.'

'Let's do our best to put it behind us then,' Philip said, as they finally came to a place where he could make the necessary turn. 'Maybe a drink and a nice dinner when we get back to Yogya will cheer us up. Have you been to that new place yet, the Puri Artha?'

'No, but I've heard it's lovely.'

'Then it might be the right place for putting our irrational fears to rest.'

'Great,' she said, feeling a little less sure that their fears were so irrational but glad that at least they had faced up to their demons. They had come here, taken a look at the path the lava had taken and come away unscathed.

Set in an open courtyard bordered by flowering plants dotted with flickering oil lamps and enhanced by the slightly hypnotic *gamelan* music emanating from the bar, drinks and a delicious dinner in the beautiful dining area of the Puri Artha Hotel gradually drove Tess's vague apprehensions about Mt Merapi to the back of her mind.

Philip also found himself relaxing and drifting into a more positive mood.

They were still lingering over their coffee when Mary Kent surprised them by coming over to their table.

'What luck to find you here!' she said, 'Derek and I are having a drink with a new Australian couple who have just arrived, Mark and Tabitha Carpenter. Mark is an irrigation engineer like Derek and will be working with him on the project. Come join us when you've finished your coffee, we're in the bar and I'm eager for them to meet a few people. It's Tabitha's first time overseas and Yogya isn't the easiest place in the world to adjust to. Better still, don't wait until you've finished your coffee, come now. A waiter will bring it for you.'

Finding her urging hard to resist, Tess and Philip got up and followed her.

Mary had barely finished the introductions when Derek announced, 'The Carpenters are keen mountain climbers so I've been telling them about our plans for Mt Merapi.'

'We're not really climbers,' Tabitha put in hastily, 'not with ropes and cleats and that sort of thing anyway. We just like to go walking in the mountains.'

'That sounds like climbing to me,' Mary said.

Tess echoed this opinion.

'Anyway your Mt Merapi plan sounds like good fun,' Mark said. 'Tabitha and I would really like to join in if we can.'

'Of course you can,' Derek replied, 'the more the merrier.'

'Most of us are going,' Philip said, referring to the English speaking community, 'and we're all really looking forward to it,'

Tess looked at him in astonishment. He was sounding like someone who had never known a moment's fear, rational or otherwise, of volcanoes.

Philip, noticing the rather amazed expression on her face, took it to stem from admiration for his change in attitude, whereas she was actually thinking what a cool liar he was.

'Are you a climber too?' Mark asked, turning to Tess.

'No,' she replied, shaking her head.

'But you're coming along on this one, aren't you?' Derek put in, as if there were only one possible answer.

'I don't know,' she replied. Although she was fairly sure that she did know, she just didn't feel like arguing it out with Derek at that moment. After all, if Philip could massage the truth a little why couldn't she?

'You know, I want to tell you something before you go inside,' Philip said when he had driven Tess home and pulled up in front of the door.

'Oh,' she returned, not certain that she really wanted to hear it.

'Just this really: today has meant a lot to me, sharing my

feelings about Mt Merapi with someone who doesn't think I'm a complete wimp for feeling the way I do. Going over to Muntilan together, actually looking at the path the lava has taken in the past, almost makes me feel like I've come to terms with my stupid phobia, so the thought of living within shouting distance of an active volcano doesn't scare me as much as it did.'

He paused, waiting for a similar admission from her, but when none came he added, 'I hope the day has been good for you too. I'd feel awful if the shock treatment for my problem had done anything to make yours worse, given you the horrors or anything.'

'No, nothing like that,' she said, looking pensive. 'It's more that seeing the path of the lava, all cold and grey but sort of serpentine, has left me with a funny feeling.'

'Like what?'

'You'll think I'm sort of crazy –'

'No I won't.'

'Well, it's left me feeling like the mountain has something to tell me, something I almost –' then remembering Barry's reaction to the idea of almost knowing something, but not quite, and worried that Philip might feel the same, she left the end of her sentence hanging in the air. 'Do you know what I mean?'

'I can't honestly say I do. Can you –'

'Forget it,' she said. 'I don't really know what I meant

either so you absolutely mustn't worry about today. It didn't freak me out or anything, I promise.'

'That's good anyway,' he said, hoping she was telling the truth. 'I'll see you in the office tomorrow then.'

Wondering whether or not it would be a good idea to take his relationship with her any further, he watched her go up the path to her door.

During the next few days Tess had trouble getting Mt Merapi and the path of the lava out of her mind. When she gazed at it over her morning tea in front of the house, her own words as she had said them to Barry, 'something I almost know but not quite,' kept coming back to her.

How was that possible, she asked herself, how could she almost know something but not quite? Either she knew it or she didn't.

No that's not completely true, she corrected herself, sometimes there were things that slipped to the back of her mind where she couldn't quite get to them, at least not right away. She knew they were there, though, and generally she'd think of them hours, or even days, later. They'd just pop into her head when she was thinking about something else. It happened all the time, mostly for little things but she supposed it could it happen for fairly big things too. Why not?

The disappearance of the Mataram Kingdom had something to do with the path of the lava, she was sure of that. And the more she thought about that grey river of ash twisting down the mountain, the more certain she was that a boiling river of death must have come rushing down towards Prambanan at some point, submerging some things on its way, sparing others, following the contours of the land and some logic of its own. It would have washed effortlessly over wooden homes and palaces, cremating them and everyone in them as it went, even lapped around the base of the temples that had been built to propitiate the very gods who were there to protect them. Not only would that have been possible, she reasoned, it would have been highly likely.

That would mean that Darwati wasn't quite right about the lava always going down the Muntilan side of the mountain but how could she be?

So few people in that ancient Kingdom would have been able to read or write that few, if any, historical records would have been kept.

With these reflections taking hold in Tess's mind, she found herself coming to the conclusion that there had never been anything mysterious at all in the disappearance of the Mataram Kingdom. After all, with its capital built on the flood plain of an active volcano, hadn't a sudden violent tragedy been more an inevitability than a surprise?

Yet beyond the worst affected areas, she reflected, some remnants of the Kingdom's social order must have persisted. The rice farmers must have continued the changeless rhythm of their lives; the annual monsoon must have come and gone with undiminished predictability. The fertility of the soil, already sufficient to generate an agricultural surplus capable of supporting an elaborate court, must have become even greater, thanks to the addition of the newest layer of volcanic ash.

Tess became so excited about these ideas as they whirled around in her mind that she forgot about breakfast, leapt into the first passing bicycle rickshaw she saw without bothering to haggle over the price, and directed the driver to the office.

Thank heavens Philip had changed from an enemy to a friend, she told herself, and that once upon a time he had been an archaeologist too. And even more importantly, that he truly shared her interest in her thesis and she could talk to him about her ideas.

She was halfway there before she glanced at her watch and realised that, in her excitement, she had forgotten how early it was. The office wouldn't be open yet and he would still be at home. She reached up, tapped the driver on the shoulder and gave him directions to Philip's house instead.

He was just sitting down to breakfast, hair still wet from his morning shower, when she rushed through the door like a human cyclone.

'I figured it out,' she cried without preamble.

He regarded her with mute astonishment but his maid, who considered all foreigners slightly insane, was unperturbed by this odd behaviour so early in the morning. She simply motioned Tess to a chair and offered her a cup of coffee.

'What did you figure out?' Philip asked.

Her words tumbled out in a breathless jumble so it took a little guesswork on Philip's part to get it all straight but he managed it. His reaction was considerably less enthusiastic than she had hoped.

'But there's nothing new about the volcanic eruption idea,' he protested.

'Oh, I know that,' she replied impatiently, refusing to give way to her disappointment, 'but other people have just mentioned it and then thrown it into a basket of possibilities along with earthquakes and wars and epidemics as an explanation of what might have happened. They haven't followed through on any of it. They just say it was all a mystery and let it go at that. The difference is that I'm certain it was –'

She broke off as one of his old looks of condescending incredulity crossed his face.

'But don't you see the significance of all this?' she demanded, in a tone that implied as much disdain for his mental powers as he was showing for hers.

He didn't enjoy being belittled any more than she did.

'No, I don't,' he said, in his most patronising manner. 'I'm afraid you'll have to enlighten me.'

She repeated her main points, only adding, 'It shows that the court must have been very near Prambanan, just on slightly lower ground, that's all. Any idiot should be able to see that.'

'Then perhaps that's why it's clear to you,' he replied, spreading a spoonful of pineapple jam on his toast, 'but to people who are a little more aware of the complexities of this matter, it's not quite so obvious. In any case, I'm afraid I have some bad news for you. Professor Hariyanto from the Archaeology Department, you must know him, he says he knows you, was in my office yesterday afternoon looking for funding for an excavation he's planning. He says that a stone tablet inscribed in the old Javanese script, Kawi, I think he called it, has been uncovered by some farmers in a field near Tegal on the North Coast.'

A feeling of cold dread ran down her spine, one that told her she wasn't going to like what Philip was about to say,

'Apparently it's a proclamation about taxes for the entire Mataram Kingdom,' he continued, 'and it states very clearly that it is being issued in the capital and it specifically mentions Tegal.'

'But that's impossible,' she gasped.

'Professor Hariyanto didn't seem to think so. I'm afraid you're just going to have to reconcile yourself to the fact that your little theory is out the window.'

'No I'm not,' she retorted, hotly. 'Surely you must see that since the eruption of Mt Merapi and the disappearance of the capital happened at the same time, it would be absurd to think they had nothing to do with each other. One of them must have caused the other or else they both must be the result of the same thing.'

'I'm really sorry,' he said, actually sounding like he was. 'I hate to put a damper on that vivid imagination of yours but when it comes to weighing the romantic notions of a graduate student against the hard evidence presented by an experienced archaeologist, what can I do? I have to treat your ideas about Prambanan for what they are; childish fantasies.'

'But they're not!'

'Come now, you haven't a shred of hard evidence.'

'I'd think the tumbled down state of Prambanan would be evidence enough but if it isn't, don't worry. I'll get whatever evidence you need.'

'On your own,' he asked, 'without any resources at your disposal or any funds for an excavation?' He looked highly

347

unconvinced. 'I doubt it. I'd put your chances of success somewhere around zero.'

'Don't lose any sleep over it. I'll get hold of the funds I need somehow.'

'I'm sorry to have to tell you this but you won't get them from me.'

'Are you funding Professor Hariyanto?'

'I'm considering it.'

'At least I know whose side you're on then.'

'I wish you wouldn't look at it that way.'

'I wish I didn't have to,' she returned. 'Fortunately the Southeast Asia Foundation isn't the only place that has money.'

'I'm sure you're right and I'd be very interested to see what luck you have. In the meantime, you'd better have some toast. Try the pineapple jam, my cook makes it herself and it's not bad.'

'Great idea,' Tess said, and taking a large spoonful of the sticky yellow goo, she spread it across a piece of toast, hurled it across the table at him and stormed out.

I may not get my evidence in time for my thesis, she told herself as she ran out onto the street and hailed a bicycle rickshaw, but it'll be in time for the rest of my life. I just hope that bastard, Philip, feels like a complete fool when I do.

Shit, Philip thought as he heard the door slam behind

348

her, that looks like the end of trying to direct the course of her thesis. But there wasn't anything he could do about it now, not if she was going to be so irrational. Oh well, perhaps her thesis wasn't all that important anyway, perhaps it had just been an excuse for spending more time with her.

No of course it hadn't, he assured himself. Still, there were times when he almost wished he were gay. Those lucky guys didn't have to deal with women at all, well hardly at all, although he supposed they had mothers and possibly sisters too. Nevertheless, it didn't seem fair that he had to have his hormones in the so-called 'right place' when other people got off so damn lightly.

The last thing Tess was thinking about as she made her way toward Professor Hariyanto's office was her hormones. She was still on a sort of high from throwing the marmalade toast at Philip. Seeing his face covered with pineapple jam had done wonders for her spirits, it gave her a laugh whenever she thought about the astonished expression on her face.

Professor Hariyanto greeted her with the usual Javanese politeness and, in response to her questions, not only told her about the recent discovery in Tegal but gave her a translation of the inscription from old Javanese into modern Indonesian.

'When was it found?' she asked him.

'About four months ago.'

Damn, she muttered to herself, in all this time nobody ever bothered to mention it to her even though there were a number of people in the archaeology department who knew, or who should have realised, how much it would interest her.

Someone once told her that if you didn't ask the right questions, you wouldn't get the right answers, or possibly any answers at all. Well, Java was certainly an extreme example of that. At that moment she would have given a good deal to have had another piece of pineapple toast at hand so she could startle Professor Hariyanto out of his shell of politeness. But she let the moment pass, what else could she do? The Javanese had always treated her as an outsider and when it came down to it, that's what she was.

She was in a bleak mood when she left Professor Hariyanto's office. She went out into the growing heat of the morning, took out the inscription and carefully reread it.

It had been written in the year 795 and was, as Philip had told her, a proclamation issued by the raja about taxes. When she was sure she thoroughly understood it all, she crumpled it into a tight little ball and shoved it into her handbag.

Well that was that, she reasoned, she would just have to live with it.

A feeling of restlessness swept over her but there was nowhere on this crowded island that a foreigner even do anything as simple as going for a walk without being followed by hordes of children calling out 'hello, hello' every five seconds.

If she could just walk around and think about things, she mused, then maybe she could figure out what to do about her thesis, about her life too, for that matter. Even though it had been an absolute rollercoaster of a morning, she knew there must be answers out there somewhere but at the moment they were maddeningly out of her reach.

A glimpse of Kanwa, who was just disappearing into a building on the other side of the quadrangle, distracted her from her thoughts. He was so busy all the time that he was rarely at home when she went to see Mini but she remembered how nice he had been that day at the zoo.

The zoo; that was the one place in Yogya where she could saunter along shady paths, stop for a drink under the thatched roof of a wooden lean-to and, on a weekday morning, probably encounter no one but an occasional pair of lovers strolling hand in hand under the unceasing eyes of the animals.

She flagged down a rickshaw and was just negotiating an acceptable price when Darwati, crossing the quadrangle on her way to class, spotted her and came over to ask where she was going.

Her manner was friendly but Tess sensed the slight reserve her friend had shown ever since their argument about the diamonds.

'To the zoo.'

'By yourself?' Darwati gasped.

'Why not?' Then on impulse, she added, 'Why don't you come with me?'

Darwati shook her head regretfully.

'I cannot,' she said. 'I have a big examination this morning and then Sigit is meeting me afterwards.'

'Too bad,' Tess sighed, but seeing a mask of defensive coolness slip down across Darwati's face, she added hastily, 'I didn't mean that it was too bad about Sigit, I'm glad that's working out for you. I just meant that the zoo would be a lot more fun if you came too.'

Darwati's frosty mask was replaced by a warm smile that Tess found reassuring so she wished her luck on the exam, climbed into the rickshaw and started off across town.

Going to the zoo at a time when she would ordinarily be working not only gave Tess a glorious feeling of freedom but a light-hearted sense that she was being a little bit naughty, as well.

Yet as soon as she had paid the very modest admission

fee and walked in, her spirits took a downward turn.

For a moment she put this down to the fact that she had never been to a zoo alone before, it just wasn't the sort of thing people ordinarily did. But then why should she let that bother her, she wondered. After all, if she could come halfway around the world by herself, she should certainly be able to take a trip across the city to the zoo on her own. It wasn't as if she didn't know anybody there, she knew the tiger that had caused such a stir at Gajah Mada when it had ambled into the Food Science Building.

The first thing she would do, she decided, was see what had happened to him. So she did and was highly distressed with what she found.

Now gaunt and restive, the famous animal - famous around Yogya anyway - was pacing back and forth in its cage, dejection apparent in its every movement.

'You must wish like mad that you had never come here and gotten yourself into this mess,' she said, almost as if she were talking to another human being. 'Whatever you were looking for, a quick lunch I suppose, couldn't possibly have been worth ending up here.'

The tiger gave no indication of appreciating her sympathy.

'Sometimes I feel the same way,' she continued, 'today for instance. I almost wish the same thing, that I'd never come here. I know I have no right to compare my situation with yours. I'm free to walk away, I could even go to the airline office today and buy a ticket back to Philadelphia if I really wanted to. I'm fantastically lucky compared to you but I'm just not in the sort of mood to appreciate that the way I should. Nothing's going the way I had hoped. I almost feel like I'm in sort of a cage too. It's just that the bars of my cage are human bars, made up of the people around me, people who don't do anything to help me, people who won't tell me what's going on and who refuse to care about what I do.'

She could hear her voice rising to a level that was perilously close to that of a childish whine and, even though there was only an animal to hear her, she began to feel embarrassed about her stupid moaning.

Nevertheless, seemingly unable to stop herself, she continued, 'But why don't they care? Why does everyone make things so difficult for me?'

It was only then that the tiger appeared to take notice. It stopped its pacing, sat down on its haunches directly in front of her, took several deep panting breaths that not only expanded its chest but appeared to enlarge its entire body and, fixing her with a stare so penetrating that it seemed to look into her very soul, opened its massive jaws and addressed her with a thunderous roar. It resonated throughout the entire zoo and seemed to tell his fellow captives what it had heard and exactly what it thought of

354

this wimp of a girl.

Having made its point, the tiger then got back on all four feet and, with an imperious swish of its gorgeous tail, suggested that the King of the Jungle had given Tess enough of its valuable time and attention. It turned away from her and resumed its usual pacing.

Tess was convinced that something important had passed between the tiger and herself but it was a moment or two before she realised what it was.

When she did, she broke out laughing and exclaimed, 'You amazing creature, you must be the smartest tiger in the whole world. You were able to look inside me and read my thoughts, make me see what a worm I was being, feeling sorry for myself like this and blaming my troubles on everybody else. I should be glad that nobody else in the Archaeology Department seems to care much about my research. If it makes them blind to what I'm doing, they won't try to stop me from doing it and that leaves me free to do anything I want.

'And as far as Philip is concerned, I don't need his extensions or even his grants. The temple walls and the other finds nearby have already given me more than enough material for my thesis. Of course, I'm sure there's a lot more for me to uncover but my life won't be over the day I hand in the horrible thing.'

Even if Tegal was the capital at the time Professor

Hariyanto's inscription was written, that didn't mean it had always been, or always would be the capital. It might have been moved by the time Prambanan was built, that was all, and somehow, someday, she was going to show the world that she was right.

Tess lifted her head, took several deep breaths much as the tiger had done, and could almost feel herself growing taller and stronger.

'There, you incredible beast,' she continued, this time fixing it with her stare and, without realising it, speaking out loud. 'I'll gladly give you all the admiration you deserve and I won't give you a reason to put me down anymore. And if I can stand up to you, the fiercest, proudest creature in the world, I can certainly stand up to sly, slinky, selfish, miserable human beings like –'

'I hope you don't mean me,' she heard a voice behind her say. 'And I don't mean to ask a rude question or anything but have you totally flipped out?'

Whirling around, Tess saw Barry standing there with a mixture of amusement and concern on his face.

'What are you doing here?' she gasped.

'Are you the only one allowed to come to the zoo?'

'You followed me,' she cried, outraged.

'No I didn't. I just got up this morning, looked out the window and decided that it was the right sort of day for a heart to heart with a tiger. And being a pretty astute guy,

I figured that the best place to find one was at the zoo, so here I am.'

'So I see,' she said, and added ungraciously, 'just my bad luck.'

Pointedly turning and walking away, she passed several cages housing other cats, a family of scampering monkeys and three swaybacked pigs before she felt Barry's firm grip on her arm.

'Listen, I didn't follow you,' he insisted, 'not exactly anyway. I ran into Darwati and she told me she had seen you setting off for the zoo so that's why I'm here. Although I admit that having a chat with a tiger wasn't high on my list of priorities. To tell you the truth, I've never been very good at getting a conversation going with any of our stripy friends. For some reason, they never seem very eager to talk to me.'

'They're not the only ones.'

'Look, Tess, I can understand why you're furious with me. Believe me, if there was any way I could undo what happened that weekend with Cynthia, God knows, I would. But since I can't, couldn't you just bring yourself to forgive me enough to talk to me once in a while, like now for instance? Would it kill you to have a quick Coke with me in that stall over there?'

He pointed to the thatched roof lean-to not far away, with tables and stools set out in front of it. A colourful display of bottles of sticky sweet drinks on a shelf in the background alerted the thirsty visitor to its wares.

'Suppose we went over there and shot the breeze for a few minutes, do you think you could survive that?'

'I'm not too sure.'

'Take a chance then, give it a try. Just think about it, the only two English speakers in this entire bestiary quenching their thirst by themselves. Or worse, walking around with their tongues hanging out simply because they won't sit down together for ten minutes. Does that make any sense to you?'

'I guess not,' Tess admitted, 'and the truth is, I am getting a bit thirsty. If I don't have a drink with you, I'll have to have one on my own so I might as well try putting up with you.'

'Where are those women who like to build up a guy's ego,' he mused, as they made their way over to the drinks stall, 'that's what I'd like to know.'

'If you want to go look for one, don't let me keep you.'

Barry ignored this and concentrated on the selection of drinks instead.

'I guess a warm Coke's the least revolting thing we can hope for,' he concluded, sitting down at one of the tables.

After giving their order, he asked, 'Listen, are you okay?'

'Of course, why wouldn't I be?'

'Well, you've got to admit that shooting off to the zoo in the middle of the morning isn't exactly the sort of thing you usually do.'

'I don't see anything wrong with it,' she returned defensively.

'It's not a crime, I'll grant you that but you were talking to that tiger like it was Sigmund Freud or something. That's a pretty weird thing to do. I think you could use a vacation, get away from Java for a while. After all, life here is enough to drive anyone round the bend.'

'I have not been driven round the bend. It's you who are totally out of touch with your surroundings.'

'Hey, I thought we were talking about your problems, not mine,' he protested.

'I don't have a problem. You're just imagining –'

'You come here and pour your heart out to a tiger and you think you don't have a problem?'

'No, I don't. You're the one who has a problem, if you think you can live in a Javanese village without coming to terms with *Kebatinan*.'

'You mean that Javanese mysticism stuff,' he exclaimed, horrified. 'Don't tell me you've fallen for it all of a sudden?'

'No, of course I haven't. I'm just trying to understand it, that's all.'

'Don't even try,' he said. 'You'll find that it messes with your head in a way you might not be able to shake off when you want to get back to the real world, which you will when you get back to Philadelphia. No rational person can understand it. In any case, what's that got to do with your skipping out of the library and playing psychoanalyst-and-patient with that stripy character?'

'Haven't you ever heard of tigers with human souls?' she asked.

'Yes, not often though. Most people don't want to talk to foreigners about that sort of thing which is pretty understandable when you think about it. It must be damn embarrassing.'

'It doesn't embarrass me,' Tess said.

'Good God, Tess,' Barry cried, suddenly alarmed, 'you can't mean you actually –'

'Believe it?' She gave a quick laugh and then said, somewhat ruefully, 'No, I suppose I don't, not really. Not now anyway, when I'm here talking to you.'

'You better talk to me more often then.'

'Silly! I wasn't really talking to the tiger, I was sort of thinking out loud and –'

'That's a relief.'

'It's just that the tiger gave me the most piercing stare you can possibly imagine and I felt like it was looking right into my heart and into my mind too. And I was so mortified that what it found there wasn't good enough, it made me realise things about myself. Bad things that

I had never seen before.'

'Like what, for instance?'

'Like the fact that I was being weak, letting other people dictate how I felt about things. Allowing them to make me miserable when I should have been strong, should have ignored them, gone ahead and done what I really wanted. And with those amazing amber eyes right on me, it seemed as if I was getting the message straight from the tiger itself. So it couldn't be just an ordinary animal, could it?'

'A pretty big 'as if', if you ask me,' Barry said.

'But it does show that there really is something in what the Javanese mystics say about tigers,' she pointed out. 'Some of them really must have human souls.'

'Let's not jump to any conclusions.'

'I'm not jumping, I just wish I was.'

'Why do you wish that?'

'Can't you see, if you take any mystical qualities away from the tiger, you destroy an idea that could be really beautiful? I mean, just think about having this extraordinary creature actually communicating with me, even if it was to point out some unflattering truths about my character. Isn't that the most exciting thing you've ever heard?'

'No, it isn't. Like most kids, I was brought up on stories about Superman and Spider-Man and dinosaurs that rise up from the dead. They were far more exciting than some old Javanese duffer claiming that he had been to Chicago and putting it down to astral travel when, in reality, he had never been more than a few miles from his village. Hasn't it occurred to you that it might be a coincidence that you happened to figure out a few things about yourself just at the moment when that tiger was eyeing you up, probably wondering how you would taste in a sandwich?'

Noticing how her face fell at this possibility, he tried to make her feel better by adding, 'Listen to me. I know the Javanese think that the world is full of all kinds of spirits, most of them bad. And they believe that all kinds of crazy things can happen to people, like having out-of-body experiences or getting turned into animals or God knows what. But you're not Javanese, you don't really live in that world, you're just dropping in for a ten-month visit, and that's not the same thing at all. Their world isn't your world and if you let these weird Javanese ideas affect you too much, you're going to have a hell of a time when you get back to the real world, your world, my world. Everybody's going to think you've gone off the deep end.'

'The Javanese world is real too,' Tess argued, truculently.

'Real for them, maybe, but it's not real for you or me so you'd better make an effort to hang on to your sanity, in spite of what I'm sure are continuous efforts on the part of the Javanese to relieve you of it.'

'What I don't understand is how an anthropologist

can consistently refuse to see that there are things, lots of things, that we would do well to learn from the Javanese.'

'He can do it by finding out about that crazy stuff but basically leaving Javanese ideas and culture to the Javanese.'

After considering this for a moment, she gave a tentative nod and said, 'Maybe.'

'Definitely,' he said emphatically, then asked hopefully, 'Friends again?'

'Maybe,' she equivocated, not actually sure she wanted to be.

'Can I take that as a yes?'

'Take it any way you like,' she replied.

Thinking about it later that evening, she wondered whether or not it was ever possible to be friends with someone she had had sex with and concluded that it probably wasn't.

At the same time that evening, Philip was musing on the insidious effect of pineapple jam on his outlook on life and realising that, for the first time since he was a kid, he was actually damn lonely. Could it be that Tess, or rather her absence from his life, was making him feel that way? He was going to miss having her share her ideas with him, perhaps not only to improve her thesis but because of the way her face lit up whenever she talked about the Mataram Kingdom.

Then he thought about how often he had extinguished that light by putting her down. Maybe that girl he had gone out with ages ago, he couldn't remember her name, had actually had a point when she called him an insensitive bastard.

But Tess was different, he told himself, and his relationship with her, more like a mentor than anything else, was different. She was a dreamer, there was no changing that, so what choice did he have but to bring her back to reality on the subject of her thesis?

Sooner or later she would have to face up to the fact that her so-called plans for her thesis were really just dreams rooted in a kind of romantic nonsense, so wasn't he being kind when he told her the truth? What was the point of building a relationship, or researching a thesis, based on a childish fantasy?

It was bound to end in disaster with a lot of pain for both of them, or at least for him.

Then Philip caught himself. Building a relationship with Tess? What in the world had he been thinking? He must be insane. But then wasn't love just a code word for those moments of sexual insanity that human beings so often fell prey to; moments when a woman could even throw a piece of pineapple toast at you and you didn't hold it against her; moments when it actually made her seem even more attractive? Of course it would only be a woman who did something like that, no man would ever do anything so outrageous.

But never mind about all that now, he told himself. Tess and how he felt about her was the basic problem. The question was, what was he going to do about it?

Tess, by contrast, gave very little thought to Philip in the hours and days following the pineapple toast incident and she wasn't thinking about him at all as she hurried down Jalan Malioboro one Saturday morning a few weeks later. She was on her way to Toko Mirota to buy a new thermos and some peanut cookies for Holly Kent, items that should prove useful when they went 'on an explore' as Holly called it, out to one of the numerous temple sites on the Kedu Plain. But her journey was intercepted by Barry, who came charging out of the newly-opened Tip Top Ice Cream Parlour when he saw her.

'This place isn't half bad,' he reported, 'and I can definitely vouch for the coconut ice cream. Come in and give it a try.'

Tess hesitated. She wanted to get on with her plans for the day but resisting the lure of something cold and thirst-quenching in the middle of a hot Yogya morning wasn't easy. And she wasn't very good at resisting temptation, she usually succumbed.

'It seems like you're super busy these days,' Barry remarked when they were ensconced at a table and she had agreed with him about the coconut ice cream.

'I am, I'm frantic.'

'What about?'

'My thesis, what else? I've broadened my topic and changed my whole approach to everything.'

'Is that a good idea at this point?'

'Absolutely,' she said, a spark of excitement lighting up her eyes. 'It's incredible the way almost everything I've found fits in with the fantasies I used to have about life in the Mataram Kingdom. Sometimes, when I look at a panel of relief carvings it's almost like looking at an old photograph of something I'd almost forgotten but the picture brings it back. At least, that's the way I feel sometimes when –'

'Yeah,' Barry interrupted, getting the same vaguely uncomfortable feeling he had had when he found her talking to the tiger. 'Don't you think it's a little late to broaden your topic?' he cautioned, wanting to steer the conversation away from any of her off-the-wall ideas. 'Aren't you more or less at the point where most people start narrowing their topic down?'

'Probably, but you can't run your life by what other

people do can you?'

'Sometimes it can be a guide.'

'Sometimes it can be a straitjacket,' she returned. 'I was always running up against lack of evidence for what I really wanted to do.'

'And that is?'

'Find the capital of the Mataram Kingdom, of course. So instead of zeroing in on that alone, I'm going to do it in the context of a social and cultural history of Central Java during the Classical Period. After all, that really only means widening my research to include the Sailendra dynasty and then instead of scratching around for pathetic little bits of information like I've been doing, drawing on all the material around the lower levels of Borobudur, I'll be deluged with material. And how much would the life of the people have changed just because there was a different dynasty at the top?'

'Beats me!'

'Well, look at your village, probably the life there isn't all that different from what it was a thousand years ago.'

'Too right, that's the trouble with it.'

'Of course all this does give me about a million extra things to do,' she continued, 'but it's so worth it because it's changed my attitude about everything and instead of dragging myself to the library every morning, I wake up dying to get started.'

'That's a good thing then,' he admitted.

'More than good, it's great. Part of my problem was that I was doing so much library research it was like being back at Penn, except that this library was a lot hotter and the stuff I had to read was a lot harder because so much of it was in Indonesian or Dutch. But now I'm spending most of my time going around the smaller temple sites, there are about a million of them within a few hours' bus ride from here. It's so much more fun and I feel so much more in control of my topic.

'I'm not constantly bumping up against the shortage, the total absence really, of any hard data so I don't get the same sneers when I talk about it. People might look a little sceptical, I'll admit, but that's not the same thing. I'd still love more than anything to find the capital of Mataram but if I can't do that in time for my thesis, I'll just carry on looking for it afterwards. My life won't end the day I hand in my thesis, will it, and I'll still be able to go back to Pennsylvania with plenty of material to write it all up. Going around doing the research is great fun, especially when Holly comes with me and –'

'You can't mean little Holly Kent, can you?'

'Why not?'

'What's she got to do with anything?'

'She thinks that going 'on an explore' as she calls it, looking for a lost palace from an ancient kingdom, is a sort of magical adventure.'

'Isn't she a little young to have racked up much expertise in archaeology, or is she just your mascot or something?'

'No of course not, but she's a great person to talk to about my ideas.'

'A kid of five, you've got to be kidding.'

'Holly's eight.'

'Same thing. Too young to smoke, drink or have sex, in other words, useless, and certainly too young to be called in as some kind of assistant on an archaeology project.'

'It's because she's so young that she's so wonderful,' Tess explained, 'great for me anyway. She never asks awful questions like where's the evidence, what are your sources, do you read Sanskrit, do you have financing for an excavation? Not that that would make any difference because, even if I did, there would be no way of knowing exactly where to dig. It's just that I'm absolutely sure it has to be somewhere in the vicinity of Prambanan. Best of all, Holly's too young to laugh at what I know any professional archaeologist would deride as nothing more than romantic nonsense and some kind of wild goose chase. She just lets herself be caught up in the enchantment of searching for a long-lost kingdom and I love that about her.'

'It's hard to see how spending long hot hours crammed into a sweltering bus between the vegetables and the chickens, and maybe even a goat or two, can be that enchanting. Are you sure a few fallen down temples are worth it?'

'Of course I'm sure. I admit they're not huge and glorious like Borobudur or Prambanan but –'

'They're small and ignominious?' Barry suggested.

'No you idiot,' she cried, 'they may be small but the carvings on some of them are terrific. And so little has been written about them that I never know which ones are going to turn out to have some gem of information until I get there. That's what makes them so interesting. As for the goats, the chickens and the heat, things like that don't matter when it's all for a dream I've had for years. Ever since I was Holly's age, in fact.'

'They may not matter to you but I'm surprised they're not something of a deterrent for Holly.'

'They don't seem to be. She just thinks of them as making it all more of an adventure and I have to say, her enthusiasm is contagious. Looking for clues as to where the capital might have been is a lot more fun when she comes along.'

'Any luck?' he asked, trying to look like he was taking all this seriously.

'Not so far.'

'Don't you get kind of discouraged when you tramp around the countryside all day and don't come up with anything?'

'No. If clues were easy to find, the site of the capital, the royal palace and all that would already have been discovered, wouldn't they?'

'Maybe.'

'In any case,' she said, scraping the last of her ice cream out of the dish, 'I'd better be going. Holly will be wondering where I am.'

'Hold on, I'll drop you by there.'

They climbed on Big Red and no further conversation was possible until they arrived at the Kents' door.

'Will it be later this afternoon when you bring Holly back?' he asked, as she was climbing off.

'Probably.'

'Good, I might see you then,' he said, and drove off.

Tess's excursions with Holly generally ended with tea and cake at the Kents' when they returned. Derek had started playing tennis with Philip and the Carpenters after work on Saturday afternoons and he generally invited them back to the house afterwards. Knowing this, Elizabeth and some of the other English speakers took to dropping by and joining the little party.

Unfortunately for Barry, Felicia, whom he didn't much like, frequently brought her boyfriend, Paul, whom he liked even less, to these impromptu gatherings so Barry started avoiding them.

Nevertheless, one Saturday afternoon a month or so after his ice cream meeting with Tess, Barry found himself in desperate need of a little English conversation and a soothing piece of Mary Kent's coconut cake.

He had been invited to the circumcision of the village headman's great nephew, a boy of eight or nine, and such ceremonies always left him feeling a little frazzled. It was customary for the procedure to be carried out on a number of boys, all about that age, at one time and the thought of how terrified they must be lying there waiting for their turn and how awful the pain must be when they finally got the knife without the benefit of any anaesthetic; it was enough to make him feel positively sick.

He knew that coconut cake wasn't usually considered a very good remedy for a slightly queasy-feeling stomach but in this case, accompanied as it would be by a little socialising, it seemed just the thing. Tess was likely to be there too, which should make it interesting.

She wasn't there when he arrived but Mary was just cutting him a second piece of cake when he heard her voice, along with Holly's, outside the front door.

A moment later they burst onto the scene, Holly declaring that she would kill for a cup of tea, being sent off to wash first and then coming back, full of tales of the day's adventures.

It seemed there had been three goats on the bus and one of them had made a mess right next to Holly's seat so they had had to get up and move and everybody had laughed and –

'That's quite enough,' Mary had said.

'But –' Holly protested. She was not an easy child to suppress.

During the ensuing altercation, Barry's eyes followed the changing expressions on Tess's face.

He'd thoroughly botched things with this girl, he told himself. She clearly didn't want to have anything more to do with him, at least not in the way he wanted. This business of being 'just friends' wasn't his sort of thing at all, so why was he wasting time giving it a try with Tess?

He realised he had actually been the one who had suggested being friends again but he had meant it to include something a little more exhilarating. Why hadn't she figured that out and why couldn't he get her out of his mind?

He was worried about her, that was it. After all, they had had such a great time together in Bali, spectacular actually, so he couldn't simply stand back and let her go off the deep end with all this Javanese mysticism stuff. Just because it was all nonsense didn't mean that it wasn't dangerous, especially for someone as ditsy as Tess. He had heard stories about it in the village; people could be made sick by evil spells and sometimes even die from them.

The power of suggestion was strong and people who believed in them often succumbed to the symptoms called for in the wicked incantations.

Tess needed someone to look out for her, that was certain and who else was going to do it? Javanese friends like Darwati probably believed in that stuff so they wouldn't be any help at all. The Kents wouldn't be much good either; Tess wasn't close enough to any of them except Holly and she was too young to be any use. As for Philip, he was too self-centred to look out for anyone but Number One.

The only person who could really keep an eye on Tess was him and under the circumstances, this was the best vantage point from which to do it. He could watch her expression and catch bits of what she was saying and no one, least of all Tess, would be any the wiser.

He wasn't entirely correct.

Philip hadn't seen Tess very much since the morning of the pineapple jam incident. He suspected she was avoiding him and, in any case, he wanted time to sort out and understand how he really felt about her. Why risk either the embarrassment of a rejection or the dangers of an involvement unless he was very sure of what he wanted? The trouble was, he couldn't quite trust Barry not to nip in and screw up his plans. What was he up to right now, for instance, what were guys like Barry ever up to?

At least Tess was smart, she'd be able to see Barry for the womaniser he was. Or would she? She was so –

His train of thought was interrupted by Mark Carpenter, who was talking about the change in the weather.

'It's not raining anymore,' he was saying, 'so when are we going to climb Mt Merapi?'

'Let's do it while Paul's here,' Felicia said eagerly, 'it would give him chance to get some great pictures.'

Paul looked like he didn't quite share her enthusiasm for this opportunity, instead he just muttered something under his breath that nobody could hear.

'I think you're all lunatics,' Mary declared, 'but never mind. Tess, Elizabeth and I can drive up to Selo and meet you with a picnic afterwards.'

'Bring lots of beer,' said Mark Carpenter. 'We'll need it by then.'

'Actually I'd like to go on the climb,' put in Elizabeth, with a rebellious glance in Mary's direction.

'Good for you,' Barry said approvingly.

A lively discussion then broke out about the necessary gear to bring along.

'A torch; that's a flashlight on your side of the Atlantic, I believe,' Derek said, translating for the Americans, 'and plenty of extra batteries.'

'Why will we need them?' Paul demanded. 'We're not going to be up there after dark, are we?'

Derek, surprised at the question, set him straight. 'We'll be doing most of the upwards trek at night,' he said. 'That way if we leave here in the afternoon we can drive as far as Selo, pick up a guide and be at the volcanology bungalow in time to catch a few hours' sleep before starting out again. If we leave there about two in the morning, we can make it to the top in time for sunrise.'

Philip, quick to see that Paul didn't look very pleased at this plan, took full advantage of the presence of an ally. 'It would be a lot safer to forgo the sunrise and do the climb in the daytime,' he suggested.

'No need for that if we're careful,' Derek assured him.

'I'd hate like hell to leg it all the way up there and miss the sunrise,' Barry said, more to annoy Philip and that little creep, Paul, than to safeguard the aesthetic rewards of the expedition.

'The view at dawn should be fantastic,' Felicia told Paul encouragingly.

'But we'll only have a short window of time to look at it before the cloud cover comes over and cuts everything off,' Elizabeth put in.

'If you guys are afraid of the dark,' Barry said, with a wicked glint in his eye, 'you can stay back and help Mary and Tess bring the picnic.'

Everyone laughed except Philip, who went white with silent anger and Paul, who declared that he was 'only concerned for Felicia's safety.'

'Hey, just kidding,' Barry said, not entirely truthfully, 'no offence meant.'

'Sure,' Philip replied, trying to sound like a good sport but not fooling anyone.

Ignoring this exchange, Derek continued to hold forth on the practicalities of the climb; what to bring, who else might want to be included and a few helpful tips on how not to fall into the open crater of boiling lava at the summit.

On hearing this last piece of advice, Philip was nearly overwhelmed with a sense of panic. I thought I'd gotten over this, he murmured to himself, and I will. The others aren't bothered about the idea of the open crater, not even Tabitha. She's not scared; she just doesn't like the thought of a long climb. Only Tess and I are actually afraid. I can see the fear in her eyes and she's not even going. Just hearing about it frightens her. I'm stronger than she is and I'm going to go no matter how I feel about it. I'm not going to let myself be dominated by my fears and I'm not going to let that bastard, Barry, or anyone else, not even Tess, see that I'm afraid.

He took a deep breath, tried to look a little more relaxed and pasted a smile on his face but he was too late to deceive Tess. She had recognised the fear in his eyes and, thinking of the supercilious way he had treated her on the pineapple toast morning, and about a thousand other mornings, afternoons and evenings as well, she revelled in this unexpected opportunity to get back at him. She'd show him who was superior now.

'Actually I've changed my mind,' she told Derek, 'I think I'll go on the climb after all. Hearing you talk about it makes it seem too exciting to miss.'

A chorus of approval rose up from everyone except Mary, who said, 'Oh dear, I was hoping you'd keep me company,' and from Philip, who gave her a look of unspoken reproach which said that she had betrayed him.

Tess responded with a defiant flick of her plait and accepted a second piece of Mary's delicious cake.

After a further discussion of the climb, Barry decided he had had enough tea for a lifetime but he never had quite enough food, no matter how much cake he had eaten. He suggested that they all go out for a beer and some Chinese food.

'I'm afraid I've got work to do,' Philip replied.

'On Saturday night?' Barry exclaimed. 'You've got to be kidding.'

A chorus of disbelief from the others made Philip hastily change his mind and go along with the plan and soon they were all seated around a large table amidst the cheerful clang of glasses and chopsticks.

Elizabeth, excited by the prospect of the climb and relaxed by several glasses of beer, became more gregarious than usual. Intelligence and humour sparkled in her blue eyes and both Philip and Barry began to wonder why they had never really noticed how attractive she was.

Philip, with Tess still on his mind, didn't intend to act on this sudden revelation but Barry decided that he just might do something about it. After all, Tess couldn't very well think he was going to wait for her forever, could she?

Later, when they had all had a delicious feast and no more food seemed to be coming out of the kitchen, Philip announced that he would take Tess home, so Barry turned to Elizabeth and offered her a ride on Big Red.

The proprietary note in Philip's voice went unnoticed by Barry but it wasn't lost on Tess, who heard it and hated it.

'Don't bother,' she said ungraciously, 'I'll take a rickshaw.' Before anyone could stop her she ran down the street, hailed an empty one and hopped in.

'Hey, wait, I want to talk to you about –' Philip protested, but broke off in mid-sentence. He didn't want to shout and he didn't want to run after her. Either one would make him look ridiculous so he contented himself with saying goodnight to the others and getting into his car alone.

He was just pulling away from the curb when he noticed that Elizabeth and Barry were still there, laughing together about something. Then Barry got on his stupid motorbike, Elizabeth climbed on behind him and off they went, zooming around a curve in the road and out of sight.

Philip couldn't help wondering if he should be making a move on Elizabeth rather than Tess.

Barry, glorying in the feeling of the wind in his face as Big Red took them speeding down the hill behind the Garuda Hotel then up the other bank of the river to Kota Baru, was far from having similar thoughts. He had just decided that the last thing he needed was to take up with either Elizabeth or Tess.

Women, no matter who they were, somehow always managed to mess up his life so he'd do better to stay away from them for a while, at least until he was eighty or ninety. Now that he thought about it, maybe he would become a monk; that would save him time, money and aggravation. Yes, that was the ticket. The idea was so simple, he couldn't understand why he hadn't come up with it before.

It didn't take long for Big Red to overtake Tess's rickshaw. Barry called out to her and gave her a friendly wave as they passed but he was actually thinking that going home alone served her damn well right when she could have been with him.

Yet as they drove through the deserted streets of Kota Baru, he began to notice how nice it felt to have Elizabeth pressed up against his back. She was holding him very tightly; was that because she was afraid of falling off, he wondered, or did she have something else in mind? A picture of her without her clothes on flashed invitingly through his mind. Her voluptuousness was wonderfully exciting in comparison with the straight figures of the Javanese girls; not that Tess's proportions were any too generous either.

Hey watch it, he told himself, having fantasies about Elizabeth in the nude was a singularly bad idea. Or was it? Tess had turned him down, so didn't that leave him free to look elsewhere?

Yet when they got to Elizabeth's place, he didn't take her up on her invitation to come in for a coffee. He merely dropped her off at her door with a goodnight kiss, one that was friendly but nothing more.

In the meantime, watching Barry and Elizabeth racing off into the darkness together had left Tess feeling sad and isolated.

Damn you, Barry, she had thought, why did you have to go and spoil everything, letting your horrible wife or ex-wife or whatever she is, stick her hideous nose into our lives and tarnish what we had together?

But then Cynthia wasn't the one who had messed

everything up, Tess fumed, as if she were talking aloud to Barry. You were the one who did that. Cynthia didn't even know me, she wasn't the one who should have cared about my feelings. At least I found out what you were like when I did. If Cynthia hadn't come back how long would it have been until you found someone else to have sex with? Just thinking about it makes me sick, I don't even want to be friends with you anymore. And when I think how close I was coming to forgiving you.

When Tess arrived back in her room, she was surprised to see a letter and a book on her desk that hadn't been there when she had gone out.

The American stamp on the envelope caught her attention. Could it be from Mike, she wondered, but when she looked at it more closely, she saw that it had been sent to her in care of the Archaeology Department at Gajah Mada and then readdressed to her at the Southeast Asia Foundation, so it wouldn't be from Mike. Someone there, probably Ninik, must have dropped it by the house.

Opening it, she was surprised to see a cheque fall out onto the floor. This was nothing compared to her astonishment when she caught sight of the signature. It read, 'love Cynthia', and was followed by two interlocking triangles with smiling faces on them.

Tess's first impulse was to crumple it up and toss it into the bin without reading it but curiosity got the better of her. She found she just couldn't do that so she held it up to the kerosene lamp, set about deciphering Cynthia's rambling scrawl and read –

Dear Tess,

John and I are married but whether or not we are going to live happily ever after depends on you. Will you be a darling and send me some packets of that wonderful stuff from the *jamu* lady in Barry's village. Just tell her it's for me and she will know what I want. But don't tell Barry, he's such a stick-in-the-mud he would probably disapprove.

Love,
Cynthia

P.S. You might want to try some of it yourself, a spoonful in a strong tasting drink (Barry's, not yours) should do it. Give it about twenty or thirty minutes to work and then climb into bed for the Arabian Nights and the Kama Sutra and the Loves of Aphrodite all rolled into one.

love Cynthia

How dare she send me a letter like that, Tess fumed, as words like 'how awful' and 'how preposterous' and 'how fucking absurd' whirled through her mind. Taking control of herself, she smoothed out the paper and read it again before, still in a state of stunned disbelief, she held it to the top of the kerosene lamp, watched it catch fire and burn.

As the ashes and charred scraps of paper fell to the base of the lamp, her head cleared and the events surrounding the disastrous arrival of Cynthia in her life began to fall into place.

Barry hadn't seemed glad to see Cynthia in the village that day, she reminded herself. If the only reason he had had sex with her was because she had put an aphrodisiac powder in his drink, how could he be held responsible for anything that happened under the circumstances, especially when he seemed so genuinely sorry about it afterwards?

He had even claimed not to understand how it had happened. At the time she had thought that she had never heard such a lame excuse in her life but now she realised it might actually have been true. He hadn't known because the idea of Cynthia slipping him some kind of aphrodisiac would never have entered his mind. Not that he had ever needed one when he was with her, she thought, remembering their time in Bali with a smile. So it really hadn't been any lingering attraction to Cynthia or any despicable flaw in his character that had made him have sex with her that weekend, it was the *jamu* and now that she knew that she could forgive him.

Thank you for that, she murmured silently to Cynthia and, still totally stunned by the letter, paid no attention to the unfamiliar book lying on the desk beside it.

The family's maid found it as she was tidying up the next morning, put it on a high shelf over Tess's desk, and it remained there, forgotten, for several weeks.

A few days later, Tess took the bus out Jalan Solo to the unremarkable turnoff where she could catch the rattletrap market bus that would take her within walking distance of Barry's village.

'Hey, what brings you here?' Barry asked, bounding out of his house to greet her. 'I saw you through the window and couldn't believe my eyes.'

'I came to see you, of course.'

'Great! Come on in, have a seat,' he urged, oblivious to the fact that there was no place to do it, all the chairs in the room were piled high with books and papers and weren't available for sitting on. 'I'll just see if I can rustle up some coffee, won't be a tick.'

Suddenly aware that he was about to leave Tess standing in the middle of the room looking a bit befuddled, he added, 'Oh, sorry.' Sweeping a stack of papers off one of the chairs, he said, 'I'll just throw some of this junk on the floor.'

'How do you ever find anything in this mess?' she asked.

'Easy, I just use my secret filing system, no patent pending,' he explained before disappearing into the back of the house.

He reappeared a few moments later.

'We're in luck. Siti's out the back doing laundry and she says she'll make the coffee, that means it may be drinkable.'

'Great,' she replied, feeling that - after the rough and tumble of the two buses she had had to take to get here - she could use a cup. Plunging right into what she had come to tell him, she continued, 'I got a letter from Cynthia yesterday.'

'You did?'

Astonishment bordering shock was evident in his every feature.

'Yes,' she said, enjoying his reaction.

'Why, what the hell did she want?'

'How do you know she wanted anything?'

'I know Cynthia.'

386

'She said she had gotten married.'

'That's no surprise,' Barry returned, glancing at a calendar on the wall. 'I expect that wasn't all she said.'

'No, it wasn't.'

'Well, are we playing guessing games?' he asked, a touch of impatience in his voice.

'No, of course not, it's just that it's so hard to believe what she wanted. It isn't easy to tell you.'

'Bite the bullet and tell me anyway. I can believe anything of Cynthia.'

'She asked me to save her marriage to your brother –'

'How in God's name does she expect you to do that?'

'By getting some powders from the *jamu* lady in your village and sending them to her. She claimed I could just tell her, the *jamu* lady that is, who they were for and she'd know which ones they were.'

Barry's countenance relaxed.

'Probably some of that 'stay young and beautiful' stuff,' he said. 'She was always trying out different lotions and potions but there was one of those she particularly liked.'

'I don't think that's quite the one she had in mind this time.'

'Oh. What kind then?'

'The aphrodisiac kind, the real thing.' Tess hesitated and then added, 'She didn't want me to tell you but –'

'You're kidding,' he said aghast, 'let me see that letter.'

'I can't. I burned it.'

'What the hell did you do that for?'

'No reason really, except that it made me so furious I didn't think of doing anything else. I mean she came into my life, ripped it all apart and then dared ask me to do her a favour. I just saw red, that's all.'

'Well, one thing about Cynthia is that she has absolutely no shame. If she sees something in it for her, she'll ask anybody for anything.'

'How did you ever let yourself get involved with someone like that?'

'By thinking with my dick instead of my brain, I guess. You've got to admit she doesn't hurt the eyes and I promise you, her performance in bed would give an Egyptian mummy a hard-on.'

'She had a little help, you know,' Tess said.

He eyed her suspiciously. 'What are you talking about?'

'The aphrodisiacs.'

'Not with me she didn't, I can promise you that. As you may remember from our little get-together in Bali, I don't exactly need that stuff.'

'Well she told me, or as much as told me, that she put some in your drinks sometimes.'

'Like hell she did!'

'She managed to do it without letting you know, that's what she said.'

'Either she's lying or you're making all this up.'

'You can't think I'd do that.'

'Can't I? Why wouldn't I think that someone who talks to a tiger like it's some kind of four-legged psychiatrist might get a few other crazy ideas as well? I wouldn't actually put anything past your wild imagination. But even so, to come here accusing me of being a limp rag in bed when you know perfectly well that's not true –'

'I didn't come here to accuse you of anything,' she protested. 'I came to tell you that things could be alright between us again, if you wanted them to be.'

'What things?' he asked, knowing perfectly well what she meant but not wanting to make it too easy for her. Hadn't she given him a difficult enough time?

'Well, like sex actually. You can't really be held responsible for that orgy you had with Cynthia if she put something in your drink so I've changed my mind about you being some kind of loathsome, treacherous worm.'

'Thanks a lot but let me tell you, Barry Gellert doesn't need any help to get it up when an attractive woman takes off her clothes. So you can just go back to the zoo and tell that to your stripy friend.'

'But I didn't mean –'

'Look, let's get this straight. Brother John may well need a dose or two to stiffen the old boy up, I don't know and I don't want to know, but yours truly here does not need any help from any fucking *jamu*.'

'You're taking this all wrong. You don't understand –'

'You're damn right I don't understand. Forget that coffee and get on Big Red. I want to make sure you're on the next bus back to Yogya.'

'Don't worry,' she cried, 'I'll be on it and without any help from you or your stupid bike.'

With that, she ran out the door and along the dikes between the rice paddies, running until she was out of breath and her vision was blurred by the tears that were streaming down her face.

In the days that followed, Tess took as much care to avoid Barry as he did to stay away from any place where she might possibly turn up.

He didn't go to the Kents' on Saturday afternoon even though for once he really wanted to because he knew they would all be making plans for the climb. It was only a few weeks away now.

Tess wasn't quite as successful in avoiding the Saturday afternoon gathering. At first she tried to beg off but Holly pleaded with her to stay and Mary, seeming to suspect that something was wrong, gave her a long quizzical look though fortunately didn't ask any awkward questions. But after a day spent sitting on a hard wooden bench that posed as a seat, bouncing over rutted roads in a bus that may have once been fitted out with shock absorbers even though there was no longer any evidence of them, Tess felt that she would kill for a cup of tea and a piece of cake, preferably chocolate but coconut would do. To hell with Barry, she murmured under her breath, I hate him. And maybe he won't even be here today.

She was in luck, he wasn't.

It was actually Elizabeth who looked up in the hope of seeing Barry whenever the door opened. They had run into each other on Jalan Malioboro several times recently and had ended up having a beer together in the lobby of the Hotel Garuda. Then, one day last week, they had met by design rather than by accident and had both been raving about Mary's cakes, although Barry lamented the fact that they came 'with all that tea'.

Perhaps it was just as well he didn't come today, Elizabeth told herself as she scraped up the last bit of coconut icing on her plate. It wouldn't do to see him too often. He was attractive and fun but there was something about him that made her wary, a nagging feeling that all those beers might be leading up to a little more than she wanted to take on. Casual affairs simply weren't her thing and the truth was that she actually preferred someone more serious, someone a bit more like Philip.

She knew there were people, Felicia in particular, who

thought he was cold but she didn't agree. She could see that he was just reserved, a quality she quite liked and actually preferred to Barry's juvenile sense of fun.

The only trouble was that both Philip and Barry, especially Philip, seemed to be far more interested in Tess than they were in her and why wouldn't they be? Tess was so much more attractive, had a better figure and was far livelier and more fun. She also suspected that Tess had a lot more sex appeal, although she realised that only a man would know that for sure.

In any case, it was pretty obvious that she didn't stand much of a chance with either of them. It was a pity about Philip though.

She was not surprised when, after the teapot had been refilled a number of times and the beautiful cake had been reduced to a few crumbs, Tess was the one who was offered a ride home.

'By the way, did you ever get that book I dropped by your place?' Philip asked, as he was turning the car out onto Jalan Solo.

'What book?'

'It was just one my sister sent me for my birthday and I thought it might be your sort of thing.'

'No, I never got it,' she said, completely forgetting the book that had been on her desk next to Cynthia's extraordinary letter. 'I can't imagine what could have happened to it. No one in the family reads enough English to have wanted it and even if they had, they wouldn't have just taken it without saying anything. At least, I don't think they would.'

Philip frowned. He distinctly remembered stopping by her place and handing the book to the maid but he merely said, 'If it turns up around the office. I'll make sure you get it.'

'But I can't take your birthday present,' Tess protested. 'Your sister must have sent it all the way from the States.'

'Birthdays are for kids,' he replied, 'and anyway you can just borrow it if that makes you feel any better.' Changing the subject, he added, 'I'm surprised you're going on this climb. If anyone had asked me, I'd have said it wasn't something you'd want to do.'

'Actually, I'd have thought that too,' she agreed, 'and to tell you the truth, I am a little nervous about it but I'm not going to let that put me off.'

'Good for you,' he said admiringly.

'You're going too,' she pointed out, thinking it wasn't fair for her to get all the kudos.

'Yes, but that doesn't count because I'm over all those silly feelings about volcanoes,' he bragged, not entirely truthfully.

As it happened, it was just the next morning when she was looking for an article Professor Subandi had lent her about recent temple finds on the Dieng Plateau that she noticed a book up on the highest shelf above the desk that she didn't recall seeing before.

The little maid who cleaned her room in the mornings must have put it there, she decided, although why she had chosen to put it up so high when that must have been quite a reach for her, was a mystery.

One glance at the title, DARING TO FOLLOW THEIR DREAMS: Three Men Who Changed the Face of Archaeology, was enough to tell her that it was the book Philip had been talking about. Opening it and flicking through it, she saw that it started with a section about Schliemann's discovery of Troy and how he had done battle with the scientific establishment of his day to excavate, against all apparent odds, in the place he was somehow sure was the right one. Then there was a segment on Howard Carter, his refusal to give up the search for King Tutankhamun's tomb and the mystical convictions surrounding its opening. Last of all, there was a chapter on Sir Arthur Evans and his fervent belief, sustained over more than thirty discouraging years in Crete, that he would be able to find the site of the ancient Palace of Knossos.

Good God, it looks like it's been written just for me

and it's certainly what I need to encourage me right now. Seeing a note inside the front cover, she read:

Dear Tess,

It seems there is more than one way to conduct archaeological research and more of a precedent for your way, the intuitive way, than I had realised.

Best of luck,
Philip

It must have taken a lot for him to write something like this and virtually admitting he was wrong, she thought. It's probably as close as he's ever come to an apology. Feeling awful about never having thanked him and never even acknowledging that she had received the book, she decided that she'd go and find him right away.

The trouble was that the book was in her hand and she couldn't help taking a quick look at it. She read the first few pages, then a bit more and then to the end of the first chapter. After that she was lost. She spent the rest of the day curled up on her bed totally absorbed. Eventually it began to get dark and as there was barely enough electricity to read by, she put it down and went to Philip's house to tell him how much the book, and his note, meant to her.

By the time she had flagged down a rickshaw, bargained for a good price and arrived at his house, he was relaxing with his usual pre-dinner glass of whisky and plate of cassava chips.

'Philip,' she began when she had accepted his offer of a drink but declined any of the bitter-tasting chips, 'I can't thank you enough for that book. It is absolutely fabulous, I'm loving it.'

'So you finally decided to read it,' he returned tersely.

She explained about the family maid and her genius for hiding things in weird and wonderful places.

'And I'm so very, very, very sorry, I didn't find it for so long. From the moment I saw the title I couldn't put it down, not until it got dark anyway. You must have thought I was the most dreadful person in the world not to have said anything about it before now.'

'Not quite the most dreadful,' he conceded, indulging in what, for him, was a rare moment of gallantry.

'And the note you sent with it was so…. well, it really means a lot to me.'

'That's a little hard to believe,' Philip growled.

'Why should it be? You knew me well enough to realise how important the book would be to me or you wouldn't have dropped it by.'

'Interesting for you, yes; important to you, I doubt it. It seems to me that you're prepared to go your own way regardless of what I think.'

'Well, that's true,' she conceded, 'but that's not the point.'

'What is then?'

'The point is that caring what you think and being an absolute slave to your opinion aren't the same things at all. I do care what you think and what the people at Gajah Mada think.'

'But you believe I'm trying to turn you into some kind of intellectual slave, is that it?' he asked, unable to hide his amusement.

'Frankly, yes. You're making it sound ridiculous but it's really pretty close to the truth, so close that it actually made me hate you for a while, but now I can see that you're not nearly as hateable as I thought. You even have a rather likeable side when you're not being horrible.'

Philip was conscious of a swimming sensation in his head, one that made him remember a physics professor whose lectures had always given him the feeling that he was dealing with a completely alien set of thought processes and left him thoroughly befuddled.

What the hell, he told himself with a shrug, he shouldn't even try to figure out how Tess's mind worked.

He invited her to dinner instead and, to the astonishment of both of them, they made it through the entire evening without quarrelling once.

As the day of the climb approached, a sense of excitement began to build up in Yogya's tiny foreign community. Cooks were sent to the market for peanuts and cashews to fry up with onions and chilli peppers to provide them with extra energy along the way. Precious imported raisins were bought at Toko Mirota, Silver Queen chocolate bars were tucked into backpacks and Derek's flask was filled with a single malt whisky from the duty free shop in Singapore airport. Pullovers and jackets, unthinkable items in the steaming heat of Yogyakarta, were pulled out from the depths of wardrobes or borrowed from friends.

Tess turned everything out of her cupboard in a last minute search for her torch only to find it under the bed, so by the time she joined the gathering at the Kents', most of the dozen or so climbers had already arrived.

Derek was busy sorting out who would go in which of the available cars as far as Selo, the little village nestled in the saddle between the peaks of Mt Merapi and Mount Merbabu. It was the last point accessible by car and would be the starting point for the trek itself.

'I'll go with the Carpenters in their car,' Derek was

announcing to anyone who was listening. Seeing that Tess had just arrived, he added, 'Why don't you come with us too? That will leave Philip with enough room in his car to take Elizabeth, Felicia and Paul.'

He went on to direct the other climbers into the appropriate vehicles and added, 'That will leave our car free for Mary when she drives up tomorrow with the picnic.'

After a couple of false starts - Barry had left his water bottle tied to the handle of Big Red, Felicia had forgotten to bring the jumper she was borrowing from Mary, and Derek had accidently gone off without his flask of single malt whisky - everyone was reunited with their treasured items and the small parade of vehicles was ready to set off.

The sun was nearing the horizon by the time they got to Selo but fortunately they were able to find a watchman for their cars, locate the guide and begin the short climb up to the volcanology station before the brief tropical twilight gave way to darkness.

'I'm afraid this isn't going to be the Savoy,' Derek warned, as they approached the unprepossessing bungalow where they would spend a few hours and hopefully get a little sleep before setting out on the main part of the trek.

Derek's certainly right about that, Tess thought when

she saw the interior of the bungalow.

'Are we really supposed to sleep on those things?' Felicia cried, looking in dismay at the wooden benches dotted between various pieces of electronic equipment.

'What's down here?' Elizabeth asked, starting hopefully down a narrow passage leading off the main room.

Tess followed her with similar hopes but found only three little rooms, each barely large enough to hold one, or at the most two, of the same benches. Further exploration merely revealed two more rooms, each scarcely larger than a telephone box. One had a round hole bordered by two platforms shaped vaguely like a human foot and was presumably the toilet, the other contained a vat of water for washing.

Tess wasn't bothered by these sanitary arrangements, they were smaller and more cramped than the ones in her house but she was used to them by now. Far more troubling was the prospect of getting any sleep at all on one of those hard benches. The lumpy kapok mattress she slept on in Yogya was the height of luxury in comparison.

Tired and hungry, she was almost on the point of wishing she hadn't come when she heard Barry's voice calling out, 'Cheer up kids, room service has arrived.'

Hoping that something delicious had magically dropped out of the sky, Tess hurried back to the main room only to see Barry ensconced on one of the benches triumphantly pulling a nearly full bottle of Johnnie Walker out of his backpack.

'If the chief doesn't object,' he continued, nodding in Derek's direction, 'I think a little refreshment is in order.'

The chief, whose flask was still squirreled away, was scarcely in a position to protest.

Inspired by the whisky, everybody delved into their bags for sandwiches, packets of spicy dried noodles, chocolate bars and any other food they had with them. Elizabeth handed around pieces of chicken for everyone and, between the excitement of the climb and the unaccustomed chill of the mountain air, everything tasted unexpectedly delicious.

'Four stars in the *Michelin Guide*,' pronounced Barry, when he had polished off his own store of provisions and helped himself liberally to anything else that anyone was willing to give away.

'Five stars,' asserted Derek.

'Does it even have five?' asked Felicia, doubtfully.

Elizabeth claimed that it did and Paul said that it didn't but no one was inclined to pursue the point.

One by one, they remembered that they had only a few hours to get some sleep before midnight when the serious climbing would begin. They gravitated to the benches, stretched out and tried to get what rest they could.

The Carpenters took possession of one of the small

rooms, Tess and Elizabeth shared another, Philip found a bench in the furthest one and hoped no one would join him, unless perchance it was Tess but he didn't think that was very likely. He had just lain back and closed his eyes when he heard Paul's voice saying in a loud whisper, 'Look, there're two free benches in here. They're not any wider than the others though.'

He recognised Felicia's voice whispering back, 'They'll have to do then, won't they? Fortunately I think I'm sleepy enough that it won't really matter.'

Shit, Philip thought, he distinctly didn't want company especially not those two. He tried to turn over so he wouldn't be facing them but the bench was so narrow he couldn't quite manage it, at least not without risking the ignominy of ending up on the floor. All he could do was pretend to be asleep and hope he soon would be. The problem was that not a single nerve in his body seemed prepared to relax.

Sounds of laughter and none-too-sober conversation coming from the main room didn't help but eventually he heard someone telling Barry, 'Shut up, will you, so the rest of us can get some sleep.'

Fortunately Barry did and eventually he was able to drift into a light doze. It wasn't very refreshing though, more of a nightmare really. He felt himself being enveloped in a dense fog where the only light came from the fiery insides of the volcano.

Paul, on the other side of the room, was also a victim of sleeplessness, not because of nerves but because of the nearness of Felicia. After a while, he crept over to her bench, kissed her and woke her up.

'But we can't,' she protested, 'not here.'

'Why not?'

'Because of him,' she said, motioning towards Philip.

'He's asleep.'

'He might wake up.'

'No he won't, we'll be quiet.'

He tried to lie down on top of her but she pushed him off.

'Fuck,' he said, landing with a hard thump on the concrete floor. 'Don't worry, I'm okay though,' he muttered, before adding in a sarcastic whisper, 'thanks for asking.'

He tried to climb back on top of her but she wouldn't have it so he tried using his weight to hold her down. She struggled out from under him then there was an almighty crash as one of the legs of the bench gave way and, amidst a noisy clatter of wood on cement, they were both jolted onto the floor.

Felicia was furious and Paul felt like a prize idiot. By the time they had recovered from the shock, massaged their bruises and managed to find empty benches in the main room, there was barely enough time left to get any sleep.

In Philip's view, the upset hadn't been a bad thing; at least he would finally get to have the room to himself for a little while.

'What happened?' a female voice asked from the doorway.

His eyes flew open and, switching on his torch, he saw Tess standing there.

'I heard a dreadful crash,' she was saying. 'It sounded like it came from in here.'

'It did,' he said, swinging his feet to the floor and sitting up. 'Felicia's bench broke so she went into the other room. Paul followed her in his usual puppy dog way.'

'I'm glad something woke me up,' Tess said, coming over and squeezing in beside him on his bench. 'I was having a nightmare.'

'I hadn't got to the dreaming stage yet,' he replied.

'You're a little nervous too then,' she suggested, 'sort of like me.'

'Not really,' he said. It was a lie but he didn't want to admit how very jittery he was feeling. 'Just a little uncomfortable and of course, these benches '

'Nonsense, don't try to tell me that's the reason you can't sleep. I know you better than that.'

'Okay, okay, I suppose you're right.'

'I didn't think I was nervous until I had that bad dream,' Tess said sympathetically, 'but now I know I must have been. Anyway I don't want to go back to sleep,

I'd rather stay up and talk. How about you?'

'There isn't really much point in going back to sleep now,' he said, positioning his watch to catch the stream of moonlight shining through the window. 'Everybody will be getting up again pretty soon.'

'Good,' she said, smiling at him in a way that encouraged him to reach out and lace his fingers through hers. He was about to pull her towards him when his fears about the volcano resurfaced and he released her.

That's why she doesn't see me as really hateable, he told himself. She thinks of me as pitiable and that's worse.

But he was never good at understanding women and he was wrong about Tess now. She was actually thinking how sensitive and understanding he was underneath that cool defensive exterior and how different he was from Barry.

The very thought of that beast sent a wave of anger rushing through her; their last meeting had been so ghastly, she couldn't bear to think about it.

Philip felt her shudder and, thinking it was in revulsion at his touch, quickly dropped her hand.

'What's the matter?' she asked.

He insisted that nothing was.

She didn't believe him and, convinced that she was somehow responsible for his change of mood, reached up and put her arms around his neck.

The next instant his arms were around her and they

were kissing. He wondered if he could kiss away her fear of the mountain, and his own fear too? The idea made him chuckle and she looked startled.

Perhaps a little more kissing was required at this point, or maybe even a little action under the ten thousand sweaters she seemed to be wearing but not much more than that. The privacy here was too uncertain and, unlike Paul, he wasn't prepared to do anything on a goddamn stage. He didn't imagine Tess would like that either but when they got off this damn volcano and went back to Yogya

Tess heard loud snoring coming from the other room and wondered if it was Barry. She wished he'd wake up, come down the hall and find her with Philip. What a moment that would be!

Almost within seconds, that was exactly what happened.

'Having fun, kids?' Barry enquired, keeping his tone casual and hoping they wouldn't notice the stunned expression on his face, 'or are you just sorting out the details of Tess's extension?'

'What does it look like to you?' Tess demanded.

'It looks like fun, maybe Ninik could use the same technique for me.'

'What a vile thing to say,' Tess cried.

'Yeah, I'm a pretty vile sort of guy,' he returned cheerfully.

'I think you'd better apologise to Tess,' Philip said, his voice tense with quiet fury.

'What for, surely not for admitting what kind of guy I am?'

'For being deliberately obtuse, among other things,' Philip retorted.

'There was nothing deliberate about it,' Barry replied airily. 'It just comes naturally.'

'Wonderfully perceptive of you to have realised,' Tess remarked, 'but can't you take your sudden clarity of mind elsewhere?'

'Just what I was about to suggest myself,' the unflappable Barry returned. 'The two of you had better get your kicks while you can or else put your passion on ice until tomorrow. We're going to start any minute now.'

'I'll never speak to that bastard again,' Tess told Philip, raising her voice in the hope that Barry, who had walked off down the hall, would be able to hear her. 'I hate him, I hate him, I hate him.'

'As much as you hated me?' Philip asked, laughing.

'More, hundreds of times more.'

Elsewhere, Barry found Elizabeth, leaned over, kissed her on the forehead and said, 'Wake up, sleeping beauty, the excitement's about to begin.'

Once out in the darkness, everyone fell into single file behind the guide and started up the steep, uneven path. Tess was careful to position herself just behind Philip; she reached out and caught hold of him whenever she was unsure of her footing and he, although none too confident of his own, continuously managed to steady her. Felicia actually did trip and was just saved from a nasty fall by the ever-present Paul.

At one point Elizabeth's shoe broke and they all had to stop while Barry fixed it for her, other than that their rest stops were few and far between. Derek even managed to pass the flask of whisky down the line of climbers from time to time without anyone having to break their stride.

After a while, the trail became so narrow that with each step they had to put their left foot exactly where the right foot had just been. Paul dropped his water container just as he was opening it and could only stand by and watch in dismay as its contents poured out into the surrounding undergrowth.

Eventually, the thick forest cover gave way to an expanse of low brush that - in a display of ferocity rare in the plant kingdom - attacked the human invaders with its razor-sharp edges. It ripped Felicia's too-thin trousers to shreds and left jagged slashes in all but the heaviest of clothes.

By the time the sky began turning a pinkish grey, the

punishing slope of the terrain had begun to abate and the little band of climbers found themselves on a wide and desolate expanse of barren shale.

'It's like the surface of the moon,' Tess observed.

'Yeah, except for these nasty yellow things,' Paul said, nudging one of them with his foot.

'They're the famous sulphur flowers,' Derek explained. 'You've probably heard about them.'

'If those are flowers, I'll kiss a pig,' Paul growled in reply.

'Do you have to take everything so literally?' Derek asked in amusement. 'They're actually just bits of sulphur.'

'Whatever they are,' Paul said, fishing his camera out of his rucksack, 'I've got to get a picture of them.'

As there was no longer any need to go single file, the climbers soon fanned out into separate groups with the fitter ones quickly overtaking their slower companions. Derek, Barry, the Carpenters and the guide led the most advanced group, while Tess, Philip, Paul and Felicia lagged further and further behind.

'Should we try and go a little faster?' Philip suggested, although he was already short of breath.

'No way,' gasped Felicia, whose scratched and bloodstained trousers were now glued to her skin. 'I'm already going as fast as I can.'

'With wounded legs like that, how could she possibly go any faster?' put in Tess, secretly grateful to Felicia for providing an excuse not to increase their pace.

This became especially true as they approached the slanting rim of the caldera with its gaping mouth tipped in the direction of Magelang. It seemed to loom larger and larger the closer they came and the gradient increased with every step they took.

As the ascent become more nearly perpendicular, they discovered that the shale beneath their feet was covered with powdery sand made from volcanic ash. As they tried to cross it, they slid back a step or two for every few steps forward. Sharp pieces of broken shale cut their shoes and the stench of sulphur became so overpowering that Tess had the feeling she was walking on a thousand rotten eggs.

By the time the slower group reached the lower rim of the crater, Paul was the only one whose curiosity hadn't been at least partially stifled by exhaustion. As a result, no one was next to him when he crept up to the edge of the caldera and peered down through the swirling steam into the gaping mouth of the volcano.

'How did the others get so far, so fast?' Tess wondered, catching sight of the group far above them on the upper rim. 'Do they have wings on their shoes?'

'I wish I had had wings on mine,' moaned Felicia, stretching out her aching legs.

Philip was so amazed at the fact that he was standing this close to the dreaded source of red hot magma without having a panic attack that he didn't say anything. He merely resolved to stay where he was and not court disaster by venturing any closer to the danger zone.

None of them was remotely pleased to hear Barry calling down from the higher elevation, 'Hey, you slugs, you better get a move on or you'll miss the sunrise.'

They could only give him evil looks as, to their dismay, he began retracing his steps around the perimeter of the caldera and coming towards them.

'Did you guys stop for a quick nap or what?' he taunted.

It was fortunate no one had a gun.

'Why don't you take your inane remarks and go to hell,' Paul hissed. 'And in case you can't figure out how to get there,' he added, with a nod at the steam pouring out of the volcano, 'let me suggest a convenient route.'

'Nobody asked you to come down here,' Tess said rudely.

'Wrong, Derek did, he didn't think you slowpokes should be left to your own devices. It can be kind of tricky going around here sometimes.'

'I'm not going anywhere,' Tess declared, 'not until I've had a chance to recover a bit.'

'Neither am I,' said Felicia.

'Tell Derek I'll come when I get this shot,' Paul said, pointing his lens directly down into the gaping aperture.

'Forget it,' ordered Barry, going over to the edge and

peering down. Beset by a sudden queasiness he drew away, saying, 'You can't see anything through all that steam anyway.'

'I might be able to,' Paul argued. 'It comes up in puffs and swirls. I got a quick glimpse down into the hole a minute ago so if I'm lucky, and totally ready for it, I might just be able to get the shot of a lifetime.'

'That may be, but –'

'If you think I'm going to let an opportunity for something like that get away, you're crazier than hell.'

'Make it snappy then,' Barry said. 'After climbing all this way, I'm not about to miss the sunrise just for one of your fucking photos.'

'Don't wait then, see if I care,' returned Paul, intent on finding the best angle for his shot.

'Right,' Barry said, but leaving him with one last warning, he added, 'Watch it though, this stuff isn't hard rock and if it breaks –'

'Don't worry,' Paul returned, testing the shale along the rim with his foot, 'I know what I'm doing.'

'Do you? Then you must know that it would be a lot safer if you'd lie down to take your precious pictures. You'd spread your weight that way.'

'The safest thing would be for you not to take any more pictures at all,' Tess pointed out. 'And I'm feeling better now, so let's go on up to the top.'

'Hold on a minute, will you?' asked Paul. 'There's no way I'm going to miss this shot, it's going to be incredible.' Leaning over to improve his angle, he moved his right foot to balance the consequent shift in his weight.

A sound of cracking shale, followed seconds later by the sight of Paul catapulting down towards the boiling lava, momentarily paralyzed the little group. They could only stare in stricken silence as he disappeared from view.

Eons of time passed, at least that's what it seemed like to Tess, before she saw a hand reaching up out of the swirling mist and heard a hollow voice call, 'Help.'

She didn't believe in ghosts but what other explanation could there possibly be? Surely no one could survive even for an instant in the flames of that bottomless pit. Ghosts had to exist and Paul's must be trying to lure them down to share his fiery death.

Barry, unencumbered by any thoughts of the supernatural, was the first one to react. Quickly figuring out that there must be some kind of ledge along the interior wall of the crater and that the little creep must have had the good luck to land on it, he did the only thing he could think of. He threw himself full-length onto the ground, stretched his hand down towards the bubbling lava and let the terrified photographer reach up and grab hold of his arm.

Paul clung to his rescuer with desperation and utter

panic while Barry, realising too late what the downward pull of someone's weight on his arm would mean, groped madly for something he could hold onto; a piece of shale, anything to stop him sliding down into the molten core of the earth.

Yet nothing he could lay his hands on seemed to be quite enough to stop his progress as he inched towards the yawning mouth of the abyss.

'Quick,' Tess told Philip, as she fell onto one of Barry's legs and held it for all she was worth. An instant later Philip was grasping Barry's other leg but even with their combined strength, they didn't succeed in thwarting all of his forward motion. They slowed it down but still he continued sliding ever so gradually towards oblivion.

'Run! Scream! Get help! Quickly!' Tess ordered Felicia, who stood frozen in shock. Recovering her mobility, Felicia did her best to raise the alarm but everyone on the higher rim was too intent on catching their first glimpse of the sunrise to be attuned to anything else that was going on.

Paul, nearly crazed with fright by this time, began to feel the narrow ledge that had been giving him tenuous support, start to crumble away beneath his feet. In desperation, he tried to climb up Barry's arm, hand over hand as if it were a rope. In spite of Tess and Philip's Herculean efforts to hold Barry's legs, he was slowly being dragged closer and closer to the edge. He was so near that Paul was soon able to clasp both hands around his would-be rescuer's neck.

Tess could see that Barry had no way of prying Paul's grip loose without using the hand that was contributing substantially to stopping him slide into oblivion himself. In spite of everything she and Philip were doing, they were only succeeding in reducing the speed of Barry's progress toward the lava below, not stopping it.

If only she were stronger, Tess thought. Even though she was straining every muscle she had, she knew that Philip's hold on him was the one that really counted. Where were the others, she asked herself, why didn't they come? How much longer could the two of them counter the downward pull of Paul and Barry's weight?

She felt Barry slide a little more.

'Hang on for a minute,' she told Philip, 'don't let go.'

Releasing her grip on Barry's leg, she moved at lightning speed to straddle his back and press down on him with all her strength but even then she couldn't counter the inexorable drag of Paul's weight.

Suddenly seeing in a flash what she had to do, she began prying Paul's fingers off Barry's neck, one by one.

'Stop,' Philip shouted, 'you'll be sending the guy to his death.'

She heard him but she didn't stop and, desperate as Philip was to pull her hands away and force her to do it, he didn't dare let go of Barry even for a second. It would send him plunging down into the lava along with Paul, very possibly taking Tess with them.

In any case, Philip needn't have worried. Each time Tess managed to unclasp one of Paul's fingers, it was back around Barry's neck again a moment later so she began pounding his knuckles with the side of her hand instead.

When that didn't get the result she wanted, she reached for a nearby piece of broken shale and, using all her strength, brought it down on Paul's knuckles over and over and over again until –

A pair of strong arms was pulling her away while other hands dragged Barry, with Paul still clinging to him, to safety.

When the strong arms, Derek's, released her, she sank to the ground, put her face in her hands and sobbed with relief and emotional exhaustion.

Poor Tess, Elizabeth thought as she watched her, she must really love Barry to have done what she did.

'She's a murderess,' Felicia said furiously.

She's hysterical and small wonder, thought Derek.

'What does Tess have to cry about?' Felicia exclaimed. 'You'd think she was the one who'd nearly died inside that crater.'

Who would have thought Tess would be such a cool customer, Philip marvelled. Brave, smart and with enough presence of mind to realise that if she couldn't save two people, she might at least try to save one, even if that meant doing something distinctly unpalatable like dropping Paul in –

I shouldn't have tried to stop her, he decided, I just should have done the hard part myself. I should have been the one to send the little idiot into the lava, not let her do it. But of course that wouldn't have worked, would it? She wouldn't have been strong enough to hold the two of them by herself, no matter how quickly he could have moved.

In a display of compassion that surprised even himself, Philip went over and put his arms around Tess. 'You shouldn't be crying,' he said soothingly. 'You saved Barry's life. You should be feeling very proud right now.'

Barry was lying on the ground, his head propped up in Elizabeth's lap, drinking the little whisky remaining in the flask when he heard these words.

'Here, give this to Tess,' he said, turning to hand the flask to Philip, 'she's the one who really deserves it.'

The only problem was that moving his arm was no easy task, in fact it was damn difficult and he got a vicious stab of pain in his shoulder when he attempted it. Had he dislocated it, he wondered, or more accurately, had that little photographer prick dislocated it for him? Either way, the pain was a real bitch but it was such a relief to find that, in spite of everything, he was still alive that nothing else seemed very important.

It was good just to lie there, fill his lungs with the mountain air and let people make a fuss over him. He guessed he had missed the sunrise but he had never been big on that sort of thing anyway.

His euphoric mood was shattered when he heard Derek telling Tabitha that he and Mark were going to go down to Selo for stretchers.

'Don't get one for me,' he said, sitting up in alarm. 'I'll be able to walk, just give me a few minutes to get myself together. And a little more whisky, if anybody's got some.'

'Okay, if you're sure,' Derek agreed doubtfully, but he was still troubled about Paul. The fellow was trembling uncontrollably and was clearly in shock.

'Are you going to be able to make it down to the cars, Old Man,' Derek asked, 'or do you think you might want a bit of help?'

Paul didn't seem to take in the question.

Derek discussed the situation with Elizabeth.

'It would be a lot better if Paul could walk,' he said. 'Otherwise it will be quite a wait until we get back here with the stretchers.'

'But what if Paul collapses on the way down?' she asked.

'Then of course somebody would have to go for help but if Paul's able to make it even part of the way on his own, it would be a good thing.'

Derek and Felicia took the first turn at supporting Paul while Barry, walking unsteadily but walking nonetheless, carried on under his own steam, although he couldn't help wondering if there was any muscle in his body that didn't ache.

Seeing that he was a bit wobbly, Elizabeth darted forward and put an arm around his waist.

'Now this is the kind of help I like,' he said, using his good arm to squeeze her closer.

By the time they reached the sharp-edged plants of the low brush, Elizabeth could see that he was steadier on his feet and soon he scarcely needed her at all. Paul gradually seemed to be pulling himself together after his ordeal too, she noted with approval, even though he was still muttering unintelligible things to himself.

Not even Derek, who had been keeping a close eye on Paul, was prepared to see him suddenly lurch away from his supporters, dart back through the sharp vegetation and wrap his fingers around Tess's neck.

Philip, who was the closest to Tess at that moment, immediately grabbed hold of Paul and tried his best to pull him away but without much effect. The battles he had fought in recent decades had been verbal rather than physical and he wasn't in very good shape. It was left to Barry to spring across the intervening distance, raise his one good arm and deal Paul a punishing blow on the jaw.

Shocked, dazed and completely unprepared for this kind of response, Paul staggered backwards, relinquishing his hold on Tess's neck as he went.

Seeing this as her first opportunity to try out the instructions her mother had once given her, she used her knee to deliver Paul a searing blow in the testicles, one that sent an excruciating wave of pain reverberating through his entire body.

Seeing Paul crumble to the ground, Felicia turned on Tess like a cyclone. 'What have you done now?' she cried.

'When it comes to standing there quietly while she's being strangled,' Barry intervened cheerfully, 'Tess just isn't very cooperative.'

'She's dangerous, she's got to be stopped,' Felicia retorted, running over to Paul who was still writhing on the ground. 'She's criminally insane.'

'Yeah, some people are like that,' Barry acknowledged genially. 'When a crazed killer gets his hands around their neck, they kind of lose it.' Regarding Paul's prostrate form with distaste, he added, 'When we get this toad up and moving again, we'd better make sure he's at the front of the pack where we can all keep an eye on him.'

'And it might not be a bad idea to keep Tess near the

back with several people around her in case Paul goes berserk again,' put in Philip.

'Yeah, I don't want the beer I've been looking forward to for hours delayed while someone fills out a coroner's report.'

'It doesn't look like Paul's in any shape to walk,' Derek observed.

'Tess doesn't look too great either,' Elizabeth pointed out. 'She's deathly white.' Turning to Tess, she asked, 'Do you think you're going to be able to make it?'

Tess nodded. 'Oh yes, I'm fine,' she said, not completely truthfully.

'Of course you are,' Felicia hissed, 'only the good die young.'

'Let's hope so anyway,' Barry said. 'God knows, it's what I kept telling myself while I was dangling over that hellhole up there.'

After Paul had been set none-too-gently on his feet and the downwards trek was resumed, Barry and Philip were the only ones who displayed anything like the high spirits with which they had all started out; Philip because he had actually climbed the dreaded volcano, been to the very edge of its gaping mouth and single-handedly, almost single-handedly anyway, cheated it of its prey. Certainly Tess alone would never have been able to prevent Barry and Paul from plunging into the molten lava, so when it

421

came down to it, they both owed their lives to him. Tess did too, after a fashion anyway, because of those seconds when she had been concentrating on trying to pry Paul's fingers off of Barry's neck. If the two of them had fallen into the terrifying caldera, she could well have been dragged down with them.

He wasn't going to kid himself that he had done it alone but the lion's share of the glory must surely come to him. That's what he felt like; a lion. He had battled the volcano and won. He never needed to be afraid of it again.

Barry was too busy revelling in the rare appreciation of just being alive to think of much else. He'd hate like the devil to have anybody know just how scared he'd been up there, struggling against that seemingly inexorable slide towards the fiery interior of the earth. Each time the drag of Paul's weight had pulled him forwards another inch, he had been convinced he was in for it. God only knew he would have shaken the little prick loose if he could have but now he was glad he hadn't had to. If it had come down to a 'him-or-me' proposition he was no saint but nobody, no matter how awful they were, deserved to fall into that bubbling hell and it wouldn't have been much fun for the guy who'd sent him there either. Just thinking about it made him want to throw up, yet Tess had been prepared to do that for him and had tried so hard to do it that he had thought she was going to pound his neck into a fucking pancake. God she was made of strong stuff, stronger than he had ever realised and stronger than him, that was for sure.

He hastily pushed those terrifying moments up there out of his mind. He didn't want to dwell on them or on anything related to them. He just wanted to revel in the feeling of being alive and think about the great time he was going to have when he got down off this fucking mountain. He'd start with about a hundred cold beers, well beers anyway, even if they weren't cold. Then he'd get his shoulder fixed up and after that he'd find a soft, welcoming bed with a soft, welcoming girl, maybe someone sort of like Elizabeth, in it and after they had –

But, he asked himself, was it Elizabeth he really wanted? She was a great girl, there was no doubt about that and he liked her a lot. Still, he couldn't stop his mind from flashing back to those moments when he had been pinioned up there a few feet from hell. There had been only one other person in the world who had mattered and it hadn't been Elizabeth. Soft and invitingly feminine as she was, she wasn't Tess. The trouble was, it looked like he had missed his chance and Philip was the one she wanted now.

He'd just have to see what he could do about that.

When the exhausted climbers finally got back to the volcanology station, they were greeted with cries of outrage from the people who had driven up to meet them with the picnic.

'What happened to you?' Mary demanded. 'We were starting to think you must have had some ghastly accident up there.'

'Yes, what took you so long?' someone else wanted to know.

'We've been waiting for hours and hours,' Holly declared. 'The chicken's getting cold and so am I.'

No one seemed very interested in how she was feeling. The returning climbers merely fell thankfully onto the ground and set about quenching their thirst with vast quantities of beer. Paul, to everyone's relief, slunk off into the bungalow to deal with his own private hell.

Telling Mary, Holly and the others what had happened on the mountain gradually turned into a sort of mini trial of Tess, with Felicia spearheading the prosecution while Barry and Philip voiced the case for the defence. Derek did what he could to remain neutral, saying that Tess shouldn't be blamed for what she had done but, as help hadn't actually been very far away, she might have tried to hold off a little longer before taking the near fatal step that she did.

In the end most of the group agreed with Derek, although Mary, along with Philip, Barry and Holly, held firmly to the view that Tess had only done what had seemed absolutely necessary at the time.

Tess, not caring whether people praised or blamed her, merely listened and said nothing as the arguments flew back and forth. She neither congratulated nor castigated herself, she simply knew that there was no way she could have stood by and let Barry be pulled into the caldera without doing anything. And if Paul's life would have had to be sacrificed in the process, well, that somehow didn't seem very important.

Much to Philip's astonishment, Barry came striding into his office the next day and handed him the report he had been trying to extract from him for over a month.

'Jesus, that was fast,' he exclaimed. 'I certainly didn't expect to see you this soon.'

'Yeah, I wanted to come in and talk to you so I stayed up most of the night finishing the fucking thing.'

'I really can't discuss it before I've had a chance to read it,' Philip said testily.

'Actually the report is only part of the reason I'm here,' Barry returned. 'It's really about Tess, Tess and that nut,

Paul. I'm convinced he's dangerous, totally off his head.'

'I don't know what I can do about that.'

'You can get Tess out of here and keep her out of here as long as that bastard's still around. Ninik mentioned something about a Regional Representative's Meeting in Singapore that you were going to.'

'That's right. It starts the day after tomorrow.'

'Good, take Tess with you. Then when you get back we can figure out something a bit more long term.'

'What the hell are you talking about?' demanded Philip.

'About keeping her well out of Paul's reach.'

'But what –'

'You saw his little performance up there on the mountain, that hands-around-the-neck trick, remember?'

'Vividly,' Philip returned with a grimace.

'Well if you think he's cooled down since then, you're wrong. He's still seething and I hate to think what would happen if he tried another stunt like that when there wasn't anyone around to pull him off. He may well succeed in killing her.'

'Are you sure you're not blowing all this up into more than –'

'Damn sure. I actually ran into Paul on my way over here and we had a little a chat. He started out by moaning about his lost camera but it didn't take him long to get onto the subject of Tess and I can tell you, his feelings about her are nothing short of homicidal.'

'You can be angry with someone, pretty damn furious, without actually trying to kill them,' Philip pointed out.

'Most people can, the ones who are still grounded in reality, but not Paul, at least not where Tess is concerned. He's so eaten up with rage that there's no way he's going to handle it rationally. I figured she'd be safe enough last night because she'd be with you but –'

'She wasn't,' Philip corrected him.

'Wasn't she? Well, if she was at home that would have been okay too. That family she lives with wouldn't have stood by and let some maniac barge in and strangle her. It's while she's going around by herself in the daytime that something could happen.'

'If you're expecting me to put a leash on her, I'm going to have to disappoint you. In any case, you really should be taking all this up with Tess, not me.'

'You of all people must know that Tess doesn't have much use for me anymore,' Barry said. 'I doubt that she'd listen to anything I had to say. If I told her she should get out of here for a while, go somewhere, anywhere, she'd probably dig in and refuse to move.'

Philip couldn't help smiling. He didn't agree with Barry about much but when it came to how obstinate Tess could be, they definitely saw eye to eye.

'Okay, I'll talk to her,' Philip said reluctantly, 'but she doesn't usually take my suggestions very well either.'

'Play the heavy this time,' Barry advised. 'Don't take no for an answer.'

This wasn't an assignment that Philip relished. If he showed up at the conference with one of his grantees, one that was young, attractive and female, he'd get a load of flack about sexual harassment in the office. On the other hand, if he didn't lift a finger to protect one of the Foundation's researchers from a crazed killer, how would that look?

But Philip wondered whether Paul really was the crazed killer Barry was making him out to be. Admittedly, he had had a few moments of madness up there on Merapi but in the light of what the poor guy had just been through, wasn't that sort of understandable?

Shit, Philip thought, it wasn't clear, not to him anyway, whether Paul or Barry was the one who was flipping out. The only thing that was blatantly obvious was that, thanks to some macabre twist of fate, he was the one who was going to come out of it all looking bad.

On his way home Philip decided it might not be a bad idea to stop by Felicia's place, take a look at Paul and size up the current situation himself.

He located his prey comfortably ensconced on the veranda, book in hand and a half finished bottle of beer on a table beside him.

'Felicia's not here,' Paul told him curtly. 'She's gone to Solo for the day, shopping or something.'

Much to Paul's disappointment, his visitor failed to see this as a reason to leave, so in the end he offered to rummage around in the fridge for another bottle of Bintang. He knew it was his last and was reluctant to part with it.

Returning from the kitchen with it, he droned on for a while about how awful his life had become now that he had been deprived of his camera.

Philip wondered if he was implying that this state of affairs had been engineered deliberately. He made several attempts to change the subject and when none of them worked, got up to leave. Unless it was possible to kill someone by boring them to death, he didn't believe that Paul, unpleasant little prick though he was, posed much of a threat. He was clearly a little paranoid about his camera but, other than that, he seemed sane enough. He was just incredibly self-centred. That wasn't a crime, especially not when someone had just been through what Paul had.

Nevertheless, instead of going straight home, Philip stopped by Tess's place and broached the subject of a holiday.

'Just 'til Paul's out of the way,' he stressed, and before he had quite thought it through, he found himself suggesting that she come to Singapore with him.

As he might have expected, her response to the idea that she could be in danger was, 'Don't be ridiculous.' Since this was basically his view too, he wound up the conversation by saying, 'Well, just try to be sensible then. Watch out that you're not alone anywhere.'

Tess laughed. 'Where on this crowded island could I possibly be alone?'

He laughed too and let the subject drop.

After spending the better part of the day doing errands in Yogya, Barry suddenly realised just how much he didn't feel like going back to the village. With his shoulder still keeping him from hopping on Big Red and shooting off wherever he wanted, recently he had had too continuous a dose of village life.

Maybe he'd postpone the inevitable by stopping in to see Elizabeth for a while.

It wasn't his day though; she wasn't at home.

'Fuck,' he muttered under his breath, 'why wasn't anything going his way?'

A glance at his watch lifted his spirits. It was nearly four o'clock, teatime at the Kents'. He'd go there, chew the fat with Derek and hope Mary would have made one of her lemon cakes with coconut icing.

'How do you keep from going demented out there in that village of yours, I mean, doesn't it get a bit lonely?' Mary asked a little later, as she was handing him a cup of tea.

He noticed that there were two different cakes on the table today, about half a lemon cake and a third or quarter of one that looked like banana.

'Cake,' she asked, her knife poised uncertainly between the two, 'not that the lemon really is lemon. You can't get any here, you know. I have to make it with limes.'

He didn't care what she made it with, it was always delicious.

'You're really rather stuck out there in the middle of those rice fields, aren't you?' she continued. 'Now that you can't just hop on – what do you call that thing you ride on? – and pop into Yogya whenever you feel like it.'

'Big Red; yeah, I'll be glad when my shoulder's okay again, but in the meantime I've got lots of work to do.'

'What is it you anthropologists really do anyway?'

'They keep it a secret,' put in Derek, 'that way no one can ever accuse them of not doing it.'

'Well, whatever it is can wait, can't it,' Mary said, paying scant attention to her husband and turning back to Barry. 'Why don't you come and stay with us until your shoulder's better?'

'Thanks but –'

'Or for a few days at least.'

'I don't think –'

But seeing that he looked tempted, she pressed on, 'Today is Thursday, isn't it?'

He nodded, wondering what difference that made.

'You're here now and the usual crowd will probably be here on Saturday so why don't you just stay here with us until then?'

He didn't need much persuasion.

'Okay, thanks, I just might do that,' he said.

The first light of Saturday morning was hovering on the horizon when Tess stirred in her sleep, an unaccountable wave of homesickness sweeping over her. Bacon and eggs, she thought dreamily, but who would be cooking bacon in this Muslim country? Clearly it was someone who wasn't very good at it because she was burning it badly. It was making an ominous crackling sound and it didn't smell much like the bacon at home. It smelled like –

She sniffed again, opened her eyes and leapt out of bed. The curtains were on fire and, thanks to a gust of wind, they were billowing out into the room. One of them caught on a metal prong that had been holding the glass top of the kerosene lamp in place and knocked it over. An instant later her bedspread was ablaze.

'Help,' she screamed, wide awake now, 'help, fire, help, help!'

Remembering where she was and switching into Indonesian, she ran over to her desk, scooped up the pile of thesis notes on top of it, grabbed her handbag and fled from the rapidly encroaching flames.

Her cries roused the entire family, who in turn alerted the neighbours. Someone ran to wake up the friend down the street who had a telephone, although no one held out much hope that the fire department would arrive any time soon.

Bucket brigades were formed to douse Tess's room with water from the storage vats in the surrounding houses. Men with strong arms manned water pumps while women threw wet rags on the flames. After what seemed like ages to Tess but she learned later hadn't actually been very long at all, the fire was contained and then extinguished.

A survey of the damage showed it to be far less extensive than Tess would have thought possible. Her own room had borne the brunt of it. The charred plaster walls would need a fresh coat of whitewash but the wooden timbers overhead had been declared strong enough to carry on supporting the heavy tile roof.

Although this was great news, the thought of all the thesis work she hadn't managed to save made Tess feel positively sick. Nothing else she had lost really mattered. She still had a few clothes; the ones she had worn yesterday would be at the back of the house waiting to be washed. And some reflex action had made her pick up her handbag as she had raced out of the room so she still had whatever was in it, including her passport. She would need that for identification right away if she wanted to get any money out of the bank.

But as for the thesis notes, she couldn't bear to think about all the work that had gone into them. It was too awful.

She would have buried her face in her hands and cried like a baby, if a friendly neighbour hadn't forestalled this by handing her a cup of hot sweet tea. She was drinking it gratefully when a little girl who lived down the street brought her a plate of chilli fried rice. Her first thought was that she couldn't possibly eat it but the child looked so disappointed, she felt she had to give it a try.

To her surprise it tasted good and before long she felt sufficiently energised to join in the massive clean-up that was going on throughout the house.

After a while she began to notice that, for once nobody was staring at the strange foreigner in their midst. It was quite the opposite. They seemed to be looking away and it gave her an uncomfortable feeling that something, apart from the fire, was wrong. She tried to catch what the people around her were saying but it was nearly impossible because they were all speaking Javanese. Even so, she managed to pick up enough clues to be fairly certain they were talking about the fire. After all, what else would they be talking about?

Still, the uncomfortable feeling persisted. Were they speculating about who or what might have caused it? She thought so but she couldn't be sure.

That was when a horrible suspicion crept into her mind; did they think she had been the one who had dropped the match or upset the kerosene lamp?

The very idea made her want to get as far away from everyone as she possibly could but realising that she couldn't go very far in her pyjamas, she went to the back of the house and washed a few of her clothes that were there.

Could Paul have started it, she wondered, thinking of Philip's warning? No, she told herself, surely someone would have noticed a foreign man creeping around. It must have been dark at the time but lots of Javanese people, especially women, got up well before first light and the unexpected presence of a foreign man in the neighbourhood wouldn't have gone unremarked.

That meant that it couldn't have been Paul, she decided, but if not Paul then who or what? Could the wind alone have been enough to have blown the curtain against the lamp and knocked it over? Possibly but she didn't think so and she'd better be careful, it wouldn't do to let herself develop some sort of paranoia about Paul just because of Philip's silly suspicions.

She rejoined the clean-up brigade for a while and then checked on her clothes. The hot Javanese sun dried clothes quickly and although the jeans were still a bit damp, she decided to wear them anyway. After taking a dry top off the line and telling herself that nobody really needed underwear, she got dressed, flagged down a passing rickshaw and directed the driver to the area where the Kents lived.

It was Saturday and the usual gathering would probably be there.

'Where have you been?' Holly demanded, opening the door almost before she had had a chance to knock. 'I've been waiting for you all morning. Don't you remember, we were going to explore the place where the old palace on the hill used to be? You didn't go without me, did you?'

'Of course I didn't, I wouldn't have done that. You can't imagine what happened during the night.'

'What?'

'My house caught fire and my room is a charred

burned-out mess.'

'Did firemen come?'

'Yes, eventually.'

'Did they rescue anyone?'

'No one needed rescuing by the time they got there.'

For a moment Holly looked disappointed but then, making the most of her flair for the dramatic, she flung open the door of the lounge and announced, in her best centre-stage manner, 'Tess's house has burned down. It's a –' Suddenly in need of a prompter, she turned to Tess and asked, 'What did you say it is?'

'A charred burned-out mess.'

If Holly was looking for an excited reaction to this news, she certainly found it. Questions about what happened and exclamations of dismay and sympathy, along with offers of assistance, immediately rained down on Tess from the group around the table.

'Come and stay with us until your place is liveable again,' Mary urged.

'Yes, we have plenty of room,' added Derek.

'You'll need something to wear while you're having some new things made,' Mary said. 'My sewing lady can help there. And you can rummage around in my closet any time you like although I'm afraid everything there will be several sizes too big for you.'

Turning to Felicia, who had just arrived and was being

filled in on the story, she went on, 'You must be about Tess's size, perhaps you can come to the rescue. You could lend her a few things, couldn't you?'

Felicia didn't want to refuse in front of Elizabeth and Mary and some of the others who, for reasons that were unfathomable to her, still liked Tess. The trouble was that Paul would go ballistic if he found out she was doing anything to help his number one enemy. As far as he was concerned, Tess was the devil incarnate.

'You'll certainly need a cup of tea after all that,' Mary told Tess, as she poured her one.

'To hell with tea, give her a whisky,' Derek suggested.

'Sherry would be better,' Holly countered. 'Granny always says that's the thing for nerves.'

'Your granny's right,' Tess said, giving Holly a grateful smile, 'sherry's a lovely idea.'

It proved to be up to Granny's highest expectations and Tess was just taking the last sip when Barry clocked in.

'It looks like a lively crew here today,' he observed, 'any special reason?'

Everyone tried to tell him at once. When he had managed to disentangle the various versions of events, he responded not with the exclamations of horror that seemed to be generally expected but with a quiet grimace.

It had to have been Paul, he told himself, and since Philip clearly isn't doing anything to protect Tess or at least not doing enough, it looks like it's going to be up to me.

Then he stumbled upon the question of what that would be. The answer wasn't going to be easy to come up with because - without a certain amount of cooperation from Tess - his hands were tied. After all, he couldn't exactly pick her up and put her on a plane back to the States without her consent. He'd have to settle for round-the-clock vigilance but that would be a problem too. It would have to mean either staying up all night, not a great prospect especially if it involved several nights in a row, or taking her to bed with him and there was a word for doing that against her will. Seduction would be okay but managing it would be a bit tricky at this point.

Nobody noticed the unfinished piece of cake on Barry's plate when he went over, murmured something to Mary and rather abruptly left. The conversation was still swirling around the disaster and what could have caused it.

Mary was convinced that a carelessly thrown match had started it all and most of the others, largely for lack of a better idea, tended to agree.

When Elizabeth suggested that somebody, possibly Paul, might have started the fire deliberately, everyone immediately declared that that was impossible. Admittedly he had gone berserk up there on the mountain but that must have been due to some kind of temporary insanity brought on by his terrifying experience. He was fine now and there was no way he would ever have done a dreadful thing like that.

Mary added to this argument, saying that she had run into him in Toko Mirota the other day and commiserated with him about his lost camera. He hadn't even mentioned Tess.

Derek and the Carpenters said they had played tennis with him after work on Thursday and that he had seemed perfectly normal then, nothing like a hate-obsessed deranged pyromaniac.

Several people then hinted that Elizabeth should really be more careful with her unfounded accusations. She bit her lip under the rebuke and didn't try to defend herself while the conversation shifted from the causes of the fire to the effects and Derek saw to it that Tess's glass of sherry never stayed empty for long.

She had just begun to feel a little light-headed when a dilapidated car pulled up in front of the window and Barry sprang out.

'Where did you find that horror?' Derek asked. 'It looks like it's held together with chicken wire.'

'It belongs to Kanwa's brother,' he returned rather huffily, as he picked up his half-finished cake and held his cup out to Mary for more tea.

'Whose brother?' she asked.

'Kanwa's, a friend of mine at Gajah Mada,' Barry

explained. 'I've borrowed it for a few hours.'

'Whatever for?'

'Perhaps he's taking it to an antiques fair,' Derek suggested.

Barry looked wounded. 'Is it that bad?'

'Worse,' said Mary, joining in the fun.

'Well I'm not entering it in a beauty contest,' Barry pointed out. 'All it has to do is get Tess to the airport.'

'But I'm not going anywhere,' she protested.

'You may not have planned to,' Barry said, 'but that doesn't mean you can't start thinking about it now.'

'Why would I want to do that?'

'You don't have to stay away very long,' he said, ignoring her question, 'only until that nut, Paul, gets his arse out of here.'

'Oh, you're just being ridiculous,' she returned, dismissively.

'No he isn't,' declared Philip, who had just arrived and was standing quietly by the door. 'What he's saying makes a lot of sense.'

'But he's acting as if it was definitely Paul who started the fire and I don't see how he can be so sure,' Tess protested.

'He doesn't have to be,' Philip said. 'He's not talking about convicting him in a court of law and locking him up for years. He's just talking about a little vacation for you, a week or so in Bali. How would that be?'

'It would be a colossal nuisance,' she replied ungratefully. 'And anyway, I was just there, or don't you remember?'

'Singapore, then, but you'd need your passport for that. You didn't manage to rescue that by any chance, did you?'

'I did actually. It's in my handbag.'

'There you are,' Philip said. 'Bring me the ticket stub and the hotel bill when you get back and I'll see that you aren't permanently out of pocket.'

'In the meantime,' put in Barry, looking at his watch. 'We'd better get a move on if we don't want to miss the Jakarta flight.'

'You've missed it by about three hours already,' Felicia observed, looking pleased.

'No we haven't,' Barry returned. 'There was some kind of delay on the ground in Bali this afternoon and it hasn't arrived yet. If we're lucky, we can still make it.'

'How do you know that?' Felicia asked.

'The guy I'm borrowing the car from works at the airport. He told me.' Turning back to Tess, he said, 'So where are we? Are you going to have an unexpected vacation somewhere or are you going to stay here and wait around to be strangled again, possibly a bit more effectively this time?'

'You're making it sound like it would be really stupid to stay.'

442

'You said it, I didn't.'

Everyone began talking at once, urging her to stay away from Yogya until Paul had gone.

'It's just a precautionary measure,' Derek said, 'but why not have an extra little holiday if Philip's willing to pay for it?'

'Listen, we've got to hurry,' Barry pointed out, 'or you'll miss the plane.'

'But I have to go home and pack a –'

'You don't have anything to pack,' Barry reminded her. 'It all went up in flames a few hours ago.'

'You really must go to Singapore, you know,' Mary urged. 'You've got to have some clothes and you might be able to find some decent ones there.'

Mary was right, Tess decided. She couldn't keep wearing the same things day after day, so why not let the Foundation pay for an unexpected shopping trip? She wouldn't stay long though, just long enough to treat herself to a few things, then she would come back whether Paul was still here or not.

Unaware of the different turn her life would take when she got back, she climbed into the little rattletrap car and let Barry drive her to the airport.

TWENTY YEARS ON
Java 1989 A.D.

The pilot's announcement that they would be landing in Yogyakarta in ten minutes, Allah willing, sent Tess into a fleeting panic. Was she really ready to step back into that world she had put behind her all those years ago; that world of Barry and Philip, of Mt Merapi and Prambanan, of rational research and mystical ideas, possibly even of ancient memories carried over from past lives?

She was no longer convinced about the previous incarnations but she had no doubt about the existence of Barry and Philip. One of them had probably been real enough to have given her a baby, although Mike could also have been Art's father. She had never been entirely sure.

She had been with Philip from the time she got back from her brief trip to Singapore until the night when they had had their worst row ever. It had been about her thesis, what else, and had taught her a lesson she wouldn't forget: never again would she try to live with a total control freak.

Deciding she had all the material she needed for her thesis by that time, she had gathered up the notes she had salvaged from the fire and the clothes she had bought in Singapore, scribbled a quick line to Philip and sent the houseboy out for a taxi.

'To the airport,' she had told the driver but as they were speeding along Jalan Solo, it suddenly hadn't seemed right to leave without saying goodbye to Barry. Stopping by his village, or as close as a car could get to it, would just mean a quick detour so she had tapped the driver on the shoulder and told him where to go.

As goodbyes went, it had deserved a gold star. It lasted for three days, three nights really because they had spent most of their time in bed. Eventually Barry had tied her case on the back of Big Red, taken her to the airport and promised to write. They would get together as soon as his grant was up and he got back to the States.

But she didn't like to think about those promises; they hurt too much.

That terrible letter had destroyed everything, the letter that had made her determined never to open another one from Barry.

Yet, in blocking Barry from her memory, she had had to drive so much else out as well. As soon as she had handed in her thesis, she had changed her field of interest from Southeast Asian archaeology to Greco-Roman and had consigned her experiences in Yogya to a bittersweet dream.

Mike, on the other hand, had proved to be very real. She had phoned him to let him know she was back and somehow their relationship had more or less picked up where it left off. By the time she had realised she was pregnant, it had seemed reasonably likely that Mike was the father, although she couldn't completely rule out the possibility of Philip or Barry meriting that honour.

She had hoped that it wasn't Barry but she hadn't let that thought bother her very much because she had been convinced that one glance at the baby would be enough to tell her its paternity.

The problem was that the uncooperative little rascal - she had called him Art - hadn't actually resembled any of the probable suspects. He had just looked like a baby and Mike had been such a star when it had come to all the daddy stuff, like middle of the night feedings, that she hadn't wanted to think about the possibility of Art being anyone's but his.

But that had all been a long time ago. Art was almost nineteen now and he still didn't look like any of his possible biological fathers. He had remained very close to Mike, in spite of the fact that she herself had not. Their marriage had come apart when Mike had fallen in love with his colleague's very pretty assistant, made her pregnant and, with an eagerness that made her smile, embarked on the routine of sleepless nights again.

The divorce had proceeded quite amicably. She had felt that the moral high ground just wasn't a comfortable place for her, so neither of them had taken the other to court and much of the unpleasantness that usually went with divorce had been avoided.

Three years later she had married Karl and, in a moment of carelessness after a particularly great party when they had both been a bit stoned, they had created Art's little sister, Eleanor.

The trouble was that Karl hadn't been taken with the idea of playing daddy the way Mike had been. But that was only part of the problem; the other part was the sexy graduate student who was working with him on his book. Another divorce – this time with a hefty, albeit grudging, financial contribution from Karl to cover the cost of a nanny so she could keep working – had been the result.

She had sailed through the divorce from Mike so easily that it hadn't put her off marrying again but after all the nasty battles under the beady eyes of Karl's lawyer, there was no way she was going to sign up to any more 'til death do us part' contracts. Marriage didn't really suit her anyway; between her two children, her career and all the hard work it had taken to move from a minor university on Long Island to her current position in classical archaeology at NYU, she simply didn't have the time or the energy to deal with a husband. An occasional romp in bed with someone was the most sex she could fit into her busy life.

Going back to Java hadn't figured in her plans at all. If the invitation from the Southeast Asia Foundation to attend a Symposium on Social Research in Java hadn't arrived on one of the coldest, wettest days in February, a day when an arctic wind had sent giant flakes of snow swirling through Washington Square, her response would surely have been different. But when she had opened it, the thought of tropical gardens with mangoes and papayas hanging from trees, frangipani and bougainvillea blossoming in the surrounding greenery and gentle rivulets of water rippling across the surface of sky blue swimming pools; well, it had been just too tempting to resist.

Without bothering too much about why she had been asked to such a conference after so many years of not doing any research on Java, she had written back saying she would be there.

Now, as the plane was approaching Yogyakarta, she was beginning to wonder about the wisdom of what she was doing. In all the years since she had been researching for her thesis she had avoided coming back, preferring to leave her memories of that time buried in the deepest recesses of her mind.

This meeting, one that was almost certain to be littered with former relationships, forgotten fears and past conflicts, was going to force her to look back at a time in her life that she wasn't at all sure she wanted to remember;

a time before she had made so many compromises with her dreams.

But it was useless to worry about all that now. She would just have to hope that none of her demons made their presence felt; that by some miracle Barry wouldn't be there; that Mt Merapi wouldn't erupt and that the amount of hot air inevitably generated at conferences of this sort would be kept to a minimum. If so, she might only need to stay in Yogya for a couple of days.

From the moment she stepped off the plane and looked around, she could see that almost nothing had gone unchanged in the twenty years since she had been there. It gave her a disconcerting sensation of being in a place that was both extremely familiar and totally new at the same time.

This feeling was made even more unsettling when she walked into the air conditioned lobby of the Ambarrukmo Hotel and was greeted by the tones of the traditional Javanese orchestra, the *gamelan*. Where else in the world would she hear that haunting sound?

Once in her room, she decided she had better check the schedule for the symposium before she unpacked; she was delighted when she saw that there was nothing to do until the next morning. That meant a little breathing space before she had to face up to the possibility of running into Philip, a virtual certainty since his name had been on the invitation, or worse, meet up with Barry.

What the fuck, she told herself sternly, his presence or absence didn't matter to her any more than Philip's did. It had all been too long ago. And anyway, if the prospect of seeing one or the other of them was so horrible, why on earth had she come? Getting cold feet about it now was ridiculous.

Actually, if she ran into Barry they might not even recognise each other after all these years. How much would he have changed, she wondered, or for that matter, how much had she changed? She looked at herself in the mirror over the dressing table and tried to superimpose an image of herself as she remembered it from her postgraduate days. Her long plait had been a casualty of the passing years. She wore her hair shorter now, letting if fall just an inch or two below her ears, but the colour was still the same light brown with a touch of red that it had always been. Happily, she had stayed slim and hadn't gone all wrinkly either but she was beginning to notice that soft lighting took ten years off her age.

At the moment a shower, a change of clothes and a refreshing drink would probably do more for her appearance than anything else but why just cool off in the shower when there was a beautiful pool in the hotel garden?

A few minutes later she was luxuriating in the water and telling herself that she really should be doing laps. Yet she simply couldn't focus on anything like exercise when she was surrounded by a wonderful riot of tropical colour; shades of green punctuated with the red, magenta, yellow and white of the flowering bushes and trees.

She settled on a long languid swim instead of serious laps, then took possession of a rattan lounge chair, ordered a gin and tonic and allowed the warm humid air to envelope her. With nothing to do but relax and absorb the seductive atmosphere of the garden, she inadvertently opened her mind to long, suppressed thoughts of Barry.

She pushed them away as quickly as she could, reminding herself sternly that she didn't care whether the bastard was going to be at the symposium or not so why let herself get in a flap about him? He probably wouldn't be there anyway, it was the sort of thing he would hate unless, of course, he had really matured and she couldn't imagine that would ever happen. The very thought brought a smile to her face but only for a moment. It was interrupted by the memory of that terrible day when the devastating letter from Cynthia had arrived.

It had had a Yogya postmark and a photograph of herself with Barry at the wedding of the *jamu* lady's eldest daughter enclosed. She could recall every word of the accompanying lines as clearly as if Cynthia's scented notepaper were still in front of her.

Dear Tess,

I breezed over to Indonesia for Tini's wedding and just want to drop you a line to tell you how much Barry misses you. It was all I could do to console him. It was pretty obvious he hadn't had any YOU KNOW WHAT since you left.

Why don't you give John a call, since he is by himself in New York? Philadelphia isn't very far so maybe you two can get together. He's a little annoyed with me at the moment and I'd appreciate it if you could soothe him for me. It would be a fair exchange since I've been taking care of Barry for you.

Love,
Cynthia

And there had been a pair of interlocking triangles with smiling faces on them beneath her signature.

Subsequent days had brought a letter from Barry describing Tini's wedding with no mention of the fact that

Cynthia had been there. She had also had a telephone call from John saying that he was suing Cynthia for divorce, naming Barry as co-respondent, and asking her if she would testify in court about the little sex triangle that the three of them had going.

She had been so sickened by the whole thing that she had resolved to put Barry out of her mind and out of her life forever. She just couldn't handle a relationship that involved the periodic appearance of Cynthia.

After that she had torn up Barry's letters without opening them and hung up on his phone calls. She couldn't stand to hear any more of his lies, half-truths or glaring omissions. By the time he had actually appeared at her door a few months later, she and Mike had not only been back together but were married.

The memory of that brilliant moment when, with Mike at her side, she had slammed the door in Barry's face, would linger in her mind forever.

She and Mike had stayed together for nearly five years, the last three primarily because neither of them had wanted Art to grow up in a broken home.

Out of necessity, she had taken a bit of time off for childcare and when she was able to devote herself full-time to her career again, she had resolutely abandoned anything and everything related to Java, reading her way into classical archaeology instead.

This shift in direction had proved to be a good move for reasons that had nothing to do with Barry. Job opportunities for archaeologists were hard to find and those few that did exist were generally in the more popular areas; classical or pre-Columbian.

She was just finishing her drink when she thought that Philip, hard arse though he was, had certainly been right about one thing. Following a dream to the site of Troy may have worked for Schliemann but it wasn't the way archaeology was carried out today.

What in the world could have been on Philip's mind, she wondered, when he had invited someone to this symposium who hadn't done any work on Java for twenty years? He must have had –

'Tess.'

A voice so familiar she might have heard it yesterday made her jump.

Looking up, she had no trouble recognising Barry even though laughter lines had appeared around his eyes and there were small furrows between his eyebrows. There was also a suggestion of grey in his hair but he was deeply tanned and moved with the same cheerful nonchalance she remembered as he swung onto a chair next to her.

'This is a surprise,' she said, although of course it wasn't.

Then, embarrassed at the absurdity of this assertion, she babbled on, 'I thought you must have fallen off the edge of the earth.'

'I did, I went to Australia.'

'For twenty years?'

'Seventeen.'

'Captured by a band of brigand kangaroos?'

'Held captive by the job market, actually. You know what it's been like since the Vietnam War, the last place Americans want to hear about is Southeast Asia, so any jobs for area specialists pretty much dried up overnight. The Aussies are the only ones who've had the smarts to see that Indonesia's worth bothering about. They've even gotten hold of some crazy notion that anthropology professors should be paid something more than starvation wages, so you can see why the place appeals to me. I went there on a three-year contract and have more or less been glued to the spot ever since. Nobody Stateside seems to have noticed that I'm not around, so why go back?'

'Have you married an Australian girl then?'

'Yes, two.'

'Isn't that overdoing it a bit?' she said, with a laugh.

'Some clown told me that serial monogamy was the in thing and it fitted the cool dude image I was trying to cultivate. Unsuccessfully, I might add. How about you? How many times have you braved that bone-chilling walk down to the aisle?'

'Also twice.'

'Currently enjoying the blissful state?'

'No, are you?'

'Not at the moment.'

Eyeing her empty glass, he asked, 'What are you drinking these days?'

'Gin and tonic.'

'That should hit the spot for me,' he said, signalling the waiter and ordering one for each of them.

Tess, noticing that his Indonesian, unlike her own, was still fluent, asked, 'Do you come back to Java often?

'A couple of times a year if I can manage it. I try to keep up with what's going on in the old village but it really just takes a quick look-in to do that. The wives hated it and I never could bludgeon them into staying very long.'

'You must have been hell to be married to.'

'That's what they said,' he replied cheerfully, but he didn't linger over the subject very long. Instead he launched into an account of some of the changes in Java since she had last seen it.

'This new spelling is a bitch,' he declared, 'but I guess you know about that.'

She nodded.

'Not that it's very new anymore but I still have a hard time bringing myself to write Yogya with a 'Y' instead of a 'J'.'

'Do people really pronounce it 'Yogyakarta'?' she asked.

'Only the tourists.'

Barry reached for his drink, glared at it balefully when he found it empty and ordered another round.

Tess hoped no one would notice how late she was as she slipped into the back of the room where one of the symposium's speakers was already in full flow. But Barry noticed her, looked pointedly at his watch and wagged his finger at her in mock reproof. She laughed but inwardly felt like a naughty schoolgirl and quickly turned her attention to the man who was holding forth on the podium. It took her a moment to realise that it was Philip.

How grey he is, she thought, sort of grey all over, and smaller and thinner than I remember. He was speaking in Indonesian and she was distressed at how little of it she was able to follow.

She looked around at the sea of unfamiliar faces, mostly Indonesian with a sprinkling of foreigners here and there. She thought she recognised two professors from the Archaeology Department at Gajah Mada and was fairly sure that one of them was the friend of Philip's who had uncovered the stone inscription proving, or so he claimed, that the capital of the Mataram Kingdom had been at Tegal.

God, that argument seemed like ages ago. Did she care about it anymore? Did anyone care? She had no idea.

Scanning the symposium programme for presentations on archaeology, she only found two and they were both on the Majapahit Kingdom in East Java. The rest were all on current topics.

But wasn't the official name of the symposium '20 Years of Social Research in Java'? Did that mean there had been nothing important on the Mataram Kingdom in all that time, nothing that had shown where the capital had been when the kingdom was in its glory? The buried treasure of the rajas, if it had ever existed, had clearly not come to light.

Philip finished whatever it was he had been saying and in the ensuing round of applause led by the foreigners and followed without much zest by the Indonesians, she noticed that a young woman with light brown hair and blue eyes was looking at him with what seemed like considerable affection.

The odd thing, apart from this pretty girl apparently thinking Philip was quite wonderful, was that there was something vaguely familiar about her. But she didn't look like she was more than twenty seven or twenty eight, Tess told herself. She was too young to have been in Yogya all those years ago.

The mystery was solved during the mid-morning coffee break when the girl came over and spoke to her.

'You probably don't remember me? At least you can't possibly recognise me. I'm Holly Kent.'

'Holly! I knew I had seen you before,' Tess protested. 'Whatever brings you here?'

'Prambanan, I'm working with the Archaeology Department on the restoration.'

'But how –'

'It's all because of you really,' Holly said, 'well, also because of a grant from the Southeast Asia Foundation. That's thanks to Uncle Philip, of course. You see, I never forgot those Saturday afternoons with you when we went out to the temple sites and nosed around amongst the fallen stones.'

'They were fun,' Tess agreed.

'They were exciting treasure hunts for me, so much so that I read archaeology at university and now,' she smiled happily, 'I'm here.'

After some mutual exclamations about how great all this was, Holly pulled Tess over to Philip.

Polite but cool, he didn't seem any more enthusiastic about their reunion than she was and he quickly let it be known that he was a busy man.

'Uncle Philip's always like that,' Holly whispered to her when their brief exchange was over, 'a little reserved but he's a dear. So is Auntie Elizabeth.'

'His wife?'

'You must remember her,' Holly said reproachfully. 'Wasn't she a great friend of yours? But then I suppose she wasn't married to Uncle Philip then.'

'Of course I remember Elizabeth. It was just the 'auntie' part that threw me and I had no idea she had married Philip.'

Since it was clear that Holly would not appreciate a comment along the lines of 'poor Elizabeth', Tess resisted the temptation to say it. Instead she merely asked, 'Are they living here in Yogya?'

'No, they live in Singapore. That's where the main office of the Foundation is now. It's much bigger than it used to be and has offices and projects all over the place. Uncle Philip's the director for all of Southeast Asia.'

Tess absorbed this information without enthusiasm.

'Something I can't understand,' she confessed to Holly, 'is why I was invited to this symposium when it's been years since I've done any work on Java.'

'Oh it was a conspiracy,' Holly replied, her eyes lighting up with a mischievous sparkle.

'A conspiracy?'

'Yes, together with Ninik. She is still at the office here; in fact, she really runs it now and we thought it would be such fun to see you again that we slipped your name onto the invitation list. Uncle Philip must have seen it but he didn't say anything, so here you are. Wasn't he a bit in love with you years ago?'

'Not really,' Tess insisted, although she wondered if this was quite true.

As the day wore on and papers on subjects that barely interested her were read in a language she now had to struggle to understand, she began to think that Holly had not done her a favour in putting her on the invitation list. After all, she had made a modest name for herself in classical archaeology and was not in the habit of wasting her time at events that were so peripheral to her professional interests.

Her thoughts wandered back to Holly and what she had been like as a child. She had seemed so grown-up for her age but as a young woman, she seemed rather childlike. There had always been something a little odd about her.

Glancing across the room, Tess saw that Holly had put on a pair of round gold-rimmed glasses and was listening attentively to the speaker, giving every appearance of being not only mature but quite intelligent as well.

Did I totally misjudge her, Tess wondered, or is it that there's something about her little conspiracy that doesn't quite ring true? Not that it matters really, it's all rather flattering and it will be fun to see Ninik again so I'll just concentrate on enjoying it.

It's funny though, Tess thought as her mind continued to wander. I still have the same feeling about Holly I used to have, that she's sort of a younger version of me. Seeing her makes me wonder if some young, idealistic part of me that I hadn't thought existed anymore actually does. And that's a rather exciting feeling.

Exciting perhaps but not altogether good, she realised, as the walls of the room suddenly seemed to close in on her, locking her into a world of people and emotions she wanted to repress.

The man sitting next to her brought her back to reality by passing along a note that said:

> Don't look so agonised, very few people actually die of boredom so you'll probably survive. How about a splash in the pool in about five minutes, then a well-earned drink in the bar?
>
> B.

She telegraphed her approval with a nod.

He was doing laps when she got to the pool and didn't seem to notice her arrival, so deciding it was useless to call out any kind of greeting to someone whose head was mostly underwater, she sat down on the edge and dangled her feet in the water.

'Hey, don't be such a wimp,' he called when he finally surfaced. 'Come on in.'

'I'm just taking my time.'

'We'll see about that,' he declared, and grabbing both her legs, pulled her unceremoniously into the water.

There was no way she was going to accept this kind of treatment without taking revenge so a lively game of 'splash and dunk' ensued, one in which Tess was inevitably the loser.

'Stop,' she sputtered, when breathlessness forced her to give up the struggle.

'Surrender?'

'No, truce.'

'Truces not allowed, only surrender.'

'You might be sorry you said that,' she threatened, although she wasn't quite sure just how she would make that happen.

They had the pool practically to themselves until someone else, a man too intent on his fitness program to notice them, dived in and raced blindly towards Tess. Barry grabbed her around the waist and pulled her out of the way just in time to avoid a painful collision.

He couldn't have just let that bastard bump into her, Barry told himself when the danger had passed, but at least he had let her go as soon as the guy was out the way.

What could she have done but grab hold of Barry, Tess asked herself, but at least she had broken away as soon as she could.

Yet brief as the moment of physical contact had been, it was enough to add a new element to the mood of the past hour. A sudden tension and defensive wariness sprang up between them.

Don't take me back to what I want to forget, each said silently to the other. But in spite of themselves, they were still lingering in the pool when the rapidly falling twilight began to envelope the garden.

Before long, the lamps around the pool were lit and cast their shimmering glow over the surface of the water, a glow that distorted reality and let Barry see a girl of twenty-three, her eyes shining with excitement when she talked about a vanished kingdom. And Tess saw a devil-may-care anthropologist with a mocking smile and a red motorcycle striding into her life, her feelings and her heart.

Barry, uncomfortable with images he knew couldn't be true, said, 'Come on, let's get out and find something to drink.'

'Good idea,' Tess agreed. Glad to shake off any disturbing memories, she quickly swam over to the steps, climbed out the pool and sat down at a nearby table.

When they had finished their first round of drinks and were close to polishing off their second, Barry began to lose his jocular manner and became almost hostile. 'Actually there are a couple of things that have been bugging me ever since I saw you here,' he said.

'Oh, like what?'

'Like why the hell you stopped answering my letters the way you did, just out of the blue without a word of explanation. And why you shut the door on our relationship, literally and physically. What, or more likely who, could possibly have made you do that? Surely not that fish-faced nerd you had been engaged to? Christ, he had all the warmth and passion of a cod on a slab.'

'Mike was nothing like a cod or any other kind of fish,' she protested, heatedly, 'but that's beside the point. I can't believe you didn't realise why I stopped writing. Only a prize idiot could have failed to figure it out.'

'Call me a moron then but the fact is, I'm still in the dark.'

She told him about the letter from Cynthia.

'But all that was rubbish, a total lie,' he gasped when she had finished.

'I happen to know it was true,' she retorted, furious

that even after all these years he couldn't, or wouldn't, be honest with her.

'And what makes you think you know that?'

'Things like the pictures of you and Cynthia together at the wedding, like the fact that Cynthia's letter was postmarked Yogyakarta, like all the detail you went into about the wedding in your next letter without happening to mention that your very affectionate ex-wife had been there for the occasion. All that made it pretty obvious there was something you weren't telling me.'

'Bullshit! I can't believe you let yourself be convinced by trivial stuff like that,' he said, aghast.

'It didn't seem trivial to me,' she argued, 'and that wasn't all. Your own brother, Cynthia's husband if I may remind you, told me what was going on between the two of you.'

'But he was thousands of miles away. What could he have known about anything?'

'He probably had the same stuff to go on that I did, like the picture of you and Cynthia at the wedding, for instance. Or did she manage to fake that somehow? You never mentioned that she had a talent for trick photography.'

'Don't be ridiculous. I don't know exactly what picture you're talking about but if it was one from the wedding, there wouldn't have been any need to fake it.

She was there.'

'Then why didn't you say anything about Cynthia being there when you wrote to me?'

'I didn't want to tell you because –'

'Because I might have been ever so slightly bothered by the idea of you having a romantic interlude with your ex, was that it?'

'Well, you seem to be ever so slightly bothered about it now,' he pointed out.

'Why wouldn't I be?'

'I can think of several reasons.'

'Like what?'

'First and foremost that it was a hell of a long time ago. The bride at that wedding is currently expecting her first grandchild.'

'And the second thing?'

'Didn't it ever occur to you that two people could be guests at the same wedding without falling into bed with each other?'

'Not if one of the people was Cynthia.'

Much to her annoyance, he burst out laughing. 'She would love to hear you describing her as some sort of femme fatale but I promise you, on that particular weekend her charms were wasted.'

'Do you really expect me to believe that?'

'Believe it,' he said. 'She did come to Yogya, I admit

that, but you and I were still a going thing at the time, or so I thought anyway. And since I knew about her little tricks with the *jamu* by then I didn't give her a chance to slip me any, so nothing happened. Absolutely nothing.'

'But she told me and John did too –'

'She's a liar and he's a prick. They could have told you anything.'

'But why –'

'God only knows. Maybe Cynthia wanted to get back at me, maybe she was jealous of you or maybe she was just being vicious and trying to get her claws into you. How the hell should I know?'

'But there was John's letter too, that made all the difference. Combined with the fact that you had decided not to mention an interesting bit of news like –'

'Like what?'

'Like that little conjugal visit –'

'There was nothing conjugal about it,' Barry cried in exasperation. 'I made sure of that.'

'Then what gave John the idea that it was?'

'Geography, I guess, since he knew Cynthia was back in my village. But at that point I doubt if he really cared. Knowing John, he was probably just dredging up as much dirt as possible so he could throw it around in the divorce court and keep the judge from sticking him with too much alimony. It was really shitty of him to drag you into the process of what he now refers to as offloading his bad investment. I had no idea he was doing that.'

'I never thought –' Tess began.

'Obviously you didn't think,' Barry said, with so much anger in his voice that it almost frightened her.

'You're the one who's not thinking now,' she retorted. 'I had good reason not to trust you, remember?'

'Bullshit. You didn't have an ounce of reason, not after I found out about the jamu.'

'But I –'

'But you just let that scheming little liar, together with my reptilian brother, change the direction of your life, and my life too, worse luck. And without so much as asking me if what they were saying was true, without so much as thinking that you had reason to believe in me, without thinking at all! Good God, Madame Professor Tess, an orang-utan has more brains than you.'

Getting up so suddenly that his chair went clattering onto the tile surface surrounding the pool, he stormed back into the hotel.

'Don't worry, the feeling's mutual,' she said.

Barry didn't return for any more sessions of the symposium.

When the last paper had been read and it was all over,

Tess was free to do whatever she liked for the rest of her two-week stay in Yogya. She moved to a smaller, more charming hotel built around a courtyard garden, which was not only cheaper and more simple but would be free from any danger of running into Barry or Philip.

The thought of spending hours and hours prowling around Prambanan, renewing her acquaintance with the gods and goddesses depicted on its walls and refreshing her memory of the age-old epics of the Ramayana and the Mahabharata, made her giddy with excitement.

Holly had promised to pick her up the next morning and take her out to see the renovations. She was clearly very proud of it all and was so eager to show it off that Tess hadn't had the heart to tell her that she would really rather go there by herself, the first time anyway. She couldn't imagine why this should be true and hoped she wasn't being foolish enough to think she could recapture the dreams and enthusiasm of her youth. They, along with two of Art's three possible fathers, belonged to a world that was no longer part of her life.

Yet as she was unpacking her case in the new hotel, she was seized with an overwhelming impulse to just drop everything and go out to her much-loved temple. She had the rest of the afternoon free, the hotel was near Jalan Solo and, not being a poverty-stricken postgraduate student anymore, she could just ask the girl at the reception desk to get a taxi for her.

As for Holly, well, she just wouldn't mention that she had given into the temptation to go ahead and have a peek on her own. She felt a little guilty about this but not guilty enough to change what she was about to do.

The excitement she felt when she caught her first glimpse of the temple's towering spires was followed by a moment of distress as the taxi driver went speeding past. Hadn't he understood where she wanted to go? She was about to repeat her instructions when he veered off sharply to the left, then drew up in front of the gate to a beautifully landscaped park dotted with newly planted trees and laced with inviting paths.

To her astonishment, she saw that a ticket window had been set up and she was expected to pay an entrance fee. The sum required was negligible and, if asked, she would have said she approved of the idea of having visitors contribute to the temple's upkeep. Yet on some deeper level she couldn't help feeling affronted. It was as if she were suddenly being asked to pay an entrance fee to go through her own front door.

Hastily putting this ignoble reaction aside, she took the money out of her purse and tried to give it to the ticket seller but he shook his head and pointed to a clock that said five minutes to five.

'But there's still one more hour,' Tess protested, pointing to a sign detailing the opening hours.

He grumbled that she wouldn't have time to see very much but reluctantly scooped up the money and let her go inside.

She was surprised at how many visitors, mostly Indonesians but a scattering of foreigners, were at the temple that day and it was soon clear they all would have subscribed to the ticket seller's view that it was time to leave and not time to arrive. They were all making their way down the paths toward the exit; she was the only one foolish enough to be going in the other direction.

Tess tried to convince herself that it was good so many people were coming to see Prambanan but she couldn't quite do it. The truth was that she felt she had lost something very precious to her - the feeling that the temple belonged entirely to her was eluding her now that she was no longer the only one wandering amongst the toppled images and fallen stones.

And where were those images and stones? She scarcely saw any. Everything was neat, clean, refurbished and as good as new. It had all been put back together but the soul had been left out. It was like the set for a Hollywood movie, one that had been constructed as a background for an outdoor scene where the inside was empty.

God, what a selfish bitch she was being, she told herself as she followed one of the paths to the central courtyard. She would start making up for it the moment she saw Holly in the morning but for now she would just enjoy the fact that almost all the other visitors had left.

By the time she reached the shrines to Brahma, Vishnu and Shiva and their animals there was only one person in sight, a man lounging against a stone elephant fish at the entrance to the chapel of Nandi the Bull.

She could just ignore him, she thought, and then saw she couldn't because he was pulling himself up and greeting her with a familiar grin.

'Good God,' she exclaimed, 'what are you doing here?'

'Waiting for you,' Barry said.

'But how did you know I'd be here? I didn't know myself until five minutes before I asked the hotel for a taxi.'

'I know you, so of course I knew where you'd go the second that gruesome symposium was over.'

'Then it must have occurred to you that I wouldn't be too thrilled to see you, not after some of the things you said to me.'

'Like comparing you to an orang-utan? What's wrong with that? I like orang-utans and you would too if you bothered to get to know any. They would probably remind you of some of your better students.'

'Did you just come here to be horrible?'

'No, I can do that anywhere. I came to collect the 2000 rupiahs you owe me.'

'Whatever gives you the idea that I owe you anything?'

'Don't you remember that bet we made?'

'No, what bet?'

'Convenient for you to have forgotten.'

'Refresh my memory then.'

'The one we made about romantic love, remember? You claimed that it really existed and I said it didn't so we made a bet. We'd give it another twenty years and if either of us could honestly say we had experienced it, I'd owe you a bottle of champagne. But if neither of us could make that claim, and it would have to have been a love that lasted more than five minutes, then you'd have to buy me a beer. So I've come to collect my winnings.'

'But how can you be so sure I'm not going to say romantic love really does exist?'

'Two sessions in the divorce court are a pretty strong indication that you're not.'

'You have a point,' she acknowledged with a rueful little laugh. 'I guess I'll have to stand you to that beer but hadn't we better pay our respects to Nandi before we go?' And running her hand over the scales of the elephant fish as she went, she climbed the stairs to the little sanctuary ahead of him.

'Hey, wait for me,' Barry called, catching up with her

beneath the ferocious carved face with its entire lower jaw missing, which hung above the door.

'Who's that?' he asked, glancing up at it in mock terror.

'Kala, she guards Nandi.'

'I don't like the look of her.'

'You might not turn her on either,' Tess said, laughing. Then, her mood changing, she pushed open the door to a small chamber dominated by a massive stone bull.

To Barry's dismay, and somewhat to her own, Tess found herself pressing her palms together in the traditional gesture of respect for the stone beast that she would have used all those years ago.

What the fuck am I doing, she asked herself, picturing the faces of her friends and colleagues in New York if they could see her. There was something impressive about the animal, it was so huge that it dominated the little room and it was almost too lifelike, the sculptor must have been a genius. Still, she couldn't help thinking that making prayer-like gestures to stone beasts just didn't fit with who she was now.

'Okay, now that we've had a look,' Barry said, thinking that the place was beginning to seem a little weird, 'let's go drink up my winnings.'

'Why are you in such a hurry? Now that we're here, let's have a look at Durga's chapel. There's something about it that's bothering me.'

'Durga,' he repeated, baffled, 'who, or should I say what –'

'One of Shiva's wives, don't you remember? You must have heard me talking about her, the one who has eight arms and eight hands –'

'Too many for me.'

'And rides on a tiger.'

'Not my type.'

'She's very much my type,' Tess protested. 'I just wish I could be more like her – ride on a tiger, cut off any man's head if he annoyed me, that sort of thing.'

'I'm very glad you're not.'

'But there's something about that shrine to Durga that's bothering me.'

Barry looked puzzled. 'Like what?'

'Like the fact that I distinctly remember there was a statue of Durga in the centre of the room. She was riding on her tiger and holding some kind of weapon in each of her hands. But at the same time I remember going into the room and being crushingly disappointed because it was absolutely empty. Both of those memories can't be right and it's driving me crazy so I really want to have a look. That way I can drive the false memory out of my mind.'

'Sure, if you want to but I really don't see what the problem is. You just imagined the statue would be there so of course you felt let down when it wasn't, that's all.'

'Do you really think so?' she asked, relieved to hear such a simple explanation.

'It's obvious isn't it? But if you still want to have a look, we'd better hurry. We don't have much time before they close this place up, very possibly with us in it, and I don't think these stone floors would make for very great sleeping.'

'Okay, just a quick peek,' she said, and led the way over to another stone staircase, this one on the side of the tall, intricately carved structure dedicated to Shiva.

They looked inside and saw that the small, dimly lit room was empty.

Tess knew she was being a bit of an idiot but somehow she couldn't help feeling disappointed all over again. She had wanted the other memory to be the true one.

'Come on, we'd better go,' Barry said, and started to emphasise this with a quick tug on her long plait before he realised that it wasn't there anymore and settled for grabbing her by the scruff of the neck instead.

The feeling of that long-remembered touch shot through Tess like a bolt of lightning, instantly driving everything else from her mind; everything but the possibility of being locked in the temple for the night with Barry.

'We'd better go,' she said hastily.

He agreed and, taking her hand, led her out of the

empty room, down the steep staircase and away from the memories.

Tess had trouble getting to sleep that night, wondering whether any involvement with Barry, even just as friends, was such a great idea. The end of their relationship had been so painful last time that she'd have to be a real fool to risk it happening again, wouldn't she?

The question must have been on her mind during the night because Barry, accompanied by Durga on her tiger and followed by five or six scampering elephant fish, invaded her dreams. Somehow she could see herself in the dream but it was a younger self; one who hadn't yet given up on finding the raja's gold, one whose long rope of a plait posed a constant temptation for the mischievous elephant fish who thought it great fun to jump up, catch it in their teeth and swing on it, unmindful of the fact that this was a painful proposition for her.

The dream seemed so real that when she opened her eyes in the morning she was surprised to find herself in the Puri Artha Hotel rather than back in her old room, her thesis notes scattered across her desk and the kerosene lamp standing on the table next to her bed.

But that was all such a long time ago, she reminded herself. And Holly, who didn't know she had already been there, was going to be picking her up in less than an hour to take her to Prambanan and show her the renovations.

'Do you mind if we just run into the office first?' Holly asked as they were getting in the car. 'The plans we've been working from are there and it'll be easier to explain everything we're going to do if we have them in front of us.'

'That would be great actually. The conference has been so full-on, I haven't had a chance to see Ninik yet.'

Tess found her old friend plumper and more confident than she had been in her younger days but otherwise she didn't seem to have changed very much.

She had always been a mine of information about everybody so it came as no surprise to Tess when Ninik began filling her in on what had happened in her absence.

'The house you lived in has been torn down,' Ninik said, 'and the family has moved way out somewhere on Jalan Kaliurang. Your friend, Mini, has three children, a car and a telephone now. Professor Kanwa did some moonlighting for a foreign company and is doing very well. Many tourists are coming to Yogya these days so there are lots of new hotels and restaurants, and supermarkets too, very big ones. Prices of everything have gone way up, it's not like when you were here.'

'Do you know what happened to Darwati?' Tess asked. 'We kept in touch for a while but then... well, it was my fault, really, I was terrible about writing.'

She didn't want to mention that she had put Darwati, along with everything else about Java, determinedly out of her mind.

'Life has not been good for her,' Ninik said.

'What happened, did she ever marry Sigit?'

'Yes. Her family was very upset though, Professor Kanwa didn't like him, you see, but Darwati was pregnant so what could he do?'

Any possible answer to this question was cut off by the arrival of Philip with a stack of papers in his hands. After tipping them onto Ninik's desk and giving her a flood of instructions, he appeared to take in the fact that Tess was there and invited her into his office for a coffee.

'Do we have time?' Tess asked Holly, hoping the answer would be negative. 'I'm in no rush,' Holly replied. 'There's masses of stuff I could be doing until you're ready.'

So Tess reluctantly followed Philip into the room that had been the scene of so many conversations she would rather forget.

'Tell me,' he said when he had shut the door behind them, 'how are you finding life in the world of classical archaeology?'

After giving him the short reply she felt the question deserved, she found the politeness to say, 'I want to thank you for inviting me to the symposium.'

'Did you enjoy it?'

Stretching the truth a bit, she replied, 'Very much.'

'I wasn't sure whether you would or not. As far as I can tell, you don't seem to have kept up your interest in Java.'

'I'm afraid other things are keeping me rather busy these days.'

'So I gathered. I should tell you that it wasn't actually my idea to put your name on the invitation list. It was some scheme of Holly's and Ninik's, mostly Holly's I suspect. I can't imagine that Ninik would have done it, not on her own anyway. It came at the right time though.'

'Why do you say that?'

'Some interesting new evidence has turned up regarding the capital of the Mataram Kingdom. It suggests that the last and most important of the capitals was in Temanggung, not far from the Dieng Plateau.'

Tess looked up sharply.

'What sort of evidence are you talking about?' she demanded, surprised at how antagonistic this suggestion made her feel. Wasn't it time she put her old certainty that the capital had been somewhere near Prambanan behind her?

'Inscriptions around the base of the Pringapus temple near Mount Sundoro. You've undoubtedly been there and if you hadn't been so fixated on your own pet theories you might have come up with the idea first, not that you could have proven anything without the help of an excavation.'

'Are you thinking of proving it?'

'I'm considering it actually. I could arrange financing for an excavation that would either come up with evidence to support the theory or close the curtain on it once and for all.'

'What kind of evidence? More inscriptions, more temples, maybe a palace or two?'

'Any or all of them. As you may recall, Pringapus is only a temple to Nandi so it must have been a subsidiary chapel in a much larger complex.'

'Not necessarily,' Tess snapped.

'Hear me out if you don't mind,' he returned testily. 'There appears to be an elaborate complex of structures just below the surface.'

'It's an awfully unlikely place for a capital city,' Tess said, reluctant to let go of her opposition to his theory.

'I don't agree with you. It's on high ground, therefore defensible. It's near the early religious centre of the Kingdom which, you must remember, was Dieng and it's not far from the trade routes along the North Coast.'

'Did you send me a ticket all the way out here just to

tell me this?' Tess asked icily.

'I thought talking to you in person might be useful.'

'Why?'

'To find out for sure whether you still have an interest in your old theories or whether you've given up on them.'

'I thought I had pretty much lost interest in them but now, coming back here, I'm not so sure.'

'Ordinarily I would assume that someone who hadn't done any work in this area for 20 years had dropped it definitively but in your case, well, your interest in Prambanan wasn't ordinary. I always thought there was something rather extraordinary about it.'

'I had no idea you understood me so well.'

'Perhaps you underestimated me,' he said gruffly. 'Be that as it may, can I have your word that you won't use your reputation in archaeology to raise money for a competing excavation, one that's also looking for the capital of Mataram?'

Totally gobsmacked by the question, Tess replied, 'Doing something like that would never have occurred to me.'

'Good. Can I have your word on that?'

She was about to say 'absolutely' when something made her hesitate.

'No,' she replied, after turning it over in her mind for a moment, 'I'm not going to promise away any area of freedom I have, however unlikely it may be that I'd use it. But I can tell you that, as of now, I can't foresee doing anything like that.'

'Okay, I guess I can live with that.'

'Why do you care so much anyway?'

'Because the Foundation is about to commit a large sum of money, a very large sum, to excavate the area around Pringapus and if another excavation turned up looking for the same thing in a different place at the same time, it would suggest that somebody, possibly me, hadn't done his homework. More importantly, it could drain off the matching funds we're counting on getting from other donors.'

'You seem to have thought all of this out very carefully,' Tess observed.

'Of course I have, it's my job to think things out carefully. But now, if I can be confident you won't try to launch any diversionary projects, I can say that I've got this wrapped up.'

'I would have told you all of this in a letter if you had asked,' Tess said.

'If it hadn't been for Holly's little game, I probably would have done but, one way or another, she generally manages to get what she wants. She's good at what she does though and her parents are old friends, so I tend to humour her when I can. Has she shown you what she's managed to accomplish at Prambanan?'

'We're going there this morning.'

'You'll be impressed. But getting back to what I was saying, this excavation near Pringapus will be the most ambitious project the Foundation has ever undertaken and will be quite a star in its crown, and in my crown, if it succeeds. Conversely, if it doesn't –'

He broke off, grimacing at the painful thought.

God, she thought, even after all these years it would be hell to see Philip, of all people, succeed where she had failed, to see him be the one to find the capital of the Mataram Kingdom and, worst of all, to see him prove that it had been nowhere near Prambanan. She supposed she should wish him luck but she just couldn't bring herself to do it.

She heard him say something about hopefully putting their former differences behind them and being friends.

'Always better to be friends than enemies,' was the only decent reply she could think of, before hastily making her escape.

During their tour of the restoration work, Tess showered Holly with praise for everything she had done and managed to hide her regret that Prambanan was no longer the abandoned temple she remembered. It was selfish of her, she knew, but even though it had been tumbling down and neglected, she had liked it so much better then. In those days it had seemed to belong exclusively to her. Glancing at the still-scattered stones around the remnants of the chapel of Vishnu, she secretly hoped Holly wouldn't succeed in having them returned to their proper place.

'I have a surprise for you,' Holly said as they were having fried rice and cold drinks - no longer such a rarity in Java - in the cafe across from the temple.

Tess suppressed a groan, wondering which of her favourite places was going to be tarted up for the tourist trade next.

Fortunately, that was not what Holly had in mind.

'I thought we'd stop by Wonoboyo and see Darwati on the way back,' she said. 'It's not far from here and Ninik says the two of you used to be great friends.'

'We were and I feel awful that I was so bad about writing. I'd love to see her again and find out what's been happening in her life. I gather from Ninik that she married Sigit.'

'Yes, they've got five kids now.'

'I had no idea you knew her.'

'I didn't until a few months ago, but she came down with a nasty case of typhoid and Ninik started taking her certain kinds of *jamu*, ones she absolutely swore by, plus various other things that she thought would be good for her. Food mostly.

'Anyway,' Holly continued, 'I happened to be in the office one afternoon when Ninik was getting ready to go see her. When I realised she was planning to take that dreadful bus, I offered to take her in the car. I was coming out here to Prambanan almost every day anyway so I gradually started dropping off things for her; medicine, nourishing food, things like that, and I got to know her fairly well.'

'Poor Darwati, having typhoid must have been awful. Is she totally over it now?'

'Oh yes, that was a couple of years ago. She's very thin but Ninik says that's nothing new, she was always slim. Anyway she's a darling and so is her aunt, Ibu Kartini. She lives in the same village. It's been great getting to know them and their village too. As you must know, the trouble with being an archaeologist is that you never get to see the people you're working on while they're still alive. But Ibu Kartini is the headman's wife so she's a mine of information about what goes on in the village. As if that weren't enough, she has the most extraordinary father-in-law. You may remember him, he remembers you and Uncle Philip from the old days. It's Guru Pomo.'

'Good God, he must be absolutely doddering by now,'

Tess exclaimed.

'Prehistoric but not doddering, his mind is still razor sharp.'

'Razor sharp,' Tess repeated, with an astonished laugh. 'Don't you think 'completely crazy' or 'totally spaced out' would be a better description?'

Holly smiled. 'Well, he's a firm believer in *Kebatinan*, if that's what you mean but then isn't everyone around here, in the villages at least? In that context there isn't anything strange about Guru Pomo being able to see into the past and the future.'

'I suppose you're right,' Tess acknowledged. 'It's just that I've been in New York too long to think of Javanese mysticism as anything but weird. It seems like the ravings of a lunatic to me now.'

'I know what you mean,' Holly agreed. 'If Guru Pomo lived any place but Java people would put his claims about seeing into the distant past or the future down to senility or dementia or something, but here –'

'Here it makes him some kind of holy man,' Tess said, finishing her sentence for her.

'I don't know how you feel about it,' Holly said, 'but I think the whole *Kebatinan* thing is rather interesting.'

'I must admit I was sort of caught up in it at one point but I can't bring myself to take it seriously now. What does Guru Pomo think he's seeing these days anyway, anything exciting?'

'Yes. At least I think it's exciting and you might too.'

Tess looked doubtful.

'He claims to have seen a city, an ancient city, buried under the ground just outside Wonoboyo, more or less where you used to think the capital of the Mataram Kingdom might be.'

'Wouldn't it be a scream if he turned out to be right!' Tess said, laughing. Then with a touch of regret in her voice, she added, 'But I guess we'll never know.'

'We might be able to find out,' Holly ventured.

'I doubt it.'

'The real reason I had your name put on the invitation list for the symposium,' Holly continued, 'was to get your help in doing exactly that.'

'Doing exactly what?'

'Finding out, which means excavating of course. I was afraid that if I just wrote to you about it, you might not think it was worth coming all the way out here to see the possibilities for yourself. And I wasn't at all sure how much weight you would give to Guru Pomo's claims about what he saw.'

'When I was still in New York, none at all, but just being here in Java makes me a little more inclined to –'

'To take it seriously,' said Holly, completing her sentence.

'Well, I'm not sure I'd go that far,' Tess said with

a laugh.

'You will when you see it, that's why I was so eager to get you out here. I do hope you're not absolutely furious.'

Tess was a little unsure how to react. She had every right to be going up in flames, she was sure of that, but it wasn't so easy when she was actually glad to be here. Still, that didn't change the fact that charming little Holly had a manipulative streak that was approximately the size of the Pacific Ocean.

'I'll forgive you this time,' was the only response she could come up with.

'I thought that if you actually saw it for yourself –'

'You mean there actually is something to see?'

'Yes, it's all down to the most incredible luck really. Ibu Kartini had arranged to sell topsoil from one of her fields to a landfill project, so she hired some men to shovel if off and it turned out that the place they were digging was just where Guru Pomo says he saw the ancient city.'

To Holly's disappointment, Tess showed no sign of sharing her excitement.

'Don't you think we should play it cool,' Tess said, 'until they actually turn up something interesting?'

'But they've done that, they've uncovered the outline of walls buried in the ground. At least that's what it looks like to me and I'm sure you'll think so too when you see it.'

'Perhaps,' Tess said, with a lack of enthusiasm Holly

found annoying.

She had thought Tess would be over the moon at the possibility of finding her capital city just was where she had always claimed it was.

'I could scarcely believe it myself,' Holly said, 'not until I went down there and saw it; but I've done that now and I can promise you it is real.'

'Yes but there are ruins of minor temples and monuments buried all over Java. We saw a few of them on our Saturday morning 'explores' as you used to call them, remember?'

'That's what Uncle Philip says, well, not the part about the 'explores' of course. But I should never have mentioned Guru Pomo, the moment I did he wrote the whole thing off and said it was bullshit.'

Tess, horror-struck at the idea that she was beginning to sound like Philip, asked herself what on earth could be happening to her.

'The important thing,' Holly continued, 'is that the configuration of the walls looks more like a palace than a temple to me. If I'm right, there must have been a city around it, don't you think?'

Tess had to admit this made a certain amount of sense.

'Oh I know I might be dreaming,' Holly went on, 'believing what I want to believe and all that. I'm trying not to let myself be influenced by things like our treasure hunts for the rajah's gold but I suppose I am, just a little anyway. I wouldn't admit this to anyone but you, so you must promise to keep it a secret.'

'No problem. I'm just surprised you remember it all that fondly, after all, we never found the treasure.'

'It may not be too late,' Holly said, laughing but half serious, 'who knows?'

Twenty minutes later they were crossing the narrow, wooden and rather shaky bridge leading into Wonoboyo.

'See those men over there?' Holly said, pointing to a field not far away, 'They're the ones shovelling topsoil off Ibu Kartini's land; the walls I was telling you about are just a bit further on. I'm dying to hear what you have to say about them when you've had a closer look but we'd better pay our respects to the headman first. You remember Javanese etiquette, don't you?'

'All too well,' Tess replied, wishing she didn't. 'Would it be too awful if we saw Darwati first?'

'A little bit awful,' Holly returned with a laugh, 'but I suppose we could do it anyway. We can leave the car in front of her place and get one of her kids, she has thousands, to watch it for us. Perhaps we can hire a couple of them to wash and polish it too. It's a good way to put a little money in the family's hands.'

Holly had barely pulled up in front of a small bungalow

when a child popped up from nowhere and then immediately dashed inside, presumably to report their arrival.

A moment later, a tired-looking woman of uncertain age came out to greet them.

'Look, here's Darwati,' Holly said, opening the car door.

It wasn't easy for Tess to conceal her shock. Where was the lively, laughing girl with the long hair and the short skirts, the girl with mischief in her eyes who was madly in love with the best-looking man in the world? Where was the girl she remembered?

It took a heroic effort for Tess to put questions like these out of her mind but she knew she had to do it.

Darwati, in a mixture of Indonesian and very rusty English, was inviting them into her drab living room, urging them to sit on one of the rickety wooden chairs that were scattered about and introducing them to several children, the oldest of whom was holding a baby.

'Are they all yours?' Tess asked, trying not to show that she was a bit overwhelmed. 'How many do you have?'

'Eight.'

'How wonderful,' Tess replied, making every effort to be polite.

'Oh, not wonderful. Too many, too much work, too much expensive,' Darwati said, taking the baby from her daughter and holding him up for Tess's inspection. 'Now I have fat grandson.'

Turning to her daughter, she said something in Javanese. The girl left the room and Holly was afraid she had been told to bring out glasses of ghastly sweet tea.

Shit, Holly said to herself when this proved to be true, now they would have to sit around waiting for the damn stuff to cool. She wanted to get on with showing Tess the outline of the walls but what could she do? She couldn't be rude to Darwati so she resigned herself to listening while Tess related her doings, some of them anyway, since they had last seen each other.

Darwati said as little as possible about her own life and didn't mention Sigit at all.

Eventually Tess asked, 'How is Sigit, does he still work at the airport?'

A cloud passed across Darwati's once beautiful face. 'Yes, he still at airport but not go up,' she replied sadly, 'still not manager, money not go up.' Dismissing the subject with a laugh, she added, 'Maybe next year go up, maybe next year more money. I think so.'

Tess was hardly surprised at this news. It was clear from the surroundings that they hadn't prospered. She tried to think of something encouraging to say but nothing came to mind.

Darwati, on the other hand, slipped back into her former pattern of telling Tess things she wouldn't have dreamed of telling other Indonesians, although everyone in the village probably knew them anyway and very likely before she did.

At first she struggled to use her nearly forgotten English because she wanted to keep the children from understanding.

'Sigit drink alcohol too much, money go. He does gambling too much, money go. He play bad girls too much, money go. Buy food, big problem. Pay school, big problem.'

Frustrated by her limited ability to communicate in a language too long unspoken, she sent the children out of the room and filled in the details of her story in Indonesian.

Tess thought about her friend of twenty years ago, the one who had planned to 'get rich' as a secretary in a foreign company. It made her want to go out and kill Sigit but it seemed that Darwati didn't have the same reaction. She only looked tired and resigned and, with the nervous laugh that Javanese people so often used to smooth over difficult situations, she merely summed it all up in English, saying, 'Too much big problem.'

After a while Holly, sympathetic but already familiar with Darwati's situation, took it upon herself to bring the conversation to an end. She managed to keep the courtesy call on the headman mercifully brief and was finally able to take Tess to the area where the outline of what looked like walls protruded slightly above the ground. It was about the size of a football pitch and largely covered with tangled undergrowth.

'There could be so much more that's still hidden under all this greenery,' Holly said, searching Tess's face for signs that she shared her excitement.

'Perhaps,' Tess agreed, but without sufficient enthusiasm to please her.

'Then you don't think –'

'I didn't say that,' Tess interrupted, 'but there's no way we can know what, if anything, is really there without an excavation.'

'Exactly,' Holly declared, 'that's why getting you out here to see this for yourself was so desperately important. I wouldn't stand a chance of raising the money for an excavation on my own, I don't have the experience or the connections –'

'How about your darling Uncle Philip? I'd think that as far as connections went, he'd be at the top of the tree.'

'He would if he liked the project but he doesn't so he's worse than useless. But you're well-known in archaeology, even if it's mostly classical, and you probably have connections. If you think there's a reasonable chance of finding something important under the ground here, like perhaps the capital of the Mataram Kingdom, it could make all the difference in getting the financing for an excavation. Don't you see?'

'No, I don't see,' Tess said, speaking so sharply that Holly was shocked.

'I'm sorry,' Tess added, instantly contrite, 'really I am. I can tell that there's something here and I agree that it might be interesting but there are places all over Java that are crying out for excavation. There just isn't any money for that sort of thing, you must know that as well as I do. And what is there to indicate that this place is more important than any of the others? Nothing but Guru Pomo's vision, or whatever you want to call it, and my old conviction, which I seem to have passed on to you, that the capital of Mataram was somewhere near Prambanan. Things like that wouldn't persuade any donor in the world to put up so much as a penny.'

The crestfallen expression on Holly's face made Tess feel like a monster but what could she do? Joining in her enthusiasm and raising false hopes wouldn't do her any good and there just wasn't any tactful way of letting her down.

Even so, she wasn't happy with what she heard herself saying and it preyed on her mind as they walked back to the car. What had happened to the Tess of twenty years ago, she wondered, the Tess who would have looked at the outline of those walls and been wild with excitement, the

Tess who would have been prepared to move heaven and earth to get financing for an excavation?

She had grown up, it was as simple as that. And it certainly was time, past time actually, for that to happen.

But that time hadn't yet come for Holly. Her reactions were still remarkably childlike for someone in her late twenties and her refusal to cast aside the hope of finding a lost palace with buried treasure was a clear example of that.

Tess spent the next two days prowling around Prambanan on her own, sometimes looking at it through the eyes of the person she was now but enjoying it most when she could see it as it had appeared to her twenty years ago, when she could visualise what it been like at the height of its glory. She could almost picture herself as one of the throng of worshippers bringing offerings of candles and incense to lay at the feet of the gods.

She had gone out to Borobudur the next day but found the excursion hot and tiring. In spite of its fame, it had never captured her imagination the way Prambanan had. If it had been hot in the temple she loved, she had never noticed.

Later that night, the sound of the telephone by her bed woke her from a deep sleep.

One of the kids, she thought in panic, something awful has happened.

'Hello,' she said, in a trembling voice after picking up the phone. She was overwhelmed with relief when she heard Barry's voice on the line.

'Tess, it's me,' he was saying. 'I want to see you.'

'Fine, call me tomorrow.'

'I mean now.'

'Do you know what time it is?' she demanded, peering at her watch and trying to make out the numbers in the darkness.

'Three in the morning, or thereabouts,' he said cheerfully. 'I just got off the Bima.'

'The what?'

'Don't you remember? The fast train from Jakarta.'

'That's no reason to wake me up in the middle of the night.'

'Yes it is, otherwise how can I come see you?'

'You mean you want to come now?'

'Why not?'

'Because I'm in bed, you idiot.'

'That's alright. Stay there. Just get up to let me in, that's all.'

She was about to tell him he was being ridiculous when she suddenly realised that he wasn't. Far from being an outrageous suggestion, it was exactly what she wanted.

And that was what it proved to be. The first time they made love it was passionate and intense, the second time slow and sensuous, the next time playful and fun and the time after that it was very wet, because it was sharing a shower that got them going again. It was glorious every time.

Finally they had collapsed, exhausted, on the bed and slept until the heat woke them to the discovery that the air conditioner had gone off.

The week that followed was one of the best of Tess's life: lunches with Ninik or Holly, visits to some of her remembered haunts and then heavenly nights with Barry.

The only black cloud on the horizon was the steady approach of the day she would have to get on a plane and go back to real life.

There was only one day left when the unimaginable happened.

She had just said farewell, perhaps forever, to her much loved Prambanan and was having a cold drink in the courtyard of the hotel when Holly, flushed with excitement, came rushing in.

You'll never believe what's happened,' she said, flinging

herself down at the table across from Tess. 'You've got to come with me this very minute –'

'Where?'

'Out to Darwati's village.'

'Why, what's happened to her?' Tess asked, alarmed.

'Nothing, she's fine. Come on, forget about that drink, let's go. I'll tell you about it all in the car.'

'Give me a hint at least,' Tess protested, getting up to go with her anyway.

'The treasure, the raja's gold, what we were looking for, what I was looking for anyway on all those Saturday explores we used to go on? I think they may have found it.'

'I'm lost. What the hell are you talking about?'

'My car is just outside,' Holly said, leading the way and only beginning to explain when they were on Jalan Solo.

'The workmen have made the most spectacular find.'

'What workmen?'

'The ones who've been shovelling off top soil near the underground walls I showed you.'

'Why, what have they turned up?'

'A container of some sort, made out of gold. Someone said that it looked rather like an elegant evening bag.'

'Are you sure it's gold?'

'It would have to be, wouldn't it, to be so shiny? You bury any other metal in the ground like that and it would come out tarnished.'

'I suppose so,' Tess agreed.

'But that's not all. You'll never guess what's carved on it.'

'Tell me then.'

'A winged conch shell.'

'The symbol of Vishnu,' Tess murmured, more to herself than to Holly.

'And it's in the Mataram style,' Holly said.

'Are you saying –'

'Well, it's too soon to say anything really but I think the probability that it belonged to a raja is very high. After all, who else would have had gold like that? That makes it highly likely that those walls I showed you were the walls of a palace, a raja's palace.'

Tess caught her breath. 'Are you suggesting that those walls could have a whole city around them and that it could even be the capital city of the Mataram Kingdom?'

'I wouldn't say anything at this stage to anyone but you but it does support the theory that the capital of Mataram was where you always said it was, right here near Prambanan.'

The thought sent Tess's head spinning.

'Bedbug,' Holly called out the insult – a particularly dire one in Indonesian - to the driver of a speeding bus who had nearly forced them off the road into a drainage ditch. Getting back to the subject at hand, she exclaimed,

'But I forgot to tell you –'

'You mean there's more?'

'Yes and no, well, yes actually. They've found three ceramic jars but they're still closed and I don't know whether there's anything of interest in them or not. There's a rumour floating around that they're filled with gold but it's probably just wishful thinking.'

'Why isn't anyone opening them and finding out?'

'Because they're all waiting for the headman to come home, they think it's too important for them to do it without him. That's why I was rushing you so much. I don't want to miss the big moment when they finally take the lids off, just in case there is something exciting there. But even if there isn't, the gold container alone is positively earth-shattering. You've got to see it! I just had a glance at it but it looked to me like it might well be ninth-century.'

'Mataram times,' murmured Tess.

They arrived in Wonoboyo to find that the headman still hadn't returned. Only Ibu Kartini and two of her little granddaughters were at home so everyone was still in suspense. Nevertheless the news of the gold container and the rumours of more treasure to come had flashed through the village like lightning. Practically the entire local population had gathered around the headman's house and everyone was talking in excited voices while they waited to see what would happen.

One of the few people who were missing from the crowd was Guru Pomo. Darwati had sent one of her daughters to his house with a plate of rice and vegetables an hour or so earlier and had reported that he had been sitting cross-legged on his bed meditating.

'Well, at least Philip won't be able to claim that all this commotion is just the work of a crazy old man,' Tess said, with a laugh.

'Oh my God,' Holly exclaimed, clamping her hand over her mouth, 'Uncle Philip!'

'What about him?'

'I completely forgot that he's going back to Singapore tomorrow morning and he's about to commit a lot of money to an excavation at Pringapus.'

'What is so important about that?' Tess asked, with the slight irritation she always felt when Holly went on about her 'wonderful Uncle Philip'.

'Because if this place really is what we think it is, what we think it might be anyway, I've got to tell him what's happening.'

'Now?' Tess said incredulously.

'Yes now, because he'll want to see this. It could stop him from making a colossal mistake.'

'But we can't leave now,' Tess protested, 'not before

they've opened the jars. I'd die of curiosity and so would you.'

'Don't worry, you can stay here. I'll drive as fast as that bedbug of a bus driver and I'll be back here with Uncle Philip in a tick.'

'But what if the headman comes back and they open the jars while you're gone?'

'They probably won't. If I know the Javanese, they'll discuss it for hours before they actually do anything. It's worth the risk.'

'Is it?' asked Tess, looking at her doubtfully.

'Absolutely. Don't you see what getting Uncle Philip out here can mean for us?'

'Trouble,' Tess responded promptly.

'No, silly, it means we're almost certain to get our excavation. Unless Uncle Philip's totally blind, which he isn't, he's going to have to cancel the one at Pringapus. So you see where that leaves him, don't you?'

'No.'

'It leaves him sitting atop a pile of money that's already been allocated to finding the capital of the Mataram Kingdom. And where is there the most evidence of a ninth-century palace, the site with the highest probability of having a capital city around it? Here in Wonoboyo. So with any luck he'll put the Pringapus money into an excavation here and the great thing is, we won't even have to make the usual rounds of donors and do all that ghastly grovelling and pleading to get our excavation. We'll have it on with bells on from Uncle Philip.'

'What a genius you are!' Tess cried, throwing her arms around her friend. 'Nothing gets by you, does it?'

'Hopefully not,' Holly said with a laugh. 'Anyway, I'm off. I'll get Uncle Philip and be right back. He's probably at the office now.'

It seemed to Tess that she was gone a long time and after a while she couldn't help feeling impatient. Maybe she just wasn't used to the Javanese pace of doing things anymore and, if she was honest with herself, she would have to admit that she had never quite been in tune with the Javanese predilection for talking things to death before doing them.

Nevertheless she went over to Darwati and asked, 'Is it really so important for the headman to be here when they open the jars?'

Darwati seemed shocked at the question. 'Oh yes,' she replied, 'he very important man.'

'Of course he is,' Tess agreed hastily, 'but isn't everyone curious?'

'Gold,' she replied confidently.

'How do you know?'

'Workmen look in one jar, see gold too much, make very afraid, bring it to headman.'

'What are they afraid of?'

The answer to this was beyond the reach of Darwati's English so she shifted into Indonesian and explained that the workmen had been thrilled when they had found the gold container, each one envisioning what his share of such a treasure might mean. But when they had found the first of the ceramic jars, looked inside and seen that it was filled with gold coins and jewellery, they were terrified.

Why such riches would have come to simple workmen like themselves was more than they could fathom. It had to be the mysterious forces of the spirit world at work and because they had no idea what the capricious beings of that unseen world would want from them in return, they had quickly closed the jar back up again.

They had found two more jars after that, Darwati told them, but the workmen had been too frightened to open them. When it seemed that they weren't going to come across any more, they had brought the whole lot to the headman's house, trusting him to know the best thing to do about them.

Tess, long out of the habit of seeing things in terms of a spirit world, was still trying to adjust to this line of thought when Holly's car pulled up in front of the headman's house and, to her surprise, another car came screeching to a stop behind it.

'What are you doing here?' she demanded when Barry

leapt out.

'Getting in on the action, I hope.'

'But how did you find out about it?'

'I was in the office, chewing the fat with your old friend and paramour –'

'Do you really have to dredge up all that ancient stuff?' she cried, although she was not quite able to feel annoyed on this marvellous day.

'I thought archaeologists liked ancient stuff. Why else would they delve around in the ground the way they do, like humanoid moles with wire-rimmed glasses and dirt-stained notebooks?'

'I don't have wire-rimmed glasses.'

'That's a relief. Fill me in on what's happening. Holly's version was strictly scrambled eggs.'

This was all the encouragement Tess needed to pour out every detail of the fantastic afternoon and Barry miraculously refrained from making any facetious remarks while he listened. She had just got to the discovery of the third jar when Holly interrupted her to say that Guru Pomo had agreed to see her and they could come too if they liked.

'Thanks but no thanks,' Barry said, without hesitation.

Tess's response was equally swift. 'Great,' she said, 'I'm coming.'

In the end Philip and Barry went too; Philip in order

to ensure Holly did not take everything the old fool said as golden if he were in the dark about what had transpired and Barry just to be in on things.

'Ibu Kartini says that he has finished meditating,' Holly told them, 'but he is very tired so we mustn't stay long.'

'Fine with me,' Barry said, and Philip secretly agreed.

At first glance, Tess thought Guru Pomo's room was empty but after her eyes had adjusted to the dimness, she made out the figure of a man, paper-thin and very still, lying on a bed. She wondered if she had ever seen such an old man. His skin, dry as antique parchment, was etched with a thousand tiny lines and punctuated by a sunken mouth, devoid of teeth. Only his eyes, shining with intelligence and humanity, gave evidence of the indomitable spirit that still lived within the fragile body.

Tess almost felt as if she was looking through a transparent shell and communicating directly with his soul. Could he be peering deep into the secret recesses of her mind and seeing what she couldn't?

She shivered a little at the thought and suddenly wanted to run away from those relentless eyes that saw more than she wanted them to see. Yet she wasn't able to escape their hypnotic powers. As she stood there, imprisoned by the force of the old man's spirit, her unease gradually gave way to a sense of wellbeing and it was almost like her soul was struggling to reach out towards him, to see what he saw, to know what he knew.

Was he trying to teach her something important in that moment? At first she thought that he was but when he finally spoke he addressed all of them rather than focusing on her and his words were crushingly disappointing. They were so ordinary.

'You have come back,' he said in Javanese.

Barry translated and then explained to Guru Pomo that the others had been there before but he had not.

The old eyes glistened with anger, suggesting that their owner was still sufficiently part of this world to relish a battle.

'You have been here too,' he told Barry, with unexpected firmness.

Barry didn't want to argue with anyone this ancient so he let the matter drop.

'I see the three of you, all except the girl,' he said, indicating Holly. 'I see the three of you here together but it was very long ago.'

No one tried to contradict him.

'Won't you tell us more about the ancient city you saw,' Holly asked, 'the one near the village?'

Guru Pomo closed his eyes and Tess was afraid he had gone to sleep but he soon opened them again and slowly began to describe a grand city presided over by a raja and his court.

'Do you know when it was?' Holly asked, but received no more satisfactory reply than that it was in Hindu times, before Islam had come to Java.

'Did the gold container we saw today come from that city?' she persisted.

The old man gazed at her as though disappointed in her intelligence but his voice was kind as he replied, 'Only rajas had so much gold.'

'I sure hope he saw me as a raja,' Barry said in an aside to Tess, 'with a harem full of women and stacks of gold.'

Guru Pomo didn't understand English but he heard Barry and came close to guessing the gist of what he was saying.

'You were not very important,' he told him regretfully.

'Shit,' Barry said, but let this go by without translation.

The old man then fixed his eyes on Philip. 'You were important,' he said. 'I see you very close to the raja, maybe his son, maybe his brother, but it is good you were not the raja because you were very cruel.'

Philip shifted awkwardly and managed a surreptitious glance at his watch. What was he supposed to say to that?

Guru Pomo did not appear to expect an answer. 'We go through time and we learn, we advance,' he continued reassuringly.

Holly tried to draw him back to the subject of the ancient city but he was growing tired and did little more than repeat what he had already said. A few minutes later he told them that he must sleep, closed his eyes and seemed to forget they were there.

Philip and Barry couldn't get out of the room fast enough but Holly left in a state of high elation, chatting excitedly about Guru Pomo's description of the ancient city. Tess just felt confused, she couldn't accept anything Guru Pomo claimed to have seen as having any basis in reality as it was just too preposterous. Still, it kept whirling around in her mind to the point where she began to wonder whether, in some mystical Javanese way she would never understand, he had been responsible for the gold turning up while she was still here to see it.

Shortly after they left Guru Pomo, the headman came home, heard the incredible news, inspected the gold container and surveyed the three earthenware jars. Ever the embodiment of traditional Javanese politeness, he invited his foreign visitors, along with the respected village elders, into his house.

The excitement in the air was palpable and the little room was crowded by the time they squeezed onto a low wooden bench intended for much smaller people.

Then the headman motioned to one of the workmen to take off the lid and, when this proved to be difficult, a nervous shiver ran through the room. Was it a sign, an ominous portent of dark events to come? The workman tried again. This time his efforts were rewarded and the incredulous spectators gazed in wonder as, one-by-one, he took out gold rings, necklaces, bracelets, anklets, earrings, toe rings, belts, offering bowls, water dippers, umbrella handles, dagger handles and coins. These were placed on mats where they shone with glorious radiance under the room's one fluorescent light.

A few people were allowed to examine the objects more closely and the foreigners were thankful to be included in this privileged group. Tess was transfixed by the beauty of the repoussé work on a golden bowl that depicted scenes from the Ramayana story. She peered at it so intently that people began to mistake her admiration for covetousness, and when titters of nervous laughter alerted her to what they were thinking, she hastily put the bowl down.

Insofar as the available light permitted, Holly ran her eyes over the array of treasure for any sign that it might be from a later period. Philip, thinking along similar lines, examined it for evidence that it might all be a clever antique dealer's fake, while Barry wondered what all this would mean for Tess.

When the other two jars had been opened and revealed contents similar to the first, Barry remarked, 'I'd sort of like to see where all this stuff was found.'

'Isn't it getting a bit dark?' Tess asked.

'No problem, I've got a flashlight.'

'Let's go then,' she agreed. 'Holly, you know where it is don't you?'

'Yes, I'll show you if you like.' Turning to Philip, she asked, 'Do you want to come with us?'

He nodded and, finding himself next to Tess as they walked along, said, 'I suppose you're feeling pleased with yourself.'

'Wouldn't you be,' she countered, 'if there had been a find like this near Pringapus?'

'I suppose so,' he admitted.

'At least you're honest.'

'Well, what can I do except be man enough to admit that you were right and I was wrong, that is, if all this is on the up and not some kind of hoax.'

'Do you really think it could be?'

'The workmanship on that gold's pretty damn impressive,' Barry put in.

'I don't think it's a hoax,' Holly declared.

'We'll have to see what the Archaeology Service has to say about it,' Philip cautioned.

'What are you going to do about Pringapus?' Tess asked.

'Put it on hold for the moment.'

'And then?' Holly asked.

'Why do you want to know?' he teased, although the

answer was no mystery.

'You're going to put that money into an excavation right here aren't you, with Tess and me working on it?'

'You seem to have everything figured out,' he replied, attempting to sound gruff.

'I just thought that might be what you'd want to do,' she said sweetly.

'You think too much,' he growled, but she was confident she could persuade him to see things her way.

They were crossing the wooden bridge near where the workmen had been digging when a small flickering light caught their attention.

'What the hell is that?' Barry exclaimed.

On closer inspection they saw that a candle, several sticks of incense, and some flowers had been left on top of a small mound of earth that had been shovelled from on top of the buried gold.

'It looks like some sort of offering,' Tess said, and told them what Darwati had said about role that spirits might have played in the day's events.

No one was surprised at this, they had all been in Java long enough to be used to a mystical interpretation of the world around them. But Tess, perhaps because she had been away so long, was captivated by this impromptu little shrine in a way that the others weren't and she wasn't ready to leave quite as soon as they were.

'Aren't you coming?' Barry asked when they started back towards the village.

'Not yet, I think I'll stay for a little longer. I'm tired of trying to speak Indonesian again, it's such an effort after all this time. But I don't really want to go back to the hotel either.'

'Why not?'

'I'm afraid that all of this will seem like a dream as soon as I leave it.'

'Go on ahead,' Barry called to Philip and Holly, who had already reached the bridge. 'We'll catch up with you in a minute.'

He was uncharacteristically silent as he strolled back towards Tess and said, 'I've been thinking about what the sudden appearance of all this gold is going to mean for –'

'Me too,' Tess returned. 'I've been thinking of nothing else. I can scarcely believe my luck that it's all happening while I'm here. It's such an incredible coincidence.'

'Is it? After all, luck is an archaeologist's stock-in-trade. You people never know for sure what you're going to come up with until you stick your shovel into the ground and start to dig, do you?'

'We generally have some idea. There's always a lot of preliminary work so we're usually excavating on the basis of an educated guess that there'll be something worth finding.'

'Still, improbable accidents do happen,' Barry argued. 'How about those workmen who were repairing pipes and came across all those Roman ruins right under one of the most important squares in Florence? No one expected that to happen, yet it's ten-to-one that some archaeologist who was lounging around nearby, wishing he could afford a cappuccino at Florentine prices, got the thrill of his life just like you did today.'

'What makes you so sure?'

'Florence is infested with archaeologists, art historians, Renaissance freaks, you must know the species. When you're there, you see them everywhere you look.'

'It sounds like you're very good at spotting them,' Tess said, with a laugh.

'I've had a lot of practise, one of the wives was an archaeologist. I must have been looking for someone like you but it turned out that she wasn't, unfortunately.'

'Is that supposed to be a compliment?'

'Take it any way you want. The point is there are archaeological accidents here in Indonesia all the time, you read about them in the *Jakarta* Post. A farmer turns up something in his field that some wag says is Mataram or Majapahit or something else and if an antique dealer gets to him first, the thing finds its way into the market on Jalan Surabaya. But if a nearby archaeologist pounces on it fast enough, he writes it up for a professional journal and gives himself a boost up the career ladder. It's called being in the right place at the right time, generally spelled l-u-c-k.'

Tess smiled doubtfully. 'Perhaps you're right,' she said.

'And it's not just luck,' Barry pointed out. 'Holly had a lot to do with it. She was convinced there was something under the ground here, something that might be important, so she put her conniving little brain to work and figured out a way to get you here to corroborate her theory. The interesting question now is what does all this mean for us?'

'For us?'

'Yes, for us, but let's start with you first. What are you going to do about today's little treasure trove?'

'I don't suppose I'll do anything. It's all going to be turned over to the Archaeological Service tomorrow and they'll take charge of it.'

'And you're just going to fly back to New York and forget about it, is that it?'

'I suppose so. Why not?'

'Because it's your baby. Sure, you may have put it on ice for the past twenty years but it's what you dreamed about, worked for and basically put your career on the line for. You can be damn sure that a whole gaggle of eager archaeologists is going to jump at the opportunity to work on all this gold, with or without that excavation Holly's so sure she's going to wangle out of Philip. Can you really see yourself sitting on the subway, or wherever New Yorkers spend their time, letting someone else or even your clever little protégé, write all the definitive articles about it?'

'It won't be easy.'

'And when someone in that gaggle comes up with convincing evidence that the capital of Mataram was right here near Prambanan, just where you always said it was, how are you going to feel then? What's it going to be like when all the credit for finding the capital of Mataram goes to somebody else?'

'Pretty awful, I guess.'

'That's what I thought. Even if it's just analysing the stuff that's already above ground, you've got to be the one to do it.'

'With Holly,' Tess insisted loyally.

'No worries there, she'll see to that. Now can we get around to how all this is going to affect us?'

'Unless Australia has made you into an archaeologist, I don't see that it does affect you.'

'I'm due for a long sabbatical, that's how.'

'And?' Tess queried.

'That means I'm going to be here in Central Java while you're working on –'

'But I won't be –'

'I don't believe that. I don't think you're going to be able to stay away and if our little reunion is going to turn into something a little more long-lasting, well then. If not, I'm going to change my plans, take my damn sabbatical on Mars or some place as far out of your orbit as possible.'

'What does long-lasting mean, until Cynthia pops up again?'

'It means nothing of the sort. And Cynthia has gotten out of the habit of popping up. But even if she did materialise one of these days, what could she do? Any sex appeal she ever had bit the dust years ago when I found out about the *jamu*.'

'Can I really believe that?'

'After the week we've been having, can you doubt it?'

'Yes.'

'That's a lie. We belong together, Tess. Do you really think being with me long term would be that bad?'

Her answer was cut off by the appearance of Holly.

'Sorry Tess,' she said, 'but can I tear you away? Uncle Philip's ready to get going.'

'Don't worry about me. Barry's taking me back to the hotel.'

He concealed his surprise at this but said, 'Right, the excitement is over. We're ready to leave too.'

A tantalising aroma of ginger, garlic and roasting meat greeted them at the entrance to the courtyard restaurant in the hotel. Before long they were feasting on beef in sweet soy sauce laced with fiery chillies, chicken swimming in spicy coconut milk and mounds of fluffy white rice, followed by an assortment of bananas, rambutans and mangosteens.

When they had eaten as much as they could and washed it down with glasses of cold beer, Barry said, 'Okay, now what's the story? Do I spend my sabbatical year here with you or should I take myself off to distant points of the solar system?'

'Spend it here with me,' she said, then on second thoughts added, 'but of course I'll have to apply for a leave of absence from my job and I may not get it.'

'Then resign.'

'I can't do that.'

'Why not? You'd like Australia. After we've wrapped things up here in Java, that is. Come on, let's move to the bar and have a gin and tonic while we plan out our lives.'

'Lives,' she teased, emphasising the plural, 'don't tell me Guru Pomo has convinced you we have more than one.'

'You're almost sounding like he convinced you.'

'Not really, although a few things he said did make me wonder a bit.'

'Like what?'

'Like the fact that those walls Holly showed me and the appearance of all this gold actually supports Guru Pomo's claim that he saw an ancient city here.'

'Bullshit. He probably just heard people talking about them and figured there might have been something here, a city or whatever.'

'Maybe. But saying he had seen Philip there and that he had been important and cruel. Why would he have done that if he hadn't actually –'

'That's easy. Philip thinks he's pretty important even if nobody else does, that's obvious from his manner. And Guru Pomo thinks he was cruel. That's a bit extreme but he does strike me as kind of a hard arse. I don't think you have to be clairvoyant to see that, just a good judge of character.'

'Perhaps, but he was quite insistent that he had seen us there and not Holly. How would you explain that?'

'I wouldn't even begin to try. You can't expect me to work out the reason for every twist and turn of the old fool's imagination.'

'If you believed in reincarnation you wouldn't have to, it would be obvious.'

'And you do?'

'I don't know. Out here in Java I almost believe it but when I get back to New York, I know I won't.'

'Would that go for Australia too?'

'Probably. Tell me, though, if you're so convinced that people don't have more than one life, how do you think

I knew the capital of Mataram was somewhere not far from Prambanan?'

Barry shrugged. 'I don't know, maybe a lucky guess?'

'And why do you think I've always been so drawn to Java, ever since I was a little girl?'

'Kids have imaginations, you probably had a particularly active one. And don't forget you had your Aunt Susie who –'

'Aunt Saskia.'

'Okay, Aunt Whatever Her Name Was, who probably set yours off in a big way.'

'I can't help wondering if it was a lot more than that. Don't you think the pictures in her books could have triggered memories from a previous life, ones I wouldn't otherwise have realised I had?'

'No, I don't,' Barry said firmly. 'Listen, this mystical way of looking at things may be part and parcel of Javanese life but it's not my way and it's not yours. If you let yourself become too caught up in it, you're not going to know who you are or where you belong. So let's put it out of our minds for a while and just get on with living this one.'

Feigning innocence but unable to keep a merry sparkle out of her eyes, she asked, 'And how do you suggest we go about doing that?'

'Invite me into your lair, my darling, and I'll show you how they go about it in Australia.'

EPILOGUE

IN THE TIME OF THE GOVERNORS

Java 2087

'Shit,' James Atherton muttered to himself, as a sudden burst of rain soaked him to the skin in seconds. It was a little late to look for shelter; how could he possibly be any wetter than he already was? Nevertheless, he cast his eyes around.

The nearest refuge seemed to be the Temple of Shiva so he dashed up the staircase into the small stone chamber that, according to The Guide to *Prambanan*, was the sanctuary of the goddess, Durga.

Not really my type of goddess, he decided, after giving the statue of her in the middle of the room a once-over. Her face and figure weren't bad but those eight arms were about six too many for him. The guidebook said the animal she was riding was a tiger and, as far as he was concerned, that showed pretty poor judgement. She wouldn't be likely to get to her destination in one piece, although perhaps it was different for a goddess. And what were those things in her hands anyway?

'Fuck,' a voice said from the doorway, as the most striking girl he had seen in God-only-knew how long came rushing in. She was dripping wet but somehow that only

525

enhanced her attractiveness. She had large blue eyes, mostly blue anyway but with flecks of another colour in them, a sort of greenish-grey. They sparkled with good humour that seemed to laugh at the rain. Her hair was a brownish-blonde and she had swept it back into a thick plait that started near the top of her head and swung down to the middle of her back. Best of all, she had a smile that lit up the whole world, or his world anyway.

'Hello,' she said, seemingly surprised to find someone else in the little room.

'Hello,' he returned. 'A bit wet out there, isn't it?'

'Ghastly, I'm half drowned.'

'So am I.'

'I came out here for a holiday in the sun,' she said with a laugh. 'I certainly didn't count on this.'

'Nobody did. The rainy season is supposed to be over by now.'

'I take it you're English,' she said.

'Is it that obvious?'

'Sort of. I suppose it's just as obvious that I am too. My name is Sophie Davis, by the way.'

'James Atherton.'

'Are you looking for a holiday in the sun too,' she asked, 'or am I the only idiot who didn't expect a downpour like this?'

'No, the rainy season is supposed to be over by now.

Anyway, I'm not actually on holiday. I come out to the volcanology station on Mt Merapi a couple of times a year, we have a project going with them.'

'We?'

'Oh, sorry, I'm with the School for Earth Sciences at the University of Southampton. We're working on a new system for siphoning off some of the magma.'

'Why would you want to do that?'

'To reduce the damage when there's an eruption.'

'Oh,' she said, with a shudder, 'I can't deal with things like that.'

'Why not?'

'I have a thing about volcanoes.'

'Why?'

'The idea of being sizzled alive in boiling lava just doesn't appeal to me somehow.'

'That's not very likely to happen, not with the early warning systems we have these days.'

'Is there one for Mt Merapi?'

'A very good one.'

'That thought should help but somehow it doesn't. The idea of all that terrible lava bubbling away underground still gives me the horrors. I even had a panic attack when my parents took me to Pompeii. I was only twelve at the time but I'll never forget it. My dad had to take me back to the hotel and give me some sips of whisky to calm me down.'

'If you feel that strongly about volcanoes, why did you choose a place so close to one for your holiday?'

'I didn't realise it was that close. This was very much a spur-of-the-moment trip. I just got the sack and I wanted to get away.'

'What kind of bastard would sack you?' he asked.

'A play-by-the-rules sort of bastard,' she said, thrilled that this cool-looking guy with intelligent brown eyes and floppy dark hair seemed to be so firmly on her side. 'It was all too silly. I was working in the big cat section at the Wellington Safari Park in Devon and no one was supposed to go into any of the enclosures unless there was a guard present.'

'But you did?'

She nodded. 'Just to see Rama for a minute, have a chat, scratch him behind the ears, that sort of thing.'

'And Rama is –'

'A tiger. '

'Jesus! It could have chewed you up in a matter of seconds.'

'Yes, but Rama wouldn't do that. Not to me anyway, I'm practically his mother.'

'What makes you say that?'

'He was the smallest one in his litter and his birth mother rejected him. I've been feeding him and taking care of him since he was a few days old. He thinks of me as his real mother and I think of him –' Tears welled up in her eyes but, to his relief, didn't spill over. 'He's been my baby for almost a year now and I miss him terribly.'

James didn't quite know what to say to this so he wisely didn't say anything.

Anyway,' she continued ruefully, 'there wasn't a guard around but I was just going to stay for a minute so I thought it would be fine. And it was fine, or it would have been if someone hadn't seen me and ratted on me to my boss. So I got the sack.

'But saying goodbye to Rama was just awful, I know he wonders why I deserted him. That's why I just had to get away somewhere, anywhere, and for some reason this place popped into my mind. I remembered hearing about performances of Javanese dance-dramas, the ones they call *wayang orang*, here in Yogya at this very temple, and it sounded like a wonderfully out-of-the-way place. But when I got here I found out they won't be putting one on again until June. So between that and the Mt Merapi thing, I don't think I'll stay around.'

'But you've come all this way!'

'That doesn't matter. I think Indonesia is the wrong place for me. There are volcanoes everywhere you look. I'd be better off in Bangkok or Angkor Wat or somewhere like that.'

'It seems a pity to let a phobia play such a big part your life,' he observed.

'Well, I don't know what I can do about it.'

'I do. It may not work but it's something you can try.'

'What?' she asked, in surprise.

'Face up to your fears, confront them head on. It worked for my sister. She had a phobia about bees, wouldn't have an ice cream in the park or lunch in the garden, until some boy she was mad about wanted her to go on a picnic with him. The temptation was too much so she went and, sure enough, she got stung. That wasn't any fun of course but she found out that a few bees didn't mean the end of the world. After that she just accepted them as a normal part of the British summer and didn't let them stop her from doing the things she wanted to do.'

'Do you really think something like that might work for me?'

'It might. I think it's worth a try. A group of us from the volcanology station are going to climb up to the edge of the caldera, to the top, I mean, on Sunday. Why don't you come with us?'

'What a terrifying thought,' she said, dismissing it with a laugh.

'It shouldn't be,' he replied, wondering why he felt so disappointed. After all, he had only just met her.

'The instruments we have for detecting underground

tremors are very sensitive these days,' he said, still hoping to persuade her. 'We'd know if there was going to be any danger. You'd be safer on the slopes of Mt Merapi than you would be crossing a street in Yogya, or back in London for that matter.'

To her astonishment, she found herself wanting to believe him.

'Getting to the top of a volcano might give you the feeling that you've conquered it, just what you need to get over your phobia,' he said encouragingly. 'And even if it doesn't cure you, it will be good fun.'

'Perhaps,' she said, incredulous at the thought that she was actually considering it. But she didn't want to say goodbye to this amazing guy and just let him walk out of her life. Climbing the mountain with him would mean seeing him again, getting to know him better, sharing an extraordinary experience with him. But, she asked herself, was he worth braving a volcano for?

Although she wouldn't have to be brave, there was really nothing to worry about. Or was there?

END

NOTE

In October 1990 nearly twelve-and-a-half kilograms of gold artefacts were discovered near the village of Wonoboyo. Some of the artefacts can be seen at the National Museum, Jakarta. In 1970 a tiger wandered into the Food Science Building at Gajah Mada University.